GATES OF RUIN

Christopher Mitchell is the author of the epic fantasy series The Magelands. He studied in Edinburgh before living for several years in the Middle East and Greece, where he taught English. He returned to study classics and Greek tragedy and lives in Fife, Scotland with his wife and their four children.

By Christopher Mitchell

THE MAGELANDS ORIGINS

Retreat of the Kell
The Trials of Daphne Holdfast
From the Ashes

THE MAGELANDS EPIC

The Queen's Executioner
The Severed City
Needs of the Empire
Sacrifice
Fragile Empire
Storm Mage
Soulwitch Rises
Renegade Gods

THE MAGELANDS ETERNAL SIEGE

The Mortal Blade
The Dragon's Blade
The Prince's Blade
Falls of Iron
Paths of Fire
Gates of Ruin
City of Salve

For the Magelanders

ACKNOWLEDGEMENTS

I would like to thank the following for all their support during the writing of the Magelands Eternal Siege - my wife, Lisa Mitchell, who read every chapter as soon as it was drafted and kept me going in the right direction; my parents for their unstinting support; Vicky Williams for reading the books in their early stages; James Aitken for his encouragement; and Grant and Gordon of the Film Club for their support.

Thanks also to my Advance Reader team, for all your help during the last few weeks before publication.

DRAMATIS PERSONAE

The Forted Shore
  Kelsey Holdfast, Blocker of Powers
  Aila, Demigod & Shape-shifter
  Amalia, Former God-Queen of the City

Alea Tanton
  Belinda, The Third Ascendant
  Leksandr, The Sixth Ascendant
  Arete, The Seventh Ascendant
  Silva, Belinda's Aide
  Felice, God; Governor of Lostwell
  Latude, God; Former Governor of Lostwell

Kin Dai
  Corthie Holdfast, Champion
  Naxor, Demigod; Cousin of Vana & Aila
  Vana, Sister of Aila; cousin of Naxor
  Van Logos, Former Banner Captain
  Sohul, Former Banner Lieutenant

Catacombs
  Sable Holdfast, Dream Mage
  Maddie Jackdaw, Dragon Rider
  Sanguino, Former Bloodflies Dragon
  Millen, Torduan Fugitive
  Deathfang, Lord of the Catacombs
  Ashfall, Deathfang's Elder Daughter
  Broadwing, Discontented Dragon
  Deepblue, Discontented Dragon

Burntskull, Deathfang's Advisor
Darksky, Deathfang's Mate
Halfclaw, Green & Blue Dragon
Grimsleep, Sanguino's Father

Implacatus

Edmond, The Second Ascendant
Bastion, Edmond's Enforcer

Others

Blackrose, Captured Dragon
Frostback, Deathfang's Daughter

CHAPTER 1
THE BACK-UP PLAN

Stoneship, Forted Shore – 13th Lexinch 5252

The shimmering air materialised, and a stone chamber appeared, lit by a series of narrow slit windows. Aila dropped to the cold floor, Amalia writhing and struggling beneath her. A few feet away, Kelsey landed awkwardly, her ankle buckling under her as she fell onto the stone flagstones.

'Get off me!' cried Amalia, pushing at Aila with her good hand.

'What did you do?' yelled Aila. 'Where are we?'

Amalia raked her fingernails across Aila's cheek and lashed out with her boots, catching the demigod with a painful blow down her shin. Aila let go of the former God-Queen, and Amalia rolled away, the Quadrant clattering onto the floor beside her.

'Get her!' shouted Kelsey, as she clasped her ankle. 'She has no power over you. Punch her teeth in.'

Amalia's glance darted from the Quadrant to her granddaughter, a glimmer of fear in her eyes.

'She's right,' said Aila, tensing herself to spring. 'For the first time in my life, I'm not scared of you, grandmother.'

'You should be,' said Amalia, pulling a knife from her robes.

The two immortals stared at each other in silence for a moment, and

Aila heard the cry of a gull through the slit windows, as a waft of salty ocean air drifted into the chamber. Outside, the sky was a deep blue, dazzling compared to the dim light within the stone room.

'You can't beat us,' said Aila, 'not with one good arm and no powers. Step back from the Quadrant.'

Amalia laughed as she brandished the knife. 'Try to take it. Do you have any idea how much I would enjoy cutting you to ribbons, granddaughter?'

Kelsey pulled herself to a standing position, though she was putting no weight onto her left ankle. 'I'll get round behind her.'

'No,' said Aila; 'stay where you are. If she wounds you, you won't be able to self-heal. I can take her on my own.'

Amalia lashed out with the knife as Aila launched herself at her. The blade sliced through the thin layer of clothes around the demigod's waist, sending pain shooting through her body. She shoved Amalia back, pushing her to the ground, and scooped up the Quadrant in her right hand as the wound began to heal. Aila took a few paces back, her eyes scanning the blood across the front of her clothes.

The former God-Queen laughed from the stone floor. 'And what are you going to do now, little Aila?'

The demigod glanced down at the copper-coloured device clutched in her hand. Her eyes caught Kelsey, who shrugged.

'Do you know how to use it?' said Aila.

'No,' said Kelsey.

Amalia laughed again, then raised her voice. 'Maxin!' she yelled. 'A little assistance, if you please. Bring weapons.' She smiled at Kelsey and Aila. 'Place the Quadrant onto the ground and raise your hands in the air, and then, perhaps, I will be merciful, and you won't be beaten too severely.'

'She's bluffing,' said Kelsey. 'She panicked in Yoneath, and took us to the first place she could think of, only she wasn't expecting you, Aila. She thought it would just be me.'

'That's quite true,' said Amalia. 'However, as I have a score to settle with my granddaughter, her presence here will in no way inconvenience me. As for bluffing, we shall see, won't we?'

'Where are we?' said Aila.

'Far from Yoneath,' said Amalia, getting back to her feet, 'and far from anyone who can help you. By now, the Ascendants will be destroying the bickering fools standing by the Sextant. Even Blackrose and Corthie combined will not be able to stand up to them. I was the best chance they had, and they spurned it. The only reason I helped rescue Kelsey was so that I could use her to hide from Arete and Leksandr, but I was willing to share possession of the Holdfast girl, and I was willing to transport everyone out of that hideous cavern. This is their fault, not mine.'

Aila stared at the engraved marks on the surface of the Quadrant, wishing she had paid more attention to how the device operated. The symbols and lines were meaningless to her.

Kelsey cocked her head. 'There's no one here; no one's coming. We should get that knife off her and force her to tell us how the Quadrant works.'

'Maxin!' Amalia yelled again, then shook her head. 'Where is that boy? You would think with all the gold I've paid him, he would be a little more responsive.'

Aila passed the Quadrant to Kelsey. 'You hold onto this, and I'll disarm her.'

The sound of boots thumping up a flight of stairs reached them, and a grin split the face of the former God-Queen. There was only one door leading from the chamber and it burst open. Two men entered, one holding a crossbow, the other a long-handled axe. The man with the crossbow stared into the room, his eyes settling on Amalia.

'Ma'am,' he said, out of breath; 'I wasn't expecting you.'

'Of course you weren't,' she said. 'And who is this with you? Did you use my money to hire another guard?'

'Yes, ma'am,' said Maxin; 'just as you requested. I also hired a house-keeper and a servant; I can show you the receipts...'

'Yes, well, let's not worry about the details right now. As you can see,

I have brought us a couple of... guests. The shorter one is a mortal, like you, so be sure not to damage her; she is extremely valuable.'

Maxin pointed his crossbow at Aila and Kelsey, a look of confusion on his face. 'What, uh, what should I do with them, ma'am?'

'I believe the cellar has a few dungeon-shaped rooms,' said Amalia. 'Tie them up and put them in there. We can procure shackles and chains in the town; send our new servant out with enough gold to buy some.'

Maxin bit his lip for a moment, then glanced at the man next to him. 'Get the rope.'

'Yes, sir,' the man said, then hurried away.

Amalia's eyes sparkled as she approached Kelsey. 'Bluffing, eh? Did you really believe that I wouldn't have somewhere prepared and ready? While Silva was off looking for Belinda, I found myself with a lot of time on my hands. That, added to the natural feeling of concern about Belinda's possible reaction to my presence, left me with little choice but to secure myself a small refuge, just in case. Now, the Quadrant, please.'

Kelsey narrowed her eyes. 'Forget it.'

Amalia lunged out with her hand. Kelsey hobbled backwards, but the hand was meant for Aila, and Amalia gripped her arm, sending her death powers directly into the demigod. Aila choked and fell to her knees, her skin scabbing and rotting.

Amalia smiled. 'As you can see, young Holdfast, I'm not completely powerless. I watched Belinda heal Van, remember? Now, place the Quadrant on the ground, or I will irreparably damage Aila's self-healing powers, leaving her to die a miserable and agonising death. I don't need her; I only need you.'

Aila gasped, blood coming from her lips. She remembered the God-Queen doing the same to her in the City, but she hadn't been pregnant back then, and fear ripped through her at the thought of losing the child she and Corthie had conceived. Kelsey stood in silence for a moment, as Maxin watched from the doorway, then she placed the Quadrant on the ground.

'Good,' said Amalia. 'Now, take a few steps back. That's it; a little more.'

As soon as Kelsey was a couple of yards from the device, Amalia released Aila and grabbed the Quadrant. The demigod collapsed to the stone floor, and Kelsey rushed to her side. Aila panted, closing her eyes in shame at how powerless and scared she had been. She felt inside her, and her powers sensed the life within her womb. It seemed healthy and safe, but could she be sure?

'Sorry,' she mumbled, her voice hoarse, her hand on her midriff.

'It's not your fault,' said Kelsey.

The door swung open, and the man from before entered, along with a Fordian woman who was carrying a long length of rope. They stopped and stared at the sight of Aila on the ground, her skin slowly healing.

'Don't just stand there,' said Amalia. 'Please bind our guests, and make sure the knots are tight and secure.'

'Should we gag and hood them, ma'am?' said Maxin.

'Why bother?' said Amalia. 'The walls here are so thick that no one will hear them if they scream.'

The shackles and chains took several hours to arrive. Aila and Kelsey had been led down two flights of stairs into a large system of cellars, some filled with barrels and casks, others lying empty, and were made to sit in one while Maxin watched them with his crossbow. The ropes securing their wrists were cut, and the new shackles attached with much fuss and confusion, none of Amalia's hired helpers having much experience in the art of chaining people. The window slits of the cellar were barred to prevent robberies and the two lengths of chain were attached to an iron bar, the other ends fastened to the shackles around the prisoners' right wrists. Aila had been slow to recover from the death powers inflicted by Amalia, and Kelsey's twisted ankle had also rendered her unable to flee. Finally, after more than an hour of angry words and muttered curses, the shackling was finished, and the small group led by Maxin left the cellar room, its door closed and locked behind them.

Kelsey got up from the floor as soon as they were gone, and hobbled over to the nearest window slit. She grasped the bar and shook the chains, but everything seemed secure.

'We're on the coast,' she said. 'All I can see is water.'

Aila nodded.

'The walls are ten feet thick,' Kelsey went on, 'like a fortress or something. Any idea where we could be?'

'No.'

Kelsey glanced down at her. 'You better yet?'

'I think so. This is my fault. I panicked when she grabbed my arm.'

'Don't be ridiculous; she could have killed you. I know you're probably regretting your intervention back in Yoneath, but I'm grateful that I'm not alone. Between us, we'll think of a way to get out of here.'

Aila lifted her eyes. 'Oh yeah? How?'

'I don't know. They'll get complacent if we play along for a bit. And they haven't worked out how they're going to feed us, or let us go to the toilet. They're bound to make a mistake eventually.'

Aila shook her head, and resumed staring at the damp stone floor.

'Come on,' said Kelsey; 'don't get despondent. Didn't you once tell me that you'd escaped from house arrest?'

'Yes.'

'Well, how did you do it?'

'I used my powers to impersonate lots of different people.'

'Oh. Hmm, well, that won't work this time.'

'Do you think I hadn't realised that?'

'Don't get snippy with me; I'm just trying to help.' The Holdfast woman patted down her pockets, then frowned. 'No cigarettes. Damn it. I wonder if the guards will get me some. If not, you might be in for a few days of grumpy-Kelsey, so allow me to apologise in advance.' She crossed her arms and leaned against the wall of the cellar. 'What do you think's happening in Yoneath?'

'I don't know. If Corthie has any sense, he will have fled along with the others.'

'But that would mean the Ascendants will have the Sextant.'

'I know. We failed, utterly.'

'Not necessarily. Blackrose might have destroyed it first. And there's Belinda; who knows what she'll do? I watched her kneel before Arete and Leksandr, but her heart isn't with them.'

'You don't get it,' said Aila. 'Our worlds might already be open to the Ascendants. Right now, they could be sending soldiers to the City, and greenhides to your world. Or maybe they could use the Sextant to destroy your world? Sitting here, wherever here is, we'd never know.'

Kelsey shrugged. 'I'm not giving up hope, no matter what you say.'

'Then you're living in a dream world. It's over.'

'It's not.'

'Let's see if you're still saying that after a while being chained up.'

Kelsey let out a low laugh. 'Do you think I've never been chained up before? I was in shackles for months, for exactly the same reason that I'm chained up now – my blocking powers. People who want to hide from the gods have always wanted to get their hands on me. I survived that; I'll survive this.'

'You don't know that.'

'Actually, I do.'

'Why?' said Aila, a smirk on her lips. 'Can you see into the future?'

Kelsey's eyes widened. 'I told my brother to keep that a secret.'

Aila paused. 'Eh, what?'

'Did Corthie tell you? I should have guessed he would. I hope you didn't tell anyone else.'

'What are you talking about, Kelsey? Did Corthie tell me what?'

Kelsey crouched down by Aila, keeping her weight off her twisted ankle. 'You mean he didn't tell you?'

'Is this about Van? If so, then no; Corthie wouldn't say anything about why he allowed you two to go off together. So, you can relax, sure in the knowledge that he sided with you over me.'

'Oh. Right. Well, I can see into the future. Corthie knows, and that's why he was happy for me to leave with Van.'

Aila said nothing. She could recall Karalyn saying something similar in the Falls of Iron, and she realised that if Kelsey was speaking the truth, then she could understand why Corthie hadn't told her.

'No comment to make?' said Kelsey.

'Naxor would have read it out of my mind.'

'What?'

'That's why he didn't tell me. He knew that Naxor would discover it, and, well, my cousin has proved that he can't be trusted. Are you just like Karalyn?'

Kelsey glared at her. 'I am nothing like Karalyn.'

'Except you can block powers and see the future.'

'Aye, apart from stuff like that. Also, Karalyn can decide if she wants to block someone's powers, whereas I have no choice in the matter; it just happens. The future thing, though? Aye, we can both do that, and I know I'm not going to die here.'

'What about me?'

She shrugged. 'I have no idea what happens to you.'

'Good,' said Aila; 'I don't think I want to know.'

'But you believe me, though?'

'I guess so. After everything I've seen of the Holdfasts, it wouldn't exactly surprise me.'

Kelsey nodded. 'You wouldn't have been my first choice as a fellow prisoner.'

'Do you think you're mine?'

'No, but I'm the one Amalia wants. She tortured you so that I would give her the Quadrant back, and she might do it again, you know, to keep me in line. She seems to dislike you quite a lot.'

'We've not had the best of relationships.'

'Try not to antagonise her. We've got to lull her into a false sense of security if we've any chance of getting out of here.'

Aila stretched her arms and got to her feet, Kelsey's voice starting to irritate her. She glanced around the bare chamber, but there was nowhere to sit apart from the damp, stone floor. She walked towards the door until the chain fastened to her right wrist went taut. With her left hand outstretched, she could almost touch the sturdy wooden boards of the door, her fingers just inches away.

Footsteps echoed from the cellar passageways, and she took a step back as the door was unlocked. Maxin peered into the chamber, his crossbow levelled at the prisoners. He narrowed his eyes at them, then opened the door more fully. The other guard, and a young man in his teens entered the chamber, carrying a wooden pallet. They placed it in the corner of the room, then left, leaving Maxin alone.

'This will take a few minutes,' he said. 'Don't move or interfere.'

'Do you know what would make me more cooperative?' said Kelsey.

The guard looked her up and down.

'Cigarettes,' she said.

The other two men came back in, carrying blankets and a chair. Maxin watched them as they placed them down, then they left again.

'Well?' said Kelsey.

Maxin shook his head. 'Fire hazard.'

'You're kidding, aye? Fire hazard? Is this the way it's going to be? Are you going to feed us, or is food considered to be a choking hazard?'

'You'll be fed.'

The men returned, one of them carrying a large chamber pot, which he placed alongside the bed pallet. The other had a clay jug and a wicker basket, and he laid them down onto the floor.

'That everything?' said Maxin.

'Yes, sir,' said the other guard.

'Everything except cigarettes,' muttered Kelsey.

Amalia strode into the room as the others left, though Maxin hung back at the doorway, keeping his crossbow trained on the prisoners.

'Welcome to your new home,' Amalia beamed.

Aila edged back a step.

'Don't be nervous, granddaughter; if you behave, then there needn't be a repeat of what occurred earlier. I imagine you have a few questions, so let me forestall them by telling you where we are. Have you heard of the town of Stoneship?'

Neither Aila nor Kelsey spoke.

'I didn't think you would have,' Amalia said. 'There is a string of ancient fortresses along the northern coast of Khatanax, built to repel invaders from a long-forgotten era, and Stoneship is one of those fortresses. In other words, we're as far away from Shawe Myre as it's possible to get. No one will find us here; it's cut off from the rest of Kinell, and ships rarely stop. I bought this place for a pittance; it was built into the old sea walls, and it's the perfect place to lie low for a while.'

'And then what?' said Kelsey. 'You can't be planning on staying on Lostwell forever.'

'I have no fixed plans,' she said. 'One must await events, before one can decide the next move.'

'You coward,' muttered Aila.

Amalia smiled. 'Excuse me?'

'You heard. You had a chance to help us all, and you ran away.'

'And why would I wish to help you? You and your friends destroyed my rule in the City, and I hear it is now run by mortals. But, more than that, so much more, you murdered Marcus; did you think I would forgive or forget?' She took a step closer to Aila, her eyes dark. 'I swore then that I would torture you for a millennium, so perhaps you should be grateful that I have not yet started. Your presence here irked me at first, but now I can see that you will be of use to me. I cannot kill Kelsey, but I can hurt you.'

'You've got us where you want us,' said Kelsey. 'There's no need to hurt anyone.'

The former God-Queen ignored her. 'Do you know what else I can hurt, granddaughter? Or should I say "who else?"'

Aila said nothing, and backed up against the wall by the window slit.

'Did you think I wouldn't be able to tell?' Amalia went on. 'I knew the moment I touched your skin. You have another life inside you, a tiny, fragile life.'

'What?' said Kelsey.

Amalia laughed. 'Didn't she tell you? She's pregnant. I could have easily snuffed out its life, but I didn't; I refrained. Leverage, let's call it; another reason to behave yourselves.'

Kelsey hobbled over, and raised an arm protectively in front of Aila, who said nothing, her eyes glaring at the former God-Queen with rage and fear.

Amalia laughed again, but it was a little forced. She turned away, and made as if she were inspecting their room.

'We might go back to the City,' she said, almost conversationally.

'What city?' said Kelsey.

'*The* City, Holdfast girl. The place Aila comes from.'

Aila snapped out of her shock at Amalia's words. She hadn't felt so scared for a long time, and she knew at once that she wanted to keep the baby, but she also realised that she was now under Amalia's power. She would do what she had to do to protect the life growing within her, even if that meant obeying her grandmother.

'You would go back to the City?' she said.

'I know you think me well-travelled, granddaughter,' she said, 'but I have only ever been to three worlds – this one, the City, and my homeworld.'

'Your homeworld?' said Aila.

'Yes. Did you think I appeared spontaneously one day? I was, actually, born to a mother and a father in a real place. However, my homeworld was a casualty of the god wars long ago, and is nothing more than a wasteland. Times would be desperate indeed, if I were to consider travelling back there.'

'You've never been to Implacatus?' said Kelsey.

'No, and I have no desire to. The City is the only viable option. I had wanted Belinda to come with me, but it now looks as though that is well nigh impossible. So, we wait. If the Ascendants have the Sextant, then we see what they do with it. They may decide to move into the City at once, and start extracting every ounce of salve they can find. In doing so, they would need to eliminate Yendra, which would save me the trouble of having to do it.' She crinkled her brow. 'Or, we stay here a while, and see what transpires.'

Aila watched her. Her right arm was hidden beneath the folds of her robes, but must be close to being fully healed. Amalia caught her glance and smiled.

'If we do go back to the City,' the former God-Queen said, 'we can make sure your baby is welcomed into the family. Have you yet sensed whether or not the child is immortal?'

'What?' said Kelsey. 'I thought the children of demigods turned out mortal.'

'Most do,' said Amalia, 'but Corthie Holdfast is powerful, and his abilities may well have tipped the scales. If, indeed, he is the father?' She laughed at Aila's expression. 'We'll have to take your word for it, I suppose, dearest granddaughter.'

Aila walked across the stone floor and sat on the bed pallet. She thought back to the two centuries she had spent under house arrest, and tried to remember what had got her through it. She would need to be patient, just as Kelsey had said, but her stomach was in turmoil, and her chest ached with anxiety. She closed her eyes as a tidal wave of emotion swept over her. Since leaving the Falls of Iron, no, since Irno's death, her life had been cast into a wild storm, battered by events over which she had exerted no control.

'Well?' said Amalia. 'Have you sensed it?'

Aila shook her head.

'Let me know if you do. If the child turns out to be a demigod then you may, at long last, have proved to be of some worth to me. Imagine a little Corthie by my side as we stroll through Maeladh Palace; he could fill the void left by Marcus and Kano.'

Kelsey coughed.

'Yes?' said Amalia.

'Get out of our cell; leave us alone, you creepy old hag.'

The former God-Queen's eyes lit up. 'You think you can speak to me like that?'

'Aye. What are you going to do, kill me?'

'Oh, I daresay your blocking powers would still work if I had your thumbs removed; or, indeed, your eyes or your tongue. I shall keep you alive, of course, but in what state, who can tell?'

She smirked at Kelsey, then walked from the room. Behind her, Maxin closed and locked the door, leaving the prisoners alone in the shadows and gloom of the cell. Kelsey crouched by Aila.

'Pregnant? Wow. I didn't see that coming.'

Aila laughed, but it was joyless.

'Does Corthie know?'

'Yes,' she said. 'I told him in Yoneath.'

'I hope he got away alright.'

'You know what he's like; he thinks it's his destiny to defeat the Ascendants. Unless Blackrose carried him off, I doubt anything would have made him leave that cavern.'

'If he knew where we were, and had a way to get here, then he'd leave.'

'Yes, but he doesn't know. And now… now we're stuck here, with my insane grandmother holding us captive.'

'We'll get out. In some ways, this changes nothing; we just have to play along and be patient. I don't care about stealing the Quadrant from her; she's welcome to it if she uses it to bugger off.'

'Say we do manage to get out; then what? Where would we go?'

'Corthie and Van will be looking for us; we have to hold on to that thought. They'll never find us here, so we'll have to go to them. I don't know where, exactly, but south for a start.'

Aila nodded, keeping her eyes on the stone floor. Her initial annoyance with Kelsey had passed, and she was glad that the young Holdfast woman had remained positive. Aila's thoughts, in contrast, were dark and bleak, and she felt as trapped as she had in the City.

'What Amalia was saying,' Kelsey went on; 'about the possibility that your child might be immortal; was that true?'

'I don't know. No quarter-god in the City was immortal, but no mortals there have any powers. Many quarter-gods had some sort of a power, a vestige from their demigod parent, but none that I know of had self-healing at a level that would allow them to live forever. But I think Amalia was picking up on something, something I can feel myself. I didn't want to admit it in front of her, but I have a suspicion she might be right.'

'What do you mean? Can you sense it?'

'I think, maybe; I don't know. Sometimes, it feels as though there's another self-healing power working within me, but I might be wrong. True or not, I'll do whatever it takes to keep the baby away from Amalia.'

Kelsey's eyes widened. 'Wow. Corthie might have fathered a god.' She chuckled. 'He probably won't be surprised; after all, he already thinks he is one.'

CHAPTER 2
THE NOOSE

A lea Tanton, Tordue, Western Khatanax – 17th Tuminch 5252

Leksandr raised his hand, and the trapdoors under the row of condemned prisoners opened. Their bodies fell a few feet, then jerked on the nooses with a sickening noise. Feet spasmed and twitched, while damp patches spread across the lower parts of their clothes as they swung from the line of gallows, each corpse silhouetted by the bright sunshine striking the rear yard of the Governor's residence.

'That's the last of them,' said Arete; 'the basement of the residence is now clear.'

Leksandr nodded. 'And the final tally?'

'Out of the three and a half thousand members of the merchant class arrested by Lord Renko, just over seven hundred have been executed, while another eight hundred died of mistreatment or disease. The remainder have been returned to their homes.'

'To go straight back to work, I hope? Thanks to Renko's misguided policy, the city is teetering between starvation and insurrection. His actions brought the economy to its knees.'

Arete shrugged. 'They have been ordered to resume work immediately, but many are complaining of exhaustion and sickness. On the other hand, perhaps Alea Tanton has too many inhabitants, and a cull would do the place some good. I estimate that there are at least half a million economically inactive mortals living in the slums who are nothing but a drain on resources. Perhaps we should allow the collapse of the economy to run its natural course.'

Leksandr turned to Belinda, who was sitting next to them on the wooden platform that had been erected in front of the gallows. 'Your opinion, Third Ascendant?'

Belinda frowned.

'Why are you asking her?' said Arete. 'The old Belinda might have been an experienced ruler, but this new one knows nothing about the hard choices we face.'

'It depends on what you want to achieve,' Belinda said, ignoring Arete's comment. 'If you care about the long term future of Lostwell, then we should take every practical step to alleviate the famine, and do all we can to assist the poor and unemployed in the city. If, however, you only care about keeping Old Alea secure for long enough to find Kelsey Holdfast, or to activate the Sextant, then it makes no sense to do anything to help the mortals.'

Leksandr raised an eyebrow. 'Succinctly put. See, Arete? Belinda has a talent for cutting straight to the heart of the matter.'

Arete rolled her eyes.

'Do you care about Lostwell?' said Belinda.

Leksandr shook his head, a wry smile on his lips. 'Lostwell has no future. Its oceans are poisoned, and the land groans under earthquakes and volcanoes. This world is doomed. Thousands of years of conflict have brought it to the edge of destruction, and barely a twentieth of its landmass remains inhabitable. Within a few decades, at best, they will have used up all of its freshwater, and timber supplies, and they are running out of everything else. On top of that, the climate is getting drier and hotter, thanks to the indiscriminate use of god powers during the wars. Once we have achieved our objectives, I would be tempted to put this world out of its misery.'

Belinda kept her face expressionless, despite the turmoil she was feeling. 'Could it not be fixed?'

'What for?' said Arete. 'It would be far quicker, and easier, to create a new world to replace it, if we manage to get the Sextant to work. And if we don't, then, does it matter? There are plenty of other worlds.'

'Don't say that,' said Leksandr. 'We *shall* get the Sextant to work.' His face darkened. 'We have to.'

The Sixth and Seventh Ascendants fell into silence for a moment, and Belinda could sense the fear each of them felt. She hadn't yet dared to go into their minds, conscious that she was unable to hide her presence from them, but was becoming attuned to their moods, and had watched their anxieties increase over the month that they had been in Old Alea.

'I shall spend the rest of the day meditating by the Sextant,' Leksandr said, as he stood. 'I'm close to discovering its secrets; so close.'

Around them, a company of soldiers stood to attention as the Ascendants rose from the platform.

'Belinda,' Leksandr went on, 'I want you out searching again today.'

'I search every day,' she said.

He flashed her a glance of anger. 'Then do it better. Khatanax is a small continent, and the Holdfast girl is hiding somewhere. Find her.'

'I'll do my best.'

Arete smirked. 'How do we know that she hasn't already found her? Do you believe that she would tell us?'

'Yes,' said Leksandr.

'For our sake,' she said, 'I hope you're right. We are running out of time.'

'Don't test my patience, Arete. Work with Belinda today; search alongside her. You know where I will be.'

Leksandr turned, and strode off towards the rear doors of the residence.

Arete frowned as she glanced at Belinda. 'You may have fooled him, but I don't trust you.'

'I know.'

'We should have sent you to Implacatus so that Lord Edmond, the

Blessed Second Ascendant could examine you. Leksandr is playing a risky game keeping you here, when you could easily be a traitor.'

They began to walk in the direction of the western tower of the residence, where the Ascendants had their quarters. Around them, Banner soldiers formed an escort, and they passed the gallows, where the corpses of twenty merchants were being cut down from the nooses.

'Where shall we search today?' said Belinda.

'Do you listen to anything I say?'

'Yes.'

Arete glared at her as they walked towards the base of the tall tower. 'Is that it? I accuse you of treachery, and you change the subject? Leksandr believes you need time to adjust, but I think your mind has gone. You had a reputation for wisdom and cunning, second only to the Blessed Lord Edmond himself, and now you behave like a slow-witted mortal.'

A few of the soldiers glanced over at Arete's words, but the Ascendant didn't seem to care who was listening.

'You're hiding something,' Arete went on, 'and I will find out what it is. You're in league with the Holdfasts, and are conspiring against us – is that the truth?'

Belinda said nothing.

'Well? Answer me.'

'You've already made up your mind,' Belinda said. 'If there's nothing I can say to change it, then why speak?'

They entered the cool passageways of the western tower, where officers and courtiers bowed before them. They stepped into the lift shaft, and a team of servants began turning the winch, raising them up through the levels of the tower. It had been three months since Sable Holdfast had broken her leg in the destruction of the lift, and the platform and pulleys had been recently repaired, and retained their odour of fresh wood.

Belinda closed her eyes as they ascended. Arete was still talking, but she ignored the words spoken by the Seventh Ascendant. The lift stopped on the second-highest floor, where Arete and Belinda had their rooms, occupying the quarters once lived in by Lord Maisk and Lady Joaz. Leksandr had selected the apartment on the top floor, where Lord Renko had stayed, and the Sextant was taking up most of the space in the study there, after the Sixth Ascendant had used his powers to reinforce the floor under it.

Arete followed Belinda into her rooms, where a small group of demigods were waiting. Each of them had vision skills, and were being employed daily to search Khatanax for Kelsey Holdfast. A large map of the continent lay spread across a dining table, and was covered in scrawls and markings made in red ink, denoting the places that had been searched.

The demigods stood and bowed low in front of the two Ascendants.

'I will assist today,' said Arete, her tone angry, 'as you seem to be having difficulties.' She walked to the map and peered down at it. 'Where are you up to?'

'We've searched Tordue, the Four Counties, and the Southern Cape, your Grace,' said one of the demigods.

'What about Shawe Myre?'

'Yes, your Grace. We have paid a great deal of attention to Shawe Myre, checking it every day in case Lady Amalia returns there.' The demigod glanced away. 'But, your Grace...'

Arete narrowed her eyes. 'But what?'

'Well, your Grace, we have to admit that we cannot be altogether certain if we have missed this Kelsey Holdfast. If she can truly block vision powers, then our search could pass right over her and we wouldn't know it.'

'Surely the Third Ascendant has told you how to go about looking for the girl?'

'Yes, your Grace – we have been instructed to sense for areas that are resistant to our powers, but... but, I'm afraid none of us really understands what that might feel like.'

Arete shook with rage, then turned to Belinda.

'I explained this to you some time ago,' Belinda said. 'This is why it has taken so long; we are searching for an absence, rather than a presence.'

'All I hear are excuses!' Arete cried. 'If the Blessed Second Ascendant demands blood for this, then I will offer him the heads of everyone in this room.'

The group stilled, their glances lowered.

'Get to work,' Arete said; 'I shall supervise.'

The demigods took seats around the dining table, and Belinda sat down next to them.

'We shall continue our search of Dun Khatar this morning,' she said. 'Street by street, house by house. Look for any signs in the sands of recent movement; footprints and the like. I shall take the palace.'

'No,' said Arete; 'I will search the palace.'

Belinda nodded. 'Very well.' She gestured to the group of demigods, and their eyes glazed over. Belinda focussed, and allowed her vision to leave her body. As her sight hurtled southwards over the farmlands of Tordue, she tried to think back to every word Amalia had said to her in Shawe Myre. She had gone over their conversations many times since being brought to Alea Tanton by Leksandr, looking for clues as to where the former God-Queen might have taken Kelsey, but Belinda had discovered nothing of any use. What was far from clear to her mind, was what she would do if she did manage to find them.

Several hours later, Belinda sat alone on a couch, her gaze on the sunset through an open window. Another exhausting session of searching had proved fruitless, and Arete had left with the demigods once it had ended, her frustration evident. Belinda was glad that the Seventh Ascendant had witnessed for herself how impossible the task was, and she hoped Arete would be a little more understanding in the future, though she doubted it.

If Leksandr could get the Sextant working, then Belinda reckoned that the search for Kelsey would be called off, as the Holdfast girl was far less important to the Ascendants than the massive device that sat in the apartment above her own. The Sextant was the key to the two worlds the Ascendants were looking for, and next to that, Kelsey was almost an irrelevance.

There was a tap at her door and Silva entered, her head bowed.

'Good evening, your Majesty,' she said. 'Did you make any progress in locating the Holdfast girl today?'

Belinda hesitated. She longed to confide in the demigod, but knew that Arete and Leksandr were reading her mind on a frequent basis, and she had been forced to keep her thoughts to herself. Silva believed, like the others, that Corthie Holdfast was dead, and that Belinda was now on the side of the Ascendants, and she could see that it pained her immensely.

'No, not today,' Belinda said.

Silva smiled. 'I'm sure you'll have better luck soon, your Majesty.'

'I have come to a decision,' said Belinda.

'Yes, your Majesty?'

'Yes. I want you to leave Alea Tanton.'

Silva's face fell. 'But...'

'It's for the best, Silva.'

'Have I... have I let you down in some way, your Majesty? If so, then please tell me what I can do to make it right.'

'You can make it right by leaving. I packed a bag for you this morning. Take it, and go.'

Silva began to weep. 'Why?'

'I have made my decision,' said Belinda.

'But where should I go, your Majesty?'

'Leave Tordue as quickly as you can. I am dismissing you.'

'Are you dismissing your other servants too, your Majesty; your new ones?'

'No; just you.'

'I'm sorry,' Silva sobbed, 'for whatever it is that I have done, your Majesty.'

Belinda kept her face impassive, suppressing the growing urge to hug the demigod and tell her the truth. She knew that she was acting in a cruel manner, but it was the only way. If Arete or Leksandr got hold of her before she had left the city, then her plans would be in ruins.

She pointed to the corner of the room. 'Take your bag and go. Now.'

Silva wiped her face and shuffled to the corner of the room. She picked up the bag, then turned back to Belinda.

'If anyone asks,' said Belinda, 'I am relieving you of your duties for unsatisfactory performance. Dismissed.'

Silva fell to her knees next to where Belinda sat, and wept. 'Please, your Majesty, please let me stay. I don't understand. All I've done is try to help you.'

Belinda turned away. 'Go, immediately; that's an order. Speak to no one on the way out unless absolutely necessary.'

'I will do as you command,' Silva said. She pulled herself to her feet and hurried across the room to the door. She opened it and left.

Belinda put her head in her hands, holding back her tears. Once Silva was far from the city, and out of the reach of the Ascendants, then she would find her and explain. Then, maybe, Silva would forgive her.

She took a long hot bath, trying to wash away the guilt she felt about sending Silva from Old Alea. Her great granddaughter had shown her nothing but loyalty, and Belinda knew the demigod would die for her if she commanded it. She waited an anxious hour or two, half expecting Arete to arrive at her rooms with Silva in tow, demanding to know what she was up to, but no one appeared. She dried herself, and dressed in the robes that Lady Joaz had left behind. She spotted her own set of worn fighting clothes in the wardrobe, and remembered that the front of her leather breastplate still had the hole in it made by Sable. She would need to get it repaired. Buried at the back of the wardrobe was the Weathervane, unused since arriving in Alea Tanton. She was surprised that Leksandr had let her keep it, but the Ascendants seemed to view physical combat as primitive and uncouth, something carried out by mere mortals, and had not objected to her holding on to the old sword.

Servants were tidying her quarters when she emerged from her bedroom. They bowed to her, their eyes lowered, and she ignored them. They were all spying for Arete and Leksandr, and she had determined that she was going to give them no excuse to tell tales about her to the Ascendants. A few of the servants glanced at her as she strode through the apartment. She nodded to one as she sat by a dresser, and the servant rushed over and began to pull a brush through Belinda's hair. For a while, they had tried to make small talk with Belinda, but after days of her either refusing to answer, or giving nothing but monosyllabic responses, they had given up, and the servant brushed her hair in silence.

Belinda stared at her reflection as the tangles were drawn from her drying hair. The strange woman in the mirror glared back at her, unfriendly, and unapproachable. That was how she appeared to the servants also, and it didn't bother her in the slightest. Better they thought her aloof and cold than a traitor to the Ascendants. Was that what she was, a traitor? A rebel? She didn't know. Aside from saving Corthie, and a half-hearted attempt at warning Maddie and Blackrose, she had gone along with everything the Ascendants had asked of her. She had dutifully searched Khatanax for Kelsey, though that seemed fraudulent, as she was certain that the Holdfast girl could remain hidden forever if she wished. She remembered vision mages who had hunted for Karalyn after she had disappeared several years before. At the request of the Empress, they had scoured the Star Continent for the runaway dream mage, but it had been an impossible task. Again, when Kelsey had been abducted by Sable, several mages had searched for her, but without any success. The Ascendants didn't seem to understand that the two Holdfast sisters could be in the Governor's residence, and they wouldn't be able to see them.

Amalia was a potential loose end. If she strayed more than a hundred yards from Kelsey, then her self-healing powers would become visible to Arete and Leksandr, and they would be drawn to her as the biting insects of Alea Tanton were drawn towards the flame of a candle. Aila too, for that matter, though if she and Kelsey were Amalia's prisoners, then that seemed unlikely.

The Sextant was the other unknown. Belinda had concocted vague plans to sabotage the huge device to prevent the Ascendants from using it against the two hidden worlds, but no such effort had been necessary – the Ascendants were no closer to getting it to work than they had been in the cavern of Fordamere over a month before.

The servant took a step back and waited, her hands crossed by her waist.

Belinda glanced at her reflection, nodded and stood. The servants all bowed again, and Belinda walked from her rooms, entering the central stairwell that connected the levels of the western tower. She climbed the steps to the top floor, and knocked on the door to the outer hall of Leksandr's quarters. A demigod courtier opened it and looked out.

'The Blessed Sixth Ascendant is busy, your Grace,' he said. 'He is not to be disturbed by anything other than matters relating to the Sextant.'

'The Sextant is why I'm here,' said Belinda.

'Very well, your Grace,' the demigod said. He stepped to the side and opened the door fully to allow Belinda to enter. She glanced at the doors. One of them led to Renko's old harem, where Sable had been interred for a few days, before she had killed Maisk, rejected Naxor and fled with Lady Felice's Quadrant.

The courtier knocked on the door to the study, and entered. A moment later, he came back out and gestured for Belinda to go in. She strode through the door and saw Leksandr sitting cross-legged on the carpeted floor in front of the Sextant, which was taking up half of the space in the room.

He glanced up at her, then signalled to the demigod courtier to fetch some wine and glasses.

'Sit,' he said to Belinda. 'Here; next to me.'

She walked over to the carpet and sat down on Leksandr's right.

They waited as the courtier brought over a tray and laid it down on the floor in front of them.

'That will be all,' Leksandr said to him.

The courtier bowed low, then left the room, closing the door behind him. Leksandr filled two glasses with white wine and picked one up.

'Have you brought me any insights?' he said. 'I do hope so, as I have been reflecting upon the workings of the Sextant for some time now without success.'

She stared at the huge device, seeing the complex interconnections of wood, metal and glass.

'Out of all the Ascendants,' she said, 'who has used a Sextant before?'

Leksandr took a sip of wine. 'Nathaniel and yourself, obviously,' he said. 'Theodora, the Blessed and dearly-missed First Ascendant, was the undisputed master of working the device; she created dozens of worlds with her Sextant, before it was destroyed and she was… rendered to her present condition. Simon, the Tenth Ascendant, was also known to have used a Sextant; he created Dragon Eyre with one.'

'I know that the First Ascendant is dead,' she said, 'but where is Simon?'

'He disappeared many millennia ago. Apparently, his Quadrant was damaged at the precise moment he was travelling between worlds, and he never arrived at his destination. Apart from those four, yourself included, none of the other Ascendants had a deep knowledge of how the Sextants operated. Edmond, the Blessed Second Ascendant, was present at the creation of many worlds; he assisted Theodora in her tasks for long ages, but she never allowed him full access to the knowledge required.'

'Then why did you think it would be easy? In Yoneath, you seemed to think you would be able to get it working without a problem.'

He raised an eyebrow at her. 'Arrogance, perhaps? I confess that the Blessed Second Ascendant gave me his assurance that it was activated in the same manner as a Quadrant, and perhaps he believes that to be true. I have examined every inch of the device that can be reached without attempting to dismantle it, and cannot find any mechanism by which it might be brought to life.'

'May I look at it more closely?'

'Of course,' he said, waving his hand. 'Please do.'

She stood and approached the device. It was five feet tall, and she could see over it and look down into its inner workings. It had a thick glass panel protecting the top, but the sides were open, revealing the intricate cogs and wheels that fitted together. She traced her fingers down the smooth metal of a gear lever; it felt dull and lifeless to her touch.

'Did you see the salve mines?' Leksandr asked.

Belinda frowned.

'On the world of the City, where you were living before you returned to Lostwell; did you see the mines with your own eyes?'

Her mind went straight to the large deposit of salve they had found in the mountains where Blackrose had stayed after leaving the City. 'No.'

'But you know where they are?'

'I think so. I was told that three of the palaces in the oldest part of the City have access to mines dug into the hills. I presume that's why the palaces were built in those locations. I was only inside one of the palaces, in a place called Ooste.'

'How much is left to dig out?'

She shook her head. 'I don't know.'

'And the Quadrant that transported you from there, where is it again?'

'I told you; it was taken by Karalyn Holdfast. Why are you asking about Quadrants?'

'Because, Belinda, I fear we will soon have to give the news to Implacatus that we have failed in our mission. We have the Sextant, but it is inoperable, and we have been unable to track down either a Quadrant that has been to the salve world, or a person who has used a Quadrant to get there. Any one of these three things would be sufficient to bring us success.'

'You could use a person to get there?'

'Yes, if the person had operated a Quadrant to travel to that world. The memory of their finger movements over the device would be enough. If you were in Lostwell before going there, how did you travel?'

'Karalyn Holdfast sent me; she doesn't need a Quadrant.'

Doubt shone in his eyes as he gazed at her.

'She drew power from two demigods,' Belinda went on, 'and nearly killed them in the process. She then used that power to send me to the City of Pella.'

'Then why did she need a Quadrant to travel back to her home?'

'Because she was being cautious; she was worried about time, worried about making a mistake.'

'Ah, so she's not perfect.'

'Karalyn Holdfast is far from perfect.'

'Yet I sense you still hold her in some esteem.'

'The Holdfasts are formidable opponents. I respect them.'

'You love them, I think.'

'Is this about Corthie? Are you concerned that I bear a grudge towards you for killing him?'

'Yes, though Arete is not so sure about that. She thinks you revived him. Is that true?'

Belinda stood and faced Leksandr. 'It crossed my mind, but he was too far gone. He would have been an empty shell; a monster.'

'But you were tempted?'

'I admit it; yes, I was.'

'It is good that you are honest with me, but I will have to inform the Blessed Second Ascendant about this. When I spoke about the objectives of our mission, I omitted our one success – you. As well as finding the salve world, we were ordered to bring you to Implacatus when our mission was complete. I would have taken you back there myself by now, Belinda, were it not for one slight problem: your allegiance.'

'Did I not kneel and swear an oath?'

'You did, but your subsequent actions in Yoneath have cast doubt upon your true intentions. Arete, of course, is rather more forthright about the matter; she believes that you are still a rebel, and has advised me to dispatch you to the Second Ascendant for judgement without delay. I, on the other hand, want to give you a final chance to prove your loyalty before resorting to such drastic measures. Forget the Holdfasts. I want you to find me a Quadrant that has been to the salve world, or someone who has used one to travel there. There is very little time to spare, Belinda. Any day, the Blessed Second Ascendant will send an emissary to demand an update on our progress, and when that happens I will have to inform them about the doubts Arete and I share concerning your loyalty. You have until then to prove yourself. Am I clear?'

'Very clear.'

Leksandr rolled his shoulders and settled into a meditative pose. 'You can leave now.'

Belinda inclined her head, and walked from the room. She ignored the demigod courtier on the way out and went down the stairs to her own quarters. Her head was buzzing as she swept past her servants, and she ordered those who were tidying her bedroom to leave. Alone, she sat on the bed, her stomach coiled, her chest aching.

She thought about fleeing, but where could she go? The other Ascendants would track her self-healing powers and come after her. They would be relentless, and would chase her to the far corners of Khatanax. She tried to calm her breathing. She needed to act, but running away would achieve nothing.

She lay down on the bed in the darkness, her head on the pillow as she gazed at the dark sky through the open window.

She would think of something; she had to.

CHAPTER 3
LOW

K in Dai, Kinell, Eastern Khatanax – 17th Tuminch 5252

Corthie's stomach jolted as he lay in bed. He tried to get up, but pain shot through him as soon as he moved, and he vomited across the bed and floor of the small room. He hugged himself, agony reaching every part of his body. For a moment it was so bad that he wished he could die, then slowly, it passed, and he lay back down on the wet sheets, panting, his forehead glistening with sweat.

He opened his eyes to the darkness. Even without any light in the room, his head spun, so he closed his eyes again, fighting a wave of dizziness.

Someone knocked on his door, but he ignored it.

Images of Aila swam round his head, as they had done on each of the thirty-five days since she had been taken by Amalia. He had failed her; he had failed everyone, and Aila was staring at him in his visions with accusing eyes, telling him that he was stupid to have believed he had a destiny, and demanding to know why he hadn't listened to her.

'Corthie?' came a voice through the door. 'Are you alright?'

The words came to Corthie through a fog of pain and exhaustion. Were they real, he thought, or were they just another fevered dream?

The door opened, the squeal of the hinges tearing through Corthie's head.

'By the Ascendants,' muttered Sohul from the open doorway.

'What's the matter?' came a woman's voice from somewhere else.

'Nothing,' said Sohul, as he eased himself into the small room. He closed the door behind him, and opened the shutters, pulling the warped and paint-blistered wood clear to allow the morning light to penetrate the room.

Corthie lay still.

He heard Sohul sigh. 'You have to stop doing this to yourself, Corthie,' he said. 'You're still sick; you shouldn't be drinking.'

He felt a hand touch his forehead.

'And you're burning up,' Sohul went on. 'Listen, I'll get a mop and some rags to clean this up; I'll be back in a minute.'

Corthie heard the door open and close again, and opened his eyes, keeping them narrow to avoid the light from hurting his head more than it already ached. He shifted on the bed, and felt a wet patch from the vomit touch his skin, and then the smell reached his nose, a strong odour of alcohol and bile. He began to swing his legs free from the twisted sheets, keeping his movements slow and gradual, then placed his feet onto the wooden floor as he sat up. He hugged his stomach again, fighting the searing cramps that threatened to immobilise him.

He glanced around the small room as if in a dream. Clothes lay heaped and abandoned across the floor, and some of them had been hit by the vomit, while pools of it sat on the wood by his toes. He picked up a clean-looking pair of shorts, and pulled them on. A pounding began behind his eyes, worse than any hangover he had experienced. He felt for his battle-vision. He found it, but it was too weak to do anything to help him. It felt like a tiny spark inside him, instead of the raging inferno that was usually there. His powers hadn't recovered since he had been brought back by Belinda. They were there, but were feeble and sickly compared to what they had been like before his death.

His death.

He almost laughed, but the thought of the pain it would bring stopped him. He had died, truly died in the cavern of Fordamere, and he could still remember lying on the stone ground with Leksandr's sword through his chest. After that? After that, it all became hazy, and his first clear memory was of being in the back of a wagon as it had travelled down from a valley into the plains of Kinell.

The door opened again, and Sohul re-entered with a mop, bucket, and a pile of rags. He smiled nervously at Corthie, then placed a few of the rags onto the floor to cover the pools of vomit. The call and screech of gulls came in through the open shutters, and Sohul glanced out at the view of the river for a moment, then got to work.

Corthie stared at him.

'We'll get this sorted in a minute,' the mercenary officer said, as he dipped the mop into the bucket. 'Your clothes will need a wash too, I daresay. I can take care of that this morning for you; we can't have you dressed in sweat and sick-covered clothes now, can we? We can pile them all up for now, and then I'll heat some water...'

'Stop talking,' Corthie muttered. 'The noise is hurting my head.'

Sohul fell into silence as he carried on cleaning the floor of the room. The mopping didn't take long, and when he had finished, he crouched down, and began to gather Corthie's soiled clothes into a pile.

'We'll, uh, need to wash the sheets as well,' he said in a low voice. 'Can you stand for a minute?'

Corthie remained motionless, then placed a hand on the wall and pushed himself up. The cramps in his guts flared, and he almost doubled over in pain, then managed to stagger to the room's only seat, a small wooden stool, where he sat. Sohul stripped the bed of its sweat and vomit-soaked sheets, and dropped them into the same pile as the soiled clothes.

'I'll get some clean bedding for you before lunchtime,' he said, 'in case you need to sleep this afternoon.'

Corthie wanted to punch him. Who did he think he was, treating the great Corthie Holdfast as if he were a child? Shame filled him at the thought, and he started to cry, sobbing into his hands as Sohul stood awkwardly by his side.

'I know things seem grim at the moment,' the mercenary said, 'but they'll get better; I'm sure of it.'

Corthie clenched his fists.

'Do you, uh, want any breakfast?'

He shook his head.

'Maybe later,' Sohul said. He picked up a clean shirt and passed it to Corthie. 'Put that on, and we'll let the room air for a bit, yes? I'll take care of everything else.'

Corthie stared at the shirt for a moment, then wiped his face with his hand. He had wept so often in front of the lieutenant that he no longer felt any shame in it.

'There's a jug of cool water sitting waiting for you in the galley,' Sohul said. 'I put a few slices of lemon in, just as you like it. Come on, there's a good fellow.'

Corthie pulled the shirt over his head and stood, swaying and leaning against the wooden wall. Sohul opened the door, and Corthie staggered through into the main section of the river boat, a long, narrow room with benches, a table, and a small galley kitchen. Vana was sitting on one of the benches, and the smell of her cigarettes and coffee almost made Corthie throw up again. She gave him a look as he sat down.

'Stinking out the boat again?' she said, her nose crinkling as the odour of vomit drifted into the room.

'It'll be fine,' said Sohul, as he closed the door, a great bundle of sheets and clothes in his arms. 'The shutter's open and the smell will go away soon.'

Vana shook her head. 'I'm starting to get used to it.'

Corthie stared at her as Sohul walked past with the bundle and disappeared into another cabin.

'Don't look at me like that,' she said; 'it's your own fault. You're ill, and yet you continue to drink like a fool. If you had been remotely disciplined, you might have recovered by now. Instead, you look, and smell, like death.'

'Shut up,' he muttered.

'And in all this time,' she went on, 'we're no further forward in finding my sister, or yours. Are you not ashamed?'

'I feel more shame than you could imagine.'

'Then do something about it. Get fit; look after yourself. Perhaps even stay off the alcohol for a few days? You're behaving like a child. If Aila could see you now, she'd probably wonder why she'd ever bothered with you in the first place.'

Corthie clenched his fists and glared at her. She swallowed, and edged back along the bench.

Sohul came back into the galley and filled a mug with water. He brought it over to the table and placed it in front of Corthie, then sat and lit a cigarette. Corthie unclenched his fists and sat back on the bench, his head spinning.

'We can't go on like this,' said Vana. 'Something has to change, and soon, otherwise...'

Sohul glanced at her. 'Otherwise what, ma'am?'

She bit her lip. 'Otherwise, I'm leaving.'

'You can't leave,' said Corthie.

'Really; is that right?' she said. 'Are you going to stop me?'

'I might.'

She raised an eyebrow at Sohul. 'Did you hear that, Lieutenant? Corthie says he's going to physically hold me here against my will. Are you and Van going to let that happen? And what about Naxor? Is he a prisoner too?'

'No one here is a prisoner,' said Sohul, 'but we're all on the run from the authorities and it would be advisable for us to stick together.'

'You'd get caught if you left,' Corthie said, 'and then you'd talk; tell them where we were. We can't risk it.'

Vana smiled, but said nothing.

Sohul glanced between the two of them, the lines around his eyes betraying his anxiety. Corthie took a sip from the mug of water, wondering why the mercenary had stayed. His headache started to ease a little, but his stomach cramps and general aches and pains remained.

He felt the same way as he had imagined ill people felt, but having never been ill in his life, he wasn't sure.

The door to the outside deck opened, and Naxor walked into the galley. He seemed to notice the silent tension, and he stood for a moment, glancing at where the others were sitting.

'The water's still hot,' said Sohul, 'if you were wanting coffee.'

'I've already had some today, but thank you, Sohul.' He walked over to the table and pulled off his coat. 'Nothing to report this morning,' he said, laying it over the back of a chair. 'Kin Dai's bustling, but no one is out looking for us.'

'Thank you, cousin,' said Vana.

Naxor sniffed the air.

'Corthie was sick again,' Vana said; 'all over his room, by the smell of it.'

Naxor sat and lit a cigarette. 'I'm not cleaning it up.'

'Sohul has already done it,' she said. 'He seems to enjoy playing nursemaid to him.'

'I don't hear you complaining when he makes dinner,' Corthie said. 'The fact is that you demigods are nothing but lazy, expecting the mortals to do all the work. You've had servants everywhere you've lived, haven't you? Minions scurrying about after you, wiping your arse.'

Vana smirked. 'So says the man who can't clean up his own sick.'

'Steady on,' said Naxor; 'there's no need for any of this. We're in a bit of a pickle right now, and we need to stop the bickering.'

'Yes,' said Sohul; 'I agree. I know this has been a trying time, but look at what we've achieved – we managed to get away from the Ascendants in Yoneath, and we've managed to successfully hide in Kin Dai. We have one big advantage, namely that our enemies think Corthie is dead.'

'That's an advantage?' said Vana. 'His presence here has been nothing but a liability. If we get caught, it'll be because of him. If it weren't for Aila, I'd recommend that we ditch him here, and find somewhere else to hide.'

A sudden rage bubbled up within Corthie and he hurled the mug of water at Vana. It missed her by an inch and smashed off the wall of the galley, showering her in water and fragments of pottery. She stared at him, her mouth open, water dripping from her chin.

She stood, her hands trembling.

'That was a little over the top, Corthie,' said Naxor. 'Perhaps you should lie down for a while.'

'I am so sick of the both of you,' Corthie growled. 'Bloody demigods, so smug and arrogant. You've been pampered for so long that you don't understand the first thing about real life. One of you is a coward who used to work for Marcus; you stooped so low that you would search for Aila every day, trying to find her to please your master. And the other one? A crooked liar, who would sell out everyone he knows to get his hands on a Quadrant.' A cramp gripped his stomach, and he paused, clutching his waist, his eyes closed.

'It's nice to know what you really think of us,' said Vana.

Naxor chuckled. 'I already knew.'

Corthie jumped to his feet, his teeth bared. 'Get out of my sight, before I beat the both of you to a pulp.'

Vana started, her eyes wide. She edged round the table, pulling Naxor by the arm, and they went into her cabin. Corthie sat again, the pain in his abdomen excruciating.

'Pyre's arse; I need a drink.'

Sohul said nothing, his eyes revealing his alarm. He stubbed out his cigarette and got to his feet.

'I'll, eh, take care of the laundry now, I think.'

Corthie sat in silence as the lieutenant left the galley. For a moment, the pain passed, and he glanced around as if coming out of a trance. What was he doing? Was he trying to drive them all away? No, he lost control whenever the pain swept over him and he didn't know what he was doing. He should apologise, but his legs felt like lead. He heard Vana's raised voice through the thin walls of the river boat. He couldn't make out the words, but the anger in her tone was clear. He coughed from the fug of cigarette smoke in the galley. It had been several days since he had gone out on deck, but he felt a need for fresh air, and pulled himself up. At once, his knees gave way under his weight and he toppled to the floor, sending a full ashtray and the jug of water flying.

Sohul's head appeared at a door. 'Are you alright?'

'I'm fine,' said Corthie from the floor.

'I'll come and tidy that up.'

'No! No. I can manage. You're not my nursemaid, Sohul.'

'I know that, but you're sick.'

'I can manage. Leave me alone.'

Sohul frowned, then nodded and closed the door. Corthie got up onto his hands and knees, and began picking up the broken pieces of the jug, placing the fragments into a wooden bin by the galley stove. After that, he grimaced, and cleaned up the cigarette butts, his fingers slick with ash and water. He felt his gorge rise again from the stench of smoke and vomit, but held it in, his body moving automatically while his mind retreated. When he had finished, he placed both hands onto the edge of the table and got to his feet. He leaned against the table for a moment, then staggered over to the door leading to the outside deck. He climbed the narrow stairs, taking them one slow step at a time, then emerged into the brilliant sunshine of Kin Dai.

The river boat was tied up by a pier jutting out into the great estuary that ran through the centre of the city. Hundreds of other vessels were also berthed along the shore, so many, that Naxor had informed them that about a quarter of the city's population lived aboard a boat of some kind. The sound of the gulls overhead mixed with the noise coming from the bustling wharves, where people were moving through the wide fish markets that ran along the river front. The smells were over-powering, but were better than the stench below deck. Corthie sat on the top step of the stairs, heeding the warning to keep his height incon-spicuous, and watched the life of the city go past. Wooden piers stretched through the brown river water like a spider's web, and small barges were being punted along the tight lanes that wound their way between the thick rows of houseboats. Naxor had bought the boat where they were living with the last of their money. It had been leaky and falling apart when they had first moved in, but Sohul and Van had worked for days to turn it into somewhere inhabitable, even comfortable.

Free from the stomach cramps, Corthie's mind began to wander as if it were a beast released from captivity. Aila and Kelsey shone in his mind, and how he had let them down. If he had managed to kill the two Ascendants, then he would have found them, instead of being confined to bed, sick and in near-constant pain. But it wasn't just Aila and Kelsey that he had failed; he had lost the Sextant, which meant that the Ascendants would have the power to obliterate the two hidden worlds. Maybe they had already done it; maybe the Holdings were in smoking ruins, and the City occupied by Banner forces.

How could it have happened? How could he have been so wrong? He had no destiny; his actions weren't guided by fate – it had all been an illusion, brought about by a mixture of stupidity and over-confidence. Blackrose had been right all along; she had known the truth, and had tried to persuade him, but he hadn't listened. The two Ascendants had defeated him easily, and he had lost the Clawhammer before losing his life. And then... then Belinda had brought him back. Would she have done so if she had been able to see what life he was going to lead? No doubt she had done it out of pity, but part of him wished she hadn't, and he had been allowed to die in peace.

'Don't try and stop me!' yelled Vana, as a door was slammed somewhere in the lower level of the boat.

Corthie glanced down the stairs, and saw Vana charge up them, a bag over her shoulder, and Naxor a pace behind. She stopped when she saw Corthie sitting on the top step.

'Get out of my way,' she said. 'Please.'

Corthie shifted to the side of the step, and Vana squeezed by. Naxor followed her, his expression dark.

'You can't be serious, cousin,' he said, as they both stood on deck.

'I am perfectly serious,' she said, 'and I advise you to do the same.'

'But where in Malik's name will you go?'

'I'm not sure, but there's a ship leaving from the main docks in a few hours. It's sailing south, and will stop in at Capston, before turning and heading up to Cape Armour.'

'It's too risky,' said Naxor. 'We should stay together.'

'I can't believe you're saying that, not after he nearly took my head off with that mug. He's nothing but a vile thug; too proud to admit he's wrong, and too stupid to stop drinking. If you stay here with him, it'll be the end of you, dear cousin. Come with me.'

Naxor pursed his lips, his eyes lowered.

'We have just enough money for both of us to go,' Vana went on. 'Leave the idiot mortals here to get caught; the Holdfasts have brought us nothing but ruin and despair.'

Naxor turned to Corthie. 'Do you see how upset you've made her? Perhaps an apology would be in order.'

'I don't want his apology,' she said. 'I want nothing more to do with him.'

'I'm speaking to you, Corthie,' Naxor went on. 'Apologise, and beg her to stay.'

Corthie shook his head. 'Let her go. Maybe the ship will sink and she'll drown.'

Vana raised her palms in the air as if to say 'I told you so,' then started to walk along the gangplank. Naxor glared at Corthie, then ran after her, chasing her as she strode down the pier. Within moments, both were lost in the thick crowds passing along the wide wharf, and Corthie turned his gaze back to the river.

Corthie was awoken a few hours later by the sound of boots coming down the stairs from the deck. He had gone to sleep in Vana's cabin, as his own still stank of vomit. He listened to the footsteps as they passed the door and entered the galley, then heard voices. Corthie rubbed his face and sat up in bed. A few of Vana's possessions were still lying around the small room, but she had taken most of her things with her when she had left. He leaned over and opened the shutters a little, then got out of bed. For once, his head wasn't throbbing, and his stomach had calmed down, leaving just the usual collection of aches and pains. He felt hungry too, which was unusual, his appetite having been almost wiped out by his illness. He frowned. He should stop thinking of his condition as an illness. He had died, and had then been brought back, and his flesh and organs were damaged, perhaps irreparably. He felt for his battle-vision, and found it. Despite its weakness, it still gave him hope that he would fully recover.

He opened the door and walked into the galley, where Van and Sohul were sitting by the table. Sohul was serving the captain a bowl of hot food from a large pot on the stove, and they both glanced up at Corthie's entrance.

'I heard about Vana,' said Van.

Corthie nodded.

'And Naxor hasn't returned either,' said Sohul.

'This is bad,' said Van. 'If Naxor has gone as well, then our chances of finding Kelsey and Aila are next to nothing.'

Corthie sat.

'Even if it's just Vana,' the captain went on, 'we have no idea what she'll do next. She might go straight to the Ascendants in Alea Tanton to bargain for her life.'

'She won't,' said Corthie. 'They killed her brother; she'll never willingly help them.'

'And if she's apprehended?'

'Then we're in trouble.'

Sohul placed the bowl in front of Van, laying out cutlery for him.

'Could I have some?' asked Corthie.

'Sure,' said Sohul. 'You hungry?'

'Aye, a bit.'

'Good,' he said; 'that's a good sign.'

'This is great, Sohul, thanks,' said Van, as he ate. 'As soon as I'm finished, I'll get cleaned up.'

'How was work?' said the lieutenant.

'Fine,' he said. 'I'm tired, though. Ten hours of unloading crates from ships is not my idea of fun. Still, it pays the bills, I guess.'

'And there's one less mouth to feed,' said Corthie.

Van narrowed his eyes. 'Unfortunately.'

'There was nothing we could have done to make her stay,' said Corthie. 'I heard Naxor try to change her mind, but she was having none of it.'

'And I'm sure that throwing a mug at her head had nothing to do with it.'

Corthie frowned. 'She was getting on my nerves.'

'So?' said Van. 'We've been cooped up together for a month; we're all getting on each other's nerves. We relied upon Vana to detect if any gods or demigods were close by, but more than that, she was one of us.'

'She's not one of us. She's a demigod.'

'So's Aila.'

Corthie glared at him. Sohul placed a bowl in front of him before he could speak, then the lieutenant sat on the bench. Corthie gazed at the contents of the bowl, feeling an urge to fling it against the wall. Even Van was tiring of him; he could feel it.

'What do we do now?' said Sohul.

'We wait,' said Van. 'We need to know if Naxor is returning.'

'And if he doesn't?'

Van sighed. 'Then I don't know.'

'Surely we have to wait here until Corthie has fully recovered?'

'But how long will that take?' Van said. 'There is also the possibility that he won't get any better than he is now.' He met Corthie's glance. 'You were dead for several minutes. Belinda, and I say this with all respect, but she didn't know what she was doing. I have a suspicion that she revived your heart, but that she didn't take the time to heal all of your organs; maybe she didn't realise that she was supposed to, and I didn't remind her. I've seen people brought back by the gods before, and they only took a few days to recover. I only took a few days. It's been over a month now, and I'm not seeing much improvement day-to-day.'

'But his appetite's back,' said Sohul.

'So he says, but he hasn't actually eaten anything.'

Corthie gazed at the bowl. His hunger had evaporated at some point while they had been discussing Vana. He picked up a spoon and forced down a mouthful of the thick fish soup, then almost gagged. He felt dizzy, and the pains in his stomach reappeared the moment he swallowed. He thought about Van's words, feeling that he might be correct. Nothing about his insides felt quite right, from his joints to his stomach, lungs and head. Everything ached or felt different.

'What about salve?' he said. 'Would that work?'

'Yeah, probably,' Van said. 'The problem is trying to get some. There's none to be had in Kin Dai as far as I can tell, and I've asked around. If any Banner forces were here, then we might be in with a chance of stealing some, if, that is, it's still being distributed to the soldiers. One vial might be enough.'

'Naxor had some,' said Corthie. 'He had a small flask of it.'

'I searched his room a few days ago while he was out,' said Van. 'If he has any, it isn't on the boat.'

'You searched his room?' said Sohul, his eyes wide. 'But he'd know about it; he would know you had been in there. He reads our minds; I'm sure of it.'

Van nodded. 'I made the assumption that he would find out. To be frank, I'm beyond caring what Naxor thinks about me. If he hadn't tried to snatch the Quadrant from Amalia, then Kelsey and Aila would still be with us.'

'Why are you both still here?' said Corthie. 'It can't be due to any contract we might have had.'

Sohul and Van shared a glance.

'You're right,' said Van. 'We helped save you from Fordamere, but our handshake agreements expired some time ago. I'm here for one reason; I promised Kelsey I wouldn't stop looking for her.'

'And I'm here,' said Sohul, 'because of Van. I have a great deal of respect for you, Corthie, but the truth is that the Banners of Implacatus will have black-listed both me and Van by now. I don't think I'll ever be able to return home, not after I was seen leading an attack on Banner soldiers in Fordamere. So, I stick by my captain. He is my friend, and that's what friends do.'

Corthie nodded, deflated and in pain. He stood, and walked towards his room, ignoring the glances from Van and Sohul. He entered his cabin and closed the door. The smell had receded, and the salty air of the estuary was permeating the room. He crouched down and reached under the bed, his hand searching through piles of clothes and rubbish, until his fingers touched the surface of a clay jug. He grasped it and took it out, then sat on the bed.

One benefit of his condition, he thought, as he pulled the stopper free, was that his tolerance to alcohol had plummeted. He raised the jug to his lips and drank, gulping down the cheap, harsh spirits. His throat burned, then the warmth spread like a comforting hand across his chest, easing his aches and soothing his bitter disappointment. He felt a glow of giddy well-being, and smiled, before taking another large gulp. He thought about what Van and Sohul would be thinking, but he didn't care, the drink smothering the anxiety he had felt at the table. So, they weren't there for him, so what? He didn't need them; he could clean up his own vomit.

He heard doors opening and closing, then Naxor's voice drifted through to him. He stood, gripping the jug in one hand, and staggered into the galley.

'Hey, Naxor,' he said, stumbling into the long, narrow room. 'I was hoping you'd buggered off with that bitch Vana.'

Naxor regarded him with a cool eye. 'I was sorely tempted, believe me.'

Corthie laughed. 'Why didn't you? No one wants you here.'

Van frowned at him. 'Sit down, Corthie.'

'Screw you,' Corthie said; 'screw the lot of you.'

The galley stilled.

'Em,' said Sohul; 'Naxor was just telling us that he's carried out today's vision sweep, but there's no sign of Aila or Kelsey.'

'And why in Pyre's name should we believe that little rat? He's a liar and a thief, and I should have killed him back in the City.'

'Maybe you should go to bed,' said Van.

'Why?' said Corthie, taking another long swig. 'I'm just getting started.' He shook the jug and frowned. Empty already. He dropped it, and it rolled to the side of the floor, coming to a rest by Naxor's foot. He remembered that he might have hidden another somewhere in his cabin. 'On second thoughts,' he said, swaying, 'I might lie down for a minute.'

He turned and stumbled off, colliding with the wall before making it back into his cabin. He scratched his head.

'Alright, flask,' he muttered; 'where did I leave you?'

He leaned over to look under the bed, and his right foot slipped, sending him falling. He hit the floor, his face striking the wooden boards, then his eyes closed and he fell into oblivion.

CHAPTER 4
BACK TO THE SKIES

Catacombs, Torduan Mountains, Khatanax – 18th Tuminch 5252

The wind rushed through Sable's hair as Sanguino swept round in a tight curve. Below them, the valley where the Catacombs was located was glowing red from the lava pits, while, to the east, the sun was rising over the horizon. Despite her exhilaration, Sable was concentrating hard, keeping her vision connection to the dark red dragon intact. She could feel his thoughts within her mind as she provided him with sight, complete with battle-vision. His left eye had healed to the extent that he had reasonable clarity on that side, but his right eye would never see again.

She gripped onto the leather handle attached to the harness as Sanguino banked to the left. A belt was strapped round her waist, and her booted feet were tucked into stirrups on either side of the saddle. The new harness had been finished by Millen just a few days previously, and it was working well, doing its job of keeping Sable secure on the dragon's wide shoulders.

As well as his thoughts, Sable could also sense Sanguino's emotions as he circled above the valley; he was happy, and it made her happy to know that. Each of them had been maimed and wounded, and together they had overcome every obstacle in their way, and this flight was their long-awaited reward.

'Look at the sunrise,' he called out to her; 'it is the first I have seen in a long time, and it is all the more beautiful because of that. How I have dreamed of this day, my precious rider. I despaired at times, I confess, but your spirit bore me through all trials. You knew this day would arrive; you knew in your heart that we would fly together, and so it has come to pass. The air is beneath my wings again, and the stars above us are shining with a splendour I had almost forgotten.'

Sable smiled. 'We did it together, you and I.'

'I wish to tell you something,' he said, 'something that I have been holding back until this moment. Blackrose told me that on Dragon Eyre, each dragon has three names, secret names, as well as a name by which they are known to everyone else. Her true name is not Blackrose. I don't have anything like that, but I did have a name before Sanguino. It was bestowed upon me by the dragon who fathered me, though I now curse him.'

'What is it?'

'Badblood.'

Sable smothered her disappointment. She had known that Sanguino had been named something else in his youth, but Badblood sounded like a spiteful name given by an uncaring father. On the other hand, she reflected, it also sounded like a name given to a dangerous, outlaw dragon, and she quite liked that aspect.

'Badblood,' she repeated.

'I used to hate that name,' he said, 'but coming from your lips it sounds different. I will allow you to address me by that name when we are flying, or otherwise alone, but you must not tell anyone else.'

'Alright. Badblood and Sable, saviours of Dragon Eyre; I like it.'

He laughed. 'Let's not get ahead of ourselves.'

Sable felt the pain from her waist increase. It had been healing well, following an alarming few days after her return with Maddie from Yoneath, but the strain of the flight was making it ache. She could also sense that Badblood's wings were tiring after so many days of inactivity, but that he was too proud to admit it.

'Let's go back,' she said. 'The wound in my stomach is getting sore.'

'Of course, my rider; you need to rest, so that we can fly again tomorrow.'

He started to descend, until they were level with the tallest tombs. Burntskull was peering out at them from Deathfang's lair, a bemused expression on his face, while other dragons were also watching. The hot vapours swirled up from the rivers of lava beneath them as they soared further down. Sable focussed. It would be their first landing, and it was the part she had been most concerned about, being unable to see his limbs as they extended under his body. The dragon levelled off and hovered for a moment next to the blackened square entrance to their tomb, then edged forwards into the shadows of the cavern. He landed heavily, his claws scrabbling on the stone floor of the tomb, then he brought his wings in.

Sable puffed out her cheeks in relief. Down to their right, Maddie and Millen approached, Millen with a big grin on his face. He was still limping, but had discarded the crutch he had been using for over two months.

'Were you watching?' said Sanguino, his voice full of pride.

'Of course we were, you daft dragon,' said Maddie. 'You were great.'

'How was the harness?' said Millen.

Sable smiled. 'I managed not to fall off, didn't I?'

She unbuckled the strap, and climbed down a ladder made from twisted cords of leather that was fastened to the dragon's flank. She jumped the last yard to the ground, then regretted it as the pain in her waist peaked for a moment. She clutched her side, grimacing. Maddie came up to her and put an arm over her shoulder.

'Come and sit down,' she said.

'I will stay here,' said Sanguino, as he turned to face the entrance of the tomb.

Sable glanced at him. He had remained on guard by the opening of the cavern ever since Blackrose had been captured by the Ascendants, in case any of the other dragons tried to evict them from the Catacombs. A bolt of anxiety shot through her as she watched him. If Deathfang and the others used force against him, then there would be only one outcome. She kept her face confident despite her feelings, and allowed Maddie to lead her away to the rear of the tomb. Millen followed, and they sat by the dark hearth where they ate their meals.

'How's your tummy?' said Maddie.

'Fine,' said Sable. 'A few twinges, that's all.'

Maddie frowned at her. 'Yeah, right. I saw your face when you landed; it looked as if it hurt; a lot.'

'Don't worry about me,' she said. 'It was worth the pain to get airborne today. The other dragons were staring at us in disbelief.'

Millen passed her a mug of wine. 'You did great. Flying is wonderful, isn't it?'

She took a sip and smiled. 'Yes; it was incredible; worth all of the hard work and frustrations.' She glanced at the mug. 'Nice wine.'

'Thanks,' said Maddie. 'I was a little more adventurous on my last trip into town. I also got some fancy cheese.'

Sable glanced at her. 'I hope you were careful, Maddie. Don't take any risks. If you get caught getting us supplies, then we lose the Quadrant.'

Maddie laughed. 'I see. You're not worried about what happens to me, just your precious Quadrant.'

'It's the only way we're going to get to Dragon Eyre. I wish there had been some other way to get food.'

'Are you regretting showing me how to use it?'

'I didn't show you how to use it; I showed you how to get to the nearest town in Tordue and back; and I only did that because we were desperate and had run out of everything. And, I might have been slightly delirious from my wound at the time.'

'If you showed me how to get to Alea Tanton, then I could get a far wider range of stuff.'

Sable raised an eyebrow. 'And that's the only reason you want to go to Alea Tanton? You wouldn't, say, also try to rescue a certain dragon from captivity?'

Maddie scowled. 'Well, it's been long enough. How can you sit here calmly, sipping wine, while Blackrose is chained up in that horrible city? Every day that passes is like a knife in my heart. What if they kill her? They could be torturing her as we speak.'

Millen groaned. 'Do we have to go over this again?'

'But I still don't understand,' said Maddie. 'We have a Quadrant, so why don't we just rescue her now?'

Sable frowned. Using the Quadrant to free Blackrose had become a constant refrain from Maddie, but Sable had been procrastinating. At first, it had been due to her injury; and then she had been determined that Sanguino would fly before any rescue attempt was made. Blackrose would easily be able to take the Quadrant from her by force, and then she might choose to go to Dragon Eyre before they were prepared. Sable had to delay, so that she could remain in control.

'Millen's right,' she said. 'We've discussed this. We'll rescue Blackrose when we're ready, and when we actually have a chance of succeeding. With Sanguino's flight today, we are one step closer. And remember, I've seen her – she's not being tortured; the Deadskins are treating her like a damn princess.'

Maddie nodded, but her expression remained unconvinced. Sable darted into her mind. The black dragon's rider was harbouring a hope that she would be able to work out how to make the Quadrant take her directly to Alea Tanton, but Sable was confident that she would need much more time and practice with the device before she would be able to do that. Other than that, Maddie's thoughts were filled with impatience, and a frustration that could reach boiling point at any moment. Her emotions were stretched and pulled by Blackrose's absence, and a small part of her believed that Sable would not honour her promise to rescue the dragon from captivity. The Holdfast woman was tempted to use her powers to soothe Maddie's worries, but she had been doing a lot of that in recent days, and Maddie's mind was starting to become more resistant to her methods of persuasion.

'I have an idea,' she said.

The others glanced at her.

'You know what I can do with Sanguino, yeah? We link minds, and he can see what I can see.'

'So?' said Maddie. 'I mean, it's impressive, but what's that got to do with Blackrose?'

'I hadn't finished,' said Sable. 'What if I link to you, Maddie, and then I use my powers to check on Blackrose? In theory, if I can see her, then you would be able to as well. You might even be able to pass her a message.'

Maddie's eyes flashed with hope. 'Really? Would that work?'

Sable considered. 'Did you manage to procure any keenweed?'

'Yeah. Not much, but a bit.'

'Then, let's give it a try.'

'Now?' said Millen. 'Are you not exhausted by linking with Sanguino during the flight?'

'I'm a bit tired, but if it makes Maddie feel better, then I'll do it.'

Maddie rummaged in a bag by her feet, then passed Sable a weed-stick, her hands trembling with excitement.

'Give me a moment, both of you,' Sable said. 'I want to smoke this and prepare myself.'

'Thanks, Sable,' said Maddie, as she stood. 'This means a lot to me.'

Sable smiled, and waited as she strode away, Millen limping off behind her. She turned to gaze at the pile of ash in the centre of the hearth and took a slow breath. The pain in her guts was intense, and she could feel exhaustion about to overwhelm her. She wondered why she was so determined to hide how ill and tired she felt from the others, but she knew that their hopes depended upon her, and she wanted them to believe that she was confident and in control. They were relying on her. In Blackrose's absence, the others, Sanguino included, had looked to her for leadership, and she had been trying her best not to let them down.

She lit the weedstick and inhaled, feeling her tiredness disappear almost immediately. Her aches and pains eased, and her mind was filled with a sharp clarity. She knew she would pay for it in a few hours, but she needed Maddie to believe her, and she needed to prove her worth. In truth, Sable had never felt so hopeless and alone, despite her achievements. Getting Sanguino into the air had been one of the greatest challenges of her life, and to do so without the protection of Blackrose had seemed an impossible task a month before, when she had lain fevered and close to death. On top of that, the Ascendants had the Sextant, and Corthie and Kelsey, her nephew and niece, had disappeared, while Belinda had turned to the enemy. Dragon Eyre was the last hope she had and, although she was just as desperate to rescue Blackrose as Maddie was, she knew she had to plan everything carefully. If she messed it up, there would be nowhere to go.

She glanced round, and gestured for Maddie to rejoin her. She hurried over to the hearth and sat down next to Sable.

'Give me your hand,' Sable said.

'How romantic,' said Maddie; 'I didn't know you cared.'

'Hilarious as always, Maddie.' She took the young woman's hand in hers, and focussed. 'Alright. To do this, I'll need to go into your mind, obviously, so that I can form a connection. I'm going to tether your consciousness to my own, and then I'm going to send my vision west over the mountains and all the way to Alea Tanton. We already know that Blackrose is being held in the Northern Pits.'

'No, you already know that. I have only your word for it.'

'Well, now you'll see if I've been lying or not. Are you ready?'

'Yeah.'

Sable went into Maddie's mind, and repeated what she had done to Sanguino. Her connection to him had been developed and fostered over a long time, but the tethers to Maddie would only need to last a few minutes. She pinched parts of Maddie's mind to her own, starting with her sight.

'Woah,' said Maddie. 'I'm looking out from your eyes. Is that what I look like these days? Amalia's ass, what a mess. I'm surprised I haven't been arrested in town for looking like a vagrant. At least that explains the funny looks I've been getting.'

'Steal a mirror and a hairbrush on your next visit. Right, that part's complete. Close your eyes; you'll still be able to see what I see. Let's go.'

Sable pushed her vision out of her body, and through the cavern, emerging into the valley. She heard Maddie gasp, but tried to ignore her. She moved her vision higher, then shot it out over the tops of the mountains, sending it hurtling over the ragged and barren slopes. They passed the reservoir, then began to descend, the irrigated fields of Tordue before them. Sable picked up her speed, and the land below them became a blur of motion.

I feel sick, Maddie said inside her head.

Don't talk. Let me concentrate.

Within a few moments the ocean became visible on the horizon, and Sable aimed for the vast, sprawling city that lay on its polluted shores. Along the edge of the city was a wide band of ramshackle shanty dwellings and huts, assembled from wood and animal hides, and beyond stretched the miles of slums. Sable turned to the north, skirting the city, until the walls of Old Tanton came into view. The old port town was surrounded on three sides by the tight network of slum housing, then, after that, lay the vast sprawl of Deadskins territory, home to the hundreds of thousands of Fordians descended from those who had fled the destruction of their land. In the midst of the Deadskins region lay a huge complex of high, stone buildings, and Sable slowed, approaching with care as she scanned the movements of the swarms of people in the streets. She knew the way well, having checked on Blackrose several times since she had been captured, and led Maddie straight to the building where the black dragon was being held.

We're nearly there, she told Maddie. *Remember, do not mention the Quadrant to her.*

Sable entered the building and descended into a vast cavern carved from the bedrock of the city. Two dragons were there. One, a fine, sleek, dark green beast, was being fed live goats by a legion of Fordians at the northern end of the cavern.

That is Grassworm, Sable said, *the current Deadskins champion. He is docile and obedient, which was probably how I imagine Sanguino used to be. I'd like to try rescuing him too, but we shall see.*

Never mind him; where's Blackrose?

Sable went into the shadows at the other end of the cavern, where a huge dragon was lying, chained and muzzled, her wings secured by a multitude of shackles.

Maddie sobbed.

There she is, said Sable. *Let me try to enter her mind.*

Sable approached with her vision, and pushed against Blackrose's eyes. Going into a dragon's head was different from that of humans, as she had learned from her mistakes with Frostback. It was almost like asking for permission to enter; she felt a resistance, and then the dragon allowed her in.

Hello, Blackrose; it's me again.

Sable. How is Maddie? I hope you are looking after her as I requested.

Maddie is here with me, inside my mind. I've brought her to see you.

The dragon sighed. *I wish you hadn't. I do not want her to see me like this.*

She needed to, Blackrose. I think she was starting to doubt my word. I've asked her to be patient, but she needed proof that I wasn't lying.

Maddie? Can you hear me?

Yes, said Maddie through her tears. *What have they done to you?*

Never mind that, rider; listen to me. I know that I have doubted her in the past, but you must trust Sable. She is our only hope.

Have they made you fight?

Not yet, but that day is fast approaching. I will put on a show for them, to make them believe I am pliant. It shames me, but knowing that you and Sable are working for my release keeps me strong.

I have some good news, Sable said. *Today, Sanguino managed to fly again.*

The black dragon said nothing for a moment, and Sable saw a tear escape from her right eye.

You should be very proud, Blackrose said at last; *and tell Sanguino that I am proud of him.*

I will.

Is there any word on Frostback?

I'm afraid not. She hasn't been seen anywhere near the Catacombs.

A small part of Sable's consciousness was alerted to a noise in the tomb.

We have to go, she said. *Someone's in the cavern.*

Then go with my love and blessings. And, Maddie, stay strong, for me.

I'll try, Maddie sobbed.

Sable severed the connection and got to her feet by the hearth, the keenweed clearing her mind in an instant. A dragon was hovering by the entrance to the tomb, her grey wings beating as she talked to Sanguino. Sable rushed across the cavern, leaving Maddie swaying where she sat.

'What's going on?' she said to Sanguino as she reached the entrance. She glanced up at the dragon outside. It was Ashfall, one of Deathfang's adult brood.

'I bear a message from my father,' the grey dragon said. 'He wants to speak with you both in his lair. Now.'

'Is it bad news?' said Sable.

Ashfall glanced down at her. 'Come and see.'

She beat her wings again, and ascended, circling upwards.

Sable looked at Sanguino. 'We knew this day would come. Your flight was what they were waiting for.'

'Do you think they will try to expel us, my rider?'

'Maybe. Stay here, and I'll tell Maddie and Millen to pack a bag each and then hide in Frostback's old cavern. Oh, by the way, Blackrose says that she is very proud of you. She shed a tear when I told her you flew today.'

Sanguino nodded. Even without being in his mind, their link had become so strong that Sable could feel the mixture of pride and worry that flowed through him.

He nodded. 'Don't be long.'

Twenty minutes later, Sable climbed up onto the harness and took Sanguino out for his second flight of the day. Rather than give in to exhaustion, she had smoked another stick of keenweed, and her head was buzzing as they ascended to the highest level of tombs, lifted by the swirls of hot air rising from the lava pools at the bottom of the valley. Burntskull was waiting for them as they landed heavily in the entrance of Deathfang's huge lair, his eyes tight.

'Greetings,' said Sable, as she glanced at him.

'Frostback was right, wasn't she?' said the yellow dragon.

'What do you mean?'

'You must be a witch, otherwise how could you have made a blind dragon fly again?'

Sanguino raised his claws in a flash, his great talons aimed at Burntskull. 'Do not insult my rider, or I will rip you in two.'

Burntskull chuckled. 'At least you have some spirit about you; I thought it had evaporated a long time hence. Come, Deathfang is waiting.'

He led them deeper into the huge cavern, and into the vast space at the end where Deathfang ruled from atop his pile of gold. Sable saw Ashfall stand by his left, while Darksky was on his right, her brood of three young dragons peering out from under a protective wing. Others were there too, some of whom Sable didn't recognise except for a brief glimpse of their heads as they had glanced out of their tombs at them that morning. Halfclaw was there, she noticed, the green-blue dragon that had tormented Sanguino along with Frostback when he had first arrived. Sable began to feel the dark red dragon's fear as he faced the leadership of the Catacombs.

Everything will be fine, she said in his mind. *You have nothing to fear.*

Deathfang gazed at them with a lazy expression that Sable knew he used when he was anxious or worried.

'So,' he said, 'the blind dragon flies again? How was this done?'

'With patience and hard work,' said Sanguino.

'And with a witch as a rider,' said Burntskull. 'It is the only way.'

'Is this true?' said Deathfang.

'May I speak, o mighty Deathfang?' said Sable.

'Will you try to bewitch us?'

'If I was unable to bewitch your estranged daughter Frostback, then it would seem unlikely that any trick would work upon a dragon as powerful as you.'

Deathfang stared at her. 'You may talk, but I warn you; if I suspect you are trying to use your unnatural powers on me, I will destroy you both.'

She lifted her left hand, and showed them the stump where her little finger had been. 'A god did this to me. It may not look like much to you, but we humans need our fingers.' She then lifted her tunic to show the large scar across her stomach. 'Another god did this to me, and I nearly died because of it. I lay in a fever for days, and it has taken time to heal.'

'Of what possible interest are your injuries to us?' said Burntskull.

'I am trying to prove something. I was maimed and wounded, and so was Sanguino. Alone, we are less than we are together. Together, we flew. You can call it witchcraft if you wish, but for a moment, please consider that dragons and people can sometimes help each other. Please, do not dismiss the notion out of hand.'

'Any dragon that needs a human is weak,' said Deathfang.

Sable smiled. 'Why?'

'It would be like a human needing a rat,' said Burntskull.

'A blind man may need a faithful dog to help him find his way, and to protect him.'

Burntskull laughed. 'You equate yourself to a dog?'

She shrugged. 'Better than a rat.'

'Enough,' said Deathfang. 'I get your point, witch. For many days, we have debated what to do about your presence here in the Catacombs. For a while, we continued to expect the return of Blackrose, but it seems clear that she will never come back to the Catacombs. We must presume that she is dead.'

'She is not dead,' said Sable. 'I spoke to her half an hour ago.'

There were muttered gasps from the dragons in the cavern.

'Yes,' said Sable, 'I am what you would call a witch. I used my powers to seek out Blackrose and speak with her. She is currently imprisoned within the city of Alea Tanton, after being captured by two Ascendants. We intend to free her soon. Sanguino's first flight was a necessary step in our plans.'

'Kill her now,' snarled Burntskull. 'She is the cause of Frostback's estrangement. Your former daughter was correct about this insect being a witch; and now you have heard it from her own mouth.'

'Or, I could help you,' said Sable. 'My powers are extensive. I can see anything that moves in Khatanax; I can tell you if danger approaches.'

Deathfang laughed. 'I do not require your help, insect. Now that Sanguino can fly, you are able to leave. This shall be my final act of generosity towards you, and I shall do it out of respect for Blackrose. If you leave peacefully within the next few days, you will be unharmed.'

'Why don't we come to a deal?'

'I have told you, you have nothing to offer me.'

'What if we kill Grimsleep for you? I know that he is the main cause of your worries. He is strong, and his presence on the other side of the valley is the gravest threat to your authority in the Catacombs. If we destroy him, then will you allow us to stay?'

'Now you are being ridiculous,' said Deathfang. 'For one thing, I could kill Grimsleep any time I choose, and secondly, Sanguino would be no match for him, even with you on his shoulders.'

'You are wrong,' said the dark red dragon. 'I can, and shall, slay Grimsleep.'

'You would kill your own father?' said Ashfall, her eyes wide.

'He is not my father,' growled Sanguino. 'He has cursed me, and I him. I long to meet him in combat.'

'This is a nonsense,' said Burntskull. 'We have been more than fair with you.'

'One moment,' said Deathfang. 'This amuses me. They clearly have no chance against Grimsleep, but I would enjoy watching them try.' He turned to Sanguino and Sable. 'Very well. You have a month. If you have slain Grimsleep within that time, I will allow you to stay. If you haven't, then we will descend upon your tomb with a dozen dragons and tear you all limb from limb.'

'We accept,' said Sable. 'Then, following Grimsleep's death, we shall rescue Blackrose and depart this world forever. Anyone here who wishes to accompany us to Dragon Eyre to liberate your home world will be welcome to join us. We shall slay gods by the dozen, and lay the bodies of their soldiers in heaps. It will be a noble pursuit, filled with blood and ash, and when it is concluded, the gods will fear dragons as they did in the past.'

The chamber fell silent. Sable bowed her head to Deathfang, then Sanguino turned his heavy bulk, and they made their way to the tomb entrance. The dark red dragon said nothing as he launched himself into the air, but Sable knew he was troubled.

'I'm sorry about that,' she said, as they rose into the sky.

'You should have told me what you were going to say, my rider. How am I to kill Grimsleep? He is greater in size than Blackrose. Not even Deathfang could defeat him on his own.'

'I was thinking on my feet and I couldn't figure out any other way to make them let us stay. Listen, you don't have to fight him. We have another month. We can train hard, and then leave one night, quietly.'

'I cannot. My honour is now bound to the words I spoke in there. I was telling the truth about my desire to kill Grimsleep; I loathe him, and now I have promised to face him. I cannot back down.'

Sable nodded. 'Then we're going to have to work out how to kill him.'

CHAPTER 5

EXHIBITION

Alea Tanton, Tordue, Western Khatanax – 21st Tuminch 5252

Belinda heard the roar of the crowd as soon as the air cleared. Arete slipped the Quadrant into her robes, as the four gods took in the cheers and applause of those sitting in the vast arena. Felice raised her hand and waved to the massed Blue Thumbs supporters who, in their home arena, were outnumbering the Deadskins supporters three to one. The blue-sashed crowd chanted Felice's name and she gave a broad, but fake, smile. To her right was Arete, and then Belinda, and finally Latude, who had recently been appointed patron of the Deadskins despite still being a prisoner. His ankles were fastened with thick chains, and he looked miserable as he squinted in the bright sunshine. He would be going back to his prison cell under the Governor's residence as soon as the games were finished, and part of Belinda's role that day was to prevent him from escaping.

Arete gave a brief nod, and the four gods sat, the two Ascendants in the prime seats.

'It's nice to get out of Old Alea,' said Arete, 'and I'm looking forward to watching mortals hack each other to pieces.' She glanced at Felice. 'How long have you been the patron of the Blue Thumbs?'

'About eighty years, your Grace.'

'Ha! You must have seen a lot of blood spilled in that time.'

'I have, your Grace, though the novelty has worn a little thin over the decades.'

'We should have games like this on Implacatus. It would be something to watch, and it would keep the population under control.'

Latude snorted.

Arete gave him a withering glance. 'Behave yourself, or I will flay the skin from your face.'

Belinda watched as a gate in the circular wall of the arena opened, and a troop of armed men ran out, all wearing differing types of armour. Each one of them had a blue sash tied over a shoulder, and the Blue Thumbs supporters erupted at the sight of them. At the opposite end of the arena, another gate was opened, and a stream of green-skinned men and women in rags were pushed out by guards with spears.

'They've spiced up the executions, I see,' said Felice. 'Normally, these criminals would be chained up and butchered by greenhides.'

Arete nodded. 'The greenhides are being held back for a special treat, or so I've heard.'

Belinda noticed the eyes of the Seventh Ascendant gleam with a savage joy as she watched the armed Blue Thumbs start to hunt the condemned Fordians. They took their time about it, stalking the panicking prisoners slowly, to eke out some excitement for the crowd. The first to die was a young man, cut down from behind by an axe blow that split the back of his head open as he tried to run away. He fell to the sand and the Blue Thumbs supporters cheered, while the Fordians in the crowd sat in silence, their anger almost palpable.

Belinda watched the slaughter unfold beneath her, her mind unable to fathom why the crowd loved it so much. Were people really so cruel? Or was it only some people? Might many of them be quite normal, but get carried away by the sight of violence? Whatever the reason, she knew at once that she disapproved. Certain types of criminals may deserve to be executed, but not as entertainment. Justice was not the same as entertainment.

Arete glanced at her. 'You enjoying yourself, Belinda?'

'No.'

Arete rolled her eyes, then laughed as an old woman was beheaded on the sands below them. The Blue Thumb who had killed her stooped down and lifted the head by the hair, showing it off to the crowd, while his curved sword dripped blood onto the sand.

'So brave,' muttered Latude.

'Shut up,' said Arete.

A net was cast over the last prisoner still standing, and a group of Blue Thumbs closed in, hacking downwards with their weapons until the man lay in pieces on the sands. The crowd cheered again as the Blue Thumbs warriors formed a line in the centre of the arena. They bowed in the direction of the gods and Felice stood to give them a wave and a smile.

'They like that, your Grace,' she said, as she sat again. 'With Kemal and Baldwin both dead, I am by far the longest-serving patron. The city would burn if anything unfortunate happened to me.'

Arete laughed. 'Do you think that's why we've been keeping you alive? You live because Leksandr and I find you marginally useful. You and the other gods of Lostwell are, or were, a disgrace, and your rule of Lostwell incompetent and negligent.' She glanced at Latude. 'And you were the worst of them all. Corrupt, venal and lazy. Were it not for your shortcomings, the Sixth Ascendant and I would never have had to lower ourselves into coming here.'

Felice and Latude sank into their seats, their eyes cast down.

A few yards below them, a courtier dressed in flowing white robes stood and raised his hands. 'People of Alea Tanton,' he called out, his clear voice carrying across the arena; 'today we are honoured by the presence not only of Lady Felice, patron of the Blue Thumbs, and Lord Latude, patron of the Deadskins, but also by two Blessed Ascendants! Never in the history of the games have we seen such an audience; in generations to come, people will marvel at how lucky we are.' The crowd cheered but, again, it seemed as if most of the noise was coming from the Blue Thumbs supporters, while many of the Fordian Deadskins were sitting in silence.

'Now that the executions are out of the way,' the courtier went on, 'we have a very special treat for you all. As you know, an auction was held some thirty days ago, at which a newly-captured dragon was put up for sale. The savage beast was purchased by the Deadskins...' At this, the cheers of the Blue Thumbs turned to boos and jeers, and the courtier waited for them to settle.

'Up to now,' he continued, once a modicum of quiet had been achieved, 'no one in the public has yet had a chance to glimpse this new acquisition, but today, we are fortunate indeed, for the Deadskins have transported their new champion here, so that we can all take a look at its fighting abilities. It will not, I repeat not, be participating in any competitive match today; this is more of an exhibition to whet the appetite. The first proper match with this new dragon will take place at the Northern Pits precisely one month from today, on the occasion of the final Blue Thumbs versus Deadskins match of the year. If, that is, it survives today. Therefore, I bid you, welcome Obsidia!'

Belinda frowned. She had not been anticipating the appearance of a dragon, and when it had been announced, her thoughts had gone straight to Blackrose. But Obsidia? The name meant nothing to her.

As the courtier raised his hands with a flourish, a huge gate at the end of the arena was opened and two columns of slaves emerged from the shadows, each pulling a chain. Out of the gloom appeared the head of a muzzled black dragon, and Belinda stifled a gasp. It was Blackrose. The dragon seemed not to be resisting the pull of the chains, and walked out onto the sands to a roar of noise from the crowd. For the first time during that day's events, the Fordians in the audience leapt to their feet, their cheers ringing out, while the Blue Thumb supporters hurled abuse and insults down at the dragon.

Felice scowled.

'Whatever is the matter now?' said Arete.

'This is most unfair, your Grace,' the god said. 'That new dragon should have gone to the Bloodflies, to make up for their loss of Sanguino. This means that the Deadskins have two such beasts, against the Blue Thumbs' one; while the Bloodflies have none.'

Arete shrugged. 'The Deadskins paid the most and I never argue with money.'

Blackrose moved into the centre of the arena, while the slaves retreated back through the gate. The dragon's wings were tethered, but her limbs remained free. She raised her head and gazed around at the spectators.

Belinda coiled her vision and sent it out, meeting the dragon's gaze at she stared up at the seats where the four gods were sitting.

Blackrose, she said, *I'm so glad you're alive.*

Do not speak to me, traitor. Sable has told me everything, including your part in the disaster at Yoneath. Your time will come, and I will watch as you die.

Sable's alive?

There was no response, and Belinda realised that the dragon had severed the vision connection between them. She tried to force her way back into Blackrose's mind, but found it impossible, like trying to push a hand through a stone wall.

Belinda's spirits sank, and for a moment she thought her composure would crack. Sable had told her everything? What did that mean? With a sickening realisation she understood at once what it meant. Sable had told Blackrose that Belinda had betrayed them all, and the dragon had believed her. Why wouldn't she? To all appearances, Belinda had betrayed them. There she sat, right next to one of the two Ascendants who had captured Blackrose and slain Corthie; of course she would believe that Belinda was a traitor.

'Remember we were talking about the greenhides?' said Arete. 'This is the part I've been looking forward to. Apparently, the beasts we are about to see have been starved for several days to get them in the mood.'

Another gate in the wall of the arena opened, and a terrible shrieking echoed across the sands. Belinda frowned, remembering her time in the City of Pella, as she watched five greenhides race out of the darkness and into the bright sunlight. They caught sight of the dragon immediately, and moved into an arc, their claws and teeth clattering and snapping. Blackrose remained motionless, her eyes watching them as they edged towards her. The crowd began to simmer with excitement, while many Fordians were screaming words of encouragement at Blackrose, or "Obsidia", as they chanted her name.

Arete nudged Belinda with her elbow. 'Who's your money on?'

'I don't gamble.'

Arete rolled her eyes again. 'Fine. Who do you think is going to win?'

'The dragon.'

'I don't know about that,' Arete said; 'it looks a bit scared to me. It's just standing there.'

The low shrieking from the greenhides was almost inaudible as the roars and shouting from the crowd rose into the blue sky. The five beasts had their heads low, their talons scraping through the sand. Then, as if they had coordinated their attack, they pounced. Their strong back legs dug into the ground and they sprang at the dragon.

Blackrose reacted at once. She was unable to use her teeth, but her right forelimb swung out, and her thick claws ripped right through the closest greenhide to a roar from the watching Fordians. The other four leapt at Blackrose, their talons scoring her thick hide, and she swept her tail at them, bowling two over. In seconds she had torn the pair still standing to shreds, their dark green blood spraying across the sand. One of the others jumped up, and sank its teeth into the dragon's right flank, its talons slashing the black scales. Blackrose ignored it for a moment, and went after the last one, crushing it under her weight until it lay still. She turned to the one biting her side. She drove her muzzled head at it, knocking it loose, then, with both sets of claws, she tore it in half.

The crowd seemed almost delirious to Belinda – they were standing and screaming as if they had lost their senses. Blackrose picked up a severed chunk of greenhide flesh, and hurled it into the rows of Blue Thumbs supporters, spattering them with green blood. On the other side of the arena, the Fordians cheered and screamed in joy.

'Obsidia!' they called out, chanting her name again, as the Blue Thumbs supporters simmered in anger.

'My,' said Arete, 'she does put on a decent show. I'm tempted to go to the Northern Pits next month, to watch her in a real match.'

The large gates of the arena opened, and two lines of slaves emerged, holding the dragon's chains. Accompanying them were a dozen heavily armed guards with large crossbows. Blackrose glanced at them, then strode towards the tunnel entrance without any need for forceful persuasion; her head held high as the Fordians roared their approval.

Latude chuckled. 'My money wasn't completely wasted, I see.'

Felice stared at him. 'What do you mean? Did you give gold to the Deadskins to buy this beast?'

He winked at her. 'I might have done.'

She turned to Arete. 'That is explicitly against the rules. The gods are not supposed to use their personal funds to help their own teams.'

Arete shrugged. 'Who cares?'

'That dragon belongs to the Deadskins in more ways than one,' Latude said. 'Do you not recognise her? She used to be called Blackrose, and was the Deadskins champion for a decade some years ago. I was merely righting an old wrong.'

'Why did they rename her?' said Belinda.

'They're embarrassed. They sold her to some dealer because they thought she was useless and worn out, and they don't want to admit that they were wrong.' He glanced at the Fordians celebrating in the stands. 'I wonder if any of those fools realise the truth. It'll get out, eventually, but, as the Sacred and Holy Seventh Ascendant just said – who cares?'

Felice frowned, but said nothing.

With the dragon exhibition over, the sands were cleared of the greenhide remains, and the proper games got underway, with a dozen warriors from each team entering the arena to another sustained roar from the crowd. Belinda settled into her seat, and pretended to be interested.

'What did you think of it all?' said Leksandr to Belinda once the gods had returned to Old Alea.

'It was appalling; pointless.'

'I didn't think you'd enjoy it,' he said, filling her glass with wine. 'I find it frightfully boring, myself. After thirty millennia of watching mortals kill each other, the excitement rather pales.'

'Arete didn't seem to think so.'

'The Seventh Ascendant retains a fascination with death, rekindled, I think, by her close brush with it in Fordamere. Your friend Corthie Holdfast came quite close to killing her.'

Belinda took a sip of wine as she sat on the long couch in the Ascendant's private rooms. 'I have been searching for a suitable Quadrant, as you commanded,' she said. 'I am determined to find one for you. I need to prove myself, I understand that.'

Leksandr glanced at her, then gave a slight nod.

'This evening,' she went on, 'I intend to keep working. I will revisit Fordamere, and try to retrace the steps of those who fled before your arrival.'

'Why?'

'There were some demigods from the salve world there; companions of Corthie Holdfast. It is possible that one of them might have used a Quadrant.'

'Are these the same demigods who were related to Count Irno of the Falls of Iron?'

'Yes.'

Leksandr nodded again, and she wondered if he believed her. She wanted to check, to enter his mind to see what he really thought of her, but he would know as soon as she tried. It was true that lying was coming easier to her, but was she giving too much away?

'Were they also your friends?' he said after a pause.

'No. They were not my friends.'

'Off you go, then,' he said, 'and good luck.'

She got up from the couch, bowed her head, and left his rooms, her head spinning. She had almost told him more than she had meant to, her desire to assuage his doubts nearly overcoming her need to keep certain things secret. She knew perfectly well that Naxor had used a Quadrant to get to and from the City of Pella many times and, although she despised him, if he were caught then the location of the salve world would be discovered. Her memory was good, but she could easily be tangled up in the lies and half-truths she had espoused and if that happened, then they would know for sure that she was working against them.

She hurried to her own quarters, dismissed the prying servants, and threw up in the toilet, her stomach coiled tightly. Her heart was pounding as she crouched on the floor of the bathroom, and she began to feel that Leksandr could see through her fabrications and denials. He knew; he must, and was playing with her, using Arete to make her think that he was on her side, when all along the two Ascendants were in complete agreement. If that were true, then they were waiting for her to make a mistake that would lead them to Naxor, or to the God-Queen's Quadrant. Paranoia and doubts filled her, and she realised she was afraid.

Her thoughts went to Silva. It had been four days since she had dismissed the demigod from her service, and not a single person in the Governor's residence had commented on the fact that she was no longer around. Perhaps she had been taken into custody, and was being questioned, or tortured in the basement of the residence. Belinda washed her face and lay down on her bed, wanting to curl up into a ball and hide, or fall asleep and never wake up. Instead, she forced herself into a sitting position, and sent her vision through the half-closed shutters.

It took her over three hours to find her great granddaughter. The demigod was on the back of a wagon, heading south-east along a dusty road that led from Tordue to the Four Counties and the Fordian Wastes. There was a gap in the ring of mountains that almost enclosed Tordue, and her wagon was a few miles from a large earthen embankment that stretched across it. The demigod was sitting amid piles of luggage and goods, and a couple of other passengers were resting next to her.

Belinda almost cried out in relief when she saw her, and she dived into her mind without any hesitation.

Silva!

The demigod nearly jumped in surprise.

Silva, it's me.

Your Majesty?

Yes. O, Silva, I'm so sorry about sending you away like that; I'm sorry about everything. I've made so many mistakes, but please know that I love you, and I didn't want you to think that I had dismissed you because I was unhappy with you, I...

Her rushed tumble of thoughts trailed off as tears spilled down her face.

Your Majesty, please, slow down. What do you mean?

Corthie's alive, Silva. I revived him after Arete and Leksandr killed him. They don't know, and I couldn't tell you; I knew they would read it from your mind. I'm trying my best to work against them, even though everyone thinks I'm on their side now, but it's hard, so hard, and I don't know how long I can keep it up.

Silva quietened, and Belinda could sense her sympathy, and the turmoil in her mind. She looked into the demigod's memories, and could clearly see the feelings of betrayal and hurt that she had caused her great granddaughter.

Do you mean, Silva said after a while, *that you tricked me into going away? Am I still in your service, your Majesty?*

If you'll have me, Silva.

Your Majesty, never doubt that, never. This makes me so happy... I must try to be calm, so that no one else on the wagon can see how I'm feeling right now, but I'm worried that I might start crying at any moment. Please, tell me what you need me to do.

I'm not sure. Part of me just wanted to have an honest conversation with you, and this was the only way I could think of that would work. I've missed you; I feel so alone. Arete suspects me, but Leksandr is acting as though he trusts me. I think he's lying, but I can't tell without going into his head, and then he would know. What should I do?

You're asking for my advice, your Majesty?

I am.

To answer that, your Majesty, I must first know what it is that you want.

Belinda hesitated. What did she want?

I want to defeat the Ascendants. I want to free Lostwell, and the other worlds, from their rule. I want my friends to be safe.

Then I should search for Corthie, your Majesty. Alone, the two Ascendants would overcome you; but with him by your side? He nearly defeated them in Fordamere; together, you would stand a good chance of winning. Do you have any idea where he might be? I cannot sense his powers, so I will not be able to locate him that way.

I left him with Van, but he might be with Naxor.

I can look for Naxor.

We must be very careful. Leksandr told me that they could find the City of Pella with anyone who has ever used a Quadrant to travel there; in other words, Naxor would be able to give them all the information they need.

I understand.

Go to Cape Armour, and from there take a ship to Kinell. If Corthie fled from Yoneath, Kinell would be the place he would have most likely fled to. I will search there too, and let you know if I find them.

As you wish, your Majesty. In the meantime, I advise that you do every-thing the Ascendants ask of you; you must make them believe that you are on their side, and then, when we are strong enough, we shall strike.

I'll track your progress, and make contact every day. Thank you, Silva. Were it not for you, I would despair.

Stay strong, your Majesty.

Belinda broke off the connection and took a deep breath. She wiped the tears from her face and stood. Her heart was still racing, but it was with exhilaration and hope, rather than anxiety. Even though nothing had really changed, she felt better for having had someone to share her feelings with. She strode to the window and gazed out over the city. She frowned. Pillars of smoke were rising from over the slums, and then she became aware of shouts coming from the courtyard below her. Had something happened?

She made her way out from her quarters, and saw Arete on the landing, surrounded by demigod courtiers.

'What's happening?' Belinda said.

Arete looked at her as if she were mad. 'Did you not feel that?'

'I was in a vision trance; I felt nothing.'

'You need to fix that, immediately,' Arete said. 'The city has just experienced its worst earthquake in a century, and you felt nothing? Did you not leave even a small part of your consciousness behind to stay aware of your surroundings?'

Belinda lowered her eyes, feeling like a child being berated by an angry adult. She hadn't known that it was possible to remain aware of what was going on around her while she was using her vision powers, and didn't want to ask how it was done, in case she appeared ignorant or foolish.

'We're sending troops out into the lower city,' Arete went on, 'to assist with the casualties.'

'How bad was it?'

'Use your vision to see for yourself,' Arete said; 'I'm too busy to do everything for you.'

She strode off down the stairs, the small crowd of demigods scurrying to keep up. Belinda remained at the top of the steps for a moment, then went back into her rooms. She poured herself a glass of water and sat down by the window. Everything in her quarters seemed fine, then she noticed that a picture hanging on the wall was a little askew. There was also a thin layer of dust covering the small table where her glass was sitting, and she looked up to see a crack in the ceiling. The Sextant lay somewhere in the rooms above her, and she worried for a moment that its great weight might send it falling through the floorboards, even though Leksandr had assured her that he had used his powers to strengthen the beams beneath it. She walked into her small study, which she knew for certain was not located under the Sextant, and gazed out of the window. Her vision pulled free of her body, and she sent it across the high plateau of Old Alea so that she could look down on the lower city.

The Shinstran districts were in chaos. Tenements had collapsed, and fires were raging through parts of the slums. Debris filled the streets, and a dazed population was gathering in the open areas. The neighbouring fortress was also burning, and long sections of its outer walls were in ruins. Moving north, the Torduan and Fordian districts were in the same condition as those where the Shinstrans lived, and Belinda watched as bodies were removed from a building that had fallen over. She brought her vision back and lowered her head.

Then she remembered Blackrose. She sent her sight back out, and raced it over the city. The Central Pits where she had seen the games that morning were still standing, though a couple of the auxiliary buildings next to the main arena were damaged. A little to the north, on the main road that traversed the entire length of the city, a convoy had paused, and amid it was the largest wagon she had ever seen. It was almost as wide as the road, and over a dozen gaien were attached to its harness. The wagon was covered, but there were a few gaps in the reinforced sides, and she sent her vision through. Inside, the huge black dragon was sitting, her eyes staring out through a small air hole.

Belinda pushed her vision at the dragon's eyes, and they yielded.

What do you want, traitor? Blackrose said, as soon as she entered the dragon's mind.

To see if you were alright. And I'm not a traitor, I'm a friend.

The dragon laughed. *Is that why you stabbed Sable? Is that how friends behave?*

Sable attacked me; I was defending myself. Please believe me. I'm trying to help; I'm trying to work against the Ascendants, while making them think I'm on their side. I'm not doing a very good job, I realise that, but my heart remains with you, and Corthie, and...

Corthie? If you cared so much about Corthie, then why did you let him die? That is the rumour I am hearing; that the two Ascendants cut him down.

They did, but I revived him. Damn it. I didn't want to tell you, because if one of the Ascendants reads your mind, then they'll discover the truth.

Blackrose hesitated.

I know Sable hates me, Belinda went on, *and I understand why.*

You had better not be lying to me, the dragon said.

I'm not. Is Sable alive, do you know?

She is.

Belinda gasped in relief. *And does she still have the Quadrant?*

What Quadrant?

She had a Quadrant when she attacked me. She used it to take Maddie away with her; I assumed you knew.

Belinda felt a rumble of anger rise within the dragon.

You are filling my head with lies and half-truths in order to deceive me, the dragon said. *Go. I want nothing more to do with you.*

Nothing I have said to you is a lie.

I will see about that.

Blackrose cut the link between them, and Belinda withdrew her vision from the wagon. She didn't understand. The conversation had been going better than she had hoped, right up until she had mentioned Sable. Then it dawned on her; Sable hadn't told the dragon about the Quadrant.

Had she ruined everything by telling the dragon the truth – had she spoiled Sable's plans? Blackrose's rage with the Holdfast woman would be ferocious if she had been keeping from her the fact that she possessed a Quadrant.

Belinda almost smiled. Sable would finally get what she deserved, and Belinda only hoped she would be there to witness it.

CHAPTER 6

PLAYING ALONG

Stoneship, Forted Shore – 21st Tuminch 5252

'And then,' Kelsey went on, 'when Corthie was eight, Karalyn was kicked out of the house again for trying to split up our parents, and Keir and I went to work right away. Without Karalyn to protect him, he was at our mercy. I was a pretty evil ten-year-old, I should add, and Keir was even worse.' She paused for a moment, and peered at the base of the window bar that she had been unsuccessfully trying to dig out for over a month. 'Anyway,' she went on, raising the purloined spoon to begin scraping the mortar again, 'we started...'

'I get the picture,' said Aila from where she sat on the bed pallet. 'You and your older brother were horrible bullies. I'm not sure why you're telling me all this; it's not exactly making me think any better of you.'

Kelsey blew the dust from the base of the bar. 'I just thought you should know a bit more about Corthie when he was young, that's all. I don't care what you think of me.'

'Why did you hate him so much?'

'Well, that's the funny thing; his incessant cheerfulness used to get on my nerves, but I never actually hated him. It was all just a way to get at Karalyn, who we *did* hate, with a passion. Karalyn used to tell us off all the time for being mean to Corthie, so we kept doing it to annoy her.'

'What did your parents do about it?'

'Not much. Mother was away most of the time, governing the Holdings from the capital. Father tried to rein us in, but we used to run rings round him. Pyre's arse, I regret that now. We were almost as mean to father as we were to Corthie.' She stopped her work, her eyes cast downwards. 'I'll never forgive myself for not telling father how much he meant to me. He died saving my life, and Keir's too, when a god attacked us. Despite everything we'd done to him, he didn't hesitate, he just charged right in, and she killed him.'

Aila watched as the young Holdfast woman closed her eyes. 'That's awful,' she said. 'I don't want to take anything away from what happened to you, but my father was also killed in front of me.'

'Was he?' said Kelsey. 'Sorry.'

'Prince Michael executed him for rebelling against the God-King and God-Queen.'

'Amalia, you mean?'

'Yeah. She was the all-powerful God-Queen back then.'

'Did she order it?'

'She didn't need to; Prince Michael was really in charge. His divine parents had retired from running the City by that point. She would have known though, and approved.'

Kelsey glanced at her. 'Do you want to kill her?'

'I used to, though I would never have imagined being in a position where I would have been able to. She was the most powerful god in the City; she could have killed me with a look.'

Kelsey wiped her eyes and tried to smile. 'Not while I'm around.' She clenched the spoon in her fist and got back to work. 'You should tell me more about the City. I don't mind telling you stuff, but sometimes, I think that you're sitting there wondering when I'm going to shut up.'

'What do you want to know?'

'Well, about the sky, for a start.'

'The sky?'

'Aye. I heard Belinda say that there was something wrong with your world, and that the sun only rises a little way, and then goes down again.'

'Yes, that's true.'

'I've been thinking about that.'

'Why?'

Kelsey paused from her work again. 'Well, I have a theory. If, right, the sun is pretty much on the horizon, then wouldn't the sky often look like it's sunrise or sunset?'

'Compared to Lostwell, I suppose. The sky is usually pink or red, although it's blue sometimes. At night, it's purple, because the sun doesn't dip too far below the horizon. It never gets completely dark.'

Kelsey nodded. 'I'd like to see that.'

Aila frowned at her. 'Don't say that in front of Amalia; she'd whisk us there in no time.'

The sound of footsteps approached through the thick door, and Kelsey slipped down from the window and hid the spoon under the bed. The door opened, and the young servant walked into the room with a tray.

'Morning, ladies,' he said.

'Good morning,' said Kelsey. 'No Maxin today?'

'He left to go into town,' the young man said as he placed the tray on the ground.

Kelsey picked up a book and threw it over to him. 'Here. We've finished that one. It would be great if you could get us some more.'

'Funnily enough, that's one of the things on Maxin's list. I'd be wary of what he buys you, though; his reading skills aren't up to much. Oh, em, don't tell him I said that, eh?'

'Get me some cigarettes and it's a deal.'

The servant smiled, and retreated from the room and locked it again.

Kelsey grunted. 'Pyre's knackers, I'm so sick of pretending to be friendly to these arseholes.'

'It was your idea,' said Aila, as she got off the bed to inspect the contents of the tray, 'and, I must admit, it has kind of worked. They never bring crossbows with them when they give us meals any more, and he would never have stood there for a chat when we were first put in here. All the same, it hasn't got us out, has it?'

Kelsey brandished the blunt and bent spoon. 'Whereas, this might well do the trick.'

Aila picked up the tray. 'If you say so. Are you still craving a smoke?'

Kelsey scraped the spoon against the mortar. 'Now that you mention it, no, not really.'

'Then you should stop. I mean, you've done the hard bit.'

Kelsey laughed. 'My mother would disown me. Actually, that's a good reason to do it; to annoy her. Anyway, how was I, you know; was I unbearable?'

'You were a nightmare for oh, about twenty days. That's why I don't want you to restart; I don't think I could handle being in your company if you had to stop again.'

'That's fair, I suppose. You haven't been much fun, either, Miss Aila, just so you know. You're like the opposite of Corthie; I've never met anyone as pessimistic as you. How does he put up with it? I can feel the negativity radiate off you at times.'

'Corthie and I balance each other out, I think,' she said. 'Well, we did until he got it into his head that he was destined to slay the Ascendants; that was a step too far for me. I was also extremely annoyed with him for not telling me why he allowed Van to go off with you.'

Kelsey shrugged as she scraped the mortar. 'I'm quite proud of him for that. Holdfasts stick together, even when we fight and argue among ourselves. If you're a lucky girl, you might get to be a Holdfast one day, who knows? We'll see if mother approves.'

'Half the time, I don't know if you're joking or not. You hate your mother, but you're unswervingly loyal to her as well.'

'It's called being part of a family. I know you demigods don't... oh.' She stopped scraping.

'What is it?'

'Well,' she said; 'you know that I was only really doing this scraping malarkey to pass the time, but, eh, come and take a look.'

Aila placed the tray onto the bed and walked to the window ledge. At the base of the thick bar, a large chunk of mortar had come loose. Kelsey wedged the spoon under it and it slipped free, revealing the end of the iron bar. She took hold of the shackle and eased it through the gap, freeing her chain from the bar. She smiled at Aila, then did the same with her chain.

'Wait,' said Aila. 'They'll notice as soon as they walk in.'

'Then we rush them, and run for it.'

'What, with each of us trailing ten-foot lengths of chain behind us? They're still attached to our wrists, if you hadn't noticed.'

'We passed a little workshop in the basement when we were put in here. There's bound to be hammers and stuff we could use to get rid of the chains.'

'But they'll hear us.'

'Pyre's arse, Aila! Come on, this is the chance we've been waiting for. We can stop sitting here passively, and actually do something. I'm fed up being a damsel in distress, waiting for the boys to rescue us.'

Aila frowned. Kelsey was right. She tried to summon the spirit of Stormfire. She was unable to use her powers to mask herself, but everything Stormfire had done had really been done by her. Her heart began to pound at the thought.

'Right,' said Kelsey; 'here's the plan. We eat, then we sit by the door and wait for the next time someone comes in. And then we go for it. You can fight, can't you? I mean, I can't, but you can, aye?'

'Yes, I can fight.'

Kelsey grinned. 'That's more like it. Now you're thinking like a Holdfast.'

The waiting was excruciating. Kelsey and Aila crouched or sat by the door, their chains piled behind them, as the day slowly went by. Kelsey had tried to pass the time by playing word and guessing games, but

Aila's nerves were shredded, and all she could think about was Amalia's touch, which could bring her death in seconds. Apart from that, she might get a crossbow bolt in the guts, and she remembered how awful that felt. There were a million problems with Kelsey's plan, but the young Holdfast woman refused to listen to them, at one point sticking her fingers in her ears and singing to drown out Aila's objections.

Eventually, the light in the basement cell dimmed as evening approached, and footsteps bringing their dinner approached down the hallway outside. Kelsey's eyes narrowed, and she nodded to Aila. They moved to the side of the door, so that they would be out of sight when it opened.

Aila handed the end of her chain to Kelsey and tensed.

I am Stormfire. I am Stormfire, she repeated in her head. She didn't need the disguise. She could do it.

The key sounded in the lock, and the door was pushed open. It was the young servant again. He peered into the room, and his smile faded as he glanced at the seemingly empty cell.

Aila pounced. She sprang up, a length of chain in her hands, and wrapped it round the young man's throat, hauling him backwards. He dropped the full tray, its contents clattering to the ground, and stumbled, pulled off balance by Aila. Kelsey scooped up the jug of water from the floor and smashed it down onto the man's head. It broke, and the man cried out, and stopped struggling, his hands at his neck as Aila choked him.

'He's still conscious,' Aila said. 'Hit him again.'

Kelsey glanced at the broken jug, then clenched her fist and punched the man in the nose. He yelled as blood gushed down his face, and she punched him again. Aila hauled him into the cell as he groaned in pain.

'I've got the key,' Kelsey said, her fist bruised. 'Come on.'

They picked up the chains and ran out of the cell, and into a long passageway with rooms leading off on either side. They shut and locked the cell door, then Kelsey led the way, glancing into each room as they went.

'In here,' she said, and rushed into a room on the left. It was lit by a narrow window by the ceiling, and contained work benches and racks of tools. Kelsey dropped her chains onto a bench, and began rooting through the tools. They tried a set of bolt-cutters, but the chains were too strong, and they couldn't get the long handles to close. Kelsey then tried a hacksaw, but the blade was old and rusty, and she gave up after a minute of fruitless sawing.

'They used a hammer to drive in the pins,' she said, eyeing the rack of tools. She selected a large hammer, and brought it down on the thick iron pin holding the shackles to the chain. 'Ow!' she cried, as the hammer struck the band round her wrist. 'Pyre's arse, that hurt.'

'And it made a racket,' said Aila. 'This is no good; we have to get out of here before someone else comes downstairs.'

'There's bound to be a blacksmith in town; maybe we could ask them to remove them.'

'We'd need gold to bribe them to keep their mouths shut.'

Kelsey continued to peer around the room. She found a long steel pole, narrow enough to fit through the links of the chain. She clamped her shackle into a vice, then drove the pole into the link closest to her wrist, and began to twist it. The chain links clumped together, and soon she was straining to twist it further.

'Help me,' she muttered.

Aila grabbed the other end of the pole, and together they twisted it a few more revolutions. Aila and Kelsey heaved at the pole, and the link gave, sending Aila flying to the ground. She glanced up and saw Kelsey grinning, the chain lying free on the floor.

'You next,' said Kelsey.

Aila got up and placed her arm into the vice.

'What's all that noise?' came a shouted voice from the passageway. 'The mistress is trying to sleep.'

Kelsey grabbed a hammer and dashed to the door, holding herself flat against the wall. Maxin pushed the door open and strode in. His eyes went straight to Aila, who was standing staring at him, her wrist clamped in the vice. Kelsey swung her arm, and the end of the hammer connected with the back of Maxin's skull with a crack, and he toppled to the ground and lay still. Kelsey stared at him, as blood began to seep onto the cold, stone floor.

'Did I just do that?' she said, her eyes wide.

'Stop staring and help me get the chain off,' Aila said.

Kelsey didn't respond, her eyes fixed on the body of Maxin. 'Is he dead?'

'I don't know,' said Aila, 'and I don't really care. Get over here; I can't twist the chain off on my own.'

'You don't care that I might have just killed someone?'

'He was working for Amalia.'

'So, you're saying he deserved it? You sound like my mother.'

'Please, Kelsey. If Amalia comes down those stairs, we could be in trouble; we have to get out of here.'

The young Holdfast woman dragged her eyes away from the body, and took a few steps forward. Her right hand was still clutching the bloody hammer. She stared at the pole that Aila had rammed through a link in her chains as if she seeing it for the first time.

'Kelsey?'

'I'm just like my brothers now; a murderer. I didn't mean it, I...'

Maxin spluttered from the floor, and emitted a low groan of pain.

'There; see?' Aila said. 'He's not dead. You're not a murderer. Now, please, Kelsey, help me.'

She dropped the hammer and took the other end of the pole from Aila, and together they began turning it. As before, the chains bunched together, and then the link snapped and Aila pulled her wrist from the vice as the chain fell to the ground. Aila ran to the body of Maxin, and crouched by it. He was still breathing, so she began to rifle his pockets.

'Oh,' said Kelsey. 'I thought for a minute that you were going to help him.'

Aila found a leather wallet, and slipped it into a pocket. She then hauled the man's long coat off, and pulled it on, the sleeves long enough to hide the shackle on her right wrist.

'And I thought I'd be the one who froze,' Aila said, as Kelsey stared at her, her hands shaking. 'How have you managed to live this long without resorting to physical violence?'

Kelsey said nothing.

'Come on,' Aila said, grabbing her arm.

They went to the door of the work room and Aila peered out. The passageway was in silence, but a loud groaning was coming from the cell where they had locked the young servant.

'We should have killed them both,' she muttered, as she half-dragged Kelsey out of the room.

They ran along the passageway until they reached the stairs, then Aila stopped at a small storeroom, and stuffed her coat pockets with food. When they were full, she turned for the stairs, and nudged Kelsey along as they ascended. At the top of the steps was another passageway, with a large door on the right. It was barred with three beams, and the two women lifted them from their brackets and laid them on the floor. Aila pushed the door open, and blinked from the bright evening sunshine. Ahead of them was a series of stairs built onto the side of a huge wall, and beyond that, a small town was laid out. Wooden houses lined the streets, and dozens of chimneys were sending grey smoke up into the blue sky. Gulls called and shrieked overhead, and the air reeked of the ocean. Aila stared at the view for a moment, then led the way down the steps to the cobbled ground level. The high, thick walls encircled the small town completely, and looked ancient compared to the structures in the interior. On the left was a tall arch, and through it Aila could see a harbour with a stone jetty protruding outwards into the ocean. Several vessels were tied up, but there was nothing larger than a fishing boat. A hundred yards to the right was another arch, which led to the open countryside beyond, and Aila selected that direction.

They were walking along the street, trying to blend in with the locals, when a cry rose up behind them. Aila turned, and saw Amalia standing at the front door of the house built into the walls.

'Stop!' she cried, her eyes landing on the two escaping women.

'Keep walking,' said Aila; 'ignore her.'

She linked arms with Kelsey and they kept going. The street was busy with people. A few had turned to glance at the woman shouting from the top of the stairs, but none paid Aila or Kelsey any attention, despite the state of their clothes and their unkempt appearance. Amalia charged down the steps and started running along the street after them.

Aila saw a tavern to their left, and they ducked in through the open door. Inside, a large fire was roaring in a central hearth, and the place was filled with the odour of cooking meat. They walked to the bar and waited for a stout, middle-aged man in an apron to approach.

'How can I help you, ladies?' he said.

'We're looking for some dinner, please,' said Aila, 'and maybe a room for the night. How much would it be?'

'It's ten silver pennies per room,' he said, 'and two each for dinner. Take a seat, and I'll have someone bring over the food. Would you be wanting something to drink with your meal?'

'Ale, and lots of it,' said Kelsey.

The man smiled. 'Sure thing, ma'am.'

'Give us a moment to think about the room,' said Aila.

The man nodded, and the two women walked to an empty table next to the fire, Aila glancing at the main entrance.

'Did she see us come in?' said Kelsey as they sat.

'I'm not sure,' said Aila. She slipped the wallet out of a pocket, and looked through its contents.

'How much do we have?' said Kelsey.

'Five gold sovereigns, and about twenty in silver. Not much.' She tossed the empty wallet into the fire. 'We may have to steal some more.' She glanced at Kelsey. 'How are you feeling?'

'A bit better. Sorry about before; I... I just...'

'It's alright; you don't have to explain anything. You did what you had to. If you hadn't hit him, we'd be back in our cell by now.'

'I embarrassed myself. Keir would be laughing if he'd seen me. And Corthie would be rolling his eyes. As for mother, she...'

'Stop it, Kelsey. You may be a Holdfast, but you're not a killer; you don't need to compare yourself to the rest of your family. From now on, I'll handle any violence that's required.'

Kelsey looked at her. 'How many people have you killed?'

'I can't honestly remember.'

'Pyre's arse; you can't remember? It must be tons, then.'

'Not as many as Corthie. And I've been alive for nearly eight centuries; don't forget that.'

A serving girl approached their table with a tray, and began to set out cutlery, along with two large mugs of ale.

'Thanks,' said Aila. 'Could you please tell the barman that we'll take that room for tonight?'

'Yes, ma'am.'

'Also, what's the best way to get out of town? Do wagons leave for the south?'

'Yes, ma'am, but the next caravan isn't due to depart for a few days. It goes all the way to Kin Dai.'

'Thanks.'

The front door of the tavern swung open, and Aila and Kelsey turned to see Amalia stride in. She was wearing robes, but her right arm was bare, and fully healed. She saw them sitting at the table and smiled broadly.

'My girls,' she cried; 'there you are!'

She walked over to the table and sat. 'Are you eating? Good idea. Girl, set a place for me too, and I'll have some wine.'

The serving girl nodded. 'Yes, ma'am.'

Amalia waited until she had walked back to the bar, then she turned to Aila and Kelsey.

'You treacherous little bitches.'

'Treacherous?' said Aila. 'You locked us up; what were we supposed to do? Smile and nod along?'

Amalia pretended to look shocked. 'By abandoning me, you are betraying your own world, dearest granddaughter. If the Ascendants find me, then nothing will stop them from locating and occupying Tara. Do you want to see our enemies in Maeladh Palace?'

'So, now you want to talk reasonably? It's a little late for that.'

'Surely we can come to a deal; a mutually beneficial deal?'

'You had your chance, and instead you locked us up for a month.'

'Aye,' said Kelsey. 'Why don't you crawl back into whichever hole you emerged from, and leave us alone? Better still, give us the Quadrant, and then your beloved world will be safe.'

Amalia looked like she was about to launch into a rant when the serving girl returned with a tray.

'Your wine, ma'am,' she said.

The former God-Queen glowered at her, then took the mug of wine and drained it. 'Another.'

The serving girl nodded and hurried away.

'You two,' Amalia said, 'are finished. Where will you go? Do you even know where we are, or how to get out of this place? I was using you to keep safe, but I was keeping you safe at the same time. Did I torture or humiliate you? Did I starve you?'

Aila gave a wry smile. 'You have quite a low bar for hospitality.'

'Is Maxin alright?' said Kelsey.

'Why?' said Amalia. 'Are you going to pretend to be concerned for his welfare, after you clubbed him with a hammer?' She seethed for a moment, then tried to smile. 'Listen, come back to my apartment, and we can talk things over. What do you want? I'm sure we can reach a compromise.'

'Forget it,' said Aila. 'If you think I'd trust you after what you did to us, you must think I'm a bigger idiot than Marcus.'

Amalia's face changed and she leapt to her feet. 'If I could use my powers, I'd kill you now!' she yelled, pointing her finger in Aila's face. 'I'd level this stupid town in minutes and slaughter everyone. Have you forgotten who I am? I am the mighty God-Queen, and I'm sick of pandering to mortals who should be on their knees before me. You dare to talk about Marcus?' She picked up a knife from the array of cutlery on the table. 'I should cut your eyes out and gut you, you miserable, ungrateful wretch…'

Her words were cut off as two burly men grabbed her arms. One forced the knife from her hand.

'I'll kill you too, you stupid mortals! I'll kill you all!' Amalia cried, as she was hauled back and bundled to the ground. She tried to touch one of the guards with her fingers, but her wrists were pulled behind her by gloved hands.

The barman ran over. 'I've called for the town guard,' he cried. 'No one threatens my customers.'

Amalia spat at him. 'Insect! You loathsome beasts; do you know who I am?'

'No, and I don't care,' said the barman, wiping the spittle from his face. He nodded to the two men holding her. 'Take her to the warden's office; they can deal with her.'

The two men pulled the former God-Queen to her feet, and dragged her out of the tavern as she struggled in their grip.

The barman turned to Aila and Kelsey. 'Sorry about that, ladies. Do you know that woman?'

'We've never seen her before in our lives,' said Aila. 'She just walked over to our table and sat down.'

'What a strange woman,' said Kelsey. 'And we were just minding our own business. She was probably drunk.'

'I was starting to get a bit worried,' said Aila. 'Thanks for intervening.'

The barman nodded. 'Well, the meal and drinks are on the house, by way of an apology. A night in the town cells should sober her up.'

'Thanks,' said Kelsey.

'No problem,' he said, then turned and walked back to the bar.

Aila smiled.

'I hope the town cells are within a hundred yards of here,' said Kelsey, 'otherwise the wardens are in for a bit of a shock.'

'It's a small town,' said Aila; 'we should be safe for the night.'

'And tomorrow?'

Aila sipped her ale. 'Tomorrow, before the sun is up, we head south.'

CHAPTER 7

GOING NOWHERE

Kin Dai, Kinell, Eastern Khatanax – 2nd Luddinch 5252

'We're never going to find them, are we?' said Corthie.

Van glanced across the galley table at him. 'We can't give up.'

'I'm not saying we should give up, only that it's pointless. It's simple – my sister's powers are blocking Naxor's searches.'

'Yes,' said Sohul, 'but she'll be blocking the Ascendants as well.'

Corthie shook his head. 'We're wasting our time.'

'Then what should we do?' said Van. 'I'm open to suggestions.'

'There's nothing we can do,' said Corthie. 'Everything is hopeless.'

He reached for the bottle of spirits and filled his mug as the others glanced at him.

'I fail to understand why you keep buying him alcohol,' said Naxor.

Van shrugged. 'If I didn't, then he'd only go into the city to drink there. This way, at least we can contain him.'

'Don't talk about me like I'm not here,' said Corthie.

'You know,' said Van, 'we're not even certain that the Ascendants are still on Lostwell. They have the Sextant, yeah? If they were following their plan, then they might already have invaded the salve world. Naxor, could you check Alea Tanton from here? That might give us a better idea of what we're dealing with.'

'No,' said the demigod; 'it's too far away for me to reach. Maybe we should follow Vana's example, and get a boat. We could go back to Capston in the Southern Cape, and renew our search from there.'

'It's too risky,' said Van. 'All it would take is for one sailor to talk about seeing Corthie, and the authorities would be all over us.'

'Then perhaps I should go alone?' said Naxor.

Corthie almost choked on the spirits. 'Forget it. With everything you've done, what makes you think we'd trust you?'

'Because, if I'm caught, the Ascendants would kill me. If there were any benefit in running away, I would have left with Vana, believe me.'

'We'll have to leave at some point,' said Sohul. 'We can't stay in Kin Dai forever.'

Van glanced at Corthie. 'How's your battle-vision?'

Corthie thought for a moment. He had checked his powers that morning, as he always did, and it was true that they were stronger than at any time since leaving Yoneath. His health in other regards had also been slowly improving; he was sick less often, and sometimes an hour would go by without any stomach cramps. His appetite had also made fitful improvements, but he was still a shadow of his former self, mentally and physically.

'A little better,' he said at last, 'but not enough.'

'Then we stay,' said Van. 'We have no choice. Based on recent evidence, I now believe that Corthie is starting to recover, but we'll need him at his best if we're going to stand any chance.'

Naxor frowned as he watched Corthie drain his mug. 'That might take a while if he keeps drinking like that.'

'You lost the right to criticise me when you tried to snatch Amalia's Quadrant.'

'I was trying to stop her fleeing.'

'No, you weren't,' he said. 'You were being the same old Naxor, looking out for yourself.'

Naxor smirked. 'You know, Amalia's arm will have healed by now, and she'll have realised that Aila is pregnant; her powers will sense it if she touches her. Don't you think you should be doing everything in your power to get back to your old strength?'

'He has a point,' said Van.

'There is no point,' said Corthie. 'Maybe, if he'd come even remotely close to finding them, but he hasn't. And won't.'

Naxor stood. 'I'm going for a walk.'

'But,' said Sohul, 'we called this little meeting to discuss…'

'There's clearly nothing to discuss,' said the demigod as he strode for the steps leading to the deck. 'Corthie's given up.'

The others watched him leave, then Sohul also got to his feet.

'I'm going to bed,' he said, and walked away.

Van frowned, then poured himself a measure from the bottle.

'You joining me in getting drunk tonight?' said Corthie.

'You have to sort yourself out,' he said. 'You've gone from the most optimistic and confident person I've met, to a…'

Corthie glared at him. 'To a what?'

'To a whiny defeatist. The old you would slap the new you around the face.'

'I'm just being realistic.'

'No, you're not; you're being pathetic. I've held my tongue in front of the others, but I'm getting sick of it. Your sister and Aila are out there, somewhere. The old Corthie would never stop searching for them.'

'Then the old Corthie was an idiot. We lost; don't you understand? It's over. The two hidden worlds are probably under attack, and Implacatus has won. The Ascendants are invincible.'

Van shook his head. 'How can you say that? I watched you fight two of them, and you nearly beat them on your own. Have you the slightest notion of what that means? No one's got that close to defeating them in millennia, and what's more – you have a second chance. If they knew you were alive, then they'd fear you.'

Hope flickered in Corthie's heart, then he refilled his mug and took another sip. Hope was what had got him killed; a blind hope in his own destiny. It was better to hope for nothing; in that way he would never be let down again. He found the thought liberating. If he stopped hoping for things, then maybe his worries would disappear as well. For all he knew, his world could be in smoking ruins, his family dead. Aila and Kelsey might be dead too. What did that leave him? Nothing.

'I thought I could change things,' he said, 'but I was wrong. Sometimes, I wish Belinda had left me dead.'

Van shook his head. 'Do you think I've never been defeated? I've been involved in many wars, many battles; and we lost our fair share. The Banner of the Golden Fist taught us to treat each failure as an opportunity to learn from our mistakes. We'd analyse what went wrong, but rarely was any blame apportioned to individuals. They would criticise you for breaches of etiquette, or drunkenness, or an untidy appearance, but not for tactical errors. Corthie, you made a tactical error – you thought you could take on two Ascendants on your own. You were wrong. What does that teach you? That you're useless? That everything is hopeless? The real lesson is that, next time, you need support.'

Corthie laughed. 'You sound like Gadena.'

'Good. I respect Gadena. It's a pity you didn't listen to him.'

'I didn't need to; I beat everyone he put up against me.'

'That's your problem right there; you've never experienced defeat. Kelsey used to talk about your mother, about how she was a ruthless, no-nonsense warrior; a war leader.'

'Aye, that sounds about right.'

'And how did she behave after a defeat? What would she say to you now?'

Corthie considered for a moment, despite knowing the answer. 'She would tell me to stop acting like a baby, but that's how she deals with everything. She thinks sheer will power can overcome any odds. I watched her get her arse kicked by Asher, who was one of the gods who invaded our world with Belinda and Agatha. She was the one who killed my father.'

'Did she give up after that?'

'No. She started training again as soon as possible, and the next time she met Asher, she killed her. I didn't see it, but Kelsey told me what happened.'

'I wish Kelsey were here right now.'

Corthie narrowed his eyes. 'I'm sure you do.'

'That's not what I meant, though, yes; I do miss her. It's just that I think Kelsey might be better than me at getting you out of this hole. I think you need another Holdfast to remind you who you are.'

'And, who am I?'

Van shrugged. 'The greatest mortal warrior who has ever lived. You said so yourself.'

'That was the old Corthie.'

Van said nothing, and lit a cigarette.

'Open a window,' muttered Corthie, then he drained his mug, feeling the harsh spirits burn his throat. He went to refill his mug, then realised the bottle was empty. 'Hey,' he said; 'where's the other bottle?'

'What other bottle?' said Van. 'That was it.'

'You're kidding me? I thought we had another bottle of... of whatever it is we're drinking.'

'It's vodka, and no; we're out.'

'But I'm only getting started.'

'Tough. Go to bed.'

'No.'

'Fine; stay up.'

'Get more vodka.'

'I'm not your servant, Corthie.'

'I'll get some myself, then.' Corthie stood, and glanced around for his boots.

'You can't be serious,' said Van, eyeing him.

'Why not? A walk would do me good. We've been in Kin Dai for ages; it's time I saw some of it. All you need to do is point me in the right direction, and I'll find somewhere selling booze.'

'Sit down; you're drunk.'

'Aye, but not drunk enough. Nowhere near drunk enough.' He spied his boots and pulled them out from under the chair where they had been, then sat on the bench and began to put them on.

'Corthie, this is a joke, right? You know you can't go wandering about Kin Dai. What if you're recognised?'

'Come on. No one's going to have the faintest idea who I am. Maybe if I'd gone out when we first got here, when what happened was still fresh in people's minds, but everyone thinks Corthie Holdfast is dead.'

'All the same, you can't jeopardise everything now.'

Corthie glanced up from lacing his boots and laughed. 'Jeopardise it? The Ascendants have the Sextant; what else could go wrong?'

'Alright, you win,' said Van. 'I'll go out and buy some.'

'Too late. I'm in the mood for going out now. You should be pleased. I must be getting better, if I feel up to a night out.'

'You can't go.'

'Are you going to try to stop me? Will you wake up Sohul, and ask him to help? You know how that will end; I'm more than a match for both of you, even though I'm still sick.'

Corthie finished lacing up his boots and stood. 'Coming?'

Van stared at him. 'Don't walk out that door, Corthie.'

He laughed, and strode for the entrance. Stomach cramps struck him as he moved, but they were mild in comparison to the ones he had been experiencing for so many days, and the vodka was helping to take the edge off them. He swayed a little, but kept going. Van cursed behind him, and he smiled as he reached the steps. The night sky was dark, and the stars were out. Corthie gazed up at them for a moment from the bottom of the stairs, then started to climb, breathing in the salty estuary air. Noises were coming from many of the other house boats berthed close by, and little lamps lit up their decks and filtered through the shutters of countless cabins. Corthie stepped onto the deck, and stretched his arms as if awakening.

'You're an asshole,' said Van, coming up the steps next to him.

'It's a beautiful night,' said Corthie.

'It is. Now, come on; let's go back downstairs.'

'No, I'm going out and that's that. I can compromise, though. If you come along, then we can go somewhere that you know. That way, I won't be wandering around aimlessly looking for a drink. You can pick where we go. You must know a few places.'

'I've been out with the guys from work after a few shifts, but I'm not sure I should take you somewhere I might be known.'

'Tell them that I'm an old friend from a Banner.'

'I haven't told any of them that I used to be in a Banner. It might not be the most popular move in these parts. The government of Kinell might love Implacatus, but not many of the locals do.'

Corthie started walking towards the pier. 'I'm sure you'll think of something.'

There was a narrow walkway connecting the river boat to the pier, and Corthie strode across it, his guts starting to churn. The alcohol in his brain was over-riding his anxiety, but he still felt it in the pit of his stomach. He reached the pier and turned for the long wharf, where the fish market was closed up for the night. At the end of the pier were stone steps cut into the side of the wharf, and he climbed them, then stood on the open street, the city of Kin Dai before him. He smiled. For forty days he had been stuck on the cramped boat, and he felt alive again. To the left, the harbour front was lit up with lanterns, and small alleyways stretched away from it, almost hidden between the high stone buildings. A noise was rising from that direction, a noise Corthie knew well. Taverns.

Van joined him on the wharf, a deep frown creasing his face.

'Left sounds promising,' said Corthie.

'There are a lot of sailors' bars that way,' said Van. 'We need to be careful.'

They walked along the wharf for several minutes, passing rows of house boats tied up at the long, spindly piers that jutted out into the waters of the wide estuary. A few people were out on their decks, enjoying the warm evening air, and Corthie's height attracted a few glances. Van selected one of the many alleys leading off the wharf; it was narrow, and had garlands of flowers stretching between the high buildings on either side. At least a dozen taverns were open along the long stretch of the alley, and each seemed busy.

'So, this is what I've been missing?' said Corthie.

'This is a bad idea,' said Van. 'One drink and then we go back?'

Corthie laughed. 'Not a chance.'

Van led the way to a tavern. Its front door was open, and music was coming from the interior. They went inside, and a few heads turned to stare as they walked into the bar. Corthie glanced around. The place was half-full, and the patrons were clustered round small tables close to a low stage where a handful of musicians were playing. Van chose a table near the door, and they sat.

'Say nothing,' Van whispered, as a barmaid approached them.

'What can I get you boys?' she said, her eyes glancing at Corthie.

'Ale,' said Van.

'And some of that vodka,' said Corthie.

'I'll need the money up front,' she said. 'Sorry, boys, but you're not regulars.'

Van reached into a pocket and withdrew a leather pouch. He counted out some coins and handed them over.

'Here's twenty for now,' he said. 'Keep the ale coming.'

The barmaid took the money, smiled and walked back to the bar.

'What did I just tell you?' he said to Corthie. 'Your accent is out of place here.'

'So's yours.'

'Yes, but I sound like I might be from Alea Tanton, whereas you?'

'We could say I'm from Capston.'

'That won't work; this bar's full of sailors who will have been down to the Southern Cape.' His eyes darted around the tavern. 'People are already starting to stare.'

'Relax,' said Corthie. 'It'll be fine.'

The barmaid brought a tray over to their table and unloaded two large mugs of ale, and two small glasses of vodka.

'Where are you boys from, then?' she said.

Van smiled. 'We're from a place called none-of-your-business.'

The barmaid scowled and returned to the bar. Corthie picked up the mug of ale and took a long drink.

'My sister,' he said.

'What about her?'

'Are you in love with her?'

Van's smile disappeared.

'Well?' said Corthie.

'I get the feeling,' Van said, 'that you won't be happy with whatever answer I give.'

'Then just say the truth.'

'The truth? I wish I knew. I think about her all the time, and I don't want anything bad to happen to her.'

'You think about her?'

'Yeah, I do.'

'But you don't know if you love her?'

'I have to be honest with you; she told me about... you know, her visions.'

'Did she? I didn't think she was going to.'

'She laid it all out for me, about how she'd seen a vision of us together in the future. I guess she thought it would help explain her actions, but...'

'But what?'

'Come on. Visions of the future? You're joking, right?'

Corthie shrugged. 'If that's what she saw, then that's what's going to happen.'

'You believe it?'

'My other sister can do it, so why not Kelsey? Did you think she was just making it up to ensnare you?'

'Maybe.'

Corthie shook his head. 'She was devastated by that vision; it broke her heart. Imagine being told who you're going to end up with, when you don't even like the person.'

'I don't have to imagine; that's what happened to me. Wait a minute, she doesn't like me?'

'She thought you were an arrogant arsehole. At least, she did when I last spoke to her. I have to warn you; if you treat her badly, I will break you in two.'

'But we've no idea if we'll ever find her again.'

'You still don't get it – if she saw you together, then it will happen. Right now, you're as good as immortal. Whatever happens tonight, you won't die.'

'I thought you didn't believe in fate or destiny any more.'

'This is completely different. It's not fate, more an inevitability. It used to drive my other sister crazy. These visions are a curse.'

Van sipped his vodka. 'You Holdfasts are insane. And anyway, if you believe all that, then why are you so full of despair? You said before that everything was hopeless. It can't be that bad, not if you know your sister is alright.'

'I'm glad Kelsey's alive, but I wasn't in the vision, nor was Aila. I could die tonight.'

Van glanced round at the other tables. 'Judging by the amount of stares we're getting, there's a decent chance of that happening. We should get out of here.'

'But this is a port town. They must be used to seeing strangers.'

'Not any more. The only foreigners they've seen around here recently are Banner soldiers. This is not my first time in Kinell; I was posted here a few years back, as part of a peace-keeping operation when the locals rose up against the rulers of Alea Tanton. It wasn't a full scale war, but it got quite nasty.'

Corthie frowned. 'Now you tell me.'

Two sailors got up from a crowded table and walked over to them, while their comrades watched.

'Lads,' said one; 'enjoying yourselves?'

'Aye,' said Corthie.

'Good, good. Now drink up, and get out.'

'Why?'

'You're not welcome here,' growled the other sailor, his features tight as if he was having difficulty controlling his temper.

'My friend is right,' said the first sailor. 'You're either Banner soldiers or spies, and we don't like either in our tavern.'

'You hate the ruling gods, do you?' said Corthie.

The second sailor opened his mouth, but his colleague stopped him. 'We're not saying that; we're not falling for that old trick. Just finish your drinks, and leave.'

Van nodded. 'No problem. We'll be on our way in a moment.'

'No, we won't,' said Corthie; 'we're staying put. No one tells me where I can and can't drink. Now, would a spy say that?'

The tavern stilled.

'You're a big lad,' said the first sailor, 'but there are thirty boys in this tavern. You sure about those odds?'

Corthie shrugged. 'Bring it on.'

'Wait!' said Van. He glanced at Corthie. 'Shut up. Look,' he said, turning back to the sailors; 'my friend here has had a little too much to drink. We'll take your offer and leave; we don't want any trouble.'

'Speak for yourself,' said Corthie; 'I quite fancy some trouble.'

An older man approached, his empty hands raised. 'Please, take this outside.' He pointed at Corthie. 'And you're barred. I knew you were no good the moment you walked in.'

'They're Banner scum,' shouted one of the sailors from the table. 'Everyone in this tavern remembers what it was like when they occupied this city.'

Van stood, and the second sailor swung a fist at him. Van dodged back a step, and the blow glanced off the side of his face. The rest of the sailors in the tavern got to their feet, shouting. Corthie finished his drink and felt for his battle-vision. It was still weak, but it gave him a rush to feel it course through him. A sailor aimed a punch at him, and he raised his hand and grabbed the fist as it was about to connect with his face. He pulled the sailor's arm towards him, then brought it down against the edge of the table, breaking it. Two other sailors attacked him from the side, raining blows down onto him, and he rose to his feet, a broad smile on his face, and waded into the fight.

Twenty minutes later, Corthie and Van were staggering along the wharf. Corthie's fists were bruised and cut, and blood was coming from a wound on the side of his face, but he hadn't felt as good in a long time. Next to him, Van wasn't quite as happy. One of the sailors had clubbed him over the head with a bottle. It hadn't broken, but a large bump was forming on the top of his skull, and he scowled in pain as they made their way past the rows of house boats.

'That was great,' said Corthie.

Van said nothing.

'And you did alright,' Corthie said to him; 'you're not too bad in a fight, well, at least until that guy battered you over the head. You should have got out of his way.'

'There's something wrong with you, Corthie.'

'Why, because I like a fight? It was weird; normally I would have destroyed the lot of them, but with my battle-vision still sluggish, and with all the aches and pains, it actually made it quite even. We would have won, though, if you hadn't let yourself get clubbed. Did you see the guy I threw into the bar?' He laughed. 'He did a somersault in the air and landed upside down.'

'We're lucky the town militia didn't turn up.'

'I would have beaten them up too.'

Van shook his head at him as they turned and followed the narrow pier to their boat.

Naxor was sitting in the galley smoking a cigarette when they descended the steps from the deck. He glanced up at them, and his eyes widened.

'What happened? I nearly panicked when I got back and realised that you two weren't here. Have we been discovered?'

'Calm down,' Corthie said. 'We were just out for a drink.'

'Then why is there blood on your face? And you, Van, are you alright?'

'We got into a bar fight,' said the former mercenary, sitting heavily on the bench.

Corthie pulled a full bottle of vodka from his clothes. 'And look what I snatched on the way out.'

'But Corthie's not supposed to leave the boat,' Naxor cried. 'You endangered us all, Van; how could you allow it?'

'Next time,' said Van, 'you try to stop him.'

'There won't be a next time,' said Naxor.

'Shut up,' said Corthie as he opened the bottle. 'I'm going out again tomorrow night.'

'What?' said Van.

'Aye. It's time I got myself back into shape, just like you were saying earlier. I could feel my battle-vision getting sharper as the fight went on. And it's made me hungry, too. In fact, I haven't felt this good since Yoneath; this alive.' He glanced at his bruised knuckles and took a swig. 'I'm getting better, I can feel it, but sitting in this boat isn't going to help. I'm going to get fit, and then we're going to find Aila and my sister.'

Naxor and Van glanced at each other.

'Don't worry,' said Corthie; 'they thought we were Banner spies; they had no idea who I really was. I'll see if they fancy a re-match tomorrow. Now, let's get hammered.'

CHAPTER 8

THE SON RISES

C atacombs, Torduan Mountains, Khatanax – 12th Luddinch 5252
        'That's the plan,' said Sable. 'What do you think?'

Millen and Maddie glanced at each other, their faces reflecting the red glow of the lava below them.

'I have a slightly more sensible plan,' said Maddie; 'we use the Quadrant to rescue Blackrose. You're all better now after being stabbed, and Sanguino's been out flying every day. What else are we waiting for? Why do we need to fight Grimsleep?'

'Us three sitting here don't need to,' said Sable. 'It's Sanguino. I've already suggested to him that we leave, but Sanguino sees it as a matter of honour. But this is it; after we do this, we'll get Blackrose.'

Maddie narrowed her eyes. 'You promise?'

'I promise. And there's more. I think a few other dragons are on the verge of agreeing to come with us to Dragon Eyre. It's hardly an army, but it's better than just Blackrose and Sanguino. We can use the fight with Grimsleep to make them commit.'

'Which dragons?' said Millen.

'Well, Broadwing, for a start.'

'Who?'

'Silver body, black wings. He's about the same age as Blackrose, but has been sidelined by Deathfang and his cronies for decades. He's a big dragon, as his name suggests. And Deepblue.'

'What, that scrawny little thing?' said Maddie. 'She's even smaller than Burntskull.'

'She's tired of being pushed around,' said Sable. 'This is our choice – if we fight Grimsleep, then we'll have two other dragons to show Blackrose when we free her. If we flee, we'll have none.'

'Is that it?' said Maddie. 'A reject, and the tiniest dragon in the Catacombs?'

'Alright, Maddie,' said Sable; 'instead of complaining all the time, why don't you make the decision? Come on. Weigh up all of our options and tell us what to do.'

Sable darted into her mind as Maddie's brows furrowed. She could see the logic in Sable's plan, but didn't want to admit it, and there was still a niggling sense of guilt in her thoughts about keeping the truth of the Quadrant from Blackrose. Sable suppressed her desire to meddle; she needed Maddie to agree without any covert persuasion.

'I have questions.'

'Go on,' said Sable.

'When we free Blackrose,' she said, 'how are we going to explain that we have the you-know-what in our possession?'

'Leave that to me.'

'That's not good enough, Sable. You must have some idea.'

'I have plenty of ideas. My main one at present is that I tell her we've raided Old Alea and stolen one from the gods. In order for this to work, we'll need a diversion, which Broadwing and Deepblue can provide.'

Maddie chewed her lip for a moment. 'I hate lying to her.'

'I'll take the blame if it all goes wrong.'

'But I went along with it,' said Maddie. 'She'll know.'

'Maybe, but she thinks I'm a manipulative witch. We'll say I forced you to do it.'

Maddie groaned. 'Fine, we'll do it your way.'

'What about me?' said Millen. 'Don't I get a say?'

Sable eyed him. 'Well?'

He glanced down at the rough map that Sable had etched into the sand by the entrance of the tomb. 'What if Grimsleep refuses to come out of his cave?'

'He won't. He can't turn down a challenge and expect to remain in charge of the outlaw dragons on the other side of the valley. And, if by some incredible chance he does, then we can still claim victory. We'll have plenty of witnesses.'

'What if he uses fire more than once?'

'We've been over this; dragons might bathe each other in fire when they first start fighting, but it's just for show. Flames don't hurt them. I only need to make it through that first burst.'

'What if he gets help from the other dragons that live there?'

'Those witnesses I mentioned; they'll join in if the rules that govern fights are broken.' She smiled. 'Any more objections?'

He gazed at her for a moment, then blinked. 'No; I'm fine with it.'

'The plan needs all of us to play our part; each of us has a vital role. Are you clear on what you need to do?'

Maddie and Millen nodded.

Sable stood. 'I'll tell Sanguino, and we'll let Deathfang know that it's going to be tomorrow at dawn.'

Several hours later, Sable sat alone by the edge of the tomb, smoking a cigarette. It might be her last, she thought; if the plan failed, then it would be. The idea of possible failure didn't make her anxious; if anything, it just made her more determined to succeed. She felt a thrill run through her; she would soon be involved in a dragon fight to the death, and she realised that she had missed the excitement of being in danger. It was tempered a little by her concern for Sanguino; she didn't want him getting hurt.

She wondered if she should send a message to Naxor. She had discovered his whereabouts a few days previously, living with Corthie, Van and another Banner officer in a boat in Kin Dai. By the looks of things, they seemed to be doing nothing but sitting around getting drunk, despite Kelsey and Aila being missing. Perhaps she should look for her niece herself, but she knew how difficult that would be. She had also been spying on Belinda in Alea Tanton. The traitor was still working for the Ascendants, and the Sextant was where it had been since they had returned with it from Yoneath. She had managed to get into Leksandr's head for a few minutes, and had sensed the extreme frustration he felt regarding his inability to get the Sextant working, and his worry that Edmond, the Second Ascendant, would hold him responsible for the failure. He also had a suspicion that Belinda might not be completely loyal, which had made Sable think for a moment. It would be funny if the Ascendants turned on her; it would be exactly what Belinda deserved.

She took a drag on the cigarette and went over the plan in her mind. She felt a little guilty for extending the length of time that Blackrose was in captivity, but everything needed to be perfect. She tried to picture herself in Dragon Eyre; was that what she wanted – to go to another new world? Yes, she craved it, like she craved the feeling that came with the risks she took. She stubbed the cigarette out and stood, then noticed Sanguino directly behind her.

'I didn't want to disturb your thoughts, my rider,' he said. 'This plan of yours; it isn't entirely honourable.'

She put her hands on her hips. 'Neither am I.'

'Double-crossing and tricks are not in a dragon's nature.'

'No, but they're in mine, and we want to win, don't we? If you're having doubts, then we can forget the whole thing and flee, just as I advised before.'

He bowed his head. 'No. I could never live with myself if we did that. I must face Grimsleep.'

'Then, let's go.' She gestured to Millen and Maddie, who were standing close by, ready. Millen held up the large leather covering that he had fashioned.

Sable's nose crinkled. 'It stinks.'

'Yeah, well, it would, I guess. It's been smeared in...'

She held her hand up. 'I don't want to know. As long as it survives the initial burst of flames I can put up with the smell. Climb on.'

Maddie pulled herself up the rope ladder running down Sanguino's flank, a large bag over her shoulder, then Millen followed, after folding up the leather sheet. Sable glanced outside for a moment. There was still an hour before dawn, and they had been up all night. She patted her pocket, locating the sticks of keenweed she had secreted, as well as one of dullweed, in case it all went wrong and she needed something to numb the pain.

'Are you ready?' said Sanguino.

She nodded, then climbed up to the dragon's shoulders, settling down between Maddie and Millen, who were already strapped in. Millen had been constantly modifying the harness, as well as making the large sheet and another harness for when Blackrose was free, and it easily accommodated the three humans. Sable linked her mind to the dragon. After so much practice, it felt like slipping a hand into a glove.

She glanced at her colleagues. 'It's time for step one. Sanguino, let's go.'

Sanguino and Sable returned to the Catacombs just as the first rays of dawn were appearing over the eastern horizon. They flew up to Deathfang's lair, where Burntskull and Ashfall were waiting.

'Is today the day?' said Burntskull in an amused tone.

'It is,' said Sanguino, hovering by the entrance. 'Will Deathfang be coming to witness?'

'No,' said Burntskull. 'Instead, he is sending his daughter, Ashfall, to watch what happens. I hear a rumour, however, that Broadwing is going?'

'That is correct. Deepblue also.'

Burntskull laughed. 'Why? What benefit will those two bring? They are cowards, weak.'

'They also wish to witness.'

'Very well. Do not be surprised if they flee at the first sign of Grim-sleep.' He turned to Ashfall. 'Make sure you watch everything that happens; I'm looking forward to hearing all about Sanguino's death when you return.'

Ashfall made no response as she launched herself from the edge of the tomb. She and Sanguino circled higher, then began to fly east over the lava fields towards the far side of the valley.

'What is that terrible smell?' said Ashfall.

'My rider can answer that.'

'It's this,' said Sable, holding up the large leather sheet. 'I'm going to cover myself in it when we face Grimsleep.'

Ashfall looked incredulous. 'And why would you do such a thing? Do you think the odour will put him off?'

'What? No. You'll see.'

Sable arranged the sheet as they flew, securing the straps that Millen had sewn onto each corner. It was thick and heavy, and she hated the smell and how uncomfortable it felt as she pulled it up over her shoulders, leaving her head and arms free.

'Everyone believes you will fail,' said Ashfall.

'Not everyone,' said Sable.

'Every dragon, I meant. The opinions of insects barely count.'

They saw Broadwing and Deepblue circling as they reached the halfway point between the two sides of the wide valley. The small blue dragon looked scared. Sable knew that she had never ventured to the far side of the valley before, and it had taken all of Sable's powers to persuade her not to back out. Her mind was relatively pliant, for a dragon, and she was one of the few in the Catacombs that had proved susceptible to her powers. Next to her, Broadwing was enormous, as large as Sanguino, but much sleeker, his silver body glimmering in the early morning light. Despite his size, he had a reputation for avoiding confrontation, and was known to have backed down before much smaller challengers.

'Here you are,' he said. 'I thought perhaps that you had changed your minds.'

'That's what you were hoping, wasn't it?' said Ashfall. 'Your presence surprises me, as does Deepblue's. What do you hope to gain by coming along?'

'Sanguino asked us to be his witnesses,' said Deepblue, her voice almost lost in the wind.

'I gathered that,' replied Ashfall; 'I'm just amazed that you both said yes.'

'Where are the others?' said Broadwing. 'I had assumed that Death-fang and some of his council would be joining us today.'

'He sent me,' said Ashfall. She stared at him, as if daring him to ask why, and he looked away.

Sable could guess the reason, but she kept her mouth shut. Death-fang was afraid of Grimsleep; they all were, and she knew that Sanguino's stock had risen considerably in the Catacombs by his mere act of challenging him.

They set off eastwards, Sable happy to melt into the background, to ensure that Sanguino was the focus of attention. This day was all about him, and she needed to make sure that he took the credit if they were successful.

The rivers of lava stretched for miles before slowing and hardening into dark basalt, and they flew over the cracked and broken ground as the mountains ahead of them grew larger. Deep ravines cut across the valley, along with ridges and ragged cliffs, where lava poured into basins. The heat rose, as did the thick vapours, which swirled around them. In the distance, Sable caught sight of a pair of dragons flying over the mountains.

'We've been seen,' she said to Sanguino.

'Indeed. Look at them, fleeing back to their caves. No doubt Grim-sleep will soon be informed that Catacombs dragons are on their way.'

She sensed a flicker of doubt in his mind.

'Are you going to be all right with this? Patricide is taken very seri-ously among humans.'

'And among dragons also, my rider, but Grimsleep is no longer my father.'

They flew until the mouths of the caves where the outlaws lived became visible, then they paused for a moment, circling.

'I shall remain here,' said Ashfall. 'I will witness what occurs.'

'I think I will stay here too,' said Broadwing. 'I will come to your assistance, Sanguino, if others get involved.'

Ashfall snorted. 'I wouldn't depend upon that.'

Deepblue hesitated. While Sable was linked to Sanguino, she wasn't able to go into the small dragon's mind to reassure her, and she looked terrified.

Tell Deepblue she can stay too.

'Deepblue,' said Sanguino, 'please remain here with the others. I shall press on alone.'

'Are you sure?' said the blue dragon. 'I mean, I will, if you say so.'

'I do.' Sanguino moved ahead, then turned to face the other three dragons. 'What I am about to do, I do to redeem myself, and to bring peace and security to the Catacombs. If I am victorious, I shall return with the head of the tyrant who seeks to oppress us; and if I fall, I would ask only that you honour my name.'

'We shall,' said Ashfall. 'Two months ago, Sanguino, you were a blind and feeble dragon; yet today you prove your courage. I wish my father were here to see it, but in his absence I wish you good luck; may you tear out the throat of that vile beast, and leave his flesh for the worms to devour.'

Sanguino tilted his head, then turned and sped off, his speed surging as he raced over the last two hundred yards towards the caves.

I know the part you fear most, said Sable in his mind. *Be brave; it is the victory that matters, nothing else.*

Twenty yards from the caves, Sanguino halted, hovering over the ruined ground, which was covered in the scattered bones of hunted animals.

'Where is Grimsleep?' he bellowed. 'Will the coward known as Grimsleep emerge, or is he too scared to face me?'

A green dragon swooped down from the mountains, then darted into a cavern, its head turning to watch. Other heads poked out from the row of caves, all staring at Sanguino. Sable readied the leather sheet, getting ready to burrow beneath it.

'I must assume,' Sanguino called out, 'that Grimsleep is too craven to face me. Or perhaps he is feigning deafness, pretending that I am not here. That would not surprise me. Everyone knows he is a snivelling coward; nothing but a bully who takes pleasure in tormenting the weak. Why do you all put up with such a worthless leader?'

A low growling laugh came from one of the caves, and Grimsleep's head emerged from the shadows.

'I thought for a moment I was dreaming,' he said, his eyes glowing, 'but no, it really is my former son, come to die.'

'Come out and fight,' cried Sanguino, 'and we will see which of us is to die.'

Grimsleep yawned and stretched his forelimbs. 'I heard Blackrose has run off; did she tire of your pathetic and feeble ways?'

'You told me I would never fly again, yet look at me. You were wrong then, and you are wrong now.'

The huge black and red dragon eased his massive bulk out of the cave, and unfurled his great wings. He glanced around at the other dragons.

'This won't take long. Watch and learn.'

He beat his wings and rose up into the sky, then unleashed a torrent of flames down at Sanguino. Sable was ready, and she ducked under the thick covering as Sanguino was bathed in fire. He reared up to protect her from the worst of it, then let loose with his own flames as Grimsleep descended to attack him from above. His jaws opened, and Sanguino lashed out with his talons. Sable knew that he was temporarily blinded by her being under the thick cover, and she flung it off, her hands scalded from touching the scorched and burnt leather. She unclasped the buckles and let it fall; it had done its job.

As soon as Grimsleep closed with Sanguino, the dark red dragon turned and fled.

Grimsleep laughed. 'See? He flees! Too late, however. There will be no escape for you this day.'

The black and red dragon surged after Sanguino, his speed catching him up as the younger dragon hurtled away, heading south-west away from the caves.

Be brave, Sable said; *stick to the plan.*

This part pains me so.

I know, my beloved Sanguino, I know. It'll be over soon.

Grimsleep was gaining on them with every moment that passed, and Sable concentrated with all her strength, using her battle-vision to guide Sanguino's reactions. They dived down into a deep ravine, where a river of lava was flowing, and raced along it, Grimsleep only yards behind. The ravine twisted through the broken landscape of dark basalt, and Sanguino kept low as he sped along. The cliffs grew higher on either side of the narrow canyon, and the bottom was filled with molten rock. Ahead, the ravine came to an abrupt end, where a broad pool of lava bubbled and steamed, and Sanguino banked sharply to avoid hitting the cliffs. He turned, and landed on a ledge of rock by the banks of the molten pool. Grimsleep reared up, his claws out.

'There's nowhere to hide,' he growled down at Sanguino. 'You should have stayed in your miserable tomb on the Catacombs, pining for Blackrose. Where is your mother now?'

'Blackrose was a better parent than you ever were,' said Sanguino.

'Then where is she? I wonder; was it her fear of me, or her contempt for you that made her leave?' His eyes caught sight of Sable. 'I see you have an insect upon your shoulders; it was most considerate of you to have brought me breakfast.' He laughed. 'I will savour the taste of her flesh once you lie dead and broken before me.'

Sable cast her vision up to the side of the cliff.

Now, Maddie!

At the top of the cliff, she could see two figures among the rocks, each wielding the tools they had brought. Together, they broke down the little dam that Sanguino had made the night before, sending a torrent of liquid rock pouring from the side of the cliff. Lava burst down into the ravine, showering Grimsleep with molten rock. His right wing dipped under the weight, his thick skin smoking and burning, and he screamed in pain. At the same time, Sable broke her connection to Sanguino and drove her powers into the huge dragon's mind, his agony lowering his resistance to her. She filled him with a blinding terror as more lava covered his right wing and the rear of his body; the stench of burning scales and dragon flesh filling her nostrils.

She reconnected to Sanguino and he surged forwards, his jaws opening. Grimsleep's front talons were raised, but Sanguino swept past them, his teeth clamping round Grimsleep's throat, and his own claws ripping down the chest of the huge dragon. Bones crunched and snapped in Grimsleep's neck as Sanguino closed his jaws, and Grimsleep's body began to fall. His tail hit the lava pool, then his rear limbs sank into the abyss of molten rock. Sable gripped onto the harness as waves of heat and vapours enveloped them. Sanguino beat his wings, using all of his great strength, and tore through Grimsleep's neck, severing the huge, scarred head. The rest of him fell into the pool amid an eruption of steam and vapours as Sanguino retreated, his father's head gripped in his front claws. He flew to the end of the ravine and collapsed onto the rocky ledge. A plume of lava had sprayed across his left flank, and the scales were blistered and angry-looking, and Sable could feel the pain tear through him.

You did it, my brave Badblood.

Sanguino gazed down at the head of Grimsleep on the rocks next to him. 'I did.'

Sable shot her vision back up to Maddie.

Perfect timing, Maddie, perfect. Now hide; Ashfall and the others are coming.

She saw them scurry into the rocks of the cliffside as three dark specks approached through the sky. Ashfall was in the lead, with Broadwing and Deepblue behind her. Deathfang's daughter raced towards them, then stared down in disbelief. Half of Grimsleep's headless body lay next to the pool of lava, while the other half was submerged beneath the molten rock. Her eyes went to the monstrous head lying by Sanguino, and she let out a gasp.

'You did it!' cried Deepblue, coming closer.

The small blue dragon swooped down and landed next to Sanguino, her nose sniffing at the burns along his flank.

'How?' said Ashfall, hovering above them. 'We saw you flee in terror.'

'I tricked him,' said Sanguino. 'I made him think I was scared, and then I turned here, made my stand, and slew him. With my own teeth, I tore out his throat. The beast is dead.'

Ashfall tilted her head, as if bowing before him. 'I underestimated you.' A laugh escaped her. 'My father will have trouble believing this, but I am a witness.'

'As am I,' said Broadwing. 'This was a mighty deed, Sanguino.'

'I told you,' said Deepblue; 'I told you he could do it.'

Sable smiled, feeling the intense pride swelling through Sanguino. It had been her plan, and her stubbornness that had cajoled them into carrying it out, but she was content for the dark red dragon to take all the glory. She lifted her hands from the harness grip, and noticed that they were scalded and shaking. Her clothes were ruined from the flames, and she started to feel the pain from the burns she had received.

'Go back to your father,' Sanguino said to Ashfall, 'and bear him the news. I shall follow on in a moment, and I shall deliver the head of Grimsleep to Deathfang as I swore I would.'

Ashfall tilted her head again, then beat her grey wings and soared away to the west. Sanguino sagged as soon as she had departed, as if exhaustion and pain were about to overcome him.

'Deepblue,' said Sable. 'Maddie and Millen are up on the cliff, as they too wished to witness the fall of Grimsleep. Please bring them down here, and be careful; humans are very fragile.'

'I shall,' she said, then took off.

'My rider,' Sanguino said once they were alone; 'without you, none of this could have happened. You are bonded to me now, and I to you. I never thought it possible that I could love a human, but I love you. Promise me that you will be my rider forever.'

'I promise.'

'And I make this promise to you; I will protect you, always. You are mine.'

Deepblue returned, a human clasped in each forelimb, and set them down gently next to Sanguino. Maddie ran towards the dark red dragon, and clambered up the harness as quickly as she could. She stared at Sable for a moment, her eyes wide, then threw her arms around her.

'Ouch,' groaned Sable. 'Careful. I got a little bit scorched back there.'

'A little bit?' said Maddie. 'Malik's ass, Sable, that was insane. You are insane.'

Millen joined them, and they strapped themselves into the harness.

'Are you ready?' said Sable.

'I am,' said Sanguino.

He gripped onto Grimsleep's gigantic head with his forelimbs, as Deepblue soared upwards to join Broadwing, who was circling overhead.

'Let's go home,' said Sable. 'We'll take the head to Deathfang, and after that, I think I might need to go for a little lie down.'

CHAPTER 9
THE VOW

Alea Tanton, Tordue, Western Khatanax – 12th Luddinch 5252

Belinda walked into Leksandr's study, and the demigod courtier closed the door behind her. The room was in semi-darkness, with the shutters closed to keep out the bright sunshine. The Sixth Ascendant was sitting on the floor in front of the Sextant, his eyes closed.

'You asked for me?' said Belinda.

Leksandr said nothing. Belinda frowned and remained where she was, watching the Ascendant for any signs of movement. His chest was rising and falling, but he seemed to be deep in meditation.

'Leksandr?'

Nothing. Belinda sighed and sat down on one of the chairs by the wall. She had been summoned, no doubt, to provide an update on her search for a Quadrant related to the salve world, but perhaps he had forgotten. She glanced around the room, then settled in the chair to wait.

Her thoughts went to Silva, and she wondered how her great grand-daughter's search was going. She had been contacting her most days, and during the previous morning had spoken to her after she had arrived by ship in Capston in the Southern Cape. The rumours swirling

CHRISTOPHER MITCHELL

around the town all said that Belinda had surrendered to the old enemy, and that the rebellion was finally at an end; and the news had saddened Belinda. Silva's spirits remained high, however, and her mission had given her new purpose. Belinda had ensured that the vision gods and demigods who were sweeping the continent looking for Kelsey had finished with the Southern Cape, and she had directed them to move their search northwards to Kinell, starting with its capital Kin Dai. Belinda's own search had also moved there, after she had re-visited the cavern of Fordamere by vision. It had been painful to gaze upon the unburied bodies of the slaughtered Fordians that littered the streets and plazas of the Yoneath, and her hatred of the Ascendants had grown. Within the cavern itself, she had followed the tunnels where she had seen Van and Sohul take Corthie, but beyond that the trail had gone cold.

Aside from the searches, the rulers of Old Alea had been occupied with the aftermath of the great earthquake that had struck twenty days previously. Thousands had died; exactly how many, no one would ever know, as no regular census was maintained in the city, and the slums that had been affected were inhabited by untold numbers of the poor. Tens of thousands had been rendered homeless, not only by the earthquake, but by the devastating fires that had raged for days, incinerating entire districts. With winter looming, starvation was going to finish off many more, but neither Arete nor Leksandr seemed concerned by the toll on mortal lives; keeping the population pliant and under control was of far more importance to them. Both the Bloodflies and the Blue Thumbs had hosted games since then, in an attempt to persuade everyone that normality had been restored, but the city granaries were almost empty, and the free food dole had been suspended. Soldiers were being recruited rapidly, in expectation of the riots that would inevitably follow once the markets ran out of anything to sell.

She began to grow impatient, and sent a tendril of her vision powers across the room to Leksandr. His eyes were closed, leaving her unable to access his mind, not that she would have been brave enough to do it. She stood, and paced the room for a moment, then her eyes caught on a wall display above the cold hearth. A round iron shield was pinned to the wall, and below it was an old sword. She swallowed, her gaze going from the sword to Leksandr. She walked to the hearth before she could stop herself, her steps light. The sword looked like it hadn't been moved from the wall in many years, and the blade was tarnished and stained.

It would still work, she told herself. Leksandr was unarmed, and oblivious to her presence. She remembered the promise she had made to herself to kill them. There had never been an opportunity to do so, but it was also true that she hadn't gone out of her way to try. Her fear had kept her cautious, and she had never progressed from fantasising about their deaths to putting any such plan into operation. Her hand reached for the blade.

The door swung open and Arete strode into the room.

'Leksandr,' she cried, not seeming to even notice Belinda; 'get up.'

Belinda turned, her arm dropping to her side.

'What are you doing here?' said Arete, her eyes beginning to narrow. 'What were you up to just now?'

Belinda frowned. 'I'm waiting for Leksandr; he summoned me.'

'Why didn't you just wake him?'

'I didn't want to interrupt his meditation, or whatever he's doing.'

Arete rolled her eyes, then stepped forward and shook Leksandr's shoulder. 'Wake up.'

The Sixth Ascendant's eyes opened, and he glanced around the room. 'Yes?'

Arete frowned. 'Bastion's here.'

Leksandr face fell. 'When?'

'Just now. He appeared in the residence's main reception hall.'

'Did he come alone?'

'Yes. He wants to see us.'

'I'm sure he does.' He shook his head. 'I suppose we should get it over with.'

'Who's Bastion?' said Belinda.

Arete stared at her. 'He particularly wants to see you.'

'He's an Ancient,' said Leksandr. 'The Blessed Second Ascendant's emissary.'

'That's one word for it,' said Arete.

'If he's here,' said Leksandr, 'then he will be acting with the full authority of the Second Ascendant behind him; and anything you say or do will be reported back to Implacatus; in fact, he might well decide to take you back with him.'

A surge of panic swept through Belinda, but she kept her appearance calm.

'We need to decide what we're going to tell him,' said Arete.

Leksandr smiled and got to his feet. 'He's probably listening to us as we speak.'

'Why are you acting as if you're scared of him?' said Belinda. 'He is an Ancient; you are Ascendants.'

'He is the Blessed Second Ascendant's sword, fist and shield; his most trusted advisor and lieutenant. He is also almost as old as the Ascendants. It would be wise for you to understand that his word will always be taken over ours.'

'Wise indeed,' said a low voice from the door.

The others turned. A man in a simple black cloak and sandals was standing in the doorway. He was unarmed, and carrying nothing apart from a small shoulder bag. He walked into the room.

'Lord Bastion,' said Leksandr, bowing; 'I was just explaining who you were to the Third Ascendant.'

'I know. I heard.'

Arete also had her head bowed, but Belinda kept her chin up as Bastion approached her. He stopped when he was inches from her face and stared, his dark eyes boring into her. He nodded, then turned and walked over to the Sextant.

'Explain,' he said, his eyes fixed on the device.

'Well, my lord,' said Leksandr. 'We seized the Sextant in a successful operation some...'

'I know what occurred. Explain why you haven't returned to Implacatus.'

Belinda glanced at him. 'How do you know what occurred?'

Bastion said nothing, his eyes on the device.

'The Third Ascendant,' said Leksandr, 'has, as you may know, lost her memory, and she doesn't yet understand the correct etiquette for these, uh, situations. She didn't mean any offence by her question, you see, she...'

'I'm still waiting for your explanation,' said Bastion.

'Of course, my lord; yes. Well, the Seventh Ascendant and I decided that we would remain here to complete all of our objectives. The Sextant was only one, and there is still work to be done here on Lost-well. There is the matter of the Holdfasts, a family of mortals who are also in possession of god-like powers. We have slain one, but the others have so far eluded our detection. And the Sextant itself, of course, requires further examination in order to get it operational.'

'You had one objective,' said Bastion. 'Secure the supply of salve. Why have you failed?'

'The Holdfasts have frustrated us at every turn.'

'That's what Lord Renko said, and you know what happened to him.'

'With all respect to you and the Blessed Second Ascendant, I'm not sure you fully grasp the importance of these mortals. They are completely impervious to our powers, and have powers of their own. What's more, they come from a world where a significant proportion of mortals have powers. Nathaniel created it; it was his last act, I believe.'

Bastion paused for a second as if taken aback. 'Do you have proof of this?'

Leksandr pointed at Belinda. 'The Third Ascendant has been to this world.'

'Has she, indeed?' said Bastion. He drew his eyes from the Sextant and turned them towards Belinda. 'Is this so, Third Ascendant?'

'It is.'

'How did you come to be shielded? I cannot penetrate your mind.'

'One of the Holdfasts did it.'

'Why?'

'To protect me.'

'They were your friends?'

'Yes.'

'And now?'

'Now, I have knelt and sworn allegiance to the Second Ascendant.'

A hint of a smile crept across Bastion's lips. 'My master is minded to dismiss the Sixth and Seventh Ascendants from their positions of authority on this operation, and place you in charge in their stead.'

'My lord,' said Arete, her voice strained; 'we cannot be sure of her loyalty. She should be removed from Lostwell and interrogated by the Blessed Second Ascendant himself.'

Bastion glanced at her for a moment. 'I shall take neither course. The Third Ascendant will remain here, and Leksandr shall continue in his position as the leader of this operation. Fulfil your primary objective, or you shall be punished.' His eyes tightened. 'A world of mortals with powers? I must learn more and return with this information to Implacatus. Belinda, come with me.'

Bastion's questioning of Belinda lasted several hours and, under his unblinking eyes, she heard herself give away more than she had ever told Leksandr and Arete about the world of the Holdfasts, and her expedition to the City of Pella. He said almost nothing, letting her talk, and her words filled the awkward gaps as if silence was unbearable. With an effort, she managed to rein herself in once the questions had returned to events on Lostwell, and stopped short of revealing the truth about Corthie, or the mission that she had given to Silva.

He finally averted his eyes from her when she had finished. 'I have a message,' he said, 'from my master to you. He wishes you to know that his personal feelings towards you haven't altered in ten thousand years. He is looking forward to your reconciliation, but for that reconciliation to be complete, you must honour the word you gave to him, and become his bride upon your return.'

Belinda blinked. 'My word?'

'Yes, Belinda. You may have lost your memories, but my master remembers everything. Before you left Implacatus to join Nathaniel, you were pledged to Edmond, my master. You were to be his queen, not Nathaniel's. My master has ordered that you may only return to Implacatus if you agree to honour the vow you made to him.'

'And if I disagree?'

'Then the war begins again, only this time I imagine it will be considerably shorter. There is only you left, after all. I shall leave you to consider, and return to my master.'

He placed the shoulder bag onto his lap, pushed his hand inside it, and disappeared.

Belinda stared at the empty chair for a moment, then stood and walked to an open window. Outside was a view of the ocean, and she watched the waves roll in from the west. Why had Silva never mentioned anything about a vow she had made to Edmond? Was Bastion lying? That seemed unlikely, as it was the basis for his decision to leave her in Khatanax rather than take her back to Implacatus.

She needed answers, so she shot her vision out, bending it south towards Capston. Mile after mile of nothing but ocean passed under her, then she turned to the east, where the sky was growing dark. It was early evening when she reached the small town on the shores of the Southern Cape. She made directly for the rented rooms where Silva was staying, and found her sitting alone at a table, eating.

She entered the demigod's mind, staying as quiet as possible. It was something she had been practising, and even with her emotions churning, she remembered to do it, rather than charge in.

Silva blinked, and frowned.

You're getting much better, your Majesty, she said. *If I wasn't so used to listening out for you, I would never have perceived your presence. Well done.*

Silva, did I promise to marry Edmond, the Second Ascendant?

Her great granddaughter fell silent.

You must tell me.

If you did, your Majesty, then this is the first time I've heard of it. But...

well, if it is true, then it would explain some things I've always struggled to understand; such as comments His Majesty King Nathaniel made, or the way you sometimes reacted whenever Edmond was mentioned. I confess, though, I don't know. Who told you?

An emissary sent by Edmond. An Ancient named Bastion.

Belinda felt Silva's anger stir. *That vile beast? He has so much blood on his hands that I doubt he'd ever be able to wash them clean. He is a violent brute, and utterly loyal to the Second Ascendant, but he doesn't lie; he doesn't need to. His powers are the equal of any Ascendant, except you, your Majesty, of course; and Edmond himself. Is he in Alea Tanton?*

He was; he's gone again already. He says I have to honour my word, or Edmond will restart the war, by which I think he meant he would send people to kill me.

He has given you time to consider?

He has.

Then flee. Whether it is a lie or not, when he returns, it will be in force, and they will kill you.

Unless I agree to marry Edmond.

What? I... Your Majesty, please, you cannot.

Don't worry, Silva, I'm not going to marry him. But if I let Bastion take me to Implacatus, then I might get close enough to Edmond to kill him.

Your Majesty, if you, I mean the old you, had thought that a wise plan, don't you think you would have tried it? If you did make a promise to Edmond, then it must have been many millennia ago, long before I was born, or when you came to Lostwell. The old you would have done anything to defeat and kill Edmond; therefore there must be a good reason why she didn't attempt what you are suggesting.

You may be right, Silva; I'll think it over. For now, I'd better let the others know that Bastion has gone.

Farewell, your Majesty.

Belinda pulled her vision back to her body. Despite Silva's admission of ignorance, she felt more certain than ever that Bastion had been telling the truth. It was impossible that Edmond could love her, not if he hadn't seen her in thousands of years, and she was at a loss to explain his motivations.

She walked out of the room and back into Leksandr's study, where the other two Ascendants were waiting.

'Bastion's gone,' she said, as they looked up at her.

'Gone?' said Arete, getting to her feet.

'Yes. I told him everything I could remember, and then he left to tell the Second Ascendant.'

'Why didn't he take you back to Implacatus with him?'

'That's between me and Bastion.'

Arete glared at her, but her anger had a tinge of fear about it. They didn't know anything about the vow she had made, Belinda thought, realising that she might be able to use the knowledge against them.

'He wants you to continue working towards your objective,' she said.

Leksandr and Arete glanced at each other.

'And you, Third Ascendant,' said Leksandr, his features drawn; 'what does he want you to do?'

'That's confidential,' she said, 'but I advise you not to hinder me in any way.'

'She has betrayed us,' said Arete. 'After everything we've done to shield her from Implacatus.'

Belinda frowned. 'You have done nothing to shield me, Arete. Leksandr has, but not you. You wanted me sent there for interrogation, but that won't be happening. I won't forget how you treated me with suspicion, or how you've tried to undermine me.'

Leksandr bowed before her. 'Third Ascendant, tell me what I should do.'

'Keep working on the Sextant,' she said. 'It is the key to locating the salve world.'

'I will, your Grace.'

'And I?' said Arete, her glance switching from defiant to deferential.

'Organise relief for the victims of the earthquake,' said Belinda. 'The people of Tordue are starving, and many have lost their homes.'

'Yes, your Grace.'

Belinda kept her eyes on them. 'I will be in my rooms if you require me.'

She walked from the study, her heart racing. Were they so easily fooled? If they could have read her thoughts, then they would have been able to see through her words, but the combination of Bastion's appearance and the fact that her mind was shielded, had transformed the two Ascendants. A new feeling surged through her, one that she had never experienced before.

Power.

It felt good. The fear that she had seen in the Ascendants' eyes had felt so good, that part of her wanted to go back into the room so she could feel it again. They feared her, and because of that, they would do whatever she ordered. The possibilities began to open up before her, and she found herself wondering what would happen if she accepted Edmond's offer. Together, they would wield power over every known world, and she would be able to use that power for good, and bring an end to injustice. She remembered Silva's warning – if it were that easy, she would have done it millennia before, but in a way she *had* done it before, except she had chosen Nathaniel over Edmond. Either way, power was power.

She reached her suite of rooms and glanced at her collection of servants, some of whom seemed to sense the change in her bearing, their bows a little more formal than they had been that morning. She would need to sift through them, discarding any whose allegiances lay with Leksandr and Arete, and surround herself only with those loyal to her, if any could be found. She could interview them one by one, delving into their minds to root out their secrets and weaknesses.

She halted in the centre of her sitting room. 'Gather round.'

The servants glanced at each other, then began to assemble before her. There were six of them, all demigods from Implacatus who had arrived in Old Alea as part of the retinue of the Sixth and Seventh Ascendants.

'Lord Bastion was here,' she said, watching their expressions as they took in the information, 'and the situation has changed. You will no longer report to the Sixth or Seventh Ascendants; you report to me. What has gone before will not count against you, but if I detect the slightest hint of disloyalty from any one of you, then you will be dismissed from my service and punished.'

A few of them looked confused, and she went into one of their minds, keeping as quiet as she was able. She sensed the demigod's mixed feelings, and her longing to run and tell Arete what was happening. She looked through some of her memories, and found conversations the demigod had held with the Seventh Ascendant, with Arete instructing her to tell her everything that Belinda said and did. The demigod's true feelings about Belinda were also evident – she loathed her, and perceived her to be dangerous and a possible traitor. Belinda considered. An example would need to be made.

Get on your knees, Belinda commanded.

The demigod cried out, her eyes widening, then she fell to her knees as if a weight had pushed her down. The other servants gasped as they watched, and Belinda could feel their fear.

Confess, Belinda thundered in the demigod's mind. *Confess your disloyalty to me.*

'I was spying on you for the Seventh Ascendant,' the demigod said, her voice strained and edged with terror. 'I was under her Grace's orders. I was only doing what I was told.'

I am the rightful Queen of Lostwell. Refer to me as 'your Majesty' when you address me. Apologise.

'I'm sorry, your Majesty,' the demigod cried.

Beg for forgiveness.

The demigod bowed her head. 'Please forgive me, your Majesty; I am unworthy to serve you.'

'Yes,' said Belinda; 'you are. Now run off to Arete, and explain to her why I have just dismissed you from your position. If you enter my rooms again, I will kill you. Understood?'

'Yes, your Majesty.'

Thank me for being merciful.

'Thank you for showing me mercy, your Majesty.'

Belinda released the demigod from the vision grip, and she got up and raced from the room, knocking over a chair in her haste to leave as quickly as possible.

'Someone pick that up,' said Belinda.

The servants all hurried to do as she bid, almost fighting to be the one who could obey her first.

'That is all for now,' said Belinda. 'Come back in the morning, and I will determine who among you is fit to serve me. Loyalty will be rewarded, disloyalty punished. Dismissed.'

Within seconds, the room had been emptied, and Belinda stood alone, revelling in her newfound power. For years, since she had awoken in the attic of the Holdfast townhouse, she had served someone else. First Karalyn, then the Empress, then Thorn, and finally Corthie. She had been an able second-in-command, always available to offer support and advice, but she had never wanted to be the one in charge. She wondered why that was. She was the Third Ascendant, the second most powerful being in existence. She had ruled before, many times, and the statues and monuments dedicated to her proved that beyond any doubt. Once, she had been known as the wise old queen, and there was no reason why she couldn't slip back into that role, no reason at all. What a simple thing it had been; all it had taken was a shift in her attitude. Silva had been right; she was a Queen.

The gods and demigods who arrived at her rooms that evening to begin their daily vision search were clearly aware of what had occurred, and each one of them bowed and addressed her as 'your Majesty' as they entered.

'As I mentioned yesterday,' she said, sitting at the head of the table, 'we are moving our search from the Southern Cape and Dun Khatar up to Kinell, starting with Kin Dai. You will be looking for a demigod with vision powers. If you sense him, you must inform me immediately.'

They began at once, their eyes glazing over, and Belinda sat back and watched them. She had been pondering the problems she faced, looking for a compromise that might prevail. She knew the leadership of the City of Pella – surely a peaceful negotiation with them could provide the salve that Implacatus desired. A plan had started to take root in her mind, a plan that would involve no one being killed. Furthermore, if it succeeded, then she would receive the plaudits for restoring the supply of the precious mineral, and Arete and Leksandr would be discredited. That was what queens did, she thought; they found solutions. Implacatus would never cease their search for salve, but if she could guarantee its supply without any need for a military occupation of Pella, then everyone would win.

Two hours passed, then a demigod blinked.

'Your Majesty,' he said, his eyes lowered.

'Yes?'

'I think I have detected a faint vision signal emanating from the city of Kin Dai, by the river estuary. It appears to be coming from a river boat.'

She went into his mind, and saw the location he had pinpointed.

'Everyone,' she said, breaking into the thoughts of the others; 'that will be all for tonight. Say nothing of this to anyone.'

The gods and demigods rose from their seats, bowed, and left the room. When they had gone, she sent her own vision out into the night sky. She crossed the fertile plains of Tordue, then soared over the mountains where the wild dragons lived and entered Kinell. It looked similar to Tordue, but its farms and fields were less organised, and its villages held free people rather than the indentured slaves of Tordue. That was another thing she would change if she gained power – there would be no more slavery.

Her vision raced north-eastwards until she reached the coast of the ocean, then she turned north until she found the city of Kin Dai. Using the image she had taken from the mind of the demigod, she focussed on the river boats that crowded the muddy estuary. Her vision landed on the vessel that the demigod had identified, and she went inside, guiding her sight down from the deck. She came to a narrow galley kitchen, with a table where four men were sitting. She smiled when she saw Corthie, then noticed that he was drunk. Next to him sat Van and Sohul, and Naxor was at the other end of the table. She scowled at the sight of him, her hatred bubbling back to the surface after being suppressed for so long. She longed to talk to Corthie, but his mind was shielded, and besides, only Naxor had the information she needed.

She entered the demigod's mind, and began rifling through his memories as quickly as she was able; searching for the last time he had used a Quadrant to travel to the salve world. She found it. It was a memory that she herself was in; the time Naxor had fled from her, Karalyn and Sable when they had first arrived in the Falls of Iron. She memorised his hand movements over the copper-coloured device, then paused. She had done what she had come to do, but she still needed to warn them, not for Naxor's sake, but for the others.

He stopped talking, as if noticing something, then blinked.

'So,' he went on, 'it was faint, but I think it might have been Amalia. The powers flickered for a moment, then ceased, and I could find no trace of her after that.'

'But if it was Amalia,' said Van, 'then clearly Kelsey couldn't have been with her. How do you explain that?'

'I can't,' said Naxor; 'I'm merely reporting what I sensed.'

'And it was up north?' said Sohul.

'Yes, in one of the ancient fortress towns along the coast – the Forted Shore, I believe it's called.'

'We should go, tomorrow,' said Corthie.

Naxor, said Belinda.

He froze. He recognised her voice, she could feel it.

'Are you alright?' said Van. 'Corthie's suggestion wasn't that crazy; this is the first clue we've gained about their possible location.'

Make your excuses and go to your cabin.

'I'm fine,' he spluttered; 'fine. Yes, I'm, eh… I just need to pop into my room for a moment.' He got up as the others frowned at him. 'I'll be back soon.'

He hurried across the galley and into a tiny cabin, then closed the door. He sat on his bed, his hands trembling.

Belinda?

Yes.

I, uh, I...

I'm not here to hurt you, although you deserve it for what you did to me.

I can explain!

Shut up and listen. The use of your powers is endangering Corthie. The Ascendants believe he is dead, and I wish it to stay that way.

How did you find us?

The Ascendants have a team of gods and demigods who have been searching for Kelsey Holdfast. They found you instead. Right now, I am the only hope you have of surviving this. I know I can't trust you, but I'm sure you are perfectly capable of acting in your own interests.

But...

Be quiet, Naxor. I need you to cease using your vision powers, immediately, and move to a different location, tonight if possible; if not, then first thing tomorrow. If you don't, then the Ascendants will discover where you are.

Why are you helping us?

I am doing this for Corthie, Van and Sohul. Hide.

Are the Ascendants still in Alea Tanton?

Yes. They have no idea how to use the Sextant.

Then the City is safe? And Corthie's world too?

For now they are, and I have a plan that will hopefully keep it that way.

A plan? What plan?'

Never mind that, Naxor. Just do as I say. And tell Corthie I love him.

She severed the link before he could say anything else to her. She felt a little disgusted with herself for having been inside his mind, but if she had saved Corthie then it would be worth it. She walked to the window and gazed down at the dark city. Her city, in truth. Khatanax was hers; Lostwell was hers, and, if she wanted it, ultimate power would be hers too. She merely needed to take it.

CHAPTER 10

A GLIMMER OF SILVER

Northern Kinell – 12th Luddinch 5252

N orthern Kinell – 12th Luddinch 5252

Aila had never been so hungry. She and Kesley had been walking for days, keeping to the main roads that wound down the eastern coast of the Forted Shore, but their lack of money had slowed their progress. Some days, they had barely covered a few miles, instead spending hours trying to find enough food to eat, and on other days they had been too tired to walk at all.

The landscape was doing little to improve their mood. Acre after acre of hillside was covered in nothing but tree stumps, and the great majority of traffic they had seen on the road was involved in transporting timber down to the large port of Kin Dai, ready to be exported to Alea Tanton. Labour camps dotted the countryside, filled with workers who went out each day to cut down more of the vast forest that had once covered the whole of Northern Kinell, leaving behind nothing but a wilderness of tangled undergrowth and the remains of the fallen trees. No attempts were being made to plant new ones, and after seeing how the City of Pella had carefully managed its own small woodlands, Aila was sickened by the waste.

They had spent several days working at one of the camps, collecting the scraps of wood that the lumber gangs had left behind, but the hours were long and hard, and the pay had been barely enough to cover a single day's food.

Kelsey had lost a lot of weight and, considering she had been slim to begin with, Aila worried about her health. As a demigod, Aila knew that her reserves of self-healing powers would keep her going almost indefinitely, but the young Holdfast woman was starting to look gaunt and ill. For the previous two days, they had veered away from the barren coast, and headed inland, closer to the edge of the forest and the labour camps. They had slept in a hut abandoned by the lumber gangs, huddling together in the cold night air among the miles of tree stumps.

The following morning, Aila awoke, her back stiff from sleeping on the rough ground. She allowed her self-healing to do its job and poked her head out of the shabby hut. All around was a wilderness of broken ground punctuated by never ending lines of tree stumps. To the south and west, smoke was rising from the edge of the forest in the distance, where the gangs were clearing undergrowth.

'There's a camp a couple of miles away,' she said to Kelsey. 'We should make for it.'

'How do you know it's there?' said Kelsey, who was still lying on the ground.

'Just a guess, really. If the gangs are already burning stuff, they must have slept somewhere close by.'

'Do you think Amalia's still looking for us?'

'She must have given up by now. Come on, get up.'

Kelsey groaned, then scrambled to the hut's entrance. 'I hate this place.'

'I know; it's horrible.'

'Maybe we should go back to Stoneship.'

'We're more than half way to Kin Dai; it'll be easier to keep going.'

'We should have... No, I'm not going to say it. You're right; we need to keep going. Though, the next time I escape from a maniac god, I want it to be with someone who can carry me on their back and run all the way to Kin Dai.'

They left the hut and Aila checked the position of the sun. In the

City, the sun was always in the same part of the sky, but she had become accustomed to its rise and fall every day on Lostwell. Kelsey had told her that it was Lostwell that moved, not the sun, but she wasn't sure if that was true, and in the situation they were in, it hardly mattered.

They began walking towards the south, following a rough track between the stumps. Aila scanned the ground as she always did when they were on the move. Once, she had found a silver coin that had bought them a loaf of bread, six apples and some cheese, which had felt like a feast, and she was determined not to miss anything else that had been carelessly dropped in the mud. Next to her, Kelsey trudged on, her hunger and exhaustion keeping her uncharacteristically quiet.

'It doesn't make any sense,' said Aila. 'Why would they cut down all the trees and not plant more?'

'They're idiots.'

'If they keep this up, there will be no forest left within a decade or so.'

'Do you think the gods care? Alea Tanton needs wood, and they'd rather cut down every tree in Northern Kinell than pause to think about the bigger picture. Khatanax is finished.'

Aila nodded. 'I'm going to steal again today.'

Kelsey said nothing.

'No complaints? No moral qualms?'

'Not any more, if it keeps us, I mean me, from starving. People who haven't eaten in days can't afford those kind of morals.'

'That's not what you said when we first started out.'

'I wasn't starving then. What's your plan?'

'When we get to the camp, you stay back and I'll go in alone and check the place out. Then I'll take on the identity of someone and help myself to whatever I can. Money, ideally, and then we can maybe rent a room with an actual bed for the night.'

After a mile and a half, Aila saw a large cluster of tents ahead of them. Small tendrils of smoke were rising from a few camp fires, and wagons and carts were parked by the side of the track.

'Alright, Kelsey,' she said; 'you stay here. I'll be back as soon as I can.'

The young Holdfast woman sat down on a tree stump. She looked tired out already, Aila thought, feeling a weight of responsibility for her. After everything she had been through, to die of hunger in the wastes of Northern Kinell seemed an ignominious way for it to end.

Aila turned, and hurried down the track. Ahead, she could make out a few figures moving through the camp, or sitting by fires, but she knew that the bulk of the workforce would already be at the forest's edge. She glanced back to check how far away Kelsey was, then considered a disguise.

You see me as an old peasant woman.

She slowed her pace to match her appearance as she walked into the camp. Kelsey had been right about hunger leading to the abandonment of morals; everywhere she looked, she was sizing up opportunities for theft, seeing the people in the camp as targets to be exploited rather than fellow human beings. She would never steal from a child, but that was about the only condition she had set herself. She watched as men unloaded sacks of grain from the back of a wagon, but it was well guarded, and grain was not much good to her or Kelsey. The guards were local militia, paid to keep order in the camps, and to ensure that the flow of timber never ceased. Quotas had to be met, as they had learned in the few days that they had worked in a camp, or there would be consequences.

The guards paid her no attention as she walked past. As she turned a corner, she saw a pile of rotting vegetables on the ground by a large tent and she walked over to take a closer look.

'Hey!' shouted a man. 'Keep your hands off; that's for the pigs, not you.'

'Do you have anything to spare?' she said.

'No, now bugger off.'

'Asshole,' she muttered, then she saw the small herd of pigs on the other side of the tent. One of those would last them a good day or two, she thought, at least until the meat went bad.

She watched as a heavily pregnant woman emerged from another tent, and she stared at her for a moment, imagining what her own appearance would look like in a few months. She was past her first trimester, but was still barely showing, and due to the way her self-healing worked, she sometimes almost forgot that she was pregnant. Even if the child within her was mortal, her powers would shield and protect it from starvation.

A well-dressed man approached, his long robes trailing in the mud. He looked like an official from Kin Dai, and had a worried expression on his face. Aila silently apologised to him, drew her knife from her belt, then walked right into his path. He came to an abrupt halt, raising his palms, and Aila fell to the ground in front of him.

'I didn't touch you,' he said.

'Sorry,' she said. 'I slipped.'

She slowly got back to her feet as he glowered at her, then she lashed out with the knife, slicing through the man's belt. She caught it with her other hand as it fell, and she bolted, her turn of speed taking him by surprise.

'Stop her!' he cried to the guards by the grain wagon.

Aila darted between a row of tents, detaching the purse and dropping the rest of the belt into the mud.

You see me as a young pregnant woman.

A moment later, three guards barged their way towards her, nearly knocking her over.

'Careful, please!' she cried.

'Sorry, miss,' said one; 'did you see an old woman go by?'

'Yes,' she said; 'just a moment ago. She was running.'

'Where?'

Aila pointed in the opposite direction, and the guards rushed away. Aila walked back to the main track leading through the camp, the purse hidden in her clothes. The man she had robbed was still standing there, a furious look on his face as he talked to a handful of other guards.

'The security in this camp is a bloody disgrace!' he shouted. 'I have enough to worry about without some old witch thieving from me in broad daylight. I want her flogged when she's found, understood?'

Aila took back her silent apology from before.

'Is the rumour true, sir?' said one of the guards.

'Yes. It's a dragon, there's no doubt about it. I'm heading straight back to Kin Dai to request immediate assistance.'

'Shall we move the camp?'

'No. Absolutely not. The work here must go on, without cessation. The dragon's not interested in stopping us.'

'But I heard it ate someone, sir.'

'Lies. A man was killed, yes, but he was torn to shreds, not eaten, and that was only because he had strayed too far into the forest. He must have disturbed its lair. We hold tight here, and carry on, and wait for the regular army to turn up to deal with it. I'm also going to request a demigod with vision powers to assist in tracking it down.' He paused, then noticed Aila's glance. 'Do you want something, girl?'

'Did you say a dragon?'

'It's of no concern to you; go back to... doing whatever you were doing.'

Aila glanced away, and began to walk back down the track. When she was out of sight, she switched her appearance to that of an old man, and continued out of the camp. Kelsey was still sitting where she had left her.

'Good news,' Aila said.

Kelsey's eyes lit up. 'You have food?'

'I have a purse.' She sat down next to the young Holdfast woman. 'And, as a benefit, the man I stole from was an asshole, so there's that too.'

Kelsey smiled. 'How much is in it?'

Aila opened the purse, and almost cried in relief. 'A lot. Enough.' She picked out six gold coins and gave them to Kelsey. 'Hide these; they'll be no good to us in the camp, but they're bound to come in handy later. That leaves at least twenty in silver. Oh, and apparently, there's a wild dragon terrorising the lumber gangs in the forest.'

'Really?'

'You don't seem very impressed.'

'I've seen plenty of flying reptiles.'

'But none that could speak.'

'I saw Blackrose for about five minutes when Van took me to Fordamere. Is there any chance at all that it's her?'

'Highly unlikely, I would imagine. A colony of wild dragons lives in the mountains a hundred and fifty miles south of here; it's far more likely to have come from there. I believe that Blackrose stayed there for a while, but I don't know what happened to her after Yoneath.'

'Maybe we should check, just in case.'

Aila stood. 'Let's eat first. Come on.'

They walked back into the camp, and made their way through the maze of tents to a small market, where they bought enough food to fill the empty bag Kelsey had been carrying. With her mouth salivating, they went to a quiet spot, sat on a dry patch of earth, and ate in silence.

'Pyre's arse, that feels better,' Kelsey said, as she licked her fingers. 'Thanks, Aila.'

'We have enough for three days, I reckon,' she said, 'but we'll need to find somewhere that will take the gold, or at least change it into smaller denominations for us. Or, we could use it to buy passage to Kin Dai.'

'How would we do that?'

'We'd have to walk back to the main coastal road and wait for a passing wagon. If we try to spend it here, it'll only arouse suspicion.'

'What about the dragon?' said Kelsey. 'We'll feel pretty stupid if we reach Kin Dai and discover it was Blackrose.'

'I told you, the chances are remote.'

'Remote, but not impossible.'

'What do you want us to do – wander off into the forest looking for a dragon? Has eating that food done something to your brain?'

Kelsey smirked. 'Maybe. What are the folk here planning to do about it?'

'They're sending for the army.'

'They're going to kill it?'

'Yes, if they can. The man also said that he was going to request a demigod with vision powers to help them. We should stay out of it; we could be in Kin Dai in a couple of days. Six gold coins should be enough to get us both there.'

Aila quietened as a couple of militia walked past where they were sitting. They looked aggrieved, and she wondered if they had been on the receiving end of a tirade for failing to find the old woman.

'Excuse me,' said Kelsey.

The guards turned.

'Can I ask you a question? Where is the dragon supposed to be?'

One of them frowned even deeper than before. 'How do you know about that?'

Kelsey shrugged. 'Word travels fast in this camp.'

'The last sighting was a little over five miles from here.'

'Is that all? That seems close.'

'Don't worry, love. We'll protect you if it comes here. Do you live in the camp?'

'Are you chatting me up?'

The guard dropped his frown. 'Might be.'

'Well, I do live here, and I might be free tonight. If, that is, you help me and my friend get a bit closer to where the dragon might be.'

'Why? Are you crazy?'

Kelsey gave him a smile. 'You might find that out tonight.'

The other guard sighed. 'We haven't got time for this.'

'Hang on a minute,' said the first guard. He turned back to Kelsey. 'There are wagons going to and from the forest edge that leave not far from here, at the western exit from the camp. Go there, and tell them Albert sent you, and they might give you a lift. The dragon was seen only a quarter of a mile from where they're cutting down the forest. What's your name?'

'I'm Betsy.'

'And I'll see you back here tonight, Betsy?'

'Alright, as long as I don't get eaten by an enormous flying snake.'

Albert grinned at her, then the two guards went on their way. Aila waited until they had disappeared behind a row of mud-splattered tents, then frowned at Kelsey.

'Betsy, eh? Sometimes, Kelsey...'

'Thanks, I know. It was a great idea, wasn't it? You're just jealous he fancied me.'

'You just ruined our chances of staying here overnight.'

'I had no intention of staying here overnight; this place is a dump. Here's what we do – we hustle a lift to the edge of the forest and find out what we can. A few questions to eye-witnesses should tell us if it's Blackrose or not, aye? If it's not, then we simply start walking to the coastal road.'

'You mean another night out in the open?'

'So? We've spent plenty of nights out in the open.'

'I shouldn't have fed you; all that food's turned your mind.'

'It has perked me up, right enough, and filled me with good ideas. Come on, Aila; this journey has been nothing but misery. It's taken us twenty days to walk sixty miles. That's an average of three miles a day.'

'I *can* count, you know.'

'I knew you weren't as stupid as you look.'

Aila shook her head and glanced away. Perhaps Kelsey's idea had some merit, she thought. It almost certainly wasn't Blackrose, but Aila could imagine Kelsey's scorn if they arrived at Kin Dai and discovered they had been wrong. And the idea of a lift taking them a few miles further south appealed.

'I have a few conditions,' she said.

Kelsey laughed. 'Let's hear them.'

'If we find out it's not Blackrose, then we leave.'

'What else?'

'Um, actually, that was it.'

Kelsey stood, picked up the bag of food and slung it over both shoulders.

'I notice you didn't agree to my one condition,' said Aila.

'That's right; it's a silly condition. We have to keep our options open.'

'But I'm pregnant; it might not be safe.'

Kelsey rolled her eyes. 'Really? You're using that excuse? You were happy to carry a knife into a camp and rob someone, but this is too much?'

'Amalia's ass,' muttered Aila as she got to her feet.

Kelsey gave her a perturbed look as she started to walk down the track. 'You can't say that; she's your grandmother.'

Aila caught her up. 'What?'

'You shouldn't refer to your grandmother's ass. It's, eh... well, it's a bit weird.'

'Shut up; it's just a saying. You've never objected to me referring to my grandfather's ass.'

'You what?'

'Malik; he was my grandfather.'

'Eww; I didn't know that. Now that I do, I would kindly ask you not to say it again.'

They walked on in silence for a moment.

'Does Amalia ever say "Malik's ass?"' said Kelsey.

'Um, I'm not sure.'

'She has a right to say it. That's it, though, just her.'

'She had him beheaded.'

'Oh. Not a happy marriage, then?'

'It might have been for the first few thousand years, who knows? It was a little bit frosty by the end, though.'

A wide track had been made by the western end of the camp, wide enough for wagons to travel on, and reinforced by a lattice of planks laid down over the thick mud. An empty wagon was sitting there as Aila and Kelsey approached, with two men standing close to the four oxen tethered to the harness.

'Hello,' said Kelsey.

The two men turned to glance at them.

'Albert said we could get a lift to the edge of the forest.'

'Did he now?' said one of the men.

'Aye, he did. How about it?'

'And how do you know Albert?'

'I'm his girlfriend. The name's Betsy. When are you leaving?'

'In two minutes.'

'Can we just climb up? We won't be any bother.'

The two men glanced at each other, then the first one nodded. 'Go on, then, lass.'

'Thanks,' said Kelsey. She hurried to the side of the open-topped wagon and climbed up onto the back, then helped Aila in as well.

Kelsey smirked at her. 'Betsy delivers the goods again.'

Aila glanced around at the dark forest. 'We need to go back.'

'Just a little further,' said Kelsey.

'But we're going to get lost if we keep going. In fact, we may already be lost.'

'Don't exaggerate. All we have to do is check where the sun is and...'

She fell into silence as they both looked up. There was no sign of the sun as far as Aila could see; the tree cover was too dense to allow much light through.

'Alright,' said Kelsey; 'we can retrace our steps. How far have we walked? We can't be more than a mile from the edge of the forest.'

Aila sat on a moss-covered tree trunk that had fallen over. 'I'm taking a break. The dragon could be anywhere; it might have flown away. And, it's probably not Blackrose anyway.'

'So you keep saying. Look, if the worst comes to the worst, we can just sit here and let the lumber gangs come to us. The rate they're cutting down the forest, that won't take long.'

She crouched down next to Aila, and they ate some of the food from the bag. Aila looked back at the way they had come as she chewed a strip of dried meat, but already she couldn't make out the path they had taken. The light was starting to fade within the forest, and every direction looked the same.

'Maybe we should stay here for the night,' she said, 'and then, in the morning, we might have a better idea of how to find our way back.'

'You mean give up?'

'We still have the gold; we can still afford to get to Kin Dai.'

Kelsey squinted into the distance, then stood and began to walk away.

'Where are you going now?' said Aila.

'Come and look at this.'

Aila sighed and got to her feet. She picked up the bag that Kelsey had left lying on the ground and followed her. The young Holdfast woman was standing close to a group of trees that looked as though a storm had struck them; their trunks were splintered and broken, and large branches were lying around like debris.

Kelsey smiled. 'What might have caused this, eh? A certain large snake with wings, perhaps?'

'I don't understand why you're so keen to meet this beast.'

'Well, for a start, if it's Blackrose, then she could fly us straight to Corthie and Van.'

Aila scowled at her. '*If* it's Blackrose, and *if* she even knows where Corthie and Van are.'

'What was her rider's name again? Maddie?'

'Yes.'

'Maddie!' Kelsey shouted into the gloom. 'Maddie!'

'Shut up! You're behaving as if there's only one dragon in Khatanax. The chances are...'

A loud crack echoed through the trees, and a flock of birds rose into the sky, startled, and flew away. A shiver ran down Aila's spine as she strained her ears to listen.

Kelsey edged closer to her. 'Something's coming.'

They stood back to back, each staring out into the shadows of the dark forest. Silence enveloped them, and it grew so quiet that Aila could hear her heart pounding inside her chest.

'Don't scream,' whispered Kelsey, 'but something's staring at me through the trees; something big.'

Aila went to turn, but a low voice froze her to where she stood.

'This is my forest; have you come to die?'

'No,' cried Kelsey, her voice high and wavering.

A large head thrust through the trees, stopping a yard from them. Its great jaws were open, and sparks were fizzing and arcing across its teeth. Above them, two red eyes were glowing like burning coals. It was too dark to discern the colour of its scales, but they seemed to shimmer like silver in the gloom.

It was most certainly a dragon, and it was not Blackrose.

Aila felt Kelsey grip her hand.

'Why have you come here?' said the dragon. 'I was expecting hunters, or soldiers, and you are neither; you are merely lost little insects.'

'Soldiers are coming,' said Aila, trying to keep her panic in check; 'and a god. They want to kill you.'

'We're here to warn you,' said Kelsey.

'You are lying,' said the dragon. 'You came to spy on me, so you could tell the soldiers where I am. You shall indeed be a warning, but not in the way you intended, as I shall kill you, and leave your remains where the other insects will find them.'

'Please don't,' said Kelsey.

The dragon raised a forelimb, and extended her long, thick claws in front of them.

'I await the truth,' she said. 'Speak, or your end will come.'

'Alright,' said Kelsey. 'I was lying, sorry; we didn't come here to warn you; we came here to, eh, well, we came here because we were looking for a particular dragon. That's right, and, eh, but you're not her, so, sorry about that. We'll just turn around and walk back out of your lovely forest; no harm done; just an honest mistake.'

'I see,' said the dragon. 'I'm going to kill you regardless, as a lesson to the insects cutting down the forest. Perhaps your deaths might give them some pause. First, though, I want you to beg for your lives.'

'You want us to beg for our lives, and then you'll kill us anyway?' said Aila.

The dragon turned her red eyes to the demigod. 'I sense that you are not as terrified as the other insect. You should be.'

She raised her claws higher, ready to bring them down. Aila's mouth fell open. If she told the dragon she was a demigod, then the beast would make certain of her death by decapitating her, or by incinerating her to ashes; if she didn't, then she might survive a mauling. But Kelsey? The young Holdfast woman had no chance.

She raised her hands. 'We're friends of Blackrose; do you know Blackrose?'

The dragon hesitated.

'And Maddie,' Aila went on. 'I know Maddie well; we're friends.'

'You know Blackrose?' said the dragon. 'How?'

'I came to Lostwell with her and Maddie.'

'And the insect known as Millen?'

Aila blinked. 'No, sorry; I don't know any Millen.'

'Sable, the witch?'

'Sable Holdfast?' said Kelsey. 'She's my mother's sister. Do you know Sable?'

The dragon drew her claws back an inch or two. 'I have had dealings with the witch.'

'We were looking for Blackrose,' said Aila. 'Do you know where she is?'

'No.'

'We last saw her in Yoneath. She came to help us, and she had another dragon with her.' Aila narrowed her eyes. 'Are you the other dragon?'

The dragon lowered her claws, and the light in her eyes seemed to dim a little. 'It wasn't my fault. I had no choice but to flee. Two Ascendants, they… I…'

'It *was* you,' said Aila. 'We're on the same side.'

Some of the fire in her eyes returned. 'I am not on the side of any insect.'

'But you're on the same side as Blackrose.'

'Blackrose is my mother.'

Kesley let out a strangled laugh.

'What?' said Aila. 'Blackrose didn't mention having a daughter.'

'She adopted me, and then I failed her. I should have died by her side, but instead I fled. It has taken me many days to recover from the death powers wielded by the two Ascendants.'

'Wait; is Blackrose dead?'

The silver dragon closed her eyes. 'I don't know.'

'We can help each other,' said Kelsey.

'I require no assistance from insects.'

'My friend is right,' said Aila. 'She has powers, a bit like Sable, except she can stop the powers of the gods. If she's with you, then no vision powers will find you, and no death powers can hurt you.'

The dragon's eyes snapped open and she stared at Aila for a long moment.

'I discern no lie,' she said after a while, 'but what you say cannot be true.'

'All the same,' said Kelsey, 'you can't kill us now. We're friends with your mother. She wouldn't be happy if you tore us to shreds, now, would she?'

The dragon's eyes glowed bright with anger. 'I cannot tell if you are lying or not. Perhaps you are related to Sable.'

'Soldiers will be coming for you,' said Aila. 'That part was true. Those same soldiers also want to catch us. Let's help each other, and together we can find out what's happened to your mother.'

The dragon squeezed her eyes closed and she seemed to tremble with rage, then she lashed out with her claws, ripping through the trunk of a tree a few yards to their left in a frenzy of noise.

'Very well!' she growled. 'I warn you, though; if you hinder me in any way, then I take your heads from your shoulders, whether you are friends of my mother or not.'

She turned, and began to move away from them, crashing her way through the undergrowth.

'I'm Aila and this is Kelsey,' said Aila, as they hurried next to her. 'What's your name?'

'Frostback.'

'Because of your silver scales?' said Kelsey. 'I like that. Would it be quicker if we flew? Could we ride on your back?'

Frostback came to an abrupt halt, her long neck turning so she could stare down at Kelsey.

'You will never ride on my back, insect; never.'

Kelsey shrugged. 'Alright; I was only asking. Are you always this grumpy?'

Frostback ignored her and started striding away. Aila and Kesley glanced at each other, then ran to chase after her.

CHAPTER 11

NO FIXED ABODE

K in Dai, Kinell, Eastern Khatanax – 13th Luddinch 5252

Corthie felt something sharp poke him in the ribs. He groaned, awakening, and wondered why his bed felt so hard.

'Is this him?' said a voice.

'Yes, officer.'

Corthie opened his eyes, his head splitting from the effects of the ruinous amount of vodka he had consumed the night before. He blinked. Daylight. He was lying by the side of a street, in the gutter. An empty bottle sat inches from his face, and next to it were a pair of boots belonging to a man.

'And he smashed up your tavern, is that right?'

'Yes, officer; just because I asked him to leave. He also attacked two of my staff, and broke the nose of one of them. He's an animal.'

Corthie tried to get up, but the spear poked him in the ribs again.

'Stay where you are, boy.'

Corthie's confusion turned to anger, and he was about to grab the spear when he realised that a small crowd had gathered round where he lay. He recognised a nearby shop front; he was close to the alleyway packed with bars and taverns, a ten minute walk from the house boat.

'Bring up the wagon,' said the man with the spear.

'What will happen to him?' said the tavern owner.

'That will be up to the magistrate. He's a big lad; he might be sent to a labour camp, or maybe he'll serve some time in the city jail.'

'Good; he deserves it.'

The tavern owner spat on him.

'That's enough,' said the militia officer; 'I want none of that. Go home; we'll take it from here.'

Corthie tried to recall what had happened the night before, but his memories were full of gaps. He remembered arguing with Naxor in the house boat; something about Belinda, and then he had gone out, but after that? Nothing. His head was pounding, and his limbs and joints ached. He closed his eyes, but then everything started to spin, and a wave of nausea overwhelmed him, and he threw up into the gutter, splashing the officer's boots.

'Gods above,' the officer muttered, stepping back. 'Where's that wagon?'

'It's here, sir,' said another voice.

'Get him in the back, and don't treat him too kindly; the bastard's just ruined my new boots.'

'Yes, sir.'

Four crossbow-wielding militiamen came into view, while another two moved round to Corthie's shoulders and began to lift him from the gutter. They heaved him up, then dragged him across the road to where a large wagon was waiting, a large, barred cage positioned upon its wide chassis. Inside were half a dozen others who had already been arrested by the militia – four men, a woman, and a young boy. The cage was unlocked and opened, then four of the militiamen pushed Corthie inside. His head struck the floor of the cage, and then his legs were shoved in and the cage was closed and locked. Corthie remained where he was, sprawled over the filthy wooden floor, and the wagon began to move, its wheels juddering over the uneven cobbles. He glanced out through the bars at the street, and caught a glimpse of Van, watching from the shadows by a market stall.

'Could you move your leg?' said a voice inside the cage.

Corthie turned. His left leg was tangled in the grimy old cloak of one of the men.

'Aye, no bother,' Corthie grunted. He pulled himself up into a sitting position and leaned against the bars.

'Rough night, lad?'

'I can't remember a thing. Where are we going?'

The man grinned, displaying his lack of teeth. 'This your first time being picked up in the old drunk wagon, eh?'

Corthie nodded at the young boy. 'He's a bit young to be drunk.'

'The lad's probably been picking pockets.'

'No, I ain't,' said the boy, 'so shut your mouth.'

The old man laughed. 'We're off to the city jail,' he said to Corthie. 'If it's your first time, you might get let off with a fine, but only if you're contrite and polite to the magistrate – he hates drunks.'

'I might have smashed up a tavern as well.'

'Then you'd better pray for a miracle, lad, cause the magistrate particularly hates violent drunks.'

'I also threw up on an officer's new boots; that I do remember.'

The old man cackled with glee.

Two of the other men in the cage were eyeing Corthie with suspicion.

'You got a problem?' he said.

'Depends,' said one. 'You Banner?'

'Nope. Why do folk round here assume I'm a Banner soldier?'

'It's your accent,' said the old man; 'it's difficult to place, it is. Where you from?'

It was an obvious question, but Corthie had no ready answer. He had tried a variety of responses in the bars and taverns he had been frequenting, but none of them had convinced anyone.

'He's a Banner deserter,' said one of the other men; 'just look at him; he'd be as well having "soldier" stamped across his forehead.'

'I have a military background,' Corthie said, 'but not with any Banner.'

'Yeah?' said the old man. 'Who have you fought?'

'Greenhides.'

Thinking it was a joke, most of the others in the cage laughed.

'If you've served here in Kinell,' said the old man, 'then you'd better watch your step in the city jail, lad.'

'I've never served in Kinell. I only arrived in Kin Dai a little while ago. And, I freely admit to knowing next to nothing about the politics of the place, or why you lot seem to hate everyone else in Khatanax. Especially the Fordians, apparently.'

'Green-skinned scum,' muttered one of the men.

The wagon pulled to the side of the road next to the waterfront, and they waited as the militia jumped down from the front and moved off into a crowd. Corthie closed his eyes against the harsh sunlight. Had he really trashed a tavern? His guts were churning, and his headache seemed to be peaking, sending bolts of pain through his skull. He remembered to check for his battle-vision and, to his surprise, found it stronger than ever, almost as strong as it had been before Yoneath. He immediately pulled on some, and his hangover eased a little. He almost cried out in relief, but kept his expression muted. Had his powers recovered? He opened his eyes and glanced around, and his battle-vision responded, flooding him with sensory information.

Great timing, he thought. His battle-vision had returned, and he was locked in the back of a drunk wagon. A memory from the previous evening flashed through him, an image of Naxor shouting about how they had to leave Kin Dai right away, and something about Belinda... That was right, Belinda had been in contact, and there was something else, good news he seemed to recall, though he couldn't remember what it was.

Four armed militiamen approached the rear of the wagon, dragging a semi-conscious man along the street. They unlocked the cage, and threw the man in before anyone could react, then quickly locked it again. Corthie pushed the fallen man from his legs. He groaned, and fell unconscious again as the wagon jolted ahead. They turned away from the waterfront and entered a network of tight streets, where many of the buildings seemed older.

'Is this the centre of Kin Dai?' said Corthie.

'It's the Old Quarter,' said the toothless man. 'The city jail is close by; not far to go.'

Corthie nodded. 'Why did you get picked up?'

'They accused me of running a gambling den,' he said. 'It's untrue, of course. Gambling's illegal in this city.'

One of the other men snorted.

'What if you're found guilty?' said Corthie.

The old man shrugged. 'I'll be fined again. They keep picking on me.'

The wagon pulled up in front of a ramshackle old building. It was several storeys tall, but its façade was crumbling. Large groups of militia were stationed outside the front doors next to a few tall palm trees, and they approached the wagon to speak to its escorts. For a long time nothing seemed to happen, then eventually the cage was unlocked, and the seven prisoners were led out, or carried, in the case of the unconscious man. The woman and boy were taken to a separate entrance, and the men were led down a set of stairs to the basement level where they were pushed into a large room that already contained a few dozen prisoners. There was nowhere to sit except for the stone floor, and once the door was locked, no guards came to check on them. Corthie's height and obvious strength drew the glances of many, and he heard a few muttered words about 'Banner scum,' but he avoided confrontation, and no one bothered him.

He spent several hours in the holding cell, and he guessed it was well into the afternoon before soldiers opened the door and gestured for him to get up. They had been coming in at irregular intervals, either taking prisoners away, or adding more into the room, without any discernible pattern that Corthie could see.

His hangover had gone by the time he was escorted up a set of stairs and into a small, cramped room, where six militiamen were waiting.

'Sit,' said an officer, gesturing to the room's only chair.

Corthie walked over to the chair and sat without a word.

'You're due to see the magistrate in ten minutes,' the officer said.

'The charges against you include the unlawful destruction of property and assaulting a citizen of Kin Dai. If you plead guilty, you'll receive a fifty day sentence in a labour camp, but if you plead not guilty, then you'll get ten years. Understand?'

Corthie's eyes tightened, and he wondered what his mother would make of Kin Dai's legal system.

The officer took out a stylus and wax-board. 'Name?'

'Aman.'

'Of?'

'Nowhere.'

The officer frowned at him. 'Place of abode?'

'Homeless.'

'Profession?'

'None.'

'Place of birth?'

'I don't remember.'

The officer nodded to one of the militiamen, and Corthie felt a stinging blow strike the back of his head. He grimaced in pain.

'Half the militia here believe you're a spy,' the officer said, leaning in close to him. 'A spy sent from Alea Tanton; a Banner soldier from Implacatus. Are you a spy?'

'No, but would a spy say yes?'

'What does Alea Tanton want? Why did they send you here?'

'Would a spy trash a tavern and fall asleep in a gutter? I don't know much about the Banners, but I do know their soldiers are professionals. Would they have sent me? I stick out here; my height, my accent. I don't like the rulers of Alea Tanton much, but even I don't think they'd be stupid enough to send someone like me.'

The club connected with the back of Corthie's head again, knocking him off the chair and onto the cold, stone floor.

'I'm going to recommend a long custodial sentence for you,' said the officer, 'just in case you're lying, but also because I don't like you.' He nodded to the militiamen. 'Take him to the magistrate.'

Corthie felt hands grip him under the shoulders, and he was

dragged through a door and into a large, ceremonial chamber, with gilt-edged paintings on the walls and fine, stained glass windows. Several clerks were sitting at desks, while over a dozen militiamen were standing guard. Behind a high bench at the end of the room, an elderly man was sitting, peering down at Corthie. A clerk handed him a clutch of wax-boards, which he glanced at.

'Aman of no fixed abode,' he said, his voice deep, 'how do you plead to the charges laid against you?'

Corthie glanced around, his head pounding.

'Your lack of response will be taken as an admission of guilt,' said the magistrate; 'do you understand?'

'I don't remember trashing any tavern,' said Corthie, 'but if witnesses said I did it, then I guess I did. Sorry. I'll try to behave better in future.'

The militia officer who had questioned him walked up to the magistrate and whispered in his ear.

'Your guilty plea is acknowledged,' said the magistrate, 'and I hereby sentence you to twenty years in a labour camp. Next case.'

Corthie stared at the magistrate in disbelief, then two militiamen guided him through another door, their crossbows jabbing into his side. He was led down a flight of stairs into a different part of the basement and shoved into a small cell. The door slammed shut behind him and he was left alone, the back of his head still aching. There was a recess in a wall with a low stone bench, and he sat, settling down to wait.

Hours passed. The only light was coming from a barred window in the door that led into the lamp-lit passageway, and he had no way to tell what time of the day it was. He grew hungry, and longed for a few pints of water to relieve his dehydration. The door opened, and he was disappointed when another prisoner was pushed in, rather than it being his dinner.

The man tripped and fell to the floor as the door was closed and locked again, then he glanced up at Corthie, a look of fear on his face. He backed away, and crouched by the other wall.

'Don't worry,' said Corthie; 'I'm not going to eat you.'

The man burst into tears. 'My life is over,' he wailed. 'Thirty years for insulting the rulers of Kin Dai, that's what the magistrate gave me; thirty years!'

Corthie watched him for a moment. 'I got twenty for trashing a tavern.'

'A tavern?' said the man. 'That doesn't sound right. You must have done something else.'

'They accused me of being a spy.'

'And are you?'

'No.'

The man wiped his face. 'That's a pity. If you were, then you might be able to help me get out of here. All I did was say that the city authorities were corrupt, which they are, and now I'm going to rot in prison. I have a wife and two young children; who will feed them now? They'll be thrown out onto the streets with nothing.'

'That seems a little unfair.'

'Unfair? It's a travesty, that's what it is. The system here in Kinell is rotten; it needs torn down. Don't you agree?'

Corthie shrugged.

'I wonder why they thought you were a spy,' the man said.

'My accent, probably.'

'It does sound strange. Where are you from?'

'Not Kinell.'

The man laughed. 'That's obvious. You sound like you might be from Implacatus, that's probably what did it. After the occupation by Banner soldier a few years back, there's a lot of mistrust here. The government might do whatever Alea Tanton commands, but only begrudgingly.' He leaned forward, his voice lowering to a whisper. 'If you were from Implacatus, then maybe you could ask your friends there to overthrow the corrupt government here in Kinell. And I could help you; I have contacts.'

Corthie narrowed his eyes. 'What kind of contacts?'

'If you agree to help me, I might even be able to get you out of this prison.'

'How?'

'You need to give me something first. You help me; I help you.'

'What do you want me to give you?'

'Answers,' he said, keeping his voice low. 'If you *are* a spy from Implacatus, then I could assist you in many ways, starting with our escape from here.'

'And if I'm not a spy?'

'I don't get it. If you're not a spy, then why didn't you just tell them where you're from?'

'How did you know I didn't tell them that?'

The man paused.

'Look, I understand that you're only doing your job,' said Corthie, 'but you're not going to get me to confess to something I didn't do. If you're done, then you can ask the guards to let you back out again.'

The man stared at him. 'Just tell me where you're from. If you truly aren't spying for Implacatus, then what harm could it do?'

'A lot. Now get out of here before I change my mind about not eating you.'

'Is your secret worth twenty years in prison?' he said, as he got to his feet. 'Think about that.' He walked to the door and banged on it. 'I've finished in here.' There was no response. 'Hello? Guards?'

A key sounded in the lock and the door opened. Two militiamen pushed the man back into the room and entered. For a split second Corthie thought they were going to attack him, but then he glanced at their faces.

'Let's go,' said Van. 'Now.'

Corthie stood. 'What about this guy?'

Naxor, also dressed in a militiaman's uniform, stared at the other man for a moment, then drew a sword and drove it through his chest.

'Was that necessary?' said Corthie, watching as the man fell lifeless to the stone floor.

Naxor cleaned the blade on the man's clothes. 'Yes. He wasn't a real prisoner; he was working for the city authorities.'

'Aye, I'd already guessed that.'

'Then you should know why we couldn't have left him alive. His blood is on your hands, though, not mine. If you hadn't been stupid enough to get arrested, then he'd still be alive.'

'Stop arguing and move,' said Van. 'Corthie, put your hands behind your back and clasp your wrists together as if they were bound. Naxor and I are escorting you to a new location, as your guards. Understood?'

Corthie nodded and did as he was told, then Van peered out into the passageway. He motioned with his fingers, and they followed him out, leaving the man lying in a pool of blood on the stone floor of the cell. Naxor closed the door and locked it, then he and Van flanked Corthie and led him down the passageway. They passed another militiaman, but he was sitting slumped in a seat by a door, his eyes closed. They went through the door, where two more guards were sleeping, their bodies propped up on a long bench.

'There's a courtyard at the top of the stairs,' whispered Van, 'and Sohul has a wagon parked just beyond the gates. We may have to run when we get out into the open. Can you manage that?'

'Sure,' said Corthie.

They climbed the stairs, and Corthie recognised the street where he had been brought in that morning. The day had passed, and lamps were illuminating the front of the city jail. Several militiamen were standing around in groups, all armed. At first, no one paid them any attention as they began to stride across the courtyard, but an officer glanced at them as they approached the gates.

'Halt,' he said. 'Where are you going?'

Naxor smiled. 'We're just going to walk out of here, if that's alright with you. If it's not, then perhaps you should have a little nap.'

The officer's eyes rolled up into his head and he collapsed to the ground.

'Someone call for a doctor!' Naxor cried, as Van starting shoving Corthie towards the gate.

Corthie and Van ran for the gate. Two militiamen hurried to block them, and Corthie powered his battle-vision, feeling a surge of euphoria as it rippled through his body. He sidestepped a lunge from a sword, and punched the first guard in the face, sending him flying through the air. He grabbed the second, and threw him into the crowd of pursuing militiamen, then he, Van and Naxor raced through the gates. Sohul was sitting on the driver's bench of a small covered wagon and the three men jumped up onto the back as the lieutenant urged the two horses harnessed to the front into action. The wagon moved off, gaining speed with every second, as Naxor leaned out of the back and sent the first row of pursuers to sleep, their comrades colliding with them as they fell to the cobbles.

Sohul manoeuvred the wagon to the left, and they joined a busy road, slowing as they entered the flow of traffic. He turned his head to glance into the back of the wagon.

'Everything fine back there?' he said.

'All good,' said Van. 'Take us south for half a mile, then we'll ditch the wagon.'

Corthie started to laugh. 'Thanks, everybody. Twenty years they gave me; can you believe that? Twenty years for ruining a tavern and breaking some guy's nose.'

Naxor frowned at him. 'If it had been up to me, I would have left you in that cell.'

'I'll bet you would have,' Corthie said. He glanced at Van. 'I assume it was your plan?'

'It was a joint effort,' said Van, 'although I do have a little experience in breaking people out of prisons. Still, it would have been a lot trickier without Naxor's vision powers. And poor Sohul's spent the entire day selling the house boat and then buying this wagon.'

'We've sold the boat?'

'Yes. It might be unwise to stay in Kin Dai after what we just did.'

'And after what Belinda told us,' said Naxor.

Corthie frowned. 'And, eh, what did she tell us again?'

Naxor shook his head at him. 'You don't remember the huge fight we had?'

'Nope.'

'Demigods with vision powers, based in Alea Tanton,' said Van; 'they found us yesterday. Well, they found Naxor. Belinda said it would be a good idea for us to leave town as soon as possible. Sohul's been sorting that as well. He's bought us passage on a ship that leaves tonight.'

Corthie nodded. 'And why were we fighting?'

'You were adamant that you weren't leaving,' said Naxor. 'You told us that there were still a few taverns in Kin Dai that you hadn't visited yet.'

'Oh. I guess I might have been acting like a drunken arsehole recently.'

Naxor raised an eyebrow. 'You guess?'

'Let's not reignite any disagreements,' said Van. 'Corthie, I saw the way you handled those two guards. Are your powers back?'

'Aye. I feel better than I've done in ages. Since, well, you know. Was there something else that Belinda told us?'

Van nodded. 'The Ascendants haven't been able to get the Sextant to work. Your world, and Naxor's, are still safe.'

Corthie puffed out his cheeks in relief. For two months he had been living with the thought that Banner soldiers or greenhides might be rampaging through his home world, and occupying the City of Pella. The images he had conjured had brought him to the edge of despair, and he felt a weight lift from him. He cleared his mind. They were getting on a ship, and leaving Kin Dai. Aila was out there, somewhere, with his sister; finding them was what mattered.

Van leaned forward and nudged Sohul. 'That's far enough. Pull over.'

The lieutenant nodded and reined in the two horses. Van and Naxor stripped out of their militiaman uniforms and pulled on civilian clothes, then they jumped down from the back of the wagon into the busy street, Corthie following them. They walked round to the front, and Sohul climbed down from the driver's bench to join them.

'Twelve gold they cost us,' he said, gazing at the two horses. 'It's a pity we don't have time to sell them.'

'Just add them to the list of things Corthie owes us,' said Naxor.

They walked into a large crowd next to a fish market, and headed in the direction of the main harbour. Corthie's height stood out, but he didn't care; he was starting to look forward to the upcoming voyage. He had enjoyed being on a ship when they had sailed from the Falls of Iron, and then from Capston to Yoneath; and he reckoned he would make a good sailor.

The streets and waterfront were well-lit by lamps hanging from the eaves of buildings, and they covered the distance to the huge harbour in under an hour. Van was careful to lead them by the busiest routes and, though they passed several detachments of militia, none took any interest in them.

A large merchant vessel was tied up alongside a broad jetty, and Sohul pointed it out to the others.

'We have two cabins,' he said, 'and I've already paid for our meals.'

'Including dinner tonight?' said Corthie. 'I'm so hungry, I could eat Naxor.'

'Yes, including dinner,' said Sohul. 'It's good to see your appetite's back.'

'And I'm going to stay off the booze for a while.'

'That might be advisable,' said Van, 'though I might have an ale or two after today's excitement.'

Sohul showed their travel documents to a small group of harbour officials and sailors at the base of a long gangway, and they were allowed to board the ship. A young deckhand took them to their cabins – Van was sharing with Corthie, and Sohul with Naxor, and they washed up and went back up onto the deck as the ship was slipping away from its moorings. A wind had picked up, and the large vessel sailed among the dozens of fishing boats and other merchant ships until it reached the enormous breakwaters at the edge of the harbour basin.

'Farewell, Kin Dai,' said Sohul, a smile on his face.

'I spoke to a sailor,' said Van; 'we can get something hot to eat in twenty minutes.'

Corthie leaned on the railings and gazed back at the lights of the city. 'And then we start the search for Aila and Kelsey. How far is it to that place; Stoneship, was it?'

The others glanced at each other.

Corthie frowned. 'What?'

'This ship,' said Sohul; 'I, uh, we needed to leave the city immediately, and this was the only vessel sailing this evening.'

'So?'

'It's not sailing to Stoneship, Corthie,' he said; 'it's taking us back to the Southern Cape.'

CHAPTER 12
HOME TO ROOST

atacombs, Torduan Mountains, Khatanax – 21st Luddinch 5252

C Ashfall's eyes narrowed as she stared at Sable. 'But you have nothing to do with Blackrose's world.'

'I know.'

'Then why are you so determined to go there? What business is it of yours?'

Sable stretched out her hand and flicked the ash from her cigarette over the edge of the tomb. 'You're right; it isn't any of my business, but I want to do what I can to help. I have other reasons. Travelling to Lostwell wasn't exactly my choice – it was either come here or be executed, but I don't like it. The earthquakes, the lava, and the fact that it never seems to rain. I mean, do you like living in the Catacombs?'

Ashfall tilted her grey head. 'It's better than the pits of Alea Tanton. I was born in that pestilent city, and was being groomed to fight for one of the teams alongside my father, or perhaps against him.'

'How did you escape?'

'It was very different in those days,' the dragon said. 'The three teams had up to a dozen dragons each, and every year more were being born in captivity. We heard a rumour from the humans who looked after us that the city authorities were going to cull our numbers, and so we revolted. Several dragons were killed in the attempt, but nineteen managed to flee, led by my father. Since then, each team has only had one dragon, or two at the most, so the humans must have learned their lesson.'

Sable glanced at the graceful dragon. Before Grimsleep's death, she had hardly said more than a few words to Sable, but since that day, Deathfang's adult daughter had started to take more interest in the 'insects' that gathered round Sanguino for protection.

'And then you came to the Catacombs?' the Holdfast woman said.

'Yes. My father challenged and killed Eventide, who used to rule here, and took charge.'

'Eventide?' said Sable, her eyes widening at the mention of the name.

'Yes,' said Ashfall; 'Deepblue's father.'

'Ah. That explains a few things. I did wonder why Deepblue held such an antipathy towards your family.'

'It is the way of dragons; the mightiest rules. Those who lived in the Catacombs before we arrived from the pits were forced to accept us, but many of them have neither forgotten nor forgiven the actions of my father. Broadwing is another one of these, and this is, I think, the reason why he and Deepblue are keen to go to Dragon Eyre with you.'

Sable smiled. 'And could you be tempted to accompany us? We could do with a dragon of your intelligence and calibre.'

'I know you could. Deepblue is weak, and Broadwing is a coward.'

'I notice you didn't answer the question.'

Ashfall stretched her forelimbs over the edge of the tomb, extending her claws. 'That's right.'

Sable nodded, wondering if the grey dragon no longer wished to continue the conversation.

'Are your wounds healed?' said Ashfall after a few moments.

'Yes, thank you.'

'Then you will be departing soon?'

'I need to scout first, but yes; soon. Blackrose has been in captivity long enough.'

Ashfall glanced down at her. 'I bullied Deepblue into revealing some of the details of your plan. You intend to rescue Blackrose on your own?'

'Yes.'

'This is disappointing. I had hoped to join any rescue attempt.'

'You want to help Blackrose?'

'I will be honest with you; Blackrose is only a part of my motivation – what I really desire is a chance to take some measure of revenge upon the rulers of that accursed city. My father's policy of keeping us away from Tordue has kept the Catacombs safe, but I sometimes feel he is being over-cautious.'

'He doesn't want to provoke the gods; he's being sensible.'

Ashfall brought her scaled head down until she was a foot from Sable's face. 'And what will stealing a dragon from under their noses do?'

Sable kept her gaze steady. 'I intend to do it in such a way that doesn't attract any attention.'

'I'm not sure my father would agree. There is a chance the gods will retaliate against the Catacombs.'

'He hasn't tried to dissuade me from going.'

'That is because he wants you all to leave. Your victory over Grim-sleep has ensured he cannot evict you from the Catacombs, not after he gave Sanguino his word, but he would be happy to see you go, especially if you take Broadwing and Deepblue with you.'

Sable nodded. 'And what about you? Would he be angry if you left?'

Ashfall glanced away. 'No. Frostback was always his favourite, at least until Darksky delivered him a new clutch of children. If Frostback returned tomorrow, my father would probably accept her back, whereas I think he is starting to consider me as a threat to his rule. Soon, I will be as strong as him, and when that day comes, he will probably challenge me, and I will have to fight him.'

'I'll be going to Alea Tanton soon,' said Sable, 'and once Blackrose is free, we intend to leave Lostwell immediately. I'd be very grateful if you decided to come to Dragon Eyre with us, and so would Blackrose.'

'Very well. I shall take a day to make up my mind.'

Sable threw the cigarette butt over the edge of the tomb and stood. 'I have to go now. Thank you for the visit.'

'You're the first insect I've spoken to since I escaped the pits, and the only witch I've ever met. I will give you an answer tomorrow regarding the expedition to Dragon Eyre. When Sanguino awakens, pass on my regards. Farewell.'

The grey dragon launched herself from the ledge, her wings extending in the warm draughts rising from the lava pools. Sable watched as she circled higher, then she disappeared over the top of the ridge. Ashfall would be a valuable addition to their team, but she knew that Deepblue would be upset by her inclusion. At least she now knew the reason, she thought. Whatever happened, at least one dragon's sense of honour would be offended, and she didn't want to get involved in dragon politics. She would ask Blackrose for her guidance, and leave it to her to make the decision.

She turned, and walked into the interior of the tomb. Sanguino was asleep in his cavern after a long flight that morning, and Maddie and Millen were sitting round the small hearth near the end of the high tunnel. She approached them and sat.

'What did she want?' said Maddie. 'And why did she only want to speak to you?'

Sable gazed into the flames of the small fire. 'She's thinking about coming to Dragon Eyre with us.'

'But Deepblue and Broadwing hate her.'

'I know. All the same, she'd be more valuable than either of them.'

'You need to tell Blackrose.'

Sable laughed. 'Yes. I intend to.'

'When? Are you going to speak to her soon?'

The Holdfast woman made a decision. She glanced up at the others. 'I'm going to rescue her today.'

Maddie's eyes widened. 'What?'

'Can you think of any reason why it shouldn't be today?'

'Well, no, but I assumed you'd think of one. You've been delaying for ages.'

Sable frowned. 'I haven't been delaying anything. We needed to get myself and Sanguino fit again, and we needed to recruit a few dragons. Millen also had to get Blackrose's new harness ready, and we required supplies.' She pointed to a pile of stacked sacks and crates. 'That stuff you've been stealing with the Quadrant; we'll need it all. It's called being prepared.'

Maddie narrowed her eyes. 'I hope Blackrose agrees.'

'I intend to tell her that I've only just managed to steal the Quadrant; she'll never know any different.'

'But Millen and I know!' cried Maddie. 'What if she uses her truth powers on us? We'd be forced to tell her what's really been going on.'

'I'll take care of that,' Sable said.

'How?'

Sable smiled. They didn't know that she had the power to remove certain memories from their minds, and she intended to keep it that way.

'Trust me.'

Maddie shook her head, her exasperation evident. Next to her, Millen chuckled, then frowned.

'Hang on,' he said. 'You're going today?'

'Yes.'

His frown deepened. 'What date is it?'

'The twenty-first,' said Sable.

'Of Luddinch?'

'Obviously.'

'Oh.'

Sable sighed. 'What does that mean?'

His brow crinkled. 'There's a huge game on in Alea Tanton today; one that will affect Blackrose. The Blue Thumbs will be visiting the Deadskins' arena, and Blackrose will probably be scheduled to fight.' He glanced towards the daylight at the end of the tunnel. 'In fact, the games will have started by now.'

Sable stared at him. 'Why didn't you tell me this before?'

'Well, you didn't give us any clues about when you were going to rescue her, and I kind of lost track of the date. Every day in the Catacombs is the same.'

Sable got to her feet, and began pacing as her thoughts whirled. How could she have been so stupid? She had been so wrapped up in preparing for their trip to Dragon Eyre that she had forgotten what was going on back in the city.

'Maybe you should wait until tomorrow,' said Millen.

'No way,' said Maddie, her eyes wide. 'Blackrose might get hurt, or worse.'

'Maddie's right,' said Sable. 'Damn it. This is my fault, but I'll fix it.'

She strode over to a pile of luggage and removed the Quadrant from a bag.

'I'm coming with you,' said Maddie, getting to her feet.

'No,' said Sable; 'it'll be too dangerous. I'll have to leave right away. Tell Sanguino when he wakes up.'

She studied the Quadrant, and poised her fingers over the engravings.

'You're not even armed,' said Maddie. 'Are you not taking a sword, at least?'

Sable shook her head. 'I won't get into the arena with a weapon.'

'Then what's your plan?'

She shrugged. 'I'll make it up as I go along. See you soon.'

'Wait!' Maddie cried.

Sable traced her fingers across the surface of the Quadrant and the cavern shimmered, then was replaced by a back alley, deep within the Fordian district of Alea Tanton. She glanced around. High tenement blocks rose on either side, and raw sewage was flowing down the centre of the alley, which led to a busy street twenty yards ahead of her. She gagged from the smell, then slipped the Quadrant into the inside pocket of her long cloak.

She knew the layout of the streets well, having scouted with her vision over the area several times. The Northern Pits were about a quarter of a mile to her left, and she could hear the low roar of the crowd in the arena. She paused for a moment, clearing her thoughts as she felt a mixture of anxiety and exhilaration pass through her body. She could do it.

She strode to the end of the alleyway. The street beyond was packed with people. Most were green-skinned, but groups of Torduans were walking down the middle of the road in the direction of the arena, flanked by militia who were shielding them from the locals. Sable began pushing her way through the thick press of Fordians towards the Torduans. She would have to pretend that she was a Blue Thumbs supporter, as no one would believe for a moment that a non-Fordian would follow the Deadskins.

A few locals stared at her as she tried to pass through them, and a man spat at her, while others shoved and jostled her.

'Blue Thumb bitch,' muttered one, his fists clenched.

She powered her battle-vision and prepared to fight, but a few members of the city militia spotted her at the edge of the crowd, and barged through the Fordians. They grabbed her, and hauled her into the middle of the road along with the other Torduans.

'Get lost, did you, miss?' said one of the soldiers, his eyes tight. 'You're supposed to stay on the main roads. The Fordians will tear you to pieces if they catch you on your own.'

'Sorry, officer,' said Sable.

'Yeah? Well, don't do it again.'

The militia turned back to their flanking positions, leaving her in the middle of a group of blue-sashed Torduans. Sable gave them a sheepish smile, and tagged along with them as they walked down the road. Ahead, the large arena of the Northern Pits loomed. Hundreds of militia were on duty around its entrances, and more lined every street that led to it.

'You were lucky, girl,' said a man next to her. 'Those green-skinned bastards could have lynched you.'

Sable nodded.

'You get separated from your friends?'

'Yeah. They had my ticket too.'

The man shrugged. 'You can buy another one at the gates.'

'And, eh... how much would that be?'

'Five silver, same as always.'

'Right, of course.'

He gave her a smile. 'You can sit with us if you want.'

'Thanks,' said Sable.

'Is this your first visit to the Northern Pits?'

'Yes. How did you know?'

'You look a little lost. You come to see the new dragon?'

Sable nodded.

'It's a disgrace, isn't it? The damn Deadskins get a second dragon, while we've only got one, and the idiot Bloodflies haven't got any. I heard that the normal rules are going to be ignored today.'

'What does that mean?'

'Well, usually, the fights are stopped before any dragon gets killed, but not today. Our boys are under instructions to kill the new beast if they can. That'll teach the Fordian assholes not to cheat.'

The group Sable was walking with entered a large plaza in front of the huge, stone arena. Buildings around it had been damaged from a recent earthquake, but the arena was still standing. A few Blue Thumbs supporters were picking up bricks and stones from the piles of rubble that lay by the edge of the plaza, and Deadskins supporters were doing the same thing on the far side of a thick line of militia.

'Stick with us after the game,' said the man who had been speaking to her; 'it's going to get rough tonight.'

It took nearly an hour to get from the plaza to their seats inside the arena. A quarter of the spectators were Torduans, while the rest of the stone benches were occupied by green-sashed Fordians. The man she had been speaking to was part of a group of around a dozen Blue Thumbs supporters, and she sat among them, trying to blend in. She recognised one or two other supporters as friends or associates of Gantu, and kept her head down. The executions had just finished when they found their seats, and the sands were being cleared of body parts by slaves with baskets.

'Here we go,' said the man, rubbing his hands together as a double line of blue-sashed warriors entered the arena from a gate.

The massed Fordians booed and jeered at their arrival on the sands, while the Torduans let out a cheer. Sable's eyes glanced around the arena. To their left, high up on a raised seating platform, three gods were sitting. She knew two – Felice, the new governor, and Latude, the former. Between them was sitting a third god, whom she didn't recognise.

'Who's that in the middle?' she said.

'That's Arete, the Seventh Ascendant,' the man said. 'I saw her at the games last month, when we hosted the Deadskins.'

Sable stared at the Ascendant for a moment. Part of her felt a little guilty that she and the others would be leaving Lostwell without defeating the Ascendants first. After all, Corthie and Kelsey were still in Khatanax, and her niece was being hunted. She wondered how they would react when they learned that she, Blackrose and the others had abandoned them. It wasn't her problem, she told herself, despite the chiding voice in her head. She had never been accepted as a Holdfast, so why should she help them now?

Her attention went back to the arena as several other gates opened and a greenhide emerged from each. They ran onto the sand then jerked back, the chains linking their ankles to the walls of the arena going taut as they strained to get at the blue-sashed warriors. Half of the greenhides, Sable noticed, were daubed in blue paint, the other half in bright green. The volume inside the arena rose as the Blue Thumb warriors arranged themselves in the centre of the sands, then a chant of 'Obsidia, Obsidia' rose up from the benches where the Fordians were sitting. A huge gate was opened, and the head of the black dragon appeared to a roar from the crowd.

'There it is,' said the man next to Sable. 'By all the gods, I hope it dies today; filthy reptile.'

Sable watched as Blackrose strode out into the arena. Her jaws were clamped within an iron muzzle, and chains were attached to her wings and her rear limbs, leaving only her front limbs free. Even so, it was clear to everyone in the crowd that she was a formidable creature, and a few of the Blue Thumbs supporters quietened in awe.

Sable tried to think of her next step. Her entire plan had been discarded, and she cursed herself for not taking one of the many opportunities to free Blackrose that had been presented to her. She could have sneaked into the training facility during the night and rescued her that way, but no; now she was going to have to attempt something that, even by her own standards, was ridiculously reckless.

On the benches just down from where the three gods were sitting, an announcer stood up, his hands raised for silence.

'Today,' he cried, his voice reaching every part of the arena, 'in the presence of the blessed Seventh Ascendant, we shall be witnessing the first contest of the new Deadskins' dragon – Obsidia!'

The crowd roared again, and many got to their feet, their fists punching the air. The Blue Thumb warriors lined up in front of the three gods and bowed their heads, then they turned to face the dragon. Several were armed with spears and long pikes, and all were clad in thick armour. Blackrose tilted her head at them, then waited. Just out of range on all sides, the greensides shrieked and snapped their claws together, desperate for anything to get close enough for them to kill.

The warriors began to advance, spreading out into an arc in front of Blackrose, their long steel-tipped pikes extended. On the right, four of them rushed forwards, and Blackrose raised her forelimb to defend herself. As soon as her attention was distracted, the warriors on the left launched a barrage of spears at her flank. Most were turned by the thick black scales, but two bit deep and the dragon cried out.

'Come on!' screamed the man next to Sable, his eyes bulging and his fists clenched. 'Kill her!'

Blackrose swiped out with her left forelimb, and one of the warriors was sent flying backwards from the blow. He landed between two green-hides, who ripped him to shreds in seconds as the crowd roared. A large net was flung at the dragon, covering her head and tangling the claws of her right forelimb, and the warriors charged forward, their pikes levelled. Blackrose retreated a few feet, but a greenhide attacked her from the rear, its teeth and claws tearing into her long tail.

Sable swallowed, and her hand moved towards the Quadrant. She pulled off the cloak, the copper-coloured device clutched in her left hand, and readied herself.

Someone tapped her on the shoulder. 'Hey, you.'

She turned, blinking.

Three angry-looking men were standing to her right.

'You used to go with Gantu, didn't you?' said one. 'It was you that got him killed, so I heard.'

'Who?' she said. 'Never heard of him.'

'Liar,' spat one of the men. 'I used to see you every day in Gantu's apartment building. You ran off with that little rat Millen.'

'You've got the wrong woman, lads,' she said.

'I even remember your weird accent,' he said. He turned to a larger group of supporters a few benches away. 'Boys, it's Sable. The bitch has come back.'

One of the men tried to grab her shoulder, and she powered her battle-vision and shoved him away. She sprang to her feet, and edged down the stone steps as dozens of faces turned to see what the commotion was.

'Get her!' cried someone. 'Throw her to the greenhides!'

She turned and ran, bounding down the steps towards the low parapet that surrounded the arena. She shoved a man carrying a tray of drinks out of her way, sending him and the wine crashing to the benches behind her, then reached the parapet and stopped, turning. A large group were charging down the steps after her, their eyes shining with hatred. Sable gulped, climbed up onto the top of the parapet, and jumped.

She fell a dozen feet through the air, then landed in the sand less than a yard from a greenhide. It lunged at her, its thick talons cleaving the air as she pushed herself backwards. The attention of the majority of the crowd was still focussed on the dragon, but many were now gazing down at Sable as she dodged the claws of the greenhide. She rolled forwards under another lunge of claws, and picked up a spear that had been thrown at Blackrose, her left hand still clutching the Quadrant. She raced away from the greenhide, and ran towards the flank of the dragon. Blackrose was bleeding from several wounds, and the heads of two spears were still embedded into her side. The shackles round her rear limbs were preventing her from being able to reach the warriors, who were darting forward with their pikes, and then retreating again before she could attack them. One of the warriors saw Sable, and stared at her for a moment open-mouthed, and Blackrose ripped him in two with her claws.

The roar from the crowd increased as more people saw Sable down on the sands. A warrior tried to grab her, but she jabbed the spear into his face and he fell screaming to his knees. Boos started to resound from the stone benches from both sets of supporters, and the announcer stood, his hands in the air as he tried to quieten the crowd. Arete was leaning forward in her seat, staring at Sable, her eyes wide.

'You?' bellowed Blackrose as she turned her neck to look down at Sable. 'I ought to kill you.'

'Shut up, you stupid lizard,' cried Sable as she reached the side of the dragon.

A warrior drove a pike at her. She dodged, but the blade ripped through the sleeve on her right arm, scoring her skin in a thin line of red. The arena was in uproar. All three of the gods were on their feet, trying to have the games halted, and Arete was pointing down at the Quadrant in Sable's hand.

'If you intend to use that thing,' said Blackrose, her eyes glowing like fiery embers, 'then do it now.'

Sable dropped the spear and slid her fingers over the device. The air shimmered, and the tomb materialised around them. Maddie screamed in surprise, then Sable noticed that one of the Blue Thumb warriors had also made the journey to the Catacombs. He was gripping onto a pike, the point of which was buried deep into Blackrose's right flank. The dragon turned, and brought down one of her forelimbs, crushed him into the floor of the cavern.

Sanguino poked his head out into the tunnel, his green eyes wide, as Millen and Maddie stared.

Sable put her hands on her knees, panting, her heart pounding.

Maddie ran towards Blackrose as if a spell had been broken, then she burst into tears as she hugged the dragon's forelimb. Millen shook his head, staring at the wounds on the dragon's flank. Then he noticed the dead warrior.

'That's Kelito!' he cried. 'You killed the captain of the Blue Thumbs.'

'Welcome back,' said Sanguino; 'we have missed you.'

'I have missed you too,' said Blackrose. 'Please remove the chains and the muzzle.'

Maddie stepped back from the dragon, her face wet with tears, then she and Millen pulled the chains from her back, releasing her wings. They then removed the iron muzzle, and Blackrose stretched her jaws.

'You're hurt,' said Maddie. 'Are you hungry? What do you need?'

Blackrose lowered her head and nuzzled Maddie's shoulder. 'We shall speak soon, rider, but before I say anything else, there is something I must do.'

She lunged out with her claws and gripped Sable tight, making her drop the Quadrant to the ground, then she strode to the edge of the tomb and launched herself into the air. Sable tried to squirm in the dragon's grasp, but the grip was so tight it was hard to breathe, and then she was dangling over the lava-filled valley as Blackrose soared into the bright sky. The dragon turned south, and they raced over the mountains, then began to cross the barren desert of the Fordian Wastes. Sable kept struggling, but it was useless, and her fear started to grow.

They flew on, passing mile after mile of nothing but the scorched and parched wastelands, until Blackrose began to descend. She dropped Sable while she was still a few yards above the ground, and the Holdfast woman fell, and rolled onto her side, gasping in pain.

'You treacherous liar,' said Blackrose, hovering above her.

'What?' said Sable. 'I don't understand; I saved you.'

'You selfish insect; how long have you been in possession of a Quadrant? And do not even think of lying to me again. If you do, I will kill you.'

Sable pushed herself up from the rocky ground, another lie poised on her lips. She stopped herself. Somehow, the dragon knew.

'I've had one since I first arrived in the Catacombs,' she said. 'I stole it from Alea Tanton before I came to find you.'

The dragon's eyes filled with rage, and fire licked around her jaws. Sable edged back, fear almost paralysing her. For a moment, she thought her life was about to come to an end, but the torrent of flames never came.

'And Maddie?' said Blackrose, her voice twisted by anger. 'Did she also know?'

'Yes, but it was my fault. I made her keep quiet about it. If you're going to kill anyone, then kill me, not her.'

'You will die, Holdfast witch,' Blackrose said, 'but not by my fire or claws. You are over a hundred miles from the Catacombs; the Fordian Wastes shall be your grave, and may rats pick over your flesh when you fall to the ground, dying of thirst. I hope your end is an agonising one.'

She beat her wings and rose back into the sky, circled once, then raced off for the north.

Sable gazed around. Nothing but flat, featureless wastes surrounded her in all directions. She had no water, or food, and the sun was beating down mercilessly upon her. She patted her pockets and found a pack of cigarettes.

She lit one, and began walking.

CHAPTER 13
PLAN, INTERRUPTED

A lea Tanton, Tordue, Western Khatanax – 21st Luddinch 5252
Queen Emily smiled from the couch where she sat. 'You've certainly given us much to think about, Belinda. It's hard to believe that it's only been a few months since you were last here in Cuidrach Palace, and harder still to believe all that has occurred on Lostwell in that time. We ought to have foreseen that salve would continue to cause us problems, but the news is worse than we could have imagined.'

The small audience chamber fell into silence. To Emily's right, King Daniel was frowning, a worried expression colouring his face, while to her left, Princess Yendra was standing, the Axe of Rand slung over one shoulder. Through the wide bay windows behind them, the sky was invisible due to a thick blanket of mist that was covering the City – the Fog of Balian.

Belinda sat still, the Quadrant resting on her knees.

'And your proposal,' said Daniel, 'how would it work in practice?'

'I suggest that you excavate a huge amount of salve, several tons if possible,' Belinda said, 'and then I shall transport it to Lostwell and allow the gods to take it. A large enough quantity could keep them satisfied for centuries.'

'But,' said Daniel, 'didn't the City used to receive champions in exchange for the salve? Are you saying that we should hand it over, free of charge?' He raised an eyebrow. 'It sounds a little like extortion to me. Would we not effectively be paying off a group of bullies? And if so, what's to stop them coming back for more?'

'If that's the price for stopping them from overwhelming your world,' said Belinda, 'then I think it's worth paying.'

'It's blackmail,' said Daniel, 'plain and simple.'

Emily glanced at him, her eyes troubled. 'How long will you be staying in the City, Belinda?'

'An hour was all I had, and most of that has now passed.'

'That's a pity,' she said. 'I do not believe we'll be able to come to a decision in that time.'

'I tend to agree with his Majesty; this sounds like blackmail,' said Yendra. 'Is there anything that the gods of this Implacatus could offer us as payment for the salve?'

'Such as?' said Belinda. 'Are you in need of champions? Haven't the greenhides been driven away from the City?'

'They have,' said Emily, 'but we have plans to eradicate them right up to the mountain chain that lies two hundred miles east of here, and then fortify those mountains to prevent any more from getting through.'

'That would require a lot of soldiers,' said Belinda.

'It would, but the benefits it would bring would be enormous. I don't suppose Blackrose would like to return? A dragon would be extremely useful for this kind of job.'

'Blackrose is currently... unavailable,' said Belinda, 'but I could look into the possibility of sending other dragons to assist you. If I do this, will you consider my proposal?'

'We will of course consider it,' said Emily. 'You have proved a wonderful servant of the City, and we owe you that, at least. Give us some time to think it over, and when you return to us, you shall have an answer.'

Belinda nodded. 'Then I shall return to Khatanax. Prepare yourselves. If Implacatus attacks, they will do so with huge numbers of mercenary soldiers, enough to defeat any Blade army that you can put together. If that happens, surrender immediately; I have seen what happens to cities that resist them.'

Emily blinked, then resumed her smile. 'Thank you for your advice.'

She stood, and Belinda also got to her feet.

'I will escort you to the roof,' said Yendra.

Belinda inclined her head towards Emily and Daniel, then walked with Yendra to the door, which a Reaper guard opened for them. They went through the corridors of the old palace, passing servants and staff, and several more guards.

'That was an interesting speech you gave,' said Yendra.

Belinda said nothing, waiting for the princess to get to her point.

'What I found most fascinating,' Yendra went on, 'was what you left out. Why is Corthie still on Lostwell, for instance? And, where is Aila, my niece?'

'I didn't tell you because I didn't want to cloud your judgement. I kept to the relevant facts regarding the Ascendant gods and their plans.'

Yendra moved to block Belinda's way. 'Then I'll ask you directly, since that seems the best way to communicate with you.' She narrowed her eyes. 'Where is Aila?'

'She was captured by Amalia.'

Shock passed over Yendra's face for a moment, before her calm demeanour reasserted itself.

'You should also know,' Belinda went on, 'that Amalia plans to return to the City. She has a Quadrant in her possession, and fears that the Ascendants will execute her if they catch her.'

'I see. Tell me, does Aila still live?'

'As far as I know.'

Yendra frowned. 'Whose side are you on, Belinda?'

Belinda hesitated, surprised at being asked such a question. 'Have my actions today not made that clear? If I wanted to betray this world to the Ascendants, then all I needed to do was tell them how to get here. Instead, I've risked everything to try to find a peaceful way out of this crisis. Do I have to die before anyone trusts me?'

'I apologise,' said Yendra. 'You give the appearance of not caring, and I made the mistake of confusing that with your true intentions. Things have been going well here since you all departed, and the news you gave to the King and Queen has disheartened me. I thought the siege of the City had ended with the destruction of the greenhides, but it seems I was mistaken.'

They resumed their walk, both gods remaining silent. The fog was obscuring the view of Pella when they stepped out onto the flat roof of the palace.

'I wish I could help in some way,' said Yendra, as Belinda held out the Quadrant.

'You can,' said Belinda. 'Start recruiting soldiers, and build some refuges that people can escape to; and mine and store as much salve as you can. I shall try to return by the end of the month, but I can't promise it.'

Yendra nodded, then Belinda activated the Quadrant. Her surroundings shimmered, and she appeared back within her locked bed chamber. She set the Quadrant to go to Yoneath, triggered it, and arrived in the deserted cavern of Fordamere. She glanced around at the devastation. She had intended to stay only for a few moments, but something caught her eye and she walked over to it, avoiding the decaying bodies strewn across the ground. She leaned over and picked it up. It was heavy, and sharp, and she nearly sliced open her fingers lifting it. She gripped it in one hand, then activated the Quadrant and travelled back to Alea Tanton.

She placed the item under her bed, then sat on the deep mattress, a vague plan forming in her mind. If she could have it repaired, it could be useful. She cleared her thoughts and went over everything that had been discussed in Pella. Daniel had been right – paying off the Ascendants in salve to stop them invading did amount to blackmail, but what choice did the City have? The gods of Implacatus would never stop hunting for the source of salve. She hoped that Emily's common sense would overrule Daniel's moral principles, but if it didn't, then at least the City had been forewarned.

She got up and unlocked her door, the Quadrant in her hand.

Several servants bowed low, their eyes lowered as she passed, and she sensed the mixture of fear and awe that she engendered in them. She left her quarters and ascended the stairs to Leksandr's rooms. He was waiting for her in his study, and turned from the Sextant as she walked in.

She passed him the Quadrant, and he slipped it into his robes.

'Did you find what you were looking for, Third Ascendant?' he said.

'Maybe.'

He nodded. 'Yoneath, was it?'

'Yes.'

'The cavern at Fordamere?'

She frowned. She would have to make something up, otherwise he would keep on with his questions.

'Indeed,' she said. 'I wanted to search the ancient temple where the Sextant had been kept.'

'Oh? That sounds interesting. May I ask what you were hoping to find?'

'You may.'

He smiled, but it was false. 'What were you hoping to find?'

'It occurred to me that something crucial to the workings of the Sextant may have become dislodged in the fire and subsequent collapse of the roof.'

He blinked. 'You mean you think there may be something missing? A part that the device needs to function? I admit that never crossed my mind.'

'Perhaps. My search was inconclusive. There appears to be nothing within the temple associated with the Sextant.'

He raised a finger and started to pace the room. 'You may be onto something. A missing part? I shall meditate on this later this evening. Now, before you leave, there are a couple of matters I wish to discuss. The first is Arete.'

'May I sit?'

'Of course,' he said, 'please do. Would you like a drink?'

'No, thank you. Arete?'

'Yes. I acknowledge that her behaviour towards you has improved since Lord Bastion's visit, but you should know that she still has her suspicions. She has mentioned to me more than once that she places no trust in you. You must be careful around her. I think it would be better if she doesn't find out about you borrowing my Quadrant; do you agree?'

'I do. Let's keep it to ourselves.'

'Excellent.'

'What if she reads it out of your head?'

'I will bury it deep. She would need to read me for many continuous hours to find something I do not particularly wish her to find. It surprises me that you are unaware of this technique, although the fact that you cannot be read yourself is probably the cause of it. You have no need to bury anything; the shields around your mind are impervious.'

'I'm sure there is much that I do not understand.'

'Feel free to ask me anything.'

'Alright. How many worlds are in existence?'

He laughed. 'Hmm. When do I begin? With Implacatus, I suppose; the first world, the originator. Hundreds of worlds have been created since the Ascendants began their rule, perhaps over a thousand. Many have been utterly destroyed, and many have drifted from our knowledge; all paths to them cut off. Who knows how many isolated worlds are out there, bereft of any connection to the others? The Sextant sitting before us is believed to be the last; apart from it, none have been seen in ten thousand years. If we manage to activate it, then not only will it find the two worlds we have been looking for, but every other world that it has created; it could reveal to us realms that have been forgotten for millennia.' He smiled. 'That was a long way to say that I don't know.'

'It seems so haphazard,' she said. 'Why isn't there some kind of record detailing where these worlds are located?'

'The knowledge required to record such things has long been lost. Without Quadrants and Sextants, we would all be marooned on our own worlds. Nathaniel was reputed to have a measure of such knowledge, enough, it was said, that he might have been able to construct a new Quadrant; but he was the last as far as I know.'

'But you must have some of that knowledge. Didn't you create the greenhides?'

He smiled again, but this time it seemed genuine. 'Yes, that was me. I assisted Theodora, the First Ascendant, when she was creating a new world. In the grand scheme, the creation of a single species next to the creation of an entire world is insignificant, but I am rather proud of what I achieved.' He sighed. 'I worked a long time on that project.'

'I have another question,' she said.

He nodded.

'How many worlds does Implacatus control?'

'Around thirty, nominally. Most of them are uninhabited; wastelands. The wars, after all, took their toll. Dragon Eyre was the most recent addition; it fell under our sway a mere two decades ago. But, if we can get the Sextant working, there will be fresh worlds for the taking.'

The sound of a door slamming came from the hallway, then the door to the study opened and Arete strode in, rage creasing her features.

'The city is in uproar!' she cried. 'Hundreds of mortals have been slaughtered at the Northern Pits.'

Leksandr frowned. 'By you?'

'No, you fool, they're killing each other. A Holdfast is responsible.'

'Arete, my dear,' said Leksandr; 'please sit and I'll get you a drink. Then you can tell us all about it.'

Arete collapsed into a chair across from Belinda, her hand rubbing her forehead as Leksandr prepared a drink for her. He brought it over and she drained it in one.

'A Holdfast has a Quadrant,' she said. 'Felice's Quadrant; the one Lord Renko left with our incompetent new governor. It was Sable.'

'Sable Holdfast?' said Belinda.

Arete stared into the mid-distance. 'She stole the dragon.'

'What dragon?' said Leksandr.

'The new one; the one we captured in Yoneath. Latude bought it for the Deadskins, and the Blue Thumbs were trying to kill it, when Sable Holdfast appeared, then took the dragon away.'

Belinda almost lost her composure. Sable had rescued Blackrose?

Part of her wanted to cheer that the black dragon was safe; the other scowled at the thought that it was Sable who had done the rescuing.

'Are we sure it was her?' said Leksandr.

'Felice recognised her from when she worked here at the residence. I have also seen her face within Lord Renko's memories; it was definitely her.'

'But why would she steal a dragon? Was she making a demonstration of her power? Was she trying to prove something to us?'

'She was trying to sow chaos in the city, and it worked. The Deadskins think that the Blue Thumbs are responsible, and they broke through the lines of militia inside the arena and started killing every Torduan they could get their hands on; while the Blue Thumbs believe that the Deadskins pulled the dragon out of the contest before she could be slaughtered on the sands. Each side is blaming the other, which is, no doubt, precisely what Sable Holdfast intended. The Northern Pits is a bloodbath, and when the Torduans discover that hundreds of their brethren have been killed, they will attack the Fordian districts.'

Leksandr's expression changed from bemused to angry. 'We'll have to send out the garrison.'

'I've already done that,' said Arete, 'for all the difference it will make. We need to get the dragon back; it's the only way to restore order.'

'The Holdfast witch could have taken the beast anywhere.'

Arete caught his glance. 'Latude has a theory about that. He says that the dragon, Obsidia, used to be known as Blackrose, and apparently, she has fought in the pits before. She was sold a decade ago, and was presumed to be dead. And then she turns up in Yoneath and attacks our forces? Latude says that there is only one place she could have been hiding all this time.'

Leksandr raised an eyebrow. 'The Catacombs?'

'Exactly. Where else in Khatanax could a dragon remain unseen?'

'It might be a good idea,' said Belinda, 'if I have my team of vision demigods search the Catacombs.'

Arete's eyes narrowed slightly. 'Thank you for the kind offer, Third

Ascendant, but I know how busy you are. I'll take this task; I will lead the search for Sable Holdfast and the missing dragon.'

'That seems sensible,' said Leksandr. 'Your mission, Third Ascendant, is far more important than the hunt for a single dragon.' He glanced back towards Arete. 'If you find them in the Catacombs, what will be our next step? Banner forces would be next to useless in that environment.'

Arete smiled. 'I'll think of something.' She stood. 'I'll get started right away.'

She gave a brief nod to Belinda, then strode from the room. The moment she had gone, Leksandr turned to Belinda.

'Sable Holdfast has a Quadrant? Please, Third Ascendant, tell me that it's a mere coincidence that I loaned you my Quadrant at the same time as this happened.'

Belinda frowned. 'Are you accusing me of helping Sable Holdfast? I detest her; she's a selfish, lying, two-faced rat. Even when I was a friend of the other Holdfasts, I loathed Sable. Believe me, Leksandr, I would never help her; never. The last time we met we tried to kill each other.'

Leksandr nodded. 'And if Arete searches, she will find nothing that contradicts your version of events?'

Belinda got to her feet and faced Leksandr, her anger simmering. 'That's right. If Sable is in the Catacombs, then Arete will also find the Quadrant she used; Felice's old Quadrant. When that happens, Sixth Ascendant, I shall expect an apology.'

His expression calmed. 'You can have one now. I apologise, Third Ascendant. My shock got the better of me for a moment. I do not believe you assisted the Holdfast woman.'

Belinda took a breath, regaining her composure. 'Thank you. I shall go back to work, and I recommend that you do the same.'

He bowed his head. 'As you wish.'

She walked from his study, and descended the steps to her own quarters on the floor below. She dismissed her servants and went to stare out of the window, her thoughts torn. Should she try to help Sable and Blackrose? If Arete was correct, would that not mean that Maddie might be in the Catacombs as well? She knew that the black dragon had planned to go to Dragon Eyre, and now it appeared that she had a Quadrant that could take her there. Another part of her hesitated. If Arete was distracted by her search for Sable, then that would give her more space to develop her own plans regarding the supply of salve. All the same, Maddie had been a friend, and Belinda had precious few of those.

She sat by the window, and sent her vision out into the clear, blue sky. She glanced north, and could see the smoke rising from the northern districts of the city. Riots and disturbances seemed to be woven into the fabric of Alea Tanton, as if they were a natural feature, along with the earthquakes. Mortals would be fighting and dying on the streets; Fordians against Torduans, their centuries-old antipathy coming to the boil once more. She hated Alea Tanton, she realised, and felt a longing for how Khatanax had been before Fordia and Shinstra had been destroyed, an age that she had lived through, but couldn't remember.

She turned from the slums and raced her vision east, crossing the irrigated plains of Tordue. Enslaved mortals were gathering in the harvests, or preparing the fields for winter, under the steady and watchful gaze of armed soldiers. Thousands of troops were needed to keep the slaves in line, and Belinda recoiled from the folly and waste of it all. She reached the mountains and climbed, passing a series of deep reservoirs. She knew the location of the main wild dragon colony, hidden in a cliffside, surrounded by rivers and pools of lava. It was impossible for any army of mortals to approach the Catacombs, let alone attack it, and the policy of the rulers of Alea Tanton had been to leave it alone in a state of nervous co-existence.

A volcano was spewing molten rock down the flank of the mountains, and Belinda came to the great rift that had once carried the main road from Fordia to Kinell. The valley floor was broken, and covered in alternating patches of basalt and lava. On the cliffs to the west, dozens of openings led into the side of the mountain, and a few dragons were circling overhead, while others could be seen within the tombs where they had made their homes.

Belinda paused, and began to scan each tomb, starting from the top. She spent only a few moments in each, working her way down the cliff-side methodically. There were more dragons living there than she had realised; dozens, with several families sharing a single tomb. At last, near the bottom of the cliff, she found Maddie. The Blade girl was sitting close to the edge of a tomb, a young man next to her, while behind them, a dark red dragon was also peering out into the valley. Belinda pushed her vision into the interior of the tomb, but there was no sign of Blackrose or Sable. She returned to Maddie, and noticed that she was clutching a Quadrant on her knees.

She entered Maddie's head.

Hello, it's Belinda.

The young woman jumped, and nearly dropped the Quadrant over the edge of the cliff.

I didn't mean to startle you.

Belinda? Hello, um, this is a surprise.

I need to speak to you about Sable and Blackrose.

Could you maybe appear in front of me, like Sable used to do? It's a lot easier to talk that way.

I've never done that before. Alright. Walk into the cavern until you are alone, and I'll try it.

Maddie got to her feet and muttered something to the dark red dragon, then walked into the semi-darkness of the tomb. Belinda knew what Maddie had meant; she had often heard Daphne and Karalyn talk about how to project an image of yourself, so that the other person would think they could see you standing in front of them. She went to Maddie's eyes, and looked out from them, then imagined herself there.

'That's better,' said Maddie. 'I can see you now. What do you know about Blackrose and Sable? I admit I'm a bit wary of you; can you read people's minds now? If so, then I guess you already know what's happened. Blackrose was here, not long ago, with Sable.'

'Where are they now?'

'I don't know. As soon as they appeared, Blackrose grabbed Sable and flew off. I think, um, that Blackrose might be doing something bad to her.'

'Why?'

'Because of the Quadrant. Sable was lying to Blackrose, telling her she didn't have one, when she did. Blackrose, as you might remember, doesn't particularly like being lied to. Wait; can I trust you? Are you working for the Ascendants now?'

A thought struck Belinda, and she cursed her lack of foresight. If Arete, or more likely, when Arete found them, she would read Maddie's mind and discover that Belinda had contacted her.

'What Sable did,' she said, choosing her words carefully, 'has caused hundreds of deaths in Alea Tanton. The teams are fighting each other; each side thinks that the other was responsible for stealing Blackrose from the arena. The Ascendants will be coming; they want to find Blackrose and Sable. You know that Sable and I hate each other, but I don't want any harm to come to you, Maddie.'

'You didn't really answer my question.'

'Your mind might be read; I must act accordingly.'

'Oh. Well, thanks for the warning, I guess.'

'I should go. Which way did Blackrose fly?'

'Towards the Fordian Wastes.'

'Take care, Maddie.'

Belinda withdrew from her mind, as frustration surged through her. She hadn't said half of what she had wanted to say, but she had still said enough to arouse Arete's suspicions further. She cursed herself again, feeling the burden of her secrets weigh upon her. She sent her vision out of the tomb, and turned south.

She searched for half an hour, and was about to give up when she saw a speck soaring through the sky. Blackrose. She decided not to attempt to make contact, aware that Arete would also discover that, and instead carried onward in the direction the black dragon had come from. She sped over the barren wastes, scanning the ground as she went, until finally, she spotted a lone figure trudging across the sands.

Sable.

Belinda longed to make contact with her, to gloat at the woman's plight. She was stranded in the middle of an enormous desert, alone and without supplies. Belinda watched for a long moment as Sable struggled along, her boots trailing through the sand. She had a fresh wound on her arm, and it was bleeding, leaving drops of blood behind her on the broken ground. Blackrose had abandoned her to die. It was no more than she deserved, Belinda thought, but her attention was drawn to Sable's eyes, and she discerned a grim determination on the Holdfast's woman's face. Belinda's gloating ceased, and she began to feel pity for her. Sable had risked everything to save Blackrose, and this was how she was being repaid. Was it possible that Sable had been misunderstood? After all, many people suspected Belinda of colluding with the Ascendants, and they were wrong. Could she have been wrong about Sable?

She cut the connection, and her vision leapt back to her body. She got to her feet, knowing what she had to do next. It was a short walk to Arete's quarters, and the courtiers allowed her to enter.

Arete was sitting with a few of her demigod assistants, and she frowned as Belinda walked into her rooms.

'Third Ascendant,' she said; 'can I help you?'

'No,' said Belinda. 'I am here to inform you of something. Alone.'

Arete nodded to the demigods, and they left the chamber.

'Well?' she said.

'I ignored your instructions and sent my vision to the Catacombs.'

'Why?'

'There is a mortal living in the Catacombs that I am fond of, and I went to warn her that you will be searching there.'

Arete sprang to her feet, rage lighting up her features. 'You warned them? You brazenly display your treachery, and then you tell me about it?'

'Blackrose has killed Sable Holdfast.'

Arete paused for a moment. 'Are you lying to me? Are you trying to stop me from doing my job?'

'I am telling you the truth. Go to the Catacombs, and you will see for yourself. The dragon feels that Sable betrayed her, and has punished her for it. The mortal I warned is a friend; her name is Maddie. Whatever else happens, I do not wish her to be harmed.'

Confusion clouded Arete's face, though the rage remained. 'I will do what needs to be done.'

'If you harm Maddie, I will kill you.'

'The mask slips at last,' said Arete. 'Your heart isn't with us; it's with our enemies, where it has always been. One day, soon, you're going to make a mistake that you will not be able to hide.' She pointed to the door. 'Get out of my quarters, most blessed and noble Third Ascendant.'

Belinda stared at her, then turned and walked back out onto the landing of the tower. What had she done? What else did Maddie know? Had the Blade girl discovered that Corthie was still alive? Belinda had to assume that Arete would read everything that was held within Maddie's memories. She walked back into her own rooms and sat, holding her head in her hands.

Time was running out. Leksandr and Arete were too powerful for her to handle alone, and the threat of Lord Bastion would only go so far. If only Sable hadn't behaved so recklessly; her actions in the Northern Pits had endangered everything. Belinda's earlier doubts evaporated, and her loathing of the Holdfast woman returned.

It was Sable's fault. Her meddling had ruined everything.

CHAPTER 14

MAKING ALLOWANCES

Northern Kinell – 21st Luddinch 5252

Aila watched as Kelsey cleaned out Frostback's lair. The young silver dragon had insisted that the 'insects' make themselves useful as a condition for her letting them stay, and Aila and Kelsey had been taking it in turns. As well as allowing them to sleep close to the dragon each night, Frostback had also been bringing them back food from her hunting trips, and Kelsey had recovered from the arduous journey across Northern Kinell.

Frostback's lair consisted of a shallow dip in the forest, a hollow surrounded by dense undergrowth and trees with a rocky slope on one side. It had been in a mess when Aila and Kelsey had first arrived, littered with gnawed bones and scraps of dead animals, while the bedding of moss and branches had been imbued with a dragon stench that had made them both nauseous. Several days of cleaning and tidying had followed, until they had got the daily routine down to an hour or so.

The dragon was keeping a close eye on Kelsey as she carried armfuls of fresh moss over to the base of the hollow where the dragon slept. She was quite beautiful, Aila thought. Her silver-grey wings shone in the moonlight, and she moved with a grace that belied her impatient belligerence. Her red eyes reminded Aila of Blackrose, and they would glow in the same way when she was angry, which was often.

'Do it properly this time,' she cajoled Kelsey, her long neck turning as she followed the Holdfast woman's movements. 'It's not a difficult job; even you insects should be able to manage it.'

'Stop complaining,' muttered Kelsey as she dropped the moss into the hollow. 'Before we arrived, you were living in your own filth; it's no wonder you need humans to help you.'

'I do not need you,' said Frostback; 'I tolerate you. You serve me, and in return, I provide you with food and protection. You can always leave if you don't like it.'

'You're always saying that, but I don't believe you. You want us to stay, don't you? You were lonely until we showed up.'

The dragon snorted. 'You have a vivid imagination.' She raised her neck and sniffed the air. 'Those goats I was tracking yesterday will be on the move.' She extended her great wings and lifted into the sky, sending a wave of cold air down into the hollow.

Aila shielded her eyes until the dragon had gone, then stood, and walked over to help Kelsey cover the ground in the fresh moss.

'Maybe we should be thinking of going,' she said to Kelsey.

'Why?'

'We're supposed to be finding Corthie and Van, and yet we're no closer to Kin Dai. You seem fit and healthy again; if Frostback won't carry us south, then perhaps we should start walking.'

Kelsey's face fell. 'But I don't want to leave.'

'What? Are you happy slaving for that flying lizard?'

'Don't call her that.'

Aila sighed. 'She's bewitched you. It's the only explanation.'

'We nearly starved to death getting here; well, I did – you would have been fine. I have no intention of going through that again. I'm not walking to Kin Dai.'

'So it's not about the dragon, it's about the walking? What if Frostback offers to take us to the outskirts of Kin Dai, would you be happy to say goodbye to her?'

'Oh, shut up. This is the happiest I've been in ages, and you just want to ruin it.'

Aila squinted at her. 'You like it here? You're happy living in the middle of a forest with no roof over our heads; happy to work every day for no thanks? Frostback is mean and spiteful...'

'No, she's not; she's just had a hard time. Her father kicked her out, and she was nearly killed by the Ascendants. Maybe I am a little bewitched, but come on, Aila – she's a dragon.'

'This is unlike you; you're usually very hard to impress, but what about Van? Corthie? I need to get back to civilisation.'

Kelsey glanced up from the moss. 'What if we could persuade Frostback to join our cause? She's already fought against the Ascendants once; if she could get over her fear of their death powers, then she might be willing to help us.'

'She doesn't seem interested. I think she was only helping Blackrose because Blackrose ordered her to. If I had to guess her motives from everything that she's said to us, then I reckon she wants to reconcile with her father Deadfang.'

'Deathfang.'

'Yes, alright; Deathfang. Let's discuss it with her when she gets back. If she's not willing to help us, then we should tell her we're going.'

Kelsey glowered at her. 'Why don't you go? You can go, and I'll stay here. You won't starve in the forest and, without me, you'll be able to use your disguise powers. Look, all I need is a chance to show her that I can protect her from the Ascendants. If that takes a little bit longer, then so be it.'

Aila suppressed her irritation. Was the young Holdfast woman being serious? There was no way Aila was going to turn up in front of Corthie only to tell him that she had left his sister in a forest with a dragon for company.

A flock of birds arose from the trees to their north, calling as they flew away. Aila turned. Frostback regularly scared the wildlife with her appearance, and the sight of birds being disturbed had become normal, but never from the north. That way lay the ever-encroaching lumber gangs, hacking, burning and sawing their way southwards, and the silver dragon did not hunt in that direction.

'Don't worry,' said Kelsey. 'The edge of the forest is still several miles away. It'll be a couple of months before they get here.'

They finished laying the carpet of fresh moss, and went to sit down by the cold remains of their little fire, where, to Frostback's disgust, they cooked the meat she brought them every day. Aila knelt by the circular pile of ashes and prepared the fire for the coming evening, while Kelsey relaxed, her eyes on the blue sky above them.

Aila was laying the last stacks of firewood next to the hearth when Kelsey sat up, her eyes narrowing.

'Something's wrong,' she said.

Aila followed her glance to the north. Smoke was rising from the forest in several places, thin wisps, which were being carried away by the wind.

'Those fires are too close,' said Kelsey. 'There's no way the lumber gangs have reached this deep into the forest by now.'

More smoke rose as Aila watched, this time from the east and west of their position, a clutch of grey tendrils clearing the roof of the forest. To the north, the volume of smoke was increasing, growing thicker and darker.

Aila stood, and stared all around them, but saw no movement in the trees. 'Damn it,' she muttered. 'I think they're trying to burn us out.'

Her boots scrambled on the dirt as she hurried up the slope of the low hillock next to the hollow. When she reached the top, she turned. She could just see over the tops of the nearby trees, and the extent of the approaching fires became apparent. To the north, half a dozen distinct pillars of smoke could be seen, and flames were visible, licking the upper branches. The fires to the east and west hadn't grown as large, but they were getting bigger, and more smoke was starting to appear from the south, cutting them off.

'We need to leave,' she called out to Kelsey, who was still in the bottom of the hollow. 'Grab everything.'

She raced back down the slope and began to gather their things, as Kelsey watched her.

'We're being surrounded,' said Aila. 'They must have discovered the lair's location. The fires to the south are still sparse; if we run, we might be able to get through that way.'

Kelsey turned to the south. There was no sign of smoke from the bottom of the hollow, and she frowned.

'Trust me,' said Aila, swinging their bag over her shoulder and taking hold of Kelsey's arm. 'Move.'

'What about Frostback?' said Kelsey, standing her ground. 'If we run, we'll get lost in the forest, and she won't be able to find us. And anyway, I'd rather burn than starve.'

'What?'

'I've told you, Aila; I can't go through that again; the thought of starving to death in the forest terrifies me.'

'Is that why you want to stay here? You're worried you'll starve if we leave?'

'You don't understand, do you? You didn't even come close to dying, but I felt it. Day after day of nothing to eat, it was turning me into a different person. I won't go through that again.'

'What about me? You're right that it would take a long time for me to die of starvation, but fire *will* kill me, and my child; Corthie's child. I can't take that risk, Kelsey.'

Kelsey said nothing, her gaze on the ground.

'I don't want to leave you here,' said Aila; 'please.'

'Pyre's arse,' Kelsey muttered; 'alright.'

They were about to move along the side of the slope when three soldiers burst through the undergrowth, crossbows in their arms.

'Halt!' cried one. 'Where is the dragon?'

Aila lifted her hands in the air. 'It flew off; it's gone.'

The three men walked forward, keeping their weapons trained on the two women. All around the hollow, smoke was billowing up into the sky, but no flames were yet visible.

'Were you the dragon's prisoners?' said one of the soldiers. 'Was it holding you hostage?'

'Yes,' said Aila, before Kelsey had a chance to contradict her.

The three soldiers relaxed a little, but continued to gaze around the lair. A shadow flitted overhead, and then a burst of fire exploded by the edge of the hollow, aimed at the three men. They dropped their crossbows, screaming as the inferno consumed them. Aila cried out in fright, and fell backwards in her haste to get away from the flames. She was about to hit the ground when something took hold of her and she felt herself lifted into the air. She glanced down, and saw a thick, scaled forelimb gripping her, the claws enveloping her chest and waist. She struggled for a moment, and caught a glimpse of the ground as it got further away. Fires were almost completely surrounding the hollow, and beyond them, dozens of soldiers were staring up.

A yard-long steel bolt sped through the air, and Frostback twisted, her long silver body darting out of the way. The dragon put on a surge of speed, and raced south over the forest, keeping only a yard or two above the tops of the trees. They passed the ring of flames and hurtled onwards.

Aila panted and shivered as the wind lashed her. She closed her eyes to stop them streaming and tried not to think about what would happen if the dragon dropped her. Her fingers were gripping onto the scales of the forelimb, while her legs were flailing about. She felt the branches of a tree hit her feet, and she yelled in pain, her voice lost to the rushing wind.

Her thoughts emptied of everything as she tried to shut out the wind, the noise, and the pain in her waist from where a claw was digging into her, and then, in an instant, it was over, and she was released onto a wide stone ledge. She groaned and opened her eyes. Her vision swam for a moment, then she realised that she was near the summit of what passed for a hill in the forests of Northern Kinell. Ahead of her, the trees seemed to go forever, and the smoke from the fires by the hollow was nothing but a tiny wisp on the horizon. She turned to her right, and saw Kelsey crouching next to her.

'That was amazing,' said the young Holdfast woman. 'Thank you, Frostback.'

'I had to drop my goat to save you,' the dragon said.

Aila glanced up, and saw Frostback's head above her, looking down at the two women. The dragon was sitting at the rear of the ledge, where a dark cave led away.

'Where are we?' said Aila.

'We are twenty miles further to the south,' said the dragon. 'Why did they do that? Why are they hunting me? You told me that soldiers were coming, but I scarcely believed it; do they hate dragons so much?'

'You were in their way,' said Kelsey.

'And didn't you kill someone?' said Aila.

Frostback stared at her.

'That's what we were told back in the camp,' said Aila. 'We heard you killed someone.'

'He walked right into my lair while I was sleeping,' said the dragon. 'I reacted in the same way I would have reacted in the Catacombs, and raised my claws to defend myself. I didn't deliberately tear him to shreds, and I even returned the body to his comrades. It is true that I detest insects, but with so many of them employed in cutting down the forest, it was not my wish to antagonise them.'

Aila frowned. 'And now you've killed another three.'

'They were threatening you, and despite your lack of worth, you are officially under my protection. It would sully my honour if I allowed those who serve me to die.'

'You have a strange concept of honour.'

The dragon's eyes glowed a fiery red. 'The honour of my kin is far superior to that of insects, who lie and cheat every day. And, were the soldiers not attacking my home? I have a right to defend my property. Even as we speak, my former lair is in flames; do you think I should have meekly surrendered? Do you take me for a coward, you ungrateful wretch?'

Aila edged back, fear racing through her. Her fingers scrabbled on the rock beneath her, but the ledge was smooth, and she braced herself as Frostback opened her jaws, a burning rage in her eyes.

'Is this going to be your new lair?' said Kelsey, her tone light. 'I like it.'

Frostback's head snapped round to face the Holdfast woman. 'What did you say?'

'The cave is big enough for us all to fit inside,' Kelsey went on, getting to her feet and brushing the dirt from the front of her clothes. 'And, even better, we can see for miles up here. There's no way anyone will be able to surprise us again.'

'That's why I chose it,' said Frostback.

'Thank you again for rescuing us; we're very grateful.'

'You might be, but the demigod isn't.'

'I am grateful,' said Aila, slowly rising to her feet, her palms outstretched. 'I am. Without you, we would have been arrested, or we'd have burned to death. All I was trying to say was that the soldiers will still be coming after you. You killed another three of them. I know you were protecting us and defending your lair, but they won't see it like that.'

'You are right,' said the dragon; 'they have become my enemies, through no fault of my own. This makes things clearer, at least. If they are my enemies, then I need to strike them before they can strike at me.' She turned her gaze to Aila. 'Thank you, demigod, for your advice. I will take it. The soldiers that attacked us will pay; all of them.'

She beat her wings and surged into the air, as Aila and Kelsey stared, open-mouthed.

'What have you done?' whispered Kelsey.

'I didn't mean that to happen,' said Aila, as the figure of Frostback grew fainter in the northern sky. 'I didn't know she was going to react that way. I was trying to tell her that we should keep flying south, to get away from the soldiers, not that she should attack them.'

'Pyre's arse; next time, just say "thank you."'

Several hours passed. Aila and Kelsey stared at the northern horizon for a long time, then explored the cave at the rear of the ledge. It went back thirty yards or so, and was dry and clean, though quite narrow in places.

'Frostback will need to reverse in,' said Kelsey, 'otherwise her bum will be sticking out of the entrance.'

Aila nodded, though her thoughts were on what the silver dragon might be doing at that moment.

'There's a little alcove further in,' Kelsey went on, peering into the gloom of the cavern. 'We could build a fire there, but it might get a bit smoky. I don't think there's any ventilation. Still, altogether it's a much better lair than the last one.'

'Does it matter?' snapped Aila. 'We won't be here long.'

'Here we go again,' muttered Kelsey.

'She took us twenty miles in under half an hour. It wasn't a pleasant experience, but it was fast. She could probably take us to Kin Dai in a couple of hours, then we could use our gold to live like royalty for a while.'

'You would just abandon Frostback?'

'Abandon her? Don't exaggerate.'

'Right now, she's off burning and pillaging, because of us, well, partly because of us. If she brings down the wrath of the Ascendants upon her, then it will be our fault. They'll kill her, unless I'm here to stop them. Do you want her death on your conscience?'

'Your reasoning is contorted, to put it mildly. We aren't responsible for her actions. Are you sure this isn't about your fear of starving?'

Kelsey shook her head. 'You say that like it's an irrational fear. If we tell her we're leaving, then she'll refuse to carry us anywhere, and then, aye, I'm a little worried about starving in the forest. My humble apologies for being mortal.'

Aila sat back down on the ledge. 'Malik's ass; we should have taken Amalia's Quadrant.'

'Hey,' said Kelsey. 'Remember our rule – no "should have" or "could have" – they're not allowed. Regret will get us nowhere.'

'So will following your plan! All I'm trying to do is get us moving.'

She turned away from Kelsey, and stared out to the north. The sun was lowering to the west, and it was starting to turn cold up on the rocky hillside. Trees dotted the summit and the slopes, but none were in front of the ledge, and a chill wind was gusting from the east. Aila wasn't sure how cold it would get over winter in Kinell, but they had no thick, warm clothes with them.

She peered forwards, noticing a small dark speck in the sky. 'Kelsey.'

'Aye?'

Aila pointed.

Kelsey wandered over from the cave entrance and crouched down next to her, a hand up to shield her eyes from the setting sun.

'I think that's her,' she said. She glanced at Aila. 'Let's give it a day or so. I know you want to get back to Corthie as soon as possible, but I'm telling you now; I'm not leaving until I can be sure that either Frostback will take us, or we have enough food for the journey. I'm sorry, but that's that.'

They watched as the dragon approached, her silver body glinting in the light from the fading sun. She circled over the hilltop a few times, then landed on the ledge as Aila and Kelsey stood. Frostback glanced at them, then dropped the carcass of a pig onto the ground in front of them.

'Your dinner,' said the dragon.

'Thanks,' said Kelsey. 'Did you decide to go hunting?'

'Clearly,' said Frostback. 'I knew you would be hungry, so I took this pig for you once I had dealt with the soldiers.'

Aila's heart fell. For a brief moment, she had thought that maybe the dragon had changed her mind.

'What happened?' said Kelsey.

'I flew back to my old lair,' said Frostback, 'and destroyed every insect that had attacked my home. Then I went further, and discovered a camp full of soldiers on the edge of the forest. I kept low, so they wouldn't see me, and then razed the camp to the ground. I burned it all, except for that pig.'

Aila groaned aloud.

'I was following your advice, demigod. And it was good advice; the soldiers had wagons full of nets, and other wagons with ballistae mounted on the back. They would have attacked me again, of that there is no doubt.' She paused, her red eyes glowing. 'You should have heard the soldiers scream. They were running around in a wild panic, this way and that; it was good sport.'

'How many did you kill?' said Aila.

'I didn't keep an exact count. Perhaps two hundred? Certainly many more than any other raid I have taken part in, except for Yoneath. My father would have been... I mean, my former father, he... never mind.' She lowered her head. 'Regardless, it is done. I am victorious, and my enemies are no more.'

Aila opened her mouth to speak, but Kelsey shot her a glance.

'You are every bit as powerful as you claimed,' said the Holdfast woman; 'not that I doubted that for a single moment.' She turned to Aila. 'Can you go and collect some firewood? I'll show Frostback our new cave.'

'Sure,' said Aila.

She turned and walked to the far end of the stone ledge, then climbed down a few feet to the earthen slope of the hillside. She knew that Kelsey wanted some time alone with the dragon; time without Aila's frown ruining things, and she understood why the Holdfast woman was acting the way she was, but the knowledge did nothing to improve the demigod's mood.

Two hundred soldiers? The authorities in Kinell would not be able to ignore that; they would have to retaliate. They had sent an armed force because Frostback had killed one man; what would they do now that two hundred had been reduced to smoking ruins?

She bent over and starting picking up wood from the ground as her mind went over the implications of Frostback's actions. Blackrose would never have behaved so rashly, but the silver dragon was young and inexperienced, like a teenager with death powers. Damn wild dragons were a menace to civilised society, and the sooner they were away from Frostback, the better.

She returned when her arms were full of wood, and she piled it up onto the ledge, then went back for more. When a full night's supply had been gathered, she climbed up onto the flat stone platform. Frostback was in the cave, with only her head, neck and forelimbs visible, like a dog looking out from its kennel. Kelsey was standing by, talking and smiling. Blood was staining the front of her clothes and her hands.

'Here's the wood,' said the demigod.

'Thanks,' said Kelsey. 'Bring it over and we'll get a fire started. I've already gutted the pig.'

Frostback watched, as Aila started carrying the wood over to the cave entrance.

'Kelsey has revealed some things to me,' said the dragon, 'which help explain your unfriendly demeanour.'

Aila frowned. 'What?'

'I hope you don't mind,' said Kelsey.

'What did you tell her?'

'That you are with child,' said the dragon. 'You are frustrated that you cannot build a nest for your young. I understand you a little better now, demigod.'

Aila's eyes widened, then anger rippled through her. 'I told you not to mention that,' she snapped at Kelsey.

'I had to,' said the Holdfast woman. 'Frostback was... well, she was...'

'I was considering killing you for your ingratitude,' said the dragon. 'But now, I will make some allowances due to your condition. When will your brood come?'

Aila stared at the silver dragon.

'She has five or so months to go,' said Kelsey. 'If you look closely, you can see her starting to show. And, I think it's only the one child.'

'All that effort for just one?' said Frostback. 'A clutch of three of four is more usual for dragons. If you are still here when the child comes, I will help you make a nest, and then I would be interested in observing the birth. I am a little unfamiliar with the method by which insects reproduce. It seems to me that eggs are far more civilised than live births, especially with all that blood. Yes, I will look after you, and make sure you have plenty to eat. No harm will come to you or your child while you remain under my protection; I swear it.'

Aila said nothing for a long moment, then she realised that the dragon was expecting a response.

'Thank you,' she said.

Frostback tilted her head. 'You are most welcome, demigod, most welcome indeed.'

CHAPTER 15

WITHOUT A CAUSE

C apston, Southern Cape, Southern Khatanax – 22nd Luddinch 5252

The four men stood by the ship's railing, watching as the harbour of Capston drew closer. The sun was halfway up the eastern sky, and it was another hot day in the Southern Cape. Corthie bit his tongue. The others had heard enough of his complaints during the voyage, and he was sick of making them.

They had gone the wrong way. His anger had initially been directed towards Sohul for buying the tickets, but he knew the lieutenant had done only what he had been told to do – get passage on any ship leaving that night. Following that, the speed of the old merchant vessel had been the next target of his ire. Nine days it had taken to plough through the seas by the eastern coast of Khatanax from Kin Dai to its destination at Capston; nine days of enforced inaction. He had paced the deck, lain in his bunk, then paced the deck again. For better or worse, the ship had been dry, with no alcohol permitted, and the sailors were looking forward to their arrival as eagerly as the passengers.

The person he was most angry with was himself. True, he had been sick and in pain, but even so, they should have left Kin Dai earlier to search for Aila and Kelsey. He had let them down again. Not only had he failed to defeat the Ascendants, he had failed to find those he loved. The idea that he had any kind of destiny felt farcical to him now, a conceit born of over-confidence and arrogance. His strength may have returned, but many of his previous assumptions had been ripped to shreds; he was strong, but he wasn't the strongest; a powerful warrior, but not the best. He wasn't invincible – push a sword through his heart and he would die like any other mortal.

'I'll be glad to get off this boat,' said Sohul. 'Yes, I know I always say that; ships and me just don't get along.'

Van smiled. 'It's been a good voyage, all things considered. The weather held, and the ocean was smooth. Could've been a lot worse.'

'It could have been a lot better, too,' said Naxor, 'especially if we hadn't had to listen to Corthie whine the entire way.'

'Fair enough,' said Corthie; 'I did whine a lot, particularly in the first few days. Knowing that Aila and Kelsey were getting further away with every mile that passed was enough to send me half-demented. So, sorry if I might have been a bit much at times.'

Van shrugged. 'It frustrated me too,' he said, 'but when you can't change something, it does no good to let it rile you up. But anyway, I appreciate the apology.'

'Yes, me too,' said Sohul; 'let's put it behind us.'

'I wonder if Vana is here,' said Naxor, his eyes on the approaching town as the ship passed the breakwaters of the harbour. 'This is where her boat was headed. She would have disembarked here, like us.'

'If she is,' said Corthie, 'then the first thing I'll do is apologise to her as well.'

Naxor nodded. 'Make sure you do that.'

Corthie bit his tongue again, suppressing the comment that was forming on his lips. His companions had a right to be annoyed with him, and for a while he was going to have to take it on the chin.

'There are no agents of the Ascendants on the quayside that I can see,' Naxor went on. 'So for now we should assume that our presence onboard has not been noticed. Getting through the harbour to a hostelry might prove otherwise, of course.'

Sohul pointed. 'There's our old ship; the one that took us from the Falls of Iron to Yoneath.'

They all turned. The vessel Sohul was pointing towards was berthed by a pier to their left. Corthie's thoughts went to the luggage they had left behind. Buried among it had been the jug of salve left over from when Blackrose had been attacked by the Bloodflies, which had been left on board with the rest of their things when they had gone to Yoneath.

'It'll be gone,' said Naxor. He sighed. 'Some lucky sailor probably sold it for a thousand in gold.'

Corthie nodded. Of the three jugs, one had gone with Maddie and the black dragon, Corthie's had been left on the ship, and Naxor had never mentioned the one that he had been given. When they had asked him about it, he had feigned ignorance at first, and had then told them a story about how he had accidentally smashed it in the Falls of Iron. Corthie knew it hadn't been in Kin Dai, and it wasn't onboard the ship they were currently on – he, Sohul, and Van had searched everywhere for it. A few doses would have been enough to have drastically shortened Corthie's recovery time, and if Naxor had been keeping it hidden from him, then it was another mark against the demigod's name.

'I'll take a look around anyway,' Naxor said. 'Who knows? I can think of a few places on our old ship where someone might have overlooked a bag.'

'And will you tell me if you find it?' said Corthie.

Naxor smiled. 'Probably.'

They sailed past the other merchant vessels by the long pier, and came in next to the high, stone wharf. Dock workers picked up the ropes thrown from the deck, and looped them round the iron cleats jutting up from the edge of the wharf. A gangway was placed between the wharf and the deck, and the passengers began to disembark. Corthie and the others joined the dozen or so merchants who had made the trip, and they ascended the wooden board up to the solid foundations of the wharf.

'That's better,' said Sohul, smiling for the first time in days.

'Follow me, chaps,' said Naxor; 'I've already scouted the way to a hostelry.'

They walked through the busy harbour, and Corthie collected a few glances from the dock workers and fishing boat crews.

'How do they feel about Banner deserters down here?' said Corthie. 'Assuming that's what they'll take me for?'

'Much the same as Kin Dai,' said Van, 'but they've never been occupied by Banner forces. The Southern Cape's too out of the way to get much attention from Alea Tanton. All the same, it would be better if you...'

'Stayed in my room?' said Corthie. 'Aye, I get it.'

The hostelry was close to the harbour, and a pair of gulls was fighting over some scraps by the kitchen door.

'It might not be as comfortable as the villa we stayed in last time,' said Naxor, 'but our reserves are a little low at the moment.'

They walked into a smoky, low-ceilinged bar and paid for a room, then took their meagre possessions up a narrow flight of stairs. Their quarters consisted of a single, cramped chamber, with four bed pallets taking up most of the floor space. Corthie picked a bed by the window and sat, while the others left to explore and procure supplies. Van was the first to return.

'There's a little garden up on the roof,' he said. 'Ramshackle, but we can sit out there in the evenings to escape the humidity inside.' He pulled a bottle of raki from his coat. 'I also got us this. Are you going to behave? We can't have you smashing up any more taverns.'

'I'll be fine,' said Corthie.

'Hmm. I've heard that before.' He smiled. 'It's usually me that people have to worry about. I've disgraced myself in a hundred different bars, brothels and smoking dens in Serene. Now I know how my friends felt.'

Corthie frowned. 'Why would you pay for a woman? I never understood that.'

'It kept my life simple,' he said. 'I used to look at married guys in the Banner, and how they would leave their wives for months at a time to go on operations or training exercises. All they did was worry about what their other halves were doing in their absence, and many of the men would stray. They were plagued with guilt and paranoia, and I had enough problems of my own without having to deal with that as well. Now, Sohul on the other hand, he stayed clear of all of that. I don't think he's set foot in a brothel in his life; oh, apart from that time he had to help carry me out of one; I was too drunk to walk.'

Corthie laughed. 'How come you never acted like that in Kin Dai?'

'I was too busy looking after you. I had a rule – never when on an operation, and being in Lostwell still feels like I'm on an operation; I haven't relaxed in months. And before you ask; I'm not about to let my guard down now.'

Naxor and Sohul entered the room, and it immediately felt cramped. The lieutenant was carrying a large basket, and Corthie could smell the cooked food that lay within.

'Let's go onto the roof,' said Van. 'There are tables and chairs up there, and a view of the harbour.'

An hour later, the four men were sitting under the shade of a canvas canopy, as the noonday sun beat down on the village of Capston. Their empty plates and bowls were piled up on a low table, and the bottle of raki had been opened. Everyone except for Corthie was smoking, Naxor having purchased some fresh tobacco from the market. Their bellies full, the conversation moved onto their next steps.

'It's obvious,' said Corthie; 'we need to go back the way we came, and head further north; that's where Naxor noticed the God-Queen's powers.'

'That was a while ago now,' said the demigod, 'and there's every chance that my deranged grandmother would have moved on. However, we have a more pressing problem – even if we wished to travel back to Kinell, we can't afford it. Most of our gold went on the horses and wagon, and the passage here; we have very little left over.'

Van narrowed his eyes. 'How long can we afford to stay here?'

'Three days.'

The men groaned.

'I'll have to get another job,' muttered Van. 'Back to unloading crates of fish again, but that will only be enough to buy food, not to fund any trip north.'

'Or we rob someone,' said Naxor. 'A rich merchant, perhaps. That would be easier than manual labour on the harbour front, and, let's be honest, a lot more fun. There's also the possibility that Vana is here in Capston; she had a fair amount of gold on her when she left.'

'Have you looked for her?' said Corthie.

'I don't need to. If she's here, then her powers will detect my presence before too long. I've already used my vision a half dozen times; I would be like a beacon to her.'

'So we wait here and see if she shows up?' said Corthie.

'Exactly. In the meantime, I can scout out some rich residences, and see if any are ripe for a midnight robbery.'

Sohul frowned, but said nothing.

'What about you?' Corthie said to the lieutenant. 'What do you think?'

'I don't know,' he said, his eyes downcast. 'I've lost sight of what I'm doing here. Everything's upside down. If I go back to Implacatus, then there's a good chance I'll be arrested for what happened in Yoneath, but I don't want to stay in Khatanax; I don't belong here. I never intended to get involved in a fight against the Ascendants, and now I'm adrift. Sorry, I don't want to sound despondent, but I did a lot of thinking on the voyage here, and I came to the conclusion that my future is bleak.'

'You and I are in the same situation,' said Van, 'and I know what you're going through. We just have to take things one day at a time.'

'At least you have a purpose,' said Sohul. 'You want to find Kelsey, because you made her a promise; and Corthie wants to find Aila as well as his sister. And Naxor, well, he'll get by no matter what happens.'

The demigod smiled as he sipped his raki. 'I'll take that as a compliment.'

'You're free to go your own way,' said Corthie to Sohul; 'you've already gone beyond any handshake contract we had, and I've no more money to pay you.'

'Thanks, but you three are all I've got,' said the lieutenant. 'My priority is to make myself useful, so you don't decide to ditch me.'

'We'd never do that,' said Van.

'I agree,' said Corthie; 'not after everything we've been through together.'

A serving boy appeared at the top of the stairwell, blinking in the bright sunshine. He approached the four men.

'Which one is Naxor?' he said.

The demigod raised a finger.

'You have a visitor,' the boy said. 'A woman.'

'Oh,' said Naxor.

'Should I send her up to see you?'

'Of course, yes. Thank you,' said the demigod.

The boy nodded then returned to the stairs and disappeared into the gloom.

'See?' said the demigod. 'All we had to do was wait. Good old Vana.'

Corthie puffed out his cheeks and readied his apology. It would have to be grovelling, and sincere. They watched the stairwell, and Naxor's smile faded as a woman emerged from the shadows onto the roof.

'It's you?' he said. 'How disappointing.'

Silva glared at him, then walked toward the table where the men were sitting. Her eyes fell on Corthie as she entered the shade of the canopy.

She bowed her head to him. 'I'm glad to see you alive and well.'

'Take a seat,' said Corthie; 'and ignore Naxor; it's good to see you, Silva. I know we mistrusted each other at first, but that seems a long time ago.'

The demigod sat. 'I still mistrust Naxor; that hasn't changed, and never will. All the same, it was his powers I sensed and without him, I wouldn't have found you.'

Naxor snorted. 'Glad to be of use.'

'I shall never forgive the way you betrayed my mistress,' said Silva.

'You broke her heart, despite being unworthy of her love. She's over you now. She's put all that behind her. I, however, shall bear her grudge for her.' She turned back to Corthie. 'Her Majesty sent me here to look for you.'

'Belinda knew I'd be coming here?' said Corthie.

'Not at first. She told me you were in Kin Dai, and I was making arrangements to sail there when she informed me that you had embarked upon a ship heading south. She needs your help, Corthie.'

Corthie felt an unfamiliar feeling flicker in his chest. It was dread, he realised.

'Her Majesty is alone,' Silva went on, 'and she cannot overcome the two Ascendants in Alea Tanton on her own; she needs you.'

Corthie got to his feet and walked to the edge of the roof, his heart racing. Memories of Leksandr pushing the sword into his heart flooded him, and he felt dizzy and sick. Behind him, he could hear the voices of the others, but he wasn't taking in their words; all he could think of was how to avoid what Silva was suggesting.

Van walked to his side and gazed out at the view over the harbour.

'I was wrong,' said Corthie.

Van said nothing.

'I was wrong about having a destiny; I was wrong about everything. If I face the Ascendants again, they will kill me again.'

'Maybe,' said Van.

Corthie felt tears in his eyes, and he grew angry with himself. Van placed a hand on his back.

'I failed,' said Corthie, wiping his eyes; 'why can't Belinda see that?'

'She knows you better than I do,' said Van. 'If she thinks you can do it, then I believe her. Come back to the table, and we'll talk. That's all – just talk.'

Corthie nodded, and they returned to their seats under the canvas canopy. Naxor raised an eyebrow as he glanced at Corthie's face, but said nothing.

'Lady Silva was just telling us,' said Sohul, 'about the Third Ascendant.'

'Yes,' said Silva. 'My mistress has been pretending to be loyal to Leksandr and Arete, but her heart lies with the common folk of Khatanax. Her Majesty has been attempting to obstruct the Ascendants, but it is only a matter of time before they realise this.'

'And the Sextant?' said Naxor.

'So far they have not been able to operate it,' said Silva. 'Lord Bastion visited. Leksandr and Arete will face the wrath of Implacatus soon if they cannot get the device to work.'

'Lord Bastion?' said Corthie.

'Yes. He is the Second Ascendant's most powerful emissary. A vile creature, who serves an even viler master.'

Sohul frowned and looked away. Silva glanced at him.

'Sohul has, um, some religious feelings about the Second Ascendant,' said Van; 'as, of course, do many who serve in the Banners.'

Silva narrowed her eyes. 'Can he be trusted? Perhaps I shouldn't be revealing secrets to someone who worships Edmond.'

'Well?' said Naxor.

'Is this what it's come to?' said Sohul. 'Are we actually considering opposing the most powerful deity in existence?' He shook his head. 'I didn't sign up for this. It's insanity, as well as deeply and profoundly blasphemous. The Blessed Second Ascendant is on a level above us all; he is the builder, the creator...'

'But you've already fought the Ascendants,' said Corthie. 'You led Fordians against them in Yoneath.'

'I know,' snapped Sohul, 'but that was different; I was under contract to you, and was obeying the rules of that contract, as any in the Banners would do. And, to be accurate, I was fighting soldiers employed by the Ascendants; I didn't actually oppose Leksandr or Arete.'

Van gave a wry smile. 'It might be time to pick a side.'

Sohul glared at him. 'Have you?'

'Yes.'

'You've always lacked respect for the gods,' said Sohul, 'and I've always overlooked it, because you were my commanding officer, and a friend. But to rebel against the Ascendants? I don't think I can.'

'My mistress is the Third Ascendant,' said Silva. 'Could you work for her?'

Sohul stared at the ground, a cigarette burning in his fingers.

'It might not come to that,' said Corthie.

They turned to him.

'I can't help Belinda, I'm sorry. I have to find Aila and Kelsey. I've let them down, and I need to put it right before I can think about doing anything else.'

Silva looked at him in horror. 'But my mistress is depending on you. Every day that passes in Alea Tanton brings her closer to danger. She risked everything to revive you in the cavern of Fordamere; how can you even consider abandoning her when she needs you the most?'

Corthie said nothing, his guts churning with a barrage of emotions.

'May I speak?' said Naxor.

'I'd rather you didn't,' said Silva, folding her arms across her chest.

'All the same,' Naxor went on, 'I do have an opinion. Firstly, I think Silva is right. What good will finding Aila and Kelsey do if we lose the worlds we come from? We've been lucky, and this may be our last opportunity to stop the Ascendants. Secondly, even if we fail in our primary objective, there will be Quadrants in Alea Tanton, Quadrants that we can use to rescue Aila and Kelsey, and then use to get off this cursed world. I do not intend to die on Lostwell.' He glanced at Silva. 'I am well aware that neither you nor Belinda will ever trust me again, and I can live with that. Having said that, I am also perfectly capable of looking after my own interests. If the Ascendants find a way to operate the Sextant, then none of us here will have a home to go to.'

'I have to agree,' said Van. 'I promised Kelsey I'd find her, and if we sail up the west coast, then Alea Tanton's on the way to where we think she might be. Could we really pass the city and not stop to help?'

'Belinda should flee,' said Corthie.

Silva shook her head. 'That, her Majesty will never do. She has fled in the past, but she has changed since those days. I think she means to stay until the end.'

'How often does she contact you?'

'Every other day, usually.'

'What?' said Naxor. 'Her vision can reach all the way down here?'

Silva smiled at him. 'Yes. Her powers are improving all the time. She could be in your head right now and you wouldn't know.'

Naxor's eyes widened. 'She isn't, is she?'

'No, but she could be.'

'The next time she speaks to you,' said Corthie, 'tell her to steal a Quadrant and come to Capston, and then we can rescue Aila and Kelsey, and get out of here.'

'Were you not listening to me?' said Silva. 'Her Majesty would never agree to that, and you should be ashamed to have suggested it. Your world is in mortal peril; would you go back there and blithely hope that your troubles were at an end? It is too late for that; the Ascendants are aware of the Holdfasts, and they will not stop until your family have been destroyed. They cannot tolerate the idea of mortals with powers that can match them.'

'Hypothetically,' said Naxor, 'if we agreed to go as far as Alea Tanton; then how would we fund the trip?'

'I have plenty of gold,' said Silva; 'more than enough for the voyage. For the two mercenaries among us, I'd be happy to draw up a contract that would see both of you well rewarded for your service. Sohul, your honour would remain intact if you worked for the Third Ascendant; she is the Queen of Khatanax, the supreme sovereign authority on Lostwell, and a far more worthy object of your pious devotion.'

'I don't need a contract,' said Van, 'though I appreciate the offer. As Sohul knows, I've always had misgivings about our illustrious Ascendants. I've seen them throw their weight around, suppressing worlds and peoples, and crushing anyone who opposes them. They will do to the hidden worlds what they have already done to Lostwell and Dragon Eyre, and the thought sickens me. When I watched Corthie fight Leksandr and Arete, a small glimmer of hope arose in me, that maybe the Ascendants could be beaten. We lost that day, but with Corthie and Belinda together? The two of them destroyed the Banner of the Golden

Fist, and they could beat Leksandr and Arete. I don't need paid for this; I'm happy to do it for free.'

'So, we may have a compromise,' said Naxor. 'We sail north, as Corthie wishes, but we go up the west coast, which will bring us close to Alea Tanton, and the Ascendants. Let's take a boat to Cape Armour, and decide what to do from there. Can we agree to that?'

Silva glared at him. 'I still don't trust you, despite your words. But, I acquiesce in this plan.'

'Me too,' said Van.

Corthie and Sohul glanced at each other.

'I would like a contract,' said the lieutenant. 'It would go some way to assuage my doubts.'

'Of course,' said Silva. 'I shall have one drawn up before we leave.' She turned to Corthie. 'And you?'

'You lose nothing by agreeing,' said Naxor, 'and you'll have plenty of time to think about it on the voyage.'

Corthie ground his teeth, then picked up the bottle of raki and filled his mug.

'Fine,' he muttered. 'Let's go to Cape Armour.'

CHAPTER 16
APOLOGY

F ordian Wastes – 22nd Luddinch 5252
    As a child, Sable had loved walking through the desert. Her parents had often taken her to the eastern region of the Holdings, where the grasslands turned into mile after mile of golden sands, a land where wild beasts roamed. Sometimes, when she had been gazing into the desert, she had tried to imagine what it would be like to be completely alone, cut off in the middle of the wasteland, and the thought had sent a thrill of horror down her spine.

The reality was worse than she had imagined. That went not only for the desert, but for her parents too. They had never told her that she was not their natural daughter, that she was, in fact, the illegitimate child of Godfrey Holdfast and Queen Miranda of the Holdings. Deep down, she still thought of herself as a Blackhold, not a Holdfast, and she had never properly digested what it meant to be the daughter of a queen.

She glanced up at the horizon, a hand shielding her eyes from the rays of the sun. Her parentage hardly mattered, not when she was about to expire from dehydration and sunstroke. On the previous day, she had walked until she had collapsed, and then she had awoken in the middle of the cold night, and walked again. The sun had arisen and still she walked, trudging along the hard, dusty ground.

The last time she had thought she was about to die, in the aftermath of Maisk's death, she had called on the name of Daphne. This time was different. Instead of beseeching her help, Sable used the memory of her half-sister to keep her going. If Daphne wouldn't give up, then neither would she, no matter how pointless and hopeless the outlook. No one would ever be able to accuse her of being weak, of giving up. She would walk until she fell over and couldn't get up again, and then she would die.

Despite her situation, she regretted nothing. If she could do it all again, she wouldn't change a thing. She had been right to keep the existence of the Quadrant a secret from Blackrose, and if the black dragon disagreed, then the black dragon was wrong. How Blackrose had discovered the truth was another matter, and Sable went over everything, trying to grasp an inkling of what had gone awry with her plan. Maddie couldn't have told her, nor Millen, and Sable herself had been very careful, yet she was convinced that the black dragon hadn't been bluffing. She had known.

Daphne pushed her way back into her mind. Why couldn't she shake the memory of her half-sister? She had barely met the woman, let alone got to know her, and yet her thoughts kept returning to the matriarch of the family. One image in particular stood out from the others – the moment Daphne had realised that Sable was a Holdfast. Prior to that, Daphne had been calling for her execution, but when Kelsey had told her the truth, her expression had undergone an immediate transformation, and she had looked at Sable with something approaching sympathy and kinship. The Empress, of course, had been outraged by Daphne's change of mind; Sable was a traitor who deserved to die, regardless of which family she belonged to, but the Holdfast matriarch had stood her ground, and her half-sister had lived.

Only to die in the Fordian Wastes, she thought. Still, every day beyond the one on which she should have been executed was a day extra, and she had been glad of the time she had spent with Sanguino.

Her bond with the dragon had made her last month one of the best in her life. Together they had flown, when everyone else had thought it impossible. They had shown the doubters; they had killed Grimsleep, and no one could ever take that away.

She pushed the dark red dragon from her thoughts, aware that it was one of the few things that might cause her steps to falter. She loved him; it was undeniable. Like him, she was broken and maimed, and they each had a past in which they had done things that had tarnished how everyone else viewed them; but despite that, they had believed in each other.

She fell to her knees, swayed, then toppled over, lying on the baked surface of the desert. The sun was climbing the eastern sky, and the heat was growing with every minute that passed.

Get up, said the imaginary voice of Daphne in her head. Rest when you are dead.

Sable struggled back to her feet, her mind swimming in a cloud of exhaustion.

'Thank you,' she muttered. 'Thank you.'

'You're welcome,' said a voice in front of her.

She blinked, her vision blurry. Was there a dragon standing next to her? It was a trick of her mind, she told herself, then collapsed to the ground again. Something nudged her, something large and scaly.

'Are you able to climb onto my back?'

Sable opened her eyes again. Something was blocking out the rays of the sun.

'I would rather you didn't die,' said the voice. 'It would cause Sanguino pain.'

Sable focussed her eyes, and saw grey scales next to her. 'Ashfall?'

A gigantic head came down, and she felt the dragon's breath against her cheek.

'Are you really here?' said Sable.

'I am.'

'Why?'

'Sanguino said he cannot live without you. It is weak of him to think in such a way, but I respect him, and when he requested that I fly out here to look for you, I could not refuse. He needs you.'

Sable drew herself up into a sitting position, the words of the dragon sinking into her. She glanced around, as if remembering where she was. She went to pull on her battle-vision, then realised that she had been burning it for hours.

Ashfall's eyes were watching her. 'Did you hear what I said?'

'Yes.'

'Sanguino has defied Blackrose in this matter. She ordered that no one attempt to rescue you.'

'Will you be in trouble with her?'

'No. Blackrose is Sanguino's mother, therefore she is responsible for his actions. He asked me to go, and she will have to take responsibility for that. If there is any conflict, it lies between them. Are you well enough to climb onto my back? I have never carried an insect that way, and I will not offer again.'

Sable placed her hands against the grey scales of a forelimb and pulled herself up.

'How long were you looking for me?'

'Since dawn,' said Ashfall. 'Blackrose refused to specify your exact location, and I have covered a hundred miles of desert.'

'Does she know you left to search for me?'

'She was sleeping when Sanguino made his request. Some of the wounds she picked up in the pits are quite severe, and I think she will need time to recover. As will you, by the look of you.'

Sable put her right foot onto the dragon's forelimb and climbed up. The sun resumed its ferocious glare as soon as she had moved out of the shadow cast by Ashfall, and she felt dizzy again.

'Hold on tight,' said the dragon.

She extended her long, grey wings, and ascended into the air. Sable grasped the folds around the dragon's shoulders, the breeze helping to lessen the heat from the sun. Ashfall gained altitude, then soared away to the north. Sable closed her eyes, and concentrated on not falling off.

'Did you truly lie to Blackrose?' said the dragon as they flew.

'Yes.'

'That was foolish.'

'It was a calculated risk.'

'Are you sorry?'

'No. I would do it again.'

A low sound like laughter came from the dragon. They flew on, and Sable retreated within herself, her grip on the dragon's shoulder the sole thought in her mind. The minutes passed, until she had lost all track of time, then they began to descend.

'Are we there?'

'Not yet.'

Sable opened her eyes, and saw the high cliffs approaching. Behind them, one of the volcanoes was spewing fresh torrents of lava down the steep mountainside. Ashfall landed on a flat ledge close to the base of the cliffs, and turned her long neck to look at Sable.

'Dismount.'

'Do I have to walk from here?'

'No. I will carry you in my forelimb.'

'Why?'

'Sanguino will be waiting, and his one good eye will be watching. I do not want to arouse any feelings of envy within him, therefore I will not carry you into the tomb on my back. You are his insect after all, not mine.'

Sable released her grip and slid down from the dragon's back. She staggered, then Ashfall's talons grasped round her waist, keeping her upright. The grey dragon took off again, and they soared over the first river of lava, low enough for Sable to feel the wave of heat that rose up from it. She coughed as the vapours enveloped them, then Ashfall started to climb as the tomb openings came into view. At least a dozen dragons were watching, their heads poking out of their homes as Ashfall approached. Sanguino lifted his neck as he caught sight of her.

Ashfall hovered by the entrance to the tomb.

'I have done as you asked,' said the grey dragon. 'I have brought your insect back.'

'You have my thanks, Ashfall,' said Sanguino. 'I will not forget this.'

Ashfall tilted her head, then dropped Sable onto the ledge at the entrance of the tomb. The grey dragon turned, then climbed away out of sight.

'Sable,' said Sanguino, his face nuzzling her as she crouched on the rough floor of the cavern. 'My rider; you are back. If you had died, I... I would have...'

'I know,' she said. 'Thank you for sending Ashfall to look for me.'

'I would have done anything to see you return to me. If Ashfall hadn't gone, I would have walked.'

'I was over a hundred miles away; you would have died.'

'Without you, my rider, I'd rather be dead. It's not just about the flying, though that is very important to me. You are dear to my heart, Sable.'

She smiled. 'And you are dear to mine.'

His good eye narrowed a little. 'Blackrose doesn't know that Ashfall went for you; she has been sleeping since yesterday evening. You shouldn't have lied to her.'

'I happen to disagree.'

'An apology to her would be in order.'

'I disagree with that too, but I'll do it for you.'

Maddie ran over, a waterskin in her hands. She passed it to Sable, and the Holdfast woman grabbed it and drank, her hands trembling from exhaustion.

'You look a right state,' said Maddie. 'Still, better than being dead. Blackrose is going to freak out when she sees you, though. Are you hungry? Stupid question, I guess. Millen is heating something up for you on the fire.'

'What about you?' said Sable, resting the waterskin on her knee for a moment. 'Are you in trouble with her Highness as well?'

'No. She blames you, completely. To her, I'm an innocent victim of your manipulation.'

'Good. Let's ensure we keep it that way.'

'But... well, it isn't really true, though, is it? I knew what we were doing.'

Sanguino's green eye glowed. 'It's not right that you should take all of the blame, my rider.'

'It is right,' said Sable. 'It was my idea; my plan. Maddie and Millen had no choice in the matter.'

'But I've used the Quadrant a dozen times to get supplies,' said Maddie.

'Yes, but you didn't know how to use it to rescue her. You would have tried had you known.'

'What about before that? I knew you had it before Blackrose was captured at Yoneath.'

'I was using my mind powers on you then.'

Maddie raised an eyebrow. 'Were you? I don't think so.'

'If I say I did, then I did, and that's all Blackrose needs to know. It's vital that your relationship with Blackrose isn't compromised. Let me take the blame, alright? Now, where's that food you promised me?'

Maddie helped Sable stand, and put an arm round her shoulder as they hobbled over to where Millen was sitting by the hearth. Sanguino turned and followed them, keeping his good eye on Sable the entire time. They sat by the fire, and Millen looked up from a pot that was bubbling over the flames.

'Sable,' he said. 'This seems familiar – me cooking your dinner while you're off doing crazy, reckless stuff.'

She smiled. 'Next time, tell me when the important games are on in the city.'

'I doubt there will be a next time. Blackrose said she's leaving for Dragon Eyre as soon as her wounds have healed. She blames you for those wounds as well, by the way.' He glanced at Maddie. 'She's going to go mental when she wakes up.'

'I will not let any harm come to Sable,' said Sanguino. 'Blackrose was too fast for me last time, and I didn't know what she was going to do. This time, I will be prepared.'

Millen spooned food from the pot into a bowl and passed it to Sable.

She took it, and began to eat, her throat sore, and her fingers still trembling. The warm food felt wonderful, and she devoured the contents of the bowl in minutes, then drank the rest of the waterskin.

'Like Blackrose,' she said, putting down the empty bowl, 'I'm going to need to sleep for a while. I've used up most of my battle-vision reserves, and when I relax, I'm liable to fall over.'

'I will protect you while you sleep, my rider,' said Sanguino. 'You need fear nothing.'

She smiled, then her eyes closed and she slid off the seat into unconsciousness.

She awoke in Sanguino's cavern, upon a low mattress with the dark red dragon's tail coiled round it. Raised voices were coming from somewhere else in the tomb.

'You're awake,' said Sanguino, his head resting on his forelimbs as he watched her.

'So too is Blackrose by the sound of it.'

'Indeed. She has discovered that you have returned.'

Sable stretched. 'How long was I asleep?'

'For a day and a night,' said the dragon. 'The dawn has come again.'

'That explains why I feel better. I'm thirsty, though.'

'There is water by the bed. Maddie left it there for you.'

She glanced down and saw the waterskin. Next to it was a pile of clean clothes, a hairbrush and another bowl filled with water, with a bar of soap next to it.

'I think she's trying to give me a hint,' Sable said. She sniffed what she had on. 'And she's not wrong. Let me get cleaned up, and then I'll face Blackrose.'

Sanguino turned, and went to the entrance of the cavern, blocking it with his bulk. Sable undressed, and washed. Her limbs were aching and stiff, and she scrubbed the sand and sweat from her skin, then gave her hair a clean in the bowl. She pulled on the clothes that Maddie had left her, and found a pack of cigarettes in a pocket, along with some matches. She lit one, and smoked it while she brushed her wet hair. It could do with a trim, she thought, wondering if she could trust Maddie to do a decent job with a pair of scissors.

She stubbed the cigarette out and stood, listening to the voices coming from the rest of the tomb. There were other dragons there, not just Blackrose.

'I'm ready,' she said to Sanguino.

The dark red dragon moved to the side and Sable walked to the entrance of the cavern. To her left, Deepblue and Broadwing were sitting in the long tunnel that led to the open air, while directly in front of her, Blackrose's head was sticking out of her own cavern.

'The traitor approaches,' said the black dragon, her red eyes burning as she stared at Sable. 'You should be dead.'

Sable put a hand on her hip. 'If I hadn't rescued you, *you* would be dead. I'm still waiting on a thank you for that.'

Maddie groaned from where she and Millen were sitting by the hearth.

'You see?' said Blackrose. 'Sable is not contrite. She is shameless. She lied to me and she doesn't care. We could have been in Dragon Eyre...'

'Yes, yes; I know,' said Sable. 'You could have been in Dragon Eyre ages ago, blah, blah. You know what, if you had, then you'd probably be dead. I did the right thing, and you can't admit it.' She shrugged. 'That's fine. I can live with your ingratitude for all that I've done for you.'

Flames flickered over Blackrose's jaws. 'Are you trying to provoke me?'

'I'm trying to make you see sense. Look at what we've achieved by being patient, instead of rushing off to Dragon Eyre at the first opportunity. We have supplies, but much more importantly, we have allies.' She pointed towards Deepblue and Broadwing, who were watching in silence. 'We have these two fine dragons, and we have Sanguino, who is able to fly again. And, if we wait a little longer, other dragons might join us.'

Blackrose's eyes burned as she stared at Sable. 'Wait even longer? Just who do you think you are? I am going home, to Dragon Eyre. My home, not yours. You have nothing to do with this expedition; you are not in charge, and it was not your decision to take.'

Sanguino nudged Sable's arm. 'Didn't you promise to say something to Blackrose?'

'Of course,' said Sable. 'Blackrose, I apologise for lying to you.'

'Another lie?' said Blackrose. 'Do you even know how to be sincere, witch?'

'I lied to you, because I believed you would take my Quadrant and immediately go to Dragon Eyre. Do you deny it?'

'A Holdfast took my Quadrant; taking yours would seem fair.'

'I said, do you deny it? Answer me.'

'I do not deny it,' said Blackrose; 'that is what I would have done.'

'You would have gone to Dragon Eyre unprepared? Right. And now you will be going with at least three other dragons, plenty of supplies, and a ton of gold.'

'What gold?'

'The gold I accumulated before I came to the Catacombs. What did you think I was doing during that period? Sleeping?'

Blackrose turned towards the hearth. 'Maddie, have you heard about this?'

'No,' said Maddie. 'Sable's never mentioned any gold to me.'

'Of course not,' said Sable. 'I was waiting to tell you all. My little secret. To be honest, you've kind of ruined the surprise, but never mind. Blackrose, will you admit to me that the circumstances of you going now are immeasurably better than if you'd gone earlier?'

'They are not "immeasurably" better, witch.'

Sable smirked. 'But they are better, yeah?'

'Where is the gold?'

'Answer my question and I might tell you.'

'Fine. I admit it. The preparations you and the others have made will stand us in good stead, but that does not excuse what you did. You don't trust me. You are a shameless liar, working for your own advantage.'

'I risked my life to save you. I have risked my life several times for you and your cause. I hardly see how dying would be to my own advantage.'

'But why?'

'Because I want to go to Dragon Eyre with you, but I didn't want to go unprepared. I knew you'd take my Quadrant, so I had to keep it a secret from you. It's really as simple as that.'

Blackrose remained silent for a moment, then scraped her claws across the floor of the cavern. 'You will not be coming to Dragon Eyre with me. You have proved that you are unworthy and a liar.'

'Then you'll also have to do without Sanguino and the gold. Your choice.'

Maddie jumped to her feet. 'Hold on a minute; let's all calm down. There's no need to make rash threats. Blackrose, please think about this. I know Sable lied to you, but you've already punished her by leaving her in the desert, and she has apologised. We can't go to Dragon Eyre without Sanguino; he's your son.'

'I can speak for myself,' said the dark red dragon. 'Mother, what Sable did was wrong, and I do not excuse it; but, if you leave her here, then I will stay by her side. She is my rider; would you be separated from Maddie? You have admitted that her plan has brought us many benefits. If you would hear my advice, I would tell you to accept her apology and forgive her.'

Blackrose turned her head away.

'What if Sable promised not to lie to you again?' said Maddie.

'Her promises are worthless,' said Blackrose. 'I believe that she could stand there and swear on all she holds dear that she would never utter a lie again, but she would not mean it.'

'And you would be right,' said Sable.

'You see?' said the black dragon, her tone almost mournful. 'Sable is incapable of sincerity. Her only virtue is that she can admit it.'

'Think how useful I would be to you on Dragon Eyre,' said Sable. 'I could help win your realm back, and you know it.'

'May I speak?' said Deepblue, her voice soft compared to Blackrose's.

They turned to her.

'Sable has been a good friend to me,' the small dragon said. 'In the Catacombs, I am treated with nothing but contempt, but Sable made me feel wanted, and useful. I know she lies, but as she said to me, humans have their lies just as we have our fire and claws. If you force her to stay here, Blackrose, then I will also stay. I will not betray my friendship with her.'

'She has bewitched you all!' Blackrose bellowed. 'Damn the Holdfasts. All the curses in the world would not suffice to satiate my anger.' She turned to Broadwing. 'And you?'

'I, uh, I will do as you say, Blackrose,' the big dragon said, bowing his head. 'You are the chief of the expedition.'

'Thank you, Broadwing,' said Blackrose. 'That settles it. I shall leave with Maddie and Broadwing, and Millen if he is willing. I have no need for disloyal companions.'

Maddie looked panicked, her eyes wild. 'Can I speak to you alone, please?'

'I already know what you will say, rider.'

'Even so, please?'

Blackrose sighed, then retreated into her cavern, Maddie hurrying after her.

Sable nodded. 'That went better than I thought.'

Millen laughed as he walked over. 'Do you ever back down?'

'Not when I'm right, and I'm usually right.'

'You have a stubborn streak, my rider,' said Sanguino. 'I sense it will get us into a lot of trouble. However, without your stubbornness, I doubt I would have flown again. I do wish you had made your apology sound a little more sincere.'

Sable lit a cigarette. 'Thank you for what you said, Deepblue; I appreciate it. And Broadwing, your loyalty to Blackrose does you proud.'

'What about the ton of gold?' said Millen.

'What about it?'

'Is it real?'

Sable looked shocked. 'Are you accusing me of making it up? That hurts, Millen. Of course it's real. I didn't weigh it though, so it might not be exactly a ton.'

'How did you get it?'

She shrugged. 'I had a Quadrant and my vision powers. I could make up a story about how difficult it was, but no, it was easy.'

He shook his head. 'That day at the Southern Pits, when you talked me into leaving with you; you were using me, yeah? You didn't care about me.'

'I do now.'

'But you didn't back then?'

'Sorry. I told you at the time that you shouldn't trust me. Does it bother you?'

'You changed my life; you turned it inside out, without a single thought for how it would affect me. All the same, I'm glad you did. I don't regret a single moment.'

The light coming from the tomb entrance dimmed for a moment as another dragon landed. It was Ashfall. She folded her wings in and strode forward, taking care to ignore Broadwing and Deepblue.

'Where is Blackrose?' she said.

'She is speaking to her rider,' said Sanguino.

Ashfall turned her glance to Sable. 'She hasn't killed you, I see. Good. I'm glad my efforts yesterday morning were not in vain.'

'Do you bear a message from your father?' said Sanguino.

'No. My father knows I am here, but he does not approve. The message I bear is from myself, and it is in response to a question your rider asked me. I was due to give my answer yesterday, but I thought it could wait until today.'

'The message is for me?' said Sable.

'It is.'

'Can it wait another few minutes? Blackrose should be out shortly, once she has made her decision.'

'Very well,' said the grey dragon.

Seeing them side by side, Sable noticed how sleek and graceful Ashfall was compared to Broadwing and Deepblue. Broadwing was bigger, but somehow seemed to carry himself in an ungainly manner, as if self-conscious, while Deepblue was the smallest adult dragon in the Catacombs, and had a defensive stance that bore testimony to the repeated bullying she had experienced throughout her life.

'What a magnificent array of dragons,' Sable said. 'Sanguino, Broadwing, Ashfall and Deepblue. I'm proud to call you all my friends. Each one of you is different, but each also possesses their own talents. Courageous, noble, graceful and intelligent. We could do great things together.'

Ashfall laughed. 'And is your talent to flatter dragons, witch?'

'It's one of them; I have a few.'

Maddie appeared in the entrance of Blackrose's cavern.

'Is she coming out?' said Sable.

'She is,' said Maddie. 'You owe me one, Sable. You'd better not let me down.'

Blackrose's head emerged from the shadows of the cavern. She stared at Sable for a moment, then noticed the presence of Ashfall. She tilted her head in welcome.

'Are you here to see me, Ashfall?' she said.

'I'm here to give my answer to Sable. Two days ago, she asked if I would like to join your expedition to Dragon Eyre. Today, I am here to say yes. If you'll have me, I will come.'

Sable grinned. 'That's great news. Fantastic. I...'

'Yes,' said Blackrose. 'It is indeed good news. I also have news. My rider has, against my own judgement, persuaded me to allow Sable to accompany us. I despise liars, and Sable is a proven liar. However, rather than risk the breaking of our company, I will tolerate her presence as Sanguino's rider.'

Sable smiled again. 'Thank you.'

'I have a few rules.'

'I'm listening.'

'Firstly, the Quadrant will remain with Maddie. You are not to touch it without my express permission. Secondly, you will guide us to the gold you talked about, and deliver it into my keeping. And finally, rather than try to extract a useless promise from you regarding your lack of sincerity, I shall make a promise to you. If I discover that you have lied to me again at any time in the future, I will rip your head off without debate or warning. You must accept these conditions if you wish to come with us to Dragon Eyre. Do you accept?'

Sable waited a moment, making a show of looking as if she were considering Blackrose's words, as the five dragons stared at her. The Quadrant clause was fine; if she truly needed to use it, she would take it and hang the consequences. The gold she had already agreed to deliver, so that was no problem, either. As for the threat regarding her lies, well, all she had to do was make sure she never got caught again.

She bowed her head a fraction. 'I accept.'

CHAPTER 17

THE EASTERN TOWER

Alea Tanton, Tordue, Western Khatanax – 29th Luddinch 5252

'Bloody dragons,' muttered Arete. 'I'll have to go in person.'

'That seems a little excessive,' said Leksandr, sipping wine from a tall-stemmed glass. 'Do we not have several thousand Banner soldiers under our command?'

'If there were just one case to deal with, then yes, but the rogue beast hiding in the forests of Kinell will also need to be addressed. The authorities in Kin Dai are frothing at the mouth, demanding assistance. Normally, I would ignore the hysterical ravings of mortals, but from the few witnesses who survived the attack on the camp, it appears to have been carried out by the same dragon that was involved with the other in the fighting at Yoneath; a young, silver female. I'll handle that one first, then proceed to the Catacombs.'

'When will you be leaving?' said Belinda.

Arete narrowed her eyes. 'Immediately. That way, you'll have less time to warn them.'

'I have already warned the mortal that I wish to be left unharmed.'

'Indeed. However, the motley collection of rebels and malcontents do not appear to have heeded your words. They are still there, skulking in their filthy tomb. I entered the mind of a weak, runt dragon named

Deepblue, and as far as I can see, the black dragon hates the Holdfast witch, and I'm almost tempted to watch them destroy each other. Were it not for the riots that are consuming the city, I would do just that.'

'The mortals want their pit dragon back,' said Leksandr.

'Yes, but the black-scaled beast shall be gifted to the Bloodflies,' said Arete, 'not handed back to the Deadskins. It was Latude's meddling that caused this situation – one dragon for each team, it's the only fair solution.'

'Perhaps we should execute Latude,' said Leksandr. 'He is bitter and resentful, and has caused us nothing but problems.'

'I agree,' said Arete. 'Then we can hang his corpse up for all to see, and blame him for the riots.'

'Do it upon your return from the Catacombs,' said Leksandr. 'You enjoy these tasks more than I. Third Ascendant, do you have anything to say on the matter?'

'No.'

'Then we are in agreement. Let's keep it to ourselves for the moment; there's little point in alarming Latude, and the other gods might get nervous if they knew.'

'Maybe we should get rid of Felice at the same time,' said Arete; 'make a clean sweep.'

'I'd rather not,' said Leksandr. 'She may be incompetent, but she shields us from having to deal with the day to day running of the city; I have no time for the tedium that would involve.'

Arete stood up from the table. 'We'll see.' She gestured to a guard by the door. 'Bring in the squad.'

The guard bowed low, 'Yes, your Highness.'

He opened a set of doors and a dozen heavily armed Banner troopers in steel plate strode into the dining room. They lined up in front of the three Ascendants and bowed.

'Is that all you're taking?' said Leksandr.

'It's all I need.' She withdrew a Quadrant from her robes and smirked. 'Behave yourselves while I'm gone.'

The air shimmered, and Arete and the dozen soldiers disappeared.

Leksandr chuckled. 'I do believe that Arete is almost excited to be going on a dragon hunt.' He glanced at Belinda. 'Do you intend to warn them again?'

'No. I sent word to my old friend when we assumed that Sable Holdfast was dead. Now that we know the truth, I have nothing else to say to them. If they choose to ally themselves to Sable, then I don't want anything more to do with them.'

He raised an eyebrow. 'You make it sound personal.'

'It is personal. Sable Holdfast is a sworn enemy.'

'There you go, thinking like a mortal again.' He shook his head. 'In a hundred years, every mortal you know will be dead; friends and enemies alike. You should try to look beyond your personal feelings; they are transient, fleeting, just like the mortals. Arete, on the other hand, will still be around in a thousand years from now; perhaps you should worry more about her enmity.'

Belinda nodded. 'I am still learning.'

'I know, and you are making mistakes. One thing, however, you may have got right – your intuition about the Sextant. I have pondered your words, and I now believe that you are correct; something, some part of the device, has been deliberately removed to render it inoperable. I assume it was you who removed it, Third Ascendant.'

'That assumption is probably correct.'

'It could be anything – a cog, a wheel, a rod; and there are several locations on the Sextant where such a part could be placed. In fact, more than one part might be missing. I intend to search Shawe Myre again; that is the most likely place where you would have hidden such a part.'

'That seems logical.'

'Indeed. We can rule out Yoneath, as it seems unlikely that you would have placed the missing part so close to the rest of the device. It is imperative that we find it before Lord Bastion returns.'

Belinda nodded. She had been keeping all thoughts of Bastion, Edmond, and her vow out of her mind. Corthie was on his way, and she had to hold out until he had time to arrive in Alea Tanton. Silva had told her of Corthie's doubts and hesitation, but Belinda had faith in him, faith that he would not abandon her. She wondered if Leksandr would lend her the Quadrant again; that way she could bring Corthie and the others directly to Alea Tanton, and they could strike while the Sixth Ascendant was alone.

'What happened to Theodora, the First Ascendant?' she said.

Leksandr stared at her in silence for a long moment. 'Perhaps you should ask Lord Bastion that when he gets here.'

'Why don't you just tell me?'

'It is not my... place to divulge such information.'

'She's dead though, isn't she? The First Ascendant is dead?'

'Oh yes. Indubitably. Very dead.'

'How did she die?'

Leksandr sipped his wine. 'The most blessed, holy, divine, sacred Second Ascendant killed her.'

Belinda frowned. 'Edmond? But why?'

Leksandr raised his hands. 'That's all I'm going to say about that. Arete may wish to tell you more; that is up to her, but I shall refrain.'

'Is it a secret?'

'The outcome – no; everyone knows that the First Ascendant is dead. The cause? Perhaps. I would be lying if I said I knew the whole story; there are secrets that Lord Edmond has never revealed to me, and I do not wish to add to the speculation and ill-informed gossip that surround the events. Now, if you'll please excuse me, I wish to begin my meditations on the missing part of the Sextant.'

Belinda stood. 'I shall leave you to your work. May I borrow your Quadrant?'

'Unfortunately,' he said, 'I will not be able to lend you my Quadrant again. The risk of Arete discovering our secret is simply too high. I'm sure you understand.'

Belinda hid her disappointment. 'I do.'

Leksandr bowed his head. 'You have my gratitude, Third Ascendant.'

She walked to the door, and the guard opened it for her. She went through to the stairs that descended through the western tower of the residence and paused. She was at a loose end. Corthie was still a few days away, and without access to a Quadrant, she would have to await his arrival. He'll come, she told herself; he wouldn't betray her; he was like a brother, and he wouldn't let her down. An idea came to her and she set off. She went down the stairs and kept going, passing the floor where she and Arete had their quarters. She rarely ventured from the western tower, and there were still parts of the Governor's residence that she had never seen.

Soldiers, courtiers and servants halted and bowed low to her as she passed. Wearing her long flowing robes, she looked the part of an Ascendant – regal and unapproachable. The Banner armourers were based on the ground floor of the main wing of the residence, and she strode along the marble-lined hallways until she could hear the noise coming from their workshop. She entered a large chamber, and a dozen Banner artificers paused from their work to bow.

'Your Majesty,' said the chief artificer; 'you honour us with your presence.'

The chamber was filled with workbenches, and shelves were loaded with ballistae parts and piles of armour and weapons. A forge sat at the rear of the chamber beneath a wide chimney, and its coals were glowing red.

'I am here about the weapon I sent downstairs for you.'

'Of course, your Majesty,' said the chief artificer. 'I have had my best men working on it.'

'Is it ready?'

'Unfortunately not, your Majesty. Let me show you.'

He led her to a crowded workbench, and removed a sheet that had been covering something.

'We're having to completely rebuild it, your Majesty. The greenhide talons themselves are still sound, but the wooden and leather parts were worn out. We're replacing all of those parts with freshly forged steel where possible, and will be welding the talons to a new head-piece. Altogether, it will be a far more formidable weapon when we have finished with it; it should last a century, or longer. Its weight will also be increased, but I trust that this will not be a problem?'

Belinda glanced at the pieces laid out on the workbench. A new metal handle was lying on the surface – a long rod of steel, with an engraved pattern of leaves and vines running down it. Next to it lay the three greenhide talons, along with a new curved steel spike that would be attached to the back of the head-piece.

'The weight will be fine,' she said.

'As you can see, your Majesty, most of the parts are here; the weapon merely needs to be assembled, and then some further decoration can be added, along with a new leather grip and strap. It will be fit for an Ascendant by the time we're through with it. I estimate it will be finished in a few days. Does it have a name, your Majesty? If so, we can engrave that upon it.'

'It is called the Clawhammer.'

The chief artificer nodded. 'There is, ah, a rumour, your Majesty, concerning this weapon. Some say that it was used to destroy the Banner of the Golden Fist at the Falls of Iron, and then it was seen in action against the Banner of the Black Crown in Yoneath. Is the rumour true, your Majesty?'

'Yes. I salvaged it from the cavern of Fordamere after its previous owner was slain. It used to belong to Corthie Holdfast.'

The chamber fell into utter silence as the artificers listened.

'Is that a problem?' she said.

'No, your Majesty,' said the chief artificer. 'The Holdfast champion was an enemy, but he had earned the respect of the Banners before he died. He was a worthy foe. We shall ensure that the work is carried out to our highest standards.'

'Thank you. Send a message when it is ready.'

The artificers bowed low.

Belinda left the workshop and began to retrace her steps to the western tower. She paused for a moment, then turned, heading towards the tower at the opposite end of the residence instead. Latude was imprisoned within a room there, and if he was going to be executed, then she wanted to see if he was holding onto any useful information first.

She entered the eastern tower, passing more soldiers who bowed before her. They asked her no questions, allowing her to walk where she pleased. She ascended to the second floor, where a row of locked chambers sat next to the stairwell. Two soldiers standing guard in the passageway glanced at her, but said nothing. She would need them to unlock the door to Latude's chamber, and she was thinking of a suitable reason when someone began thumping on the inside of one of the other doors.

She frowned. She hadn't thought that there were any other prisoners kept within the eastern tower.

'Belinda?' came a muffled voice from within the other room. 'Belinda; are you there?'

Belinda walked towards the door where the voice was coming from, her heart rate rising. It was Vana; she recognised the voice. Vana was in the Governor's residence. She glanced at the two soldiers.

'Open this door,' she said. 'I wish to speak to the prisoner.'

The soldiers bowed, and one approached with a set of keys. He selected the correct one and unlocked the door. Belinda pushed it open.

'Belinda!' cried Vana from the doorway. 'You're here to release me? At last.'

Belinda walked into the chamber and shut the door behind her.

Vana frowned. She looked rough – her clothes were soiled from travelling, and her eyes were tired and wide.

'What are you doing?' she said to Belinda. 'Aren't you here to let me out?'

'How long have you been in here, Vana?'

'Four days,' the demigod said. 'I was hiding in Alea Tanton, and then soldiers arrested me and brought me here. Didn't you know?'

'No.'

'You have to get me out; I'm going crazy in here. I've been given hardly anything to eat or drink, and they've not even allowed me to take a bath or change my clothes.'

'Have you been questioned?'

'What? Em, no, not really. A god was here; she came to see me when I arrived, but no one since then. I don't understand; I know I was in the Falls of Iron, but so were you, and you're free. Are the Ascendants going to have me killed? I've done nothing wrong.'

'Sit down for a moment,' said Belinda; 'let me think.'

Belinda took a seat, but Vana began pacing up and down the narrow chamber. It was sparsely furnished, with just a low bed and a couple of chairs, and the window was barred.

'I know you left Kin Dai a while ago,' said Belinda. 'What happened then?'

'I sailed to Capston, and stayed there, but after a few days I could sense the presence of agents – demigods, I think – searching the town, and I was worried I would be discovered, so I got another ship, this time to Alea Tanton, and I hid there instead. I was living in a horrible little place, but I thought I was safe, but then soldiers burst through my door and dragged me here.'

'And the god who visited you? Who was it?'

'She's called Felice. She came here an hour after I'd arrived. She didn't ask me any questions, though.'

'She didn't need to; she has vision powers.'

'Then she must know that I'm innocent.'

Belinda's gaze fell. 'I doubt she's interested in you, Vana, though your powers are probably the reason you're still alive.'

'That's how I knew you were in the passageway outside,' she said; 'I could sense you.'

Belinda said nothing. If Felice had read Vana's mind, then she would know Corthie was still alive, and she would know that Naxor was with him, and that Naxor knew how to get to the City of Pella. Like Silva, Vana had powers that were unusual, and Felice would have sensed that too.

'Did she say anything to you?'

'She told me that she was the governor of Khatanax, and that I would not be harmed if I cooperated, but then she left.'

'And did you sense her using her powers?'

Vana hesitated for a second. 'Yes. Am I in trouble?'

Belinda ignored the question, her mind racing through the possibilities. If Felice knew about Corthie, then why hadn't she reported that fact to Arete or Leksandr? Was she playing a game for her own advantage? The Ascendants could read Felice's thoughts, but perhaps she had buried the information, just as Leksandr had told her they could do. She glanced at Vana. The demigod knew too much, and was a threat to everything Belinda was trying to achieve. If Karalyn had been present, she would have been able to wipe Vana's memories clean of anything incriminating, but Belinda lacked that power.

'Why are you looking at me like that?' said Vana, taking a step back.

'I know what I need to do, but...'

'What do you mean? What do you need to do?'

'If the Ascendants discover what's inside your head, then everything I've done will have been for nothing.'

Vana's eyes widened. 'You're going to kill me? I knew you were ruthless, but I thought we were friends.'

'We've never been friends, Vana. You disliked me from the start.'

Vana fell to her knees, tears springing from her eyes. 'Please, Belinda, I'm begging you. None of this is my fault; I was brought to this accursed world by Naxor, and then Irno was killed and I had to go along with the others; I had no choice; I've never had a choice. And then Corthie was behaving like a pig, and I had to leave; it's not fair.' She sobbed. 'All I want to do is go home.'

'Be quiet.'

Vana fell into silence and closed her eyes, as if she expected her life to end at any moment.

Belinda stood. 'You're Aila's sister. I know I should kill you, but I can't.'

Vana burst into tears again.

'You must do something for me.'

'Anything,' said Vana.

'Tell me where Felice is right now. And Leksandr.'

'Alright.' She wiped her face, and her eyes glazed over. 'The Sixth Ascendant is in his rooms in the western tower. Felice is... she's inside a mansion two miles from here, in a large room with a dozen or so mortals; Banner officers I think, though it's hard to tell; they are armed but have no self-healing powers.' Her eyes cleared. 'What are you going to do?'

'If I can't kill you,' said Belinda; 'then someone else will have to die.'

Twenty minutes later, Belinda stepped down from a carriage, a soldier holding the door open for her. She glanced up at the entrance to Felice's mansion. The god governed Tordue from within its walls, preferring to live as far from Leksandr and Arete as was possible. Belinda had been inside a few times, always in the company of the other Ascendants, but it was more normal for Felice to be summoned to the Governor's residence if Arete or Leksandr needed to speak to her.

A courtier approached.

'Most blessed Third Ascendant,' he said, bowing. 'Governor Felice is not expecting you.'

'I know. Take me to her.'

A frown flickered across his features. 'Of course, your Majesty.'

He led her into the high-ceiling entrance hall of the mansion, where a few members of the god's staff were talking. They silenced at Belinda's approach, their glances following her. The courtier escorted her up a flight of stairs and along a corridor, then he knocked on a large door.

'One moment, please, your Majesty,' he said, then stepped inside.

Belinda waited outside the door. She was unarmed, but would find something to use, once she was face to face with Felice. A worry nagged at the back of her mind, and she released her vision powers, sending them back across the two miles to the Governor's residence. She checked in on Leksandr's study. The Ascendant was there, in his usual position, sitting cross-legged in front of the Sextant, meditating.

The courtier coughed. 'Governor Felice will see you now, your Majesty.'

Belinda walked into a large meeting room. Lady Felice was alone, standing by a window. Belinda glanced at the long meeting table. The surface was littered with papers and half-full glasses of water, as if a meeting had been interrupted.

'Third Ascendant,' said Felice; 'how may I assist you?'

Belinda waited until the door was closed behind her, then she strode towards Felice. She scanned the room as she walked, and noticed a long, iron poker by the cold fireplace. She would use that, she thought, but first she needed to know if Felice had told anyone else.

'You haven't been honest with me,' said Belinda, coming to a halt a few yards from the god.

Felice furrowed her brow. 'I don't know what you're talking about.'

'I think you do. You arrested a demigod and locked her in the eastern tower of the Governor's residence. Why didn't you tell me?'

'Ah. I see. You're talking about Lady Vana?'

'Yes. Answer my question.'

'Perhaps you should answer some of mine first, Third Ascendant. Why have you kept the fact that Corthie Holdfast is still alive from the Sixth and Seventh Ascendants? You denied having revived him, didn't you? You were lying. Furthermore, you must have known that Vana's cousin, a certain Lord Naxor, has used a Quadrant to travel to the salve world many times. Did your relationship with him cloud your judgement, or are you, in fact, a traitor?'

Belinda strode to the fireplace and picked up the poker. 'Who else knows?'

Felice laughed. 'You're going to kill me with that? Have you lost your mind, Third Ascendant?'

'Corthie once killed a god by smashing his skull in with an ashtray. I'm sure a poker will be able to do the same job. Who else knows?'

'But if I tell you that, you'll kill me. Put the poker down and talk.'

'What do you want?'

'Soldiers are waiting outside this room. One shout from me, and they'll charge in, and fill you full of crossbow bolts. Sit down, and let's discuss this like civilised people.'

Belinda walked forwards. 'It's too late for that, Felice. Tell me, or I'll rip it from your mind.'

Felice laughed again. 'Try. Go on, Third Ascendant; try to read my thoughts.'

Belinda pushed her vision out towards Felice, but her eyes were shielded by something – the thin, filmy discs that the gods used to protect their minds from invasion. Belinda blinked. Felice was prepared; she had known Belinda would be coming.

'You see?' said Felice. 'You can bash my brains in, but then you'll never know who else I told about Corthie and Naxor.'

'Or, I can hold you down and remove those... things from your eyes.'

Felice's expression changed a little. 'Now would be a very good time,' she muttered, taking a step back.

Belinda sprang at her, knocking her off her feet. She placed her free hand over the god's mouth as they fell to the floor, smothering her cry, then she laid the poker down on the ground. With a knee on the god's chest to pin her down, she reached for Felice's eyes.

The air shimmered behind her, and Belinda cried out as pain ripped through her. She glanced down, and saw the tip of a sword thrust through her chest, the blood dripping onto Felice's face. Something hit her, and she toppled to the side, the sword still lodged in her chest. She reached her hands up to push it out, then a boot kicked her in the face.

'You foolish child,' said Leksandr, standing over her with a Quadrant in his hand. 'An Ascendant you may be, Belinda, but you behave like a mortal child. You have betrayed us, and now it is time for you to pay.'

He pulled a knife from his robes and slammed it down, piercing Belinda's throat, the end of the blade embedding itself into the floorboards. Belinda squirmed and struggled, but the sword and the knife were draining her self-healing powers. Leksandr placed a boot onto her right hand, crushing it with his weight, then threw something to Felice.

'Help me get this on the Third Ascendant,' he said.

'Yes, your Grace,' Felice said. 'I was starting to get worried; I thought you weren't coming.'

'I was watching the entire thing from my study,' he said. 'I told you my plan would work. All we needed to do was wait for the Third Ascendant to incriminate herself.'

'Yes, your Grace. All the same, she nearly killed me.'

Leksandr laughed. 'I couldn't hear what was being said; I could only watch. As soon as she jumped at you, I activated the Quadrant. Sorry to say it, but you were a little expendable. Come on; don't look at me like that. This morning, Arete actually suggested that you be executed along with Latude, and I forbade it. I suspected you might prove useful, eventually.'

'Did you tell the Seventh Ascendant about Lady Vana, your Grace?'

'No. You were right to come to me with the information. Arete's temper would have probably led her to act rashly, but I imagine she will be very pleased with our day's work when she returns from hunting dragons.'

Belinda sensed Felice kneel next to her head, but her vision was blurry, and the pain excruciating. Her left hand was scrabbling at the knife lodged in her throat, but she was too weak to pull it out.

'Is it ready?' said Leksandr.

'I'm not sure,' said Felice. 'I've never attached a god-restrainer mask before.'

'It's quite simple,' said Leksandr. 'The nails go through the victim's eyes; you may have to push them in hard; give it a thump with your fist, then you do up the strap at the back.'

Felice swallowed. 'Are you sure, your Grace? She is the Third Ascendant.'

'She is a traitor and a liar. If it were up to me, I'd remove her head and mount it on the gates of Old Alea, but alas, Lord Bastion might not appreciate that when he returns. This way she lives, but will be utterly under our control. Proceed.'

A dark object was positioned above Belinda's face. Felice's hands were trembling, and she almost glanced away as she lowered the mask. Belinda stared up in panic as the two iron nails got closer to her eyes.

'For goodness' sake, Felice,' muttered Leksandr. 'Don't be squeamish. Give it a good hard push.'

Felice gagged, then brought the mask down, the nails ramming through the Third Ascendant's eyes.

Belinda screamed.

CHAPTER 18

GRATITUDE

Northern Kinell – 29th Luddinch 5252

'And then I dangled her over a pool of lava,' said Frostback, her head and forelimbs glistening in the sunlight.

Kelsey laughed. 'I wish I'd seen that.'

Aila frowned. 'I thought you liked Sable.'

'I do, well, I do sometimes; it depends what mood I'm in. She's the kind of person who needs to be dangled over lava occasionally. All the same, I'm glad she's alive. What happened next?'

Frostback tilted her head. 'I dropped her.'

'Oh,' said Kelsey.

'Her idiot protector Sanguino rescued her. Regardless, that's why I was disowned by my father. He had promised Blackrose that her pet insects would not be harmed, and I dishonoured him by trying to kill Sable.'

'Is that how you see us?' said Kelsey. 'As your pet insects?'

'In a way. You are the first humans I've really spoken to. Sable, Maddie and Millen all tried, but I didn't know them for very long, and each of them irritated me in their own way. I wonder if they are dead. Without Blackrose's protection, I cannot see how they could have survived in the Catacombs for long.'

'I hope that's not true,' said Aila. 'I don't know this Millen guy, but Maddie is a friend, and Sable? Well, Sable and I... I thought we could be friends. I don't know.'

'Sable doesn't have friends,' said Kelsey. 'Her past is littered with people she befriended, and then betrayed. I only stick by her because she's a Holdfast, albeit a reluctant one. But, you know, family's family.'

'She is a devious witch,' said Frostback.

'Still,' said Aila; 'she seemed lonely to me. As if, underneath that cocky and tough shell of hers, she's actually quite vulnerable.'

Kelsey cackled with laughter. 'You sound like one of her victims.'

Aila shrugged. 'That's what Belinda used to say.'

'And for once,' Kelsey said, 'that crazy god is correct.'

'Do you think you'll ever be able to forgive Belinda?'

'I don't know. What she did was terrible, but I got to know her a bit in Shawe Myre, and she seemed to have changed, to have grown. When Van rescued me in Yoneath, there was a moment when I was sure Belinda could have stopped him, but she didn't. One thing I am sure about – she doesn't care if I forgive her or not. She needs to forgive herself first.'

Frostback sniffed the air. It was a fine morning, the coolest day of the autumn so far. The forest stretching below them was turning orange and red in patches, next to the dark greens of the pine and spruce trees. A few clouds were drifting in from the east, the first clouds Aila had seen in months. She had almost forgotten what rain felt like, and was looking forward to it.

'I shall hunt,' said Frostback. 'The goats are getting harder to find, but I picked up the scent of some wild boars yesterday.'

'That sounds excellent,' said Kelsey.

Frostback glanced at Aila. 'And we must keep our mother-to-be well fed.'

'Thank you,' said Aila, remembering to show the gratitude that the dragon expected of her.

Frostback pulled her body from the cave and stretched her wings over the broad ledge. She turned her head to face them.

'Be good, my pet insects,' she said, then soared into the air.

They lifted their hands to shield their eyes from the swirling dust raised by her wings, then watched as she flew away to the west.

Kelsey chuckled.

'What's so funny?' said Aila.

'You, with your wide-eyed "thank you, Frostback." She has you wrapped round her little finger, well, she would if she had a little finger. Round her little claw.'

'What about you? You're happy to be a "pet insect."'

'How did Maddie become Blackrose's rider?'

'Is that a serious question? You heard what Frostback said – she swore that she'd never carry a human on her back.'

'That was just dragon hyperbole. I'll wear her down.'

'Knowing Maddie, that's probably how she did it.'

They walked to the entrance of the cave, and sat by the alcove, where a scorched and blackened circle lay, surrounded by small stones. Kelsey began to clear out the ashes from the previous evening's fire, while Aila stacked the remaining firewood.

'I wonder what Corthie's doing,' said Aila.

'Normally, I'd have a ready reply to such a question, but it seems weird to be discussing him with his girlfriend. The mother-to-be of his child.'

'You'll tell me if you have a vision about him, won't you?'

'Aye, but I've not had a proper vision in a while. I've tried looking into Frostback's eyes but I don't know if it works on dragons, and it only encourages the stupid lizard to think that I'm gazing at her in adoration.'

'How come you get to call her that, but you tell me off I say anything bad about her?'

Kelsey smirked. 'Because I'm going to be her rider.'

Frostback returned an hour later, carrying the carcass of a wild boar in her long talons. She dropped it onto the ledge, then landed.

Kelsey clapped her hands in joy. 'Roast pork tonight! Good job, o high protector of the insects.'

'I sense sarcasm in your tone,' Frostback said, 'and I do not like it.'

'That's tough, because I'm not going to change. And, strictly speaking, it was more a gentle teasing based upon feelings of affection, rather than sarcasm.'

Frostback stared blankly at her. 'You are a strange insect. Regardless, I have news, though nothing that should cause you any anxiety. I saw a small group of soldiers not too far from here, moving towards the lair. A mere dozen or so, but they have shiny steel armour that reminds me of the Banner soldiers I saw in Yoneath.'

Aila narrowed her eyes. 'Banner soldiers? Were they alone? Was anyone accompanying them?'

Frostback was silent for a moment, as if pondering. 'I did not think of that. I noticed the soldiers because their armour was glinting in the sun. There may have others with them who did not stand out. Sound advice, demigod. When I return to kill them, I will make sure that none escape. You can be quite wise at times, Aila; is that due to your extreme old age?'

Kelsey laughed.

'This isn't funny,' said Aila. 'If those soldiers belong to a Banner, then who sent them and how did they get so close to the lair without us spotting them?' She glanced at Frostback. 'You fly out two or three times a day; is this the first you've seen of them?'

'Yes, it is.'

Aila stood, and began pacing up and down the ledge. 'This could be bad, very bad.'

'You always say stuff like that,' said Kelsey. 'Try to be optimistic for once; you might like it.'

The demigod glared at her. 'Either the soldiers have just put their armour on, or they used a Quadrant to come here. If the second option is true, then it will have been a god who held the Quadrant; they would never entrust one to a soldier. If it's a god, then he or she will have been sent here to kill a dragon, so we have to assume that the god will have death powers, and battle-vision, and...'

'You're hurting my head,' said Kelsey. 'I've never heard so many "ifs" in a single sentence before. All the same; Frostback, please be careful.'

'I will eat first,' said the dragon, 'and then I will kill these new soldiers.'

Kelsey drummed her fingers off her knee. 'Maybe you should stay here, and let them come to us.'

Frostback glanced up from the carcass. 'Why? That sounds weak. They will think I am cowering in my lair.'

'I hate to say it, but maybe Aila has a point. If they've sent someone with god powers, then I'll be able to protect you from them.'

The dragon's eyes lit with anger. 'I told you not to bring that up again. I protect you, not the other way around. To imagine! The shame of being protected by an insect. Besides, your claims are ridiculous and foolish, and my opinion of you lessens every time you mention them.'

Kelsey's face fell, and she looked hurt.

'Her claims are true,' said Aila to the dragon; 'you should listen to her.'

'Nonsense,' said the dragon. 'Not even the gods can protect themselves from death powers.'

'But you know Sable has powers, and you know that Kelsey is Sable's niece. Think of Corthie as well, you've heard of his powers. The Holdfasts are different, Frostback; that's why the gods are hunting them.'

'I have seen no evidence that the gods are hunting Kelsey; the attacks of the soldiers have been directed at me. If what you say is true, then hordes of gods and their minions would be chasing her through the forest.'

'But they can't sense her; that's the entire point. Kelsey blocks all of their powers. Haven't you been listening?'

The dragon's eyes glowed. 'Be careful of your tone, demigod, or I may have to chastise you.'

Aila opened her mouth, but Kelsey put a hand on her arm. 'Frostback is being reasonable. She needs evidence, not words.'

'Sorry,' said Aila; 'you're right.'

The dragon stared at the carcass. 'Your bickering has made me lose my appetite. Sometimes, I wonder why I tolerate your presence. I shall work off my anger on the soldiers, and when I return, I will expect to receive the respect you owe me.'

She beat her wings and soared away.

'You need to be careful,' said Kelsey. 'She has a temper.'

Aila sighed. 'I know, but it's so frustrating. It's like speaking to a child; she just doesn't listen.'

They stood and watched as the silver dragon headed to the northwest. She circled in the distance, then swooped low, sending a blast of flames down into the trees below her.

'That's only a mile from here,' said Kelsey. 'Those soldiers got close.'

Frostback rose and circled again.

'Looks like you were wrong, though,' Kelsey went on. 'There doesn't seem...'

The silver dragon let out a scream. Her wings went limp, and she plummeted from the sky, falling like a stone into the forest. She crashed through the branches and disappeared from sight.

Kelsey stared, her mouth open, then she began to run.

'Wait,' cried Aila; 'what are you doing?'

'You were right,' said Kelsey, turning. 'We have to save her.'

'But...'

'Stay if you like, Aila; I'm going.'

Kelsey reached the edge of the wide ledge and leaped down into the forest. Aila stood frozen for a moment, then followed. She reached the lip of the ledge, paused, then rushed back to the cave entrance and picked up their knife. She shoved it into her belt, then ran after Kelsey. The young Holdfast woman was racing through the trees, following the track to a small stream that supplied the lair with water. Aila caught up with her by the banks of the little river, and they splashed across the shallows to the other side.

'If there are soldiers,' said Aila as they ran; 'leave them to me. Go to Frostback and I'll cover you.'

Kelsey made no indication that she had heard, her eyes on the trees ahead of them as they raced through the undergrowth. They reached a burnt part of the forest. Some of the branches were still burning, and ash was floating through the air. Aila counted the bodies of two soldiers, their steel armour blackened but intact, and they slowed. They began to creep through the trees, their eyes glancing around as if expecting an attack at any second. They arrived at a clearing, where trees had been knocked over, and saw Frostback lying there, her eyes closed. Her body was stretched out amid the broken trunks and twisted branches, and a soldier was standing by her head, a heavy crossbow in his hands.

Kelsey put a hand to her mouth as she stared at the immobile body of the dragon.

'Go left,' Aila whispered. 'Distract him, but for Malik's sake stay low in case he shoots.'

Kelsey nodded, and stole away. Aila glanced around, then took the knife from her belt. The soldier seemed to be focussed on the dragon, the crossbow pointing at her head. Aila crept through the undergrowth until she was behind him, then she heard a noise over to the left. The soldier's attention went to where the noise had come from, his eyes squinting into the gloom of the forest.

Aila tried to imagine she was Stormfire. She sprang at the soldier from behind, and with a quick motion of her hand, sliced through his throat. She leaped back a step as the soldier dropped the crossbow, his hands going to his neck, then he collapsed to the ground. Aila's eyes went from him to the bloody knife in her hand, her heart racing. She looked at the soldier's contorted face. He had been young, in his early twenties, just doing his job, and she had snuffed out his mortal life with a flick of her wrist.

Kelsey appeared before her. She stared at the body, then grabbed Aila's arm.

'Search him,' she said.

Aila blinked. 'What?'

Kelsey went down to one knee next to the soldier and began looking through his pockets, and into the hiding places behind his steel breastplate, as Aila tried to regain her composure. What was wrong with her? She had killed before, and the soldier would have shot or arrested them, yet all she could think about was the waste of life his death represented.

'Snap out of it,' said Kelsey, glancing up; 'the other soldiers can't be far away, and they'll be coming.'

Aila nodded, and peered through the trees, her hand still gripping the hilt of the knife.

'Got it,' muttered Kelsey.

'What?' said Aila again, her thoughts spinning.

Kelsey held up a small vial. 'Salve.'

Aila's eyes widened. 'How did you know?'

'I spent a lot of time with Van,' she said. 'He told me that many Banner soldiers carry this into combat, in case they're injured. Stay on guard while I try to give it to Frostback.'

'Will it work?'

'How am I meant to know? What else are we supposed to do; just leave her here to die?'

She clutched the vial in her fist and raced over to Frostback's head. Aila stared at her for a moment, then turned, her eyes scanning the forest around them. The trees were still and quiet, but she knew the Banner soldiers were professionals; they could be anywhere; they could be watching her and she wouldn't know.

A crossbow clicked.

'Don't move,' said a low voice. 'Drop the knife and raise your hands.'

Aila turned her head. A soldier was crouching in the undergrowth five yards from her, his crossbow trained on her chest.

'Last chance,' he said; 'drop the knife.'

She let go of the hilt, and the bloody knife fell to the ground. The soldier rose to his full height and stepped forward. His eyes flickered over to the dragon, but Kelsey was out of sight on the far side of Frostback's head. He spotted the body of his fallen comrade and his features hardened.

'You'll pay for that,' he said, raising his bow and aiming along its sights.

Aila stood frozen as the soldier's finger went to the trigger. She had taken a crossbow bolt before, and tried to prepare herself for the rush of agony.

A silver-scaled forelimb burst through the undergrowth, there was a glint of claws, and the soldier was torn in two where he stood, a spray of blood spattering the trees. Aila staggered back, her eyes staring at the bloody mess on the forest floor where the man had been. Nausea gripped her stomach, and she fell to her knees and threw up onto the ground.

A hand grabbed her shoulder, and she looked up to see Kelsey.

'Come on,' the Holdfast woman urged.

Frostback's head appeared in front of them, her eyes glowing bright.

'I... I owe you insects my thanks,' she said, as if the words pained her. 'You saved my life. You were right, Aila; a god is among them. We must leave, now, before the god approaches.'

There was a noise to the right, and Frostback thrust her head into the undergrowth. There was a scream, then the dragon pulled her head back, a soldier crushed between her jaws. She dropped the mangled corpse to the ground, then picked up the two women, one in each forelimb.

'Halt, lizard,' cried a voice.

They turned. A cluster of soldiers were standing to their right, forming a tight line. Behind them, a dark-skinned woman with red hair was staring at the dragon, her hand raised.

'Do you know who I am, lizard?' she said. 'Do you remember me from Yoneath? You should have died that day, but I will finish the job now.'

Frostback didn't move, her eyes widening. 'Ascendant.'

'That's right,' said the woman. 'I wanted you to see the face of the one who kills you, beast. Die.'

She pointed at Frostback. The dragon flinched, but nothing

happened. The Ascendant's mouth opened, and a flicker of fear passed over her features.

Kelsey let out a laugh from where she was clasped behind the claws of Frostback's right forelimb.

'Hi, Arete,' she said. 'The last time we met, you had me chained up and at your mercy. This time, I have a dragon with me.'

'Kelsey Holdfast?' said the Ascendant

'That's right,' she said. She glanced up at the dragon. 'Frostback, burn them.'

The dragon hesitated for a second, then unleashed a torrent of flames at the line of soldiers. Arete's hands moved, and she vanished as the stream of fire hit them. The soldiers screamed, then fell silent amid the inferno. A dozen trees went up in flames around where they had been standing, and Aila felt the heat from the fires on her face.

Frostback closed her jaws, and leaned her head forwards as the flames fell away.

'Did you get her?' said Kelsey.

'I do not see her remains,' said the dragon.

Aila tried to wriggle free of the dragon's grasp. 'She had a Quadrant; she's gone, but she might come back. We have to leave.'

Frostback ignored her, and continued to sniff the remnants of the incinerated soldiers. She raised her head after a while, then turned to Kelsey.

'I owe you an apology, Holdfast witch.'

'It's fine,' said Kelsey.

'It is not fine. I berated you for lying to me when you were telling the truth.' She closed her eyes. 'I have shamed myself; can you forgive me?'

'Of course; don't worry about it.'

'But you saved my life, twice. You gave me salve when I was dying, and then you... I can scarcely believe I am saying the words, but you stopped the powers of an Ascendant. I was wrong, so wrong.'

The dragon began to weep. Aila and Kelsey glanced at each other, and said nothing.

'Are you a god?' said Frostback. 'How is someone so small so powerful?'

'It's just as Aila said – I'm a Holdfast, and we have some funny powers.'

'Funny? No, majestic. You are a queen, Kelsey Holdfast, and I have wronged you. How can I repay you for my unkind words?'

'Eh, you could always make me your rider, you know, if you wanted to. Imagine; if I was on your back, then no god would ever be able to hurt us; we'd be invincible together.'

The dragon lowered her head. 'I am not worthy.'

'Come on, Frostback; of course you are. Most people don't believe that I have any powers when they first meet me. I can do other things too, you know, useful things, but I don't hold any grudge that you didn't believe it.'

'Are you being sincere? You think I am worthy, even after what I said?'

'Eh,' said Aila; 'perhaps we should continue this discussion at the lair? The Ascendant might return at any minute with a thousand Banner soldiers. Kelsey can repel god powers, but a crossbow bolt in the guts will still kill her.'

'You are right, demigod,' said the dragon; 'once again, your advice is sound. My apologies.'

She beat her wings, and they rose into the air. Aila groaned as they ascended, her chest and torso constricted by the grip of the dragon's forelimb around her. Frostback kept low, and soared over the trees, then rose up the slope of the hill to the lair. She landed, and deposited the two women onto the ledge.

'Aila,' said the dragon; 'I also owe you an apology. You told me that Kelsey was telling the truth, and I belittled you. You have consistently offered me good advice, and I have scorned you. My heart is riddled with shame, and my thoughts are bewildered with confusion. How could I have been so wrong?'

Aila nodded. She still felt sick about cutting the soldier's throat, but didn't want to admit it. Stormfire wouldn't have given it a second thought, but she felt a weight of guilt pressing against her chest.

'You are still angry with me, I see,' said the dragon. 'That is understandable. I have earned your ire.'

'I'm not angry with you,' said Aila.

'All my life,' the dragon said, 'I have been taught that insects are worthless, stupid, selfish liars. We killed any that ventured too close to the Catacombs, and mocked Blackrose for her weakness in befriending them. I swear to you both that I will try to change.'

Kelsey placed a palm on the dragon's face. 'You don't need to explain anything to us. We're on your side.'

'I don't deserve you, Kelsey. If I did, I would ask you never to leave me.'

'Take a breath. I can protect you from the powers of the gods, but who is going to protect me from swords and crossbows?'

The dragon's eyes lit with fury. 'I will. I would die for you, just as you risked yourself for me. Let me protect you, Kelsey; let me watch over you; let me prove that I can be worthy.'

'You don't have to prove anything to me.'

Aila frowned as she watched the Holdfast woman and the dragon gaze into each other's eyes. Kelsey was smitten; it was obvious, and the dragon now clearly felt the same. She turned and glanced out over the forest. The Ascendant could be out there, planning her next move, while Kelsey and Frostback were pledging their undying love to each other.

Tendrils of smoke were still rising from where Frostback had burned the soldiers, and the fire seemed to be growing. The forest was dry, she thought, starting to worry that they might have caused a conflagration that would devour half the forest. Flames started to appear at the tops of the trees, then some leapt the distance to other trees, and the fire continued to grow.

'Do you see that?' Aila said, squinting at the smoke and flames.

As Frostback and Kelsey turned to look, a large mass of fire began to lift up from the forest. It formed into a ball of white hot flames, then shot through the air towards them.

Kelsey cried out as Aila stared, then Frostback gathered the two women into her forelimbs and turned, her back taking the full force of the fireball. The dragon groaned in pain as the flames enveloped her. Inside the tight embrace of her claws, Aila gasped for breath, the heat overwhelming as it washed round them.

The ground began to rumble, and a crack opened up in the wide ledge, splitting it in two. Frostback tried to step away, but half of her was dragged down by the collapsing ledge. The rumbling increased into a full earthquake, and the roof of the cave fell in, sending a cloud of dust over them as the flames died away.

'Arete's back!' cried Kelsey, still wrapped in Frostback's right forelimb.

Another fireball lifted from the forest, while around them on the broken ledge, the hill itself seemed to be crumbling and sliding down into the trees.

'Fly!' shouted Aila as the second fireball was launched towards them.

Frostback looked panicked, her red eyes wide and staring. Smoke was rising from her scaled back, and blisters had appeared on her wings. She seemed to understand what Aila had said, and cleared the hillside, her damaged wings beating. The fireball struck the entrance to the lair in a mighty explosion that sent rocks bursting up into the sky. Frostback was struck by a splintered boulder, and she hung in the air for a moment, then slowly began to ascend, leaving the shattered hillside below them. A third fireball raced towards them, but Frostback flung herself out of its way, then soared upwards, ignoring the pain from her wounds. She turned south, and flew.

Frostback landed an hour later. She chose a clearing in the forest next to a stream, and almost collapsed as soon as her limbs touched the ground. She opened her talons, and Aila and Kelsey fell out, winded and slightly crushed. Aila rolled onto her knees on the grass, powering her self-healing. The nausea and pain faded, then she glanced at Kelsey, who was groaning on the ground, her arms round her chest.

Aila hurried over. Next to Kelsey, Frostback was sprawling across the clearing, panting, her eyes half-closed.

'Kelsey,' said Aila; 'do you have any of the salve left? Kelsey, listen to me.'

The Holdfast woman opened her eyes. 'My ribs,' she gasped.

'The salve, Kelsey; where is it?'

Kelsey patted a pocket, and Aila thrust her hand in and retrieved the small vial. Barely a quarter was left.

'Open your mouth,' she said.

Kelsey did so, and Aila poured in a thimbleful. Kelsey choked and writhed on the grass for a moment, then her eyes opened wide, and she sat bolt upright.

'Pyre's arse,' she cried. 'I feel amazing.'

Aila glanced at the remainder of the salve, then handed it to Kelsey. 'You give it to her.'

Kelsey nodded, took the salve, and ran to Frostback.

'Second time today,' she said, pouring the last of the contents into the dragon's mouth. Frostback shuddered, then her wounds began to fade. Kelsey threw the empty vial into the river and sat back down on the grass.

'That was close,' she said.

'Too close,' said Aila. 'We're not invincible, despite what you said before. They can still use powers on us.'

'Perhaps we were a little hasty in our evaluation of the situation,' said the dragon. 'That lesson has now been learnt, and it takes nothing away from what Kelsey did for me before.'

'You saved us this time,' said Aila. 'I thought we were going to be roasted alive.'

The dragon glanced at Aila in expectation.

The demigod sighed. 'Thank you, Frostback.'

'I was honoured to repay some of the debt I owe you. Now, I feel that Kelsey and I are on a more equal footing.' She tilted her head. 'Equal footing with an insect; whatever would my father say if he heard me utter such words?'

'Maybe we should find out,' said Kelsey.

The dragon turned to her.

'It's just a thought,' Kelsey went on. 'Maybe we could go to the Catacombs. My aunt might be there; you could dangle her over a pool of lava again.'

'I don't know,' said Frostback. 'It is unlikely that I would be welcomed if I returned, and the Ascendant might be tracking us.'

'Are you still willing to listen to my advice?' said Aila.

'I am, demigod.'

'If Sable is there, then she could reach out to Corthie with her powers, and she might be willing to help us.'

'It may be unwise to trust her,' said Frostback.

'What option do we have?' said Aila. 'If that Ascendant is chasing us, then we need help. And maybe, you know, you might be able to repair your relationship with your father.'

Frostback glanced away. 'No, I cannot. He disowned me, and sent me into exile. I would be ashamed to beg him to take me back.'

'But is that what you want?' said Kelsey. 'Do you want him to be your father again?'

The dragon closed her eyes. 'Yes. I miss my family. My elder sister is also in the Catacombs, and I even miss the three little ones – my half-brothers and half-sister, despite the fact that they have replaced me in my father's affections.' She remained silent for a moment, then opened her eyes again. 'I shall think about it. For now, the salve has made me hungry, and I must hunt again.'

'Alright,' said Kelsey. 'See if you can find another wild boar.'

'I shall. We all need to eat, especially our mother-to-be.' She glanced at the demigod.

Aila rolled her eyes. 'Thank you, Frostback.'

CHAPTER 19

CABIN FEVER

Cape Armour, Western Khatanax – 29th Luddinch 5252

Corthie sat down, sweat pouring from his forehead. For two hours he had been training, using exercises he had learned at Gadena's camp to improve his strength and fitness, as well as to pass the time until the others returned. The cabin was small, and he had been unable to carry out several of the exercises due to lack of space, but he had managed to train each day of the voyage from Capston, and he was in better shape than he had been since Yoneath.

He peered out of the grubby porthole window, the thick glass coated in salt and grime. Outside, the large harbour of Cape Armour was busy with ships, from huge grain carriers to tiny fishing boats, and he wished he could take a walk along the waterfront. They had arrived in the port the previous day, but Corthie had remained onboard, keeping out of sight. It was frustrating, but the others had insisted, and at least the enforced solitude had given him an opportunity to train more.

He swigged from a jug of water, and wiped the sweat from his face. The others were probably out enjoying themselves, visiting taverns and shops, and getting some fresh air, while he was stuck below deck in a cramped cabin. He knew it was a sensible precaution, but his boredom levels were rising, and if there had been alcohol in the room, he knew he would have succumbed to temptation.

The sun was low on the left of where he could see out of the window, which made it, in his estimation, late-afternoon. His stomach rumbled, and he longed for one of his travelling companions to return. Even Naxor would do, though preferably it would be Van with a huge basket of food and a bottle of raki. His thoughts veered to Aila, and he felt the sense of helpless frustration rise within him as he went over possible scenarios. Amalia might have taken her back to the City of Pella, or she could be imprisoned somewhere along the Forted Shore. He refused to contemplate the possibility that she might be dead, even though he knew Amalia loathed her. Kelsey was needed by the former God-Queen; she would probably be fine, but Aila had nothing to offer Amalia. And what about the baby? He knew that Aila might have decided to end the pregnancy; if her situation was hopeless, then she might have had no choice, but he desperately hoped that wasn't the case.

The cabin door opened, and Silva walked in carrying a woven shopping bag.

'Good afternoon, Corthie,' she said.

He sighed in relief. 'Thank Pyre someone else is here. I hate being shut up in this cabin.'

'I know,' she said, sitting. 'We all have our burdens to bear.'

Corthie raised an eyebrow but said nothing.

'I enquired about the shipping timetables while I was in the harbour,' Silva said, laying her bag on a little table next to her. 'The ship we are on is due to return to Capston in two days, but there's a merchant vessel leaving Cape Armour early tomorrow. I've reserved cabins on it for us and paid a deposit. It departs a few hours before dawn to catch the tide.'

'Is it going to the Forted Shore?'

'Yes, but it stops at Alea Tanton on the way. Her Majesty is due to contact me this evening; what should I tell her, Corthie? Have you decided?'

'I don't know. I can't see how I could abandon Aila.'

'Would Aila wish to see her world destroyed by Ascendants? Would she thank you if you rescued her, but allowed her world to burn?'

'She's pregnant, Silva.'

'Yes, I know. I also know that she is a demigod, like myself. I once made the mistake of carrying a mortal's child, so I believe I am in a better position than you to judge her state of mind.'

'Do you regret it?'

'Yes, hence the reason I used the word "mistake." But also no. It's complicated. Distant descendents of that union still live in the Southern Cape, but so many generations have passed that I no longer look upon them as family. The child brought me great joy, but would I do it again? No. The pain it brought outweighed the joy.'

Corthie shrugged. 'Everyone bar Aila and I thinks our relationship is a mistake.'

'Then perhaps you should heed what everyone is saying.'

'But I love her; I can't just ignore that. I have to find her.'

'Put yourself in her position and ask yourself what she would wish you to do, were she to know the choices that lie before you. You can still look for her, after you have helped the Queen. You know, when I first met you, Corthie, I took you for a boorish oaf, all muscle and no brain. I was wrong, but you are still very young.'

'I'm nearly twenty.'

'Exactly. A child. Of course, you are more than that, much more. Queen Belinda holds you in the highest regard; of all the companions she left behind when I took her to Shawe Myre, you were the only one whose parting caused her sadness. Her Majesty loves you dearly; she told me you were like a brother to her. I implore you, go to her aid as she has requested. If you wish me to get on my knees and beg, then I will do so.'

Corthie shook his head. 'You don't have to do that.'

'Then you'll go to Alea Tanton?'

'I'll think about it.'

Silva gave him an exasperated glance. 'You've been thinking about it for days.'

'And I intend to think about it some more.'

'What are you afraid of?'

Corthie glanced away. 'Dying.'

Silva blinked. 'What? The mighty Corthie Holdfast? The warrior who destroyed the Banner of the Golden Fist *and* the Banner of the Black Crown? The warrior who slaughtered untold numbers of green-hides? The only mortal warrior brave enough to stand up to the Ascendants? You're afraid of death?'

'I did all those things; you're right. I believed I was indestructible. I'm not.'

'No one is.'

'Aye, but you would survive an arrow through your heart; I wouldn't. If I get killed, then I would be leaving Aila forever, and our child would have no father. I don't fear death for my sake; I fear it for theirs.'

'If everyone felt that way, then no one would resist tyranny.'

'In the last two years, I've done more than my fair share of resisting tyranny. When does it end?'

'When there are no more tyrants.'

'Never, in other words. I'll never be free.'

'You are the greatest mortal warrior who has ever lived; it is a blessing, but also a curse.'

Corthie smiled. 'All I'm feeling at the moment is the curse, not the blessing.'

The cabin door opened before Silva could reply and Naxor staggered in. He tried to close the door but his hand slipped and he nearly fell over. He started to laugh as Silva got up and pushed the door shut.

'Oops,' he giggled.

'Are you drunk?' said Silva, taking her seat again.

'I might be a little tipsy.'

She scowled at him. 'Use your self-healing.'

'No, thank you; I'd rather remain drunk.'

'It is unbecoming for a demigod to be inebriated in public.'

Naxor pulled a face at her then collapsed onto a bed. He rolled, and then propped himself up on a couple of pillows. His hands rummaged around in a pocket, and he pulled a pack of cigarettes out.

'You're not supposed to smoke in here,' said Silva.

'I don't care,' he said, lighting a cigarette. He blew smoke at Silva and Corthie, then started laughing again.

Silva glanced at Corthie.

'I'm not getting involved,' he said. 'I'm in no position to lecture anyone about getting drunk.'

Naxor pointed a finger at him. 'Those are the truest words I've heard you say in quite a while.' He withdrew a hip flask from another pocket and offered it to Corthie. 'Go on, have a drink.'

'Thanks, but not if we have to board another ship before dawn.'

'Suit yourself,' Naxor said. 'You might change your mind once you've heard my news. It's bad; all of it is bad. Belinda has betrayed us.'

'Impossible,' snapped Silva.

'She has finally turned to the Ascendants,' Naxor said, smoke drifting up around his head. 'Word has, this very day, reached the authorities in Cape Armour, demigods using their vision to communicate, sending their little messages here and there, and spying. They'll be looking for us right now; they might even have found us.'

'What are you talking about?' said Corthie.

Naxor stared at them, his eyes wide. 'They know.'

'Know what?'

'Everything.' He shook his head, his demeanour changing from drunken joy to despair. 'They know that you're alive, for a start, and that you left Kin Dai on a ship. If that wasn't bad enough, they know that I'm travelling with you, and that I hold some very precious information inside this head of mine. Oh yes; information that the Ascendants would love to get their hands on; information that would allow them to find the City. It's so obvious. Somewhere in my memory is the action I perform with my fingers when I operate the Quadrant. That's all they need. I can't believe it didn't occur to me. I thought that only a Quadrant that had been to the City would do, but no; they can get it out of me, and they know it.'

The cabin fell into silence.

Naxor glanced at Silva. 'They know about you too, of course, but they don't care. You don't interest them in the slightest.'

'This is bad news,' she said, 'but what does it have to do with the Queen?'

'She must have cracked under pressure,' he said. 'Belinda's heart was never with us; she's one of them; an Ascendant. She must have told them everything.'

'There's another obvious answer,' said Corthie; 'Vana. What if Vana's been captured? She wasn't in Capston.'

Naxor raised an eyebrow. 'Why didn't I think of that?'

'I don't know,' said Corthie; 'maybe because you're so obsessed with the idea that Belinda hates you, that you think she'd betray us?'

'She does hate him,' said Silva, 'but not that much. If what you suggest is true, Corthie, then her Majesty could be in mortal danger. If it was Lady Vana who, willingly or not, supplied this information to the Ascendants, then Queen Belinda's position will have been compromised. The Sixth and Seventh Ascendants will know that she has not been truthful with them.'

'I still think it's more likely to have been Belinda,' said Naxor. 'Either way, this is bad.'

'Who did you read to find this out?' said Corthie.

'Someone on the Count's inner council. The gods in Alea Tanton want the locals here to notify them if they see us. I assume they've sent the same message to every corner of Khatanax.'

'Then you were right to ask me to stay in the cabin. Bollocks. What are we going to do?'

Naxor shrugged. 'Hide?'

'Ignore him, Corthie,' said Silva. 'We stick to the plan – we go straight to Alea Tanton. The Queen needs our help more than ever.'

'Or,' said Naxor, 'she's waiting for us to arrive so she can have us arrested. We'd be sailing into a trap.'

Silva glared at him. 'I do not believe that is the case.'

'Maybe so, but it's quite a risk to take. I supported you in Capston, but now? Count me out.'

Corthie frowned. 'Silva, when is Belinda due to contact you?'

'It's usually around sunset.'

He glanced out of the porthole at the darkening sky. 'We haven't long to wait. That's what we'll do; we'll wait and see what Belinda says.'

Naxor shook his head. 'That's idiotic. Do you think she's likely to confess that she's betrayed us? Don't you get it? If I'm captured, the Ascendants will have all they need to invade my world. As soon as Belinda makes contact with Silva, they'll be able to pinpoint our location, and they could be here within seconds.'

'Her Majesty already knows where we are,' said Silva. 'She knew when the ship was due to arrive in Cape Armour.'

Naxor's eyes widened. 'Then why are we still here? We need to leave at once...'

He tried to get to his feet, and Corthie punched him on the chin. Naxor's head jerked back and he slumped down onto the bed, unconscious.

Corthie glanced at Silva. 'Sorry about that.'

Silva shrugged. 'He'll be fine. It'll be sunset soon, and her Majesty will let us know what she needs.'

They lit a small oil lamp when the light in the cabin got too dim to see, and settled down to wait for Belinda. Corthie ate some of the food that Silva had brought back to the ship, then he lay on his bed, his mind going over the endless possibilities. He had guessed that, sooner or later, the Ascendants would discover that he was alive. They would be hunting him, so perhaps it made sense to strike before they could find him. The consequences of them finding Naxor would be worse, but he was sure the demigod would see sense when he sobered up.

He felt someone nudge his shoulder, and his eyes opened.

'Time to wake up,' said Van. 'We need to transfer to the other ship.'

Corthie stretched his arms and sat up. He blinked. He hadn't meant to fall asleep, and his mind was groggy. Van and Sohul were in the cabin, both smelling of raki. They were packing their bags, while trying to remain quiet. Corthie's eyes went to Naxor's bed. It was empty. He frowned, then turned to Silva. The demigod was sleeping in the chair where he had last seen her.

'Where's Naxor?' he said.

'He's gone outside to get some fresh air,' said Van.

'Did he seem sober to you?'

'Yes. We woke him up, and then he muttered something about needing to clear his head.'

'Did he tell you anything?'

Van frowned. 'Such as?'

'The Ascendants know I'm alive, and they're looking for me and Naxor. If they find him, they'll be able to use what he knows to get to the salve world.'

'What?' said Sohul, his eyes widening.

'Go look for him,' said Van to the lieutenant. 'We can't have him wandering about the ship.'

'Sure,' said Sohul. He put down his bag and slipped out of the cabin.

Corthie jumped off the bed and knelt by Silva. He shook her arm. The demigod started, her eyes snapping open, and she glanced around.

'Sorry to wake you,' Corthie said. 'What happened? What did Belinda say?'

Silva stared at him, her face paling. 'She didn't contact me. I waited and waited, and then I must have fallen asleep.'

'She didn't contact you?'

'What does that mean?' said Van.

'We don't know,' said Corthie. 'Vana might have been captured. Naxor thinks that Belinda might have betrayed us, but I don't believe that.'

'Tell me everything,' said Van.

Corthie went through all that Naxor had told them.

'This is bad,' said the former mercenary.

Corthie glared at him. 'I know. Thing is, what do we do now?'

'Let's think it through. If Belinda didn't contact Silva when she said she was going to, then that points to her being unable to do so, either because she thinks it would be too dangerous, or because she physically can't. If she had betrayed us, then surely she would have made contact, to reassure us that everything was alright. Or else, Banner soldiers and Ascendants would already be here? Damn it, there are too many variables. My best guess is that we press on, and travel to Alea Tanton as quickly as we can.'

'And what about Naxor? We can't risk them capturing him.'

'We should kill him,' said Silva. 'Then we would be sure.'

Corthie frowned. 'That's the kind of thing I'd expect Belinda to say.'

'Her Majesty had a reputation for being ruthless when she needed to be. It would be different if we knew we could trust Naxor, but we can't; he has shown time and again that he thinks only of himself. I believe he would sell us to the Ascendants to save his life.'

The door to the cabin opened and Sohul came back in.

'Well?' said Van.

'Naxor's not on the ship,' he said. 'I checked everywhere. He must have gone for a walk in town.'

'Grab your things,' said Van; 'we need to get off this boat; now.'

Sohul raised an eyebrow.

'I'll explain later,' said Van; 'let's go.'

Naxor had left his possessions by his bed, and they packed them quickly, then picked up their luggage and left the cabin. The ship was quiet, with only a couple of night-watchmen on duty, and they ascended a narrow flight of steps to the main deck. Corthie breathed in a lungful of fresh, ocean air and gazed up at the blanket of stars covering the sky. The lights from the harbour front were illuminating the taverns and port buildings, but the streets were empty.

'Where's our next ship?' said Corthie.

Silva pointed at a long, sleek merchant vessel tied up on the pier to the left of them. Sailors were out on its deck, preparing the craft for its pre-dawn departure. Silva led the others to the gangway leading down to the wharf, where a night-watchman was sitting.

'Are you all leaving us?' he said as they approached.

'Yes,' said Silva; 'we've booked passage on another vessel.'

The night-watchman nodded. 'Well, you're all paid up here, so have a good voyage, ma'am.'

'Thank you. Tell me, did you happen to see a man leave the ship a short time ago?'

'I did indeed, ma'am. He said he was going to find one of the all-night taverns, so I gave him some directions.'

'Thank you.'

The night-watchman stood to the side, and Silva strode down the gangway, the others following her with the bags. Corthie noticed that the night-watchman gave him a long glance, and he kept his head down. They reached the stone wharf and turned left, heading towards the pier where their new ship lay.

'Should I search the taverns for him?' said Sohul, as they walked.

'He won't be there,' said Van.

'How do you know that?' said Sohul. 'He may have lost track of time.'

Van frowned. 'Naxor's gone. He's run for it. The best case is that he lies low.'

'And the worst?'

Van shook his head. 'The worst is that he's already talking to the Cape Armour authorities, betraying us to save himself.'

'We don't know that,' said Corthie.

'There's too much we don't know, that's the problem. This whole thing could be a trap, but what choice do we have?'

'I should have tied him up after I punched him.'

'You punched him?' said Sohul.

'He was getting a little hysterical.'

Sohul's face fell. 'And now he's gone?'

They reached the bottom of the gangway to their new ship, and waited while porters carried several crates up onto the deck. Once the gangway was clear, Silva stepped forward and showed some documents to a small group of sailors. They examined them briefly, then gestured to her to board the ship. Two porters approached and took their luggage, and Corthie and the others followed them up the gangway.

'Welcome to my ship, ma'am,' said a tall man standing by the top of the gangway. 'I hope you have a pleasant voyage.'

'Thank you, Captain,' said Silva. 'When are we due to arrive in Alea Tanton?'

'Three days from now. If the winds are favourable, we should berth at dawn on the third day of Kolinch.' He glanced at them. 'I was told there would be five passengers in your party, ma'am, not four.'

'Ah, yes,' said Silva. 'Unfortunately, one of our group has had to drop out.'

'I see. You will still have to pay for the three cabins, I'm afraid. I hope that isn't a problem.'

'No, that will be fine.'

The captain nodded to a porter. 'These passengers have reserved the three cabins by the aft stairs. Show them the way.' He turned back to Silva. 'We are setting sail in two hours, and breakfast will be served in the galley at dawn. If you require anything on the voyage, ma'am, my door will be open.'

'Thank you, Captain.'

The porter glanced at them, then led the way to the stern of the ship, passing the two large masts in the centre of the deck. Sailors were preparing the sails for departure, and the vessel was humming with activity. The porter descended the stairs by the aft, and took them through a narrow passageway to their cabins. Silva had one to herself, and the three men were sharing the other two. They dropped off their bags, then gathered in Silva's cabin.

'I used my powers to search for Naxor,' she said as they sat.

'And?' said Corthie. 'Please don't tell me that the little rat has gone to the Count's palace.'

'He hasn't. He's currently sitting in a carriage, on the way out of Cape Armour.'

'In which direction?'

'He's on the road that leads to the Falls of Iron; the same road I took when I first arrived to look for Queen Belinda.'

'Alright,' said Van; 'so he's a rat, but not a traitor. Will Vana be able to sense his presence if he hides in the Falls of Iron?'

'No,' said Corthie; 'her range is limited to twenty miles or so.'

'Then, to be honest, we're better off without him. We'll miss his vision skills, but we won't have to worry about him getting captured in Alea Tanton.'

'What's happening in the Falls of Iron these days?' said Sohul.

'Naxor took a look yesterday,' said Van. 'He said that it's deserted. The Ascendants poisoned the land after they levelled the castle and the town. I doubt anyone's there, apart from maybe a few scavengers skulking in the caverns.'

Corthie sat forward in his chair. 'He told us that the Ascendants have a team of demigods in Alea Tanton that they're using to search Khatanax. Won't they find him?'

'It's possible, I guess,' said Van. 'Let's hope he finds a deep cave to hide in. And it'll help if he doesn't use his powers for a while.'

'He's a risk to us all. Maybe I should have killed him.'

'He probably suspected you might,' said Van. 'Well, he's out of our reach now; let's focus on what we're going to be doing next. In three days we'll be in Alea Tanton, and we've no idea what's awaiting us. Vana might be there, and Belinda might be in trouble. Any ideas?'

'If we're going on the attack,' said Corthie, 'we should do it as soon as we arrive; go straight down their throats. You know where the Ascendants live, don't you?'

'Yes; they'll be in Old Alea. The harbour where we'll berth is more than twenty miles from there…'

'Twenty miles?' said Corthie. 'How big is this city?'

'Huge. We can make our way to Old Alea, but it won't be easy getting in. The entire plateau is surrounded by walls and turrets, and the gatehouse will be heavily defended.' He glanced at the others. 'Are we set? Is this our decision – to attack?'

'You know my feelings,' said Silva. 'We attack.'

Sohul nodded. 'I'm under contract to the Third Ascendant; I say we go to her aid.'

They turned to Corthie.

He looked at each of them in turn. 'If the Ascendants know I'm alive, then they'll hunt me wherever I go. It was different when I thought I could find Aila and slip away quietly; that's not an option any more. I'll have to face the Ascendants again, and hope Belinda is by my side.'

He nodded to Van. 'We attack.'

CHAPTER 20

THE TRUE ENEMY

Catacombs, Torduan Mountains, Khatanax – 3rd Kolinch 5252

Blackrose stared down at Sable.

'You must not utter a word in here, witch,' she said. 'Do you understand?'

Sable nodded. 'Perfectly.'

The black dragon strode into Deathfang's hall, Sanguino following in behind her. Sable and Maddie glanced at each other then walked in after them. Deathfang was stretched out on his pile of gold, while Burntskull and a few of his other supporters flanked him. Ashfall was also there, her head lowered.

'Greetings to you, noble Deathfang,' said Blackrose.

Deathfang looked at her for a long moment. 'Come to steal another of my daughters from me, have you? One was not enough?'

'But, father...' said Ashfall.

'Silence,' snapped Deathfang. He glared at her. 'To think, after all we've been through, daughter, that you would desert me to follow Blackrose on her mad expedition? There will be no coming back; you realise that?'

'What do you mean, father? Are you disowning me, like you did to Frostback?'

'Of course not! I meant that any journey to Dragon Eyre will result in your death. Broadwing and Deepblue are welcome to leave; they contribute nothing to the Catacombs, but you? I had high hopes for you.'

'You have your new brood, father. Two sons and a new daughter. Darksky has never liked your older children.'

'Don't you dare speak to me about Darksky in that manner. Have I not always favoured you?'

Ashfall's eyes glimmered and she opened her mouth.

'Let's not argue,' said Burntskull. 'If Ashfall is to leave us, then let us part on cordial terms.'

'Wise words,' said Blackrose.

The small yellow dragon turned to her. 'Your wounds from the pits have healed, I see. When do you intend to leave?'

'Our party of five dragons and three humans shall be departing in a day or so.'

'And the device?' said Burntskull. 'The Quadrant? May we see it?'

Blackrose tilted her head towards Maddie. 'Show them, rider.'

Maddie reached into her shoulder bag and withdrew the copper-coloured device.

'It looks so small,' said Deathfang; 'so inconsequential.'

'The nimble fingers of humans can create such things,' said Black-rose. 'Or they could, in the case of the Quadrant. I believe the knowledge of how to construct these devices has long been lost.'

'How does it work?' said Burntskull.

'I do not know,' said Blackrose. 'I doubt anyone but the Ascendants understands that. I do, however, know how to operate it. It will take us to Dragon Eyre, or anywhere else we wish to go.'

'Damned thing,' said Deathfang; 'it will deprive me of a daughter.'

'Not if you came with us, father,' said Ashfall.

Deathfang laughed. 'Travel into the midst of a war? There are over a dozen infant dragons here in the Catacombs; do you expect me to drag them from their homes and take them to Dragon Eyre? The tombs are a hard place to live, but they are a paradise compared to that accursed world. It grieves me that you have decided to throw your life away like this.'

'We shall prevail,' said Blackrose; 'it will not be easy, but we will regain our homeland. Once that is done, and peace has been restored, I can send an emissary back here, and invite you all to Dragon Eyre. I would give you an island fiefdom to rule over, Deathfang; you would be an honoured ally.'

'Really? And why would you do such a thing?'

'As thanks for all that you have done. You could have expelled Sanguino and the humans while I was imprisoned in the pits, but you refrained.'

'Yes. I had a feeling you would return.'

'That is irrelevant. You kept your word and I am grateful. Your daughter will become a mighty chief on Dragon Eyre; perhaps even a queen one day, with her own realm.'

Deathfang's eyes narrowed. 'If she survives. The last daughter of mine to go off with you never came home.'

'We all mourn the loss of Frostback,' said Blackrose. 'She gave her life fighting the Ascendants; she was brave to the end, a credit to your line.'

'We do not know for certain that she is dead,' said Burntskull. 'She may have fled to some remote corner of Khatanax.'

Fire licked over Deathfang's jaws. 'Are you calling Frostback a coward?'

'No, my lord, no. I...'

'Only a coward would have fled,' said Deathfang. 'Broadwing would have fled; Deepblue also, if she had been brave enough to go in the first place. Not my Frostback. I was tricked into disowning her, and have paid for my folly. And now, with Ashfall's decision to leave, I am paying again.' He stared at Sable. 'I blame you, witch. You deceived me with your nefarious powers.'

Sable said nothing.

Deathfang turned back to Blackrose. 'I am glad you are removing the witch from the Catacombs, but I would advise you to be wary of her tricks. It seems to me that for every honourable member of your party, you have a dishonourable one as well. Broadwing's cowardice cancels out Sanguino's courage, and Sable's lies weigh against Maddie's loyalty. As for Millen and Deepblue, they are nothing but liabilities. Ashfall, my daughter, I fear for you amid such company.' He sighed. 'All the same, go with my blessings upon you. I cannot pretend to be happy about this, but I do not wish us to part in rancour.'

Blackrose tilted her head. 'Thank you for seeing us today, Deathfang. We shall now take our leave. I will inform you when we are due to depart the Catacombs.'

Deathfang glanced away as if bored of the conversation, but Sable could see the hurt in his eyes. Blackrose led Sanguino, Ashfall, Maddie and Sable from the cavern, and they strode to the tomb entrance.

Maddie elbowed Sable in the ribs. 'You actually kept your mouth shut. I was amazed. I was absolutely positive that you were going to say something crazy to old Deathfang in there.'

'I said I would be quiet.'

'Yeah, but I didn't believe it.'

'I'm behaving myself. Blackrose is still furious with me.'

'Indeed I am,' said the black dragon. 'Had you provoked Deathfang, I would have bitten your head off. And then, alas, I would have lost Sanguino, Ashfall and the others. The success of our expedition hangs on you behaving yourself.'

Sable nodded. 'At least until we get to Dragon Eyre.'

'As long as your mischief-making is directed at our enemies, then I shall not mind.'

Maddie climbed up onto Blackrose's harness, and Sable did the same with Sanguino. She connected her mind to that of the dark red dragon, and the three dragons launched themselves off the lip of the tomb. They circled over the lava pools for a few revolutions, then descended to Blackrose's lair. Deepblue, Broadwing and Millen were waiting close to the entrance, and moved aside to allow the others to land. Sable and Maddie clambered down from their dragons as they strode into the interior of the tomb. They gathered in Blackrose's cavern and the black dragon stood before them.

'Now that Deathfang has bestowed his blessing upon Ashfall,' she said, 'we are one step closer to leaving. Before our departure, I wish to inform you of a few things regarding Dragon Eyre. More than twenty years have passed since my realm was conquered, and I have no doubt that many things will have changed, but some constants remain. Firstly, the vast majority of my world is covered in oceans; there are no land-masses anywhere near as large as Khatanax. The humans travel between islands by ship, while we fly. Some archipelagos are hundreds of miles apart, and it is easy to get lost. For this reason, you must not fly off alone, not until you know where the main island chains lie. We will be going to my realm first, which consists of over a dozen inhabited islands. Restrict yourself to that region, and resist the temptation to explore. The stars will be unfamiliar to you, and you may not be able to find your way back.

'Secondly, you will address me as "your Majesty" from the moment we arrive in Dragon Eyre. I am a rightful queen and monarch, a legiti-mate sovereign, and no decree from the occupying forces can overturn that fact. The strategy of the invading gods was simple – they conquered the largest archipelago, then spread out, taking island chain after island chain. They devastated every island except for the ones they took in the first wave; those, they have fortified and protected.'

Sable raised a hand.

'Yes?' said Blackrose.

'Why did they invade? What do they want from your world?'

'They hate dragons,' Blackrose said. 'They wish to exterminate us.'

Sable frowned. 'That doesn't make sense. The invasion must have cost Implacatus dearly and, from what I've heard, they're still having to pay Banner forces to police their new territories. There must be more to it than just an attempt to wipe out dragons. Lostwell traded in salve; that's why they're here, and they're searching for Maddie's world for the same reason. What has Dragon Eyre got? Resources? Gold?'

'My world is comparatively poor in resources,' said Blackrose. 'Some islands have oil that bubbles up from the ground, but there is a dearth of metals. The Ascendants are not interested in plundering Dragon Eyre for its mineral riches.'

Sable snapped her fingers. 'A lack of metals? That gives me an idea.'

'I'm sure it can wait,' said Blackrose. 'Now is not the time for a debate on the motives of the gods. What we need to do is prepare. I cannot give you a plan, since none of us knows what awaits us, but you must follow my orders without question once we arrive. All that remains is to collect the gold.' Her eyes went back to Sable. 'Where is it?'

'Hidden,' she said. 'Give me the Quadrant and I'll fetch it.'

'Out of the question, witch. I have not come this far only to hand you the means to destroy my hopes.'

'Then how am I supposed to get it?'

'Tell us where it is, and we shall all go.'

'I... don't think so. If we're all going to go, then I shall go on Sanguino, and everyone else can follow us. It's about three or four hours away, I think.'

'Can I guess where it is?' said Maddie.

'You could try,' said Sable, 'but I won't confirm or deny any suggestion. Do you all remember the warning that Belinda gave Maddie? The Ascendants might well know we're here, although it's just as likely that Belinda was either panicking or lying. It's better to be safe, though. I'm not going to tell anyone whose minds could be read by Arete or Leksandr; or even by Belinda, for that matter. Sorry to be difficult, but there it is.'

Blackrose glared at her. 'Your reasoning is sound. Let's leave tomorrow at dawn. We shall load our supplies, say our farewells, and follow Sanguino and Sable to the gold, and from there – Dragon Eyre. Does anyone other than Sable have a question?'

Millen raised his hand.

'Yes?' said Blackrose.

'This is a little embarrassing,' he said.

'Go on.'

Millen glanced at the dragons. 'Maddie has Blackrose and Sable has

Sanguino. I, um, well... As you know, I made a third harness, more in hope than expectation, but it's ready. It's just that, well, which dragon will I be going on?'

Sable glanced at Blackrose. 'You must have thought of this, yes?'

'It has crossed my mind,' said the black dragon. 'The bond between a dragon and a rider has to develop over time. On Dragon Eyre, the riders were selected in their youth, and trained for years before taking on their roles. With Maddie and Sable, things were different; their bonds developed from mutual trust and affection. One simply cannot thrust a human onto a dragon and hope a bond occurs naturally. This is something we dragons need to discuss in private. Humans, please leave us.'

Sable, Maddie and Millen left the chamber.

Maddie nudged Millen as they sat by the cold hearth. 'You alright?'

He nodded, his eyes on the ground. 'Fine.'

'If you could choose,' said Maddie, 'which one would you pick? Ashfall is gorgeous, and strong. Broadwing looks the part as well, though, and you get on with him. Deepblue? Now, maybe she...'

'Stop it,' snapped Millen. 'Right now, Blackrose is presumably trying to persuade one of them to carry me. None of them want to – if they did, they would have made it clear, wouldn't they? I don't know. This is humiliating. I'd be happy to take whoever wants me.'

'You'll make it work,' said Sable. 'Whichever one volunteers, that's your chance; seize it and don't look back. We couldn't have done this without you. You made three harnesses – who else could have done that? Whichever dragon you get will be lucky to have you.'

Millen glanced at her. 'Thanks.'

Maddie scowled. 'Now I feel like a right bitch. Sorry. I do like all three of them, that's what I was trying to say; they've all got their good points. Though none of them are as good as Blackrose, obviously. I'm the queen's rider, so I think that means you're going to have to start bowing to me when we get to Dragon Eyre, and calling me "your Highness" and all that.' She burst out laughing. 'Only joking, or am I?'

Sable glanced at the young woman. 'If you earn it, I'll call you it.'

Maddie smiled. 'I heard you were a princess.'

'What?' said Millen.

'I'm not,' said Sable. 'I'm the daughter of a queen, but my birth was out of wedlock. Dear old Godfrey Holdfast, my father, was cheating on his wife. The affair went on for years, and then the queen broke it off when she fell pregnant. I was raised by the Blackholds; my aunt was married to the queen's brother, but no one ever told me who my birth parents were.'

'You used to be Sable Blackhold?' said Maddie, leaning forward in her chair.

'Yes. I still think of myself as a Blackhold, though less and less as time goes by. I found it hard to accept that I was a Holdfast at first; but I guess I'm quite similar to Daphne in some ways; I'm like a tainted version of her.'

'Daphne?' said Millen.

'My half-sister, and the mother of Kelsey, Corthie, Karalyn and Keir. Assassin, murderer, ruler, vision mage. She saved my life when the Empress wanted my head; I've never really understood that.'

'Wow,' said Maddie. 'This is more than you've ever told us before, and despite your protests, you can't deny that you've got royal blood in you.'

Sable smiled. 'If you feel you have to start referring to me as "your Highness," I won't stop you.'

Millen groaned. 'I have to travel with two women who both think they're royalty? How did my life come to this?'

'Going to Dragon Eyre can be a new start for each of us,' said Sable. 'That's why I thought I'd open up a bit; once we've left Lostwell, it'll be the three of us, together. No one on Dragon Eyre will know us.'

A shriek rang out, echoing through the tomb.

Maddie's eye's widened. 'That was Deepblue.'

They got to their feet and hurried through the cavern to Blackrose's lair. Inside, the four other dragons were staring at the body of Deepblue as she writhed on the ground. Sable and the two other humans stood back to avoid her tail, which was swinging back and forth.

'Deepblue!' cried Blackrose. 'What is wrong?'

The small, blue dragon's head lifted. Foam was coming from her jaws as if she were in great pain.

'Blackrose,' her voice groaned, 'or should I call you Obsidia?'

The others glanced at each other.

'What's happening to her?' said Broadwing.

Deepblue raised her head further, her eyes on the black dragon. 'I see you. You can run, but there is nowhere you can hide. I, the Seventh Ascendant, see you and the pathetic band you have assembled.'

'It's Arete,' said Sable. 'She's in Deepblue's mind.'

The blue dragon turned to her. 'Yes. I see you too, Holdfast. You have interfered in our business for the last time. Death is coming to you all, except for Obsidia – she has a cage in the pits waiting for her. She will...'

Sable drove her vision into Deepblue's eyes, and found the presence of Arete, her grip on the dragon's mind almost total. Deepblue was in agony, every ounce of her trying to resist the invasion of her head by the Ascendant. Sable tested Arete's powers; they were immense, but she couldn't sense Sable. She saw the fear that possessed the Seventh Ascendant – fear of Edmond, fear of the Holdfasts, fear of failure. She sensed a recent defeat caused by Kelsey Holdfast, and her hatred of the entire family. Sable smiled, and then severed the connection between Deepblue and the Ascendant as easily as blowing out a candle.

Deepblue, you are strong; you can resist Arete's powers. She cannot hurt you.

The blue dragon collapsed to the ground, panting, her eyes closed.

'I have freed her mind,' said Sable.

The others turned to her.

'I have also put some resistance into her; it might not work for long, but she should be able to repel the Ascendant if she tries again.'

'Where is she?' said Blackrose. 'Where is the Ascendant?'

Sable shrugged. 'I have no idea.'

'Then look for her. If she is close, then she may try something else.'

'Belinda was right,' said Maddie; 'they've found us.'

'Should we flee?' said Broadwing.

'If she is close, we should attack,' said Ashfall.

'Quiet,' said Sable. 'I need quiet if I'm going to search for her.'

A low, groaning, rumbling noise began. Dust fell from the ceiling of the cavern, and the dragons glanced up.

'Out of the tomb!' cried Blackrose. 'Out, before the god brings it down upon us.'

Broadwing, who was closest to the entrance, began hurrying towards the tunnel that led outside, almost knocking the three humans over in his haste. Sable ran to Sanguino, and clambered up the straps to get onto his shoulders. She connected her mind to his, an exercise that had become second nature to her. Ashfall left the cavern after Broadwing, while Blackrose nudged Deepblue.

'Get up, little one,' said the black dragon.

Deepblue got to her feet, swaying, as a large chunk of ceiling collapsed onto the ground, sending a cloud of dust upwards. A crack began to open up in the wall, and the level of noise grew to a sharp grinding of rock. Sanguino strode towards the main tunnel, as Sable glanced around. Maddie was climbing up onto Blackrose's harness.

'We must go,' said Sanguino; 'we have only moments until the entire tomb falls in.'

'Where's Millen?' Sable cried.

Sanguino reached the main tunnel. Broadwing and Ashfall had already left the tomb, and Blackrose was carrying Maddie closer to the patch of blue sky at the end of the tunnel. Sable turned, craning her neck, and saw Deepblue with Millen clasped within a forelimb.

'Let them pass first,' said Sable to the dark red dragon.

Sanguino waited, allowing Deepblue to race towards the square opening, then he followed. Behind them, the roof of Blackrose's lair had fallen in, and the dust was obscuring everything. Sable sent her vision out through it, showing Sanguino the path to take, and he hurried forwards, extending his wings as he reached the entrance. Rocks and debris showered down onto them as he launched himself from the ledge, an explosion of dust following. Sanguino surged upwards, then banked. Their tomb had been obliterated, its entrance collapsed and blocked with debris.

'Did everyone get out?' cried Blackrose.

'Yes,' said Sanguino. 'Sable and I were the last to leave.'

'Find the Ascendant, Sable,' said Blackrose, as the black dragon hovered close by.

'I can't,' she said, 'not when I'm using my powers to help Sanguino fly. I can't do both at the same time.'

'Then land. The Ascendant must be close, if she could bring down the tomb.'

A few other dragons were taking to the air to see what was happening.

'What have you done?' cried Burntskull, soaring up from Death-fang's lair.

A deafening roar of noise cut off Blackrose's response. Beyond the Catacombs, the two volcanoes both erupted, sending twin blasts of lava, burning rocks and ash into the sky. A ragged crack split the face of the cliff where the tombs lay, and ancient pillars and pediments toppled down to the valley floor. A surge of lava overwhelmed the top of the cliff, and began to pour down, entering some of the tombs, from where the terrible sound of screams echoed.

'Evacuate!' cried Burntskull. 'Get everybody out! Flee!'

Dragons shot out of the tombs, some carrying infants in their jaws or forelimbs, as the Catacombs were devastated. Some dragons emerged from their tomb with their wings on fire, their bodies spattered with lava, and others were hit by the burning rocks that were raining down like a fiery hailstorm. Deathfang appeared, a bloody wound on his right flank as he escorted Darksky and their three infants into the air.

Sable stared at the destruction. Dragons were dying; the old, the young; those who had hesitated or who had remained behind to help others. Floods of lava were cascading down the front of the cliffs, burying the tombs with molten rock. The surviving dragons circled higher and higher to escape the rain of rocks and the rising cloud of ash. The sky filled with dragons, each staring down at the catastrophe that had enveloped their homes. The two volcanoes were blasting ever more material into the air, and the flows of lava had transformed the cliffside. Not a single tomb entrance was visible; every one had been destroyed.

'Who is responsible?' said Deathfang, his voice echoing across the valley. 'Who has done this?'

'An Ascendant,' said Blackrose, rising up to join the chief where he was circling. 'She did this.'

'Where is she?'

'I don't know.'

'You brought her wrath down upon us,' cried Burntskull. 'This is revenge for your escape from the city.'

'Is that true, Blackrose?' said Deathfang.

'Should I have meekly died in the pits?' she said. 'Did you not also escape? They hate us, and fear us, that is why they have attacked.'

Deathfang said nothing, his eyes on the destruction of his home as his forelimbs gripped one of his children.

'What should we do, sire?' said Burntskull.

Rage burned in Deathfang's eyes. 'Retreat. Flee to the other side of the valley. The Catacombs are no more.'

He surged away, heading east, and the others followed, leaving the cataclysm behind them.

'I see her,' said Sable from where she sat on the barren slope. 'She's standing a couple of miles from the base of the southern volcano. She's watching us.'

'Are you sure, witch?' said Deathfang.

'I am.'

Deathfang nodded and glanced around. The survivors were stretched out along the ragged hillside, close to the caves where Grimsleep had lived. A count had been undertaken, and twenty-five dragons were missing, including six infants. The sky to the west was filled with smoke, and the rumbling of the volcanoes could be felt through the ground.

'What should we do?' said Ashfall.

'Why do you care?' snapped Deathfang. 'You were leaving us anyway.'

'You think I don't care, father? My love for you and the Catacombs is no less for my decision to go to Dragon Eyre.'

'Twenty-five dragons!' he cried, his voice strained. 'My heart burns for revenge. The accursed Ascendant did this, and she must pay, but so too must those who provoked her into this attack.' He glanced at Burntskull. 'We shall first seek out the Ascendant, and consume her with fire.'

'She will strike you down if you approach her,' said Sable.

'Be quiet, insect,' said Deathfang, his jaws open.

Sanguino moved to protect her. 'Do not speak to my rider like that. She is not to blame for what has occurred.'

'No?' said Deathfang. 'That witch has turned your mind. It was she who rescued Blackrose, was it not? It was she who engineered the slaughter among the humans that ensued. She is the reason the Catacombs have been destroyed. Frostback should have killed her that day, and I should have allowed it. You are weak, Sanguino. Sable and Blackrose must pay for this.'

'Calm yourself,' said Blackrose. 'You are doing what the Ascendant wants you to do; lashing out at your friends instead of blaming the true enemy.'

Deathfang faced her. Sparks ran across his teeth, and he raised a forelimb, the claws extended.

'You are the enemy,' he growled. 'It was always you. From the moment you arrived, you have spread dissension and estranged my own daughters from me. I should have fought and defeated you then, before you had a chance to poison the minds of the others.'

The dragons backed away, leaving Deathfang and Blackrose standing facing each other.

'I curse you,' said Deathfang; 'may rats eat your flesh, and crows peck out your eyes while you lie helpless on the barren soil.'

'I will not fight you,' said Blackrose. 'I will not do the work of the Ascendants for them.'

'Coward,' snarled Deathfang.

Blackrose's red eyes glowed with rage, and her body tensed, ready.

'Stop this nonsense,' said Sable, striding along the slope until she stood between the two dragons.

Sanguino stared at her with his good eye, but said nothing.

'I know you hate me,' Sable said to Deathfang. 'You think the destruction of the Catacombs is my fault? The Ascendants are angry because I saved Blackrose; should I have appeased them and allowed them to slay her for their own amusement? Right now, the Seventh Ascendant is watching us. She wishes to take Blackrose back to the pits; should we let her? The only reason she hasn't tried, is that she fears so many dragons in the same place – you would incinerate her if she tried to snatch Blackrose with her Quadrant. She is also hoping that you and Blackrose will fight, as an injured Blackrose would be easier to take back to Alea Tanton.'

'Then we should kill her now,' said Deathfang. 'If we all attack her, we could kill her.'

'No,' said Sable. 'She would kill some of you first, and then leave. She has a Quadrant.'

'Then what are you suggesting, witch? Do you have anything constructive to offer?'

'I can drive her away, and then we can scatter; she won't be able to track us all.'

'Scatter? You worthless insect. Do you think I built up the Catacombs only to let my kin scatter? No, we stick together; our safety is in our numbers.'

'Can you really drive her away?' said Blackrose.

Sable nodded. 'I can try.'

'Then do so.'

Deathfang glared at them both for a moment. 'Yes, witch. Do so.'

Sable sat down on the bare rock between the two dragons and relaxed. She sent her vision out, crossing the broken valley, then soaring over the remnants of the ruined Catacombs. She could sense the presence of the Ascendant, and guided her vision to the barren slopes of the southern volcano. Arete was standing there, a Quadrant in her left hand. She was using her vision to watch the dragons, and Sable entered her mind, but remained still and undetected.

Arete's thoughts were in turmoil. She wanted to seize Blackrose, but feared being trapped amid two dozen adult dragons who could kill her before she could kill them first. She was waiting, hoping that the dragons would fight each other, and then she noticed Sable's physical form, sitting on the ground. She knew the Holdfast woman was using her powers, but couldn't sense them.

Sable pushed her thoughts into the Ascendant's mind. *Quit while you're ahead. You have destroyed the Catacombs and taught the wild dragons a lesson. Dozens are dead; they will never oppose the Ascendants again. Return to Alea Tanton; your work is done.*

Arete frowned, her thoughts in confusion. Her mind was strong and, though she couldn't sense Sable's presence, she could resist her persuasion better than most. Sable tried another tack. A virile strain of paranoia snaked through the Ascendant's mind, born of millennia of mistrust and betrayal.

Forget about the dragons, Sable insinuated into her thoughts; *you should be more worried about what Leksandr is doing back in Alea Tanton. He mocks your failure with Kelsey Holdfast; he is laughing at you, and conspiring against you. He will sell you out to the Second Ascendant to save his own skin; you know this to be true. Every minute that you are away, he grows more confident, more powerful. What are you waiting for? The Catacombs have been obliterated, and who cares about getting one dragon back to the pits of the mortals? Go back, and show Leksandr that you are not fooled by his double-dealing. Go, before it is too late.*

Arete frowned, then glanced at the Quadrant. She chewed her lip for a moment, then vanished. Sable pulled her vision back and toppled over, her senses exhausted.

Sanguino's forelimb darted out, and he caught her as she fell.

'Well, witch?' said Deathfang.

'She's gone,' said Sable, struggling to keep her eyes open. 'She's gone back to Alea Tanton.'

'Good work,' said Blackrose. 'Are you alright?'

'Tired,' said Sable. 'I might have to rest for a bit. Wrestling with an Ascendant was harder than I thought...'

Sable's eyes closed, and she slipped into oblivion.

CHAPTER 21

AN END TO SUFFERING

Alea Tanton, Tordue, Western Khatanax – 3rd Kolinch 5252

Belinda longed for death. With every second that passed, she wished for the end. Death would be a mercy next to the agonies inflicted by the restraining mask, a kindness. It drove out everything from her mind, all love and hope, and any thoughts of the future. With the mask on, there was no future but pain.

Yendra had been in a mask for nearly three hundred years without dying; could Belinda last that long? She was an Ascendant, so perhaps she could remain even longer within its cruel embrace. Her wrists had been shackled to prevent her from trying to remove it, and she was lying on a cold stone floor. Sometimes she heard voices, but their words didn't register with her. Some hours, or perhaps a day, before, she had heard what had sounded like Arete's laughter, but it had meant nothing to Belinda, and had aroused no emotion within her.

Hands grabbed her shoulders. Maybe someone had decided to show her some mercy; maybe they would take a sword to her neck and end the pain forever.

Words were spoken. Was someone saying her name?

She opened her mouth to plead for death, but something stopped her.

Don't give up, she told herself; not yet.

Hands reached round to the back of her head, and the strap was unbuckled. At once the pressure on her eyes lessened a little, and then the mask was ripped from her face. Her self-healing powered up, the strain on it gone, and she sank back to the ground, panting as the pain began to ebb. The shackles round her wrists were removed next, and then the chains by her ankles fell free.

'Rest,' said a voice full of pity.

A hand took hold of hers, and squeezed gently.

'It's over,' whispered the voice. 'I'm here now; your pain is at an end. Open your mouth, just a little.'

She did so, and felt a drop of salve touch her tongue. A wave of healing surged through her body, and she convulsed. Her face felt as though it was on fire as the salve worked on rebuilding her eyes. She cried out, shaking, but the hand never let go of hers.

'That's it,' said the voice; 'that's better. Can you open your eyes?'

She tried. Her vision was sore and blurry, her healed eyes almost blinded by the light from a lamp. A face hovered over her, a face that seemed to be glowing with a pure radiance. She tried to focus, and the features on the face sharpened. It was a man. He was gazing down at her with a mixture of concern and anger. Her vision cleared. He was beautiful, perfect. He smiled, and it made her want to touch his face.

'Who are you?' she said.

'Do you not know me, Belinda?'

'No.'

'That saddens me, although I had been warned that you had lost your memories. All of the history that we share, and you remember nothing of it. But, maybe, this will allow us a fresh start together. A clean slate.'

He helped her sit up, and she rested her back against the wall of the bare chamber. They were alone in the room, she realised.

'Tell me your name,' she said.

'All right. I am Edmond.'

She narrowed her eyes. 'The Second Ascendant?'

He laughed. 'Yes. Don't look so scared, Belinda; no harm will come to you. You are safe now.'

'Where are we? Where's Leksandr?'

'He is being punished as we speak; Felice too. Their treatment of you crossed a line, and I doubt I will ever be able to forgive them for what they did to you.' His eyes darkened, and she caught a glimpse of the immense hatred that was coursing through him. 'They are lucky to be alive.'

'How long was I in the mask?'

'Four days. Can you stand?'

'I think so.'

He helped her up, and she became aware of the state of her clothes. Leksandr must have left her lying in the stone chamber, neglected and filthy, for the entire time, and she grew embarrassed.

'I need to wash,' she said, glancing away from Edmond.

'That's where I'm taking you, Belinda,' he said; 'to a bathroom, where a hot bath has been drawn for you, and fresh clothes are ready. Do you wish to have servants attend to your needs?'

'No. Thank you, I'll do it alone.'

She put some weight onto her feet, and walked on her own, feeling her cramps and aches vanish. Edmond showed her to a door, and they walked down a deserted hallway to a large, tiled bathroom. Steam was rising from the bath, and she went in.

'I will wait for you here,' said Edmond. 'Take as long as you wish.'

He closed the door, and Belinda walked to the full-length mirror that sat against a wall. She raised a hand to her mouth, her reflection making her want to throw up. Blood and pus was streaking her face, coming down in channels from each eye. Her robes were ragged and soiled, and her hair lank with sweat and matted with clumps of blood. She pulled her clothes off, and threw them into the corner of the room so they were as far away from her as possible, then climbed into the bath, sinking down into the hot water. She lay there for a moment, trying to piece together what had happened to her, then she picked up a bar of soap and got to work.

Belinda spent two hours in the bathroom, scrubbing every inch of her body, and washing her hair several times. She opened a window to let the steam escape, and pulled on the dress that had been laid out for her over the back of a chair. It wasn't her style, and she felt self-conscious as she looked at her reflection.

Four days, she thought. The worst four days of her life. She remembered freeing Naxor from a mask in the Royal Palace in Ooste, and how quickly he had seemed to recover from the experience. He had been in it for two days, and she hoped that her recovery would be as seamless. Already, her mind was trying to forget all about it, as if it had been nothing but a bad dream.

The woman in the mirror stared back at her, and Belinda frowned. Edmond had rescued her. The Second Ascendant himself was in Lostwell. She tried hard to summon some hatred for him, but how could she after he had taken her pain away? He had gazed at her as if he loved her, despite the blood, pus and vile stench. Could he really be as bad as everyone said?

She opened the door. Edmond was standing in the hallway. His glance turned from looking out of a window and he faced her, his eyes widening.

'You are so beautiful,' he said; 'like a dream. I have longed for this moment for a thousand years; no, longer.'

She looked at him. She hadn't been mistaken before; his skin seemed to glow with its own light, and his face was as perfect as any could be.

'Thank you for removing the mask,' she said.

He smiled. 'We have much to discuss. Walk with me, and we shall visit Lord Bastion.'

'Is he in Old Alea too?'

'He is. Do you know, this is the first time I have left Implacatus in five millennia? Lord Bastion has travelled through many worlds on my behalf, but only your presence here could entice me to leave my palace in Serene.'

They began to walk through the empty hallway, passing the door to the room where she had been kept.

'We shan't linger long in Lostwell,' he said. 'I have plans, many plans.'

He pushed on another door, and they entered Leksandr's study. The Sixth Ascendant was on the floor in front of the Sextant, covered in blood. His boots had been removed, and his severed toes were scattered on the thick carpet. Next to him lay Lady Felice, her skin green-hued, and her face a melted mask of bone and blood. Above them stood Bastion, his eyes on the two gods beneath him. He turned as Edmond and Belinda entered, and bowed.

'How are our prisoners?' said Edmond.

'Suffering, my lord,' said Bastion.

'Good.'

Leksandr looked up from the floor, his face mirroring the agony of his torture. 'Mercy, please...'

Edmond lashed out, kicking Leksandr in the face. He crouched down by the Sixth Ascendant and gripped his throat in his left hand. With his right, he withdrew a thin knife from his belt and used it to jab and then scoop out Leksandr's left eye.

The Sixth Ascendant screamed as blood poured from his eye socket.

'You will receive no mercy from me,' spat Edmond, pushing Leksandr back to the floor. He stood and glanced at Bastion. 'Have them removed from my presence. Let them fester in the dungeons for a while.'

Bastion nodded, then clapped his hands. Another door opened, and a man walked in. Belinda stared. It was Renko, the leader of the operation that she and Corthie had defeated in the Falls of Iron; except, something was wrong with him. His skin was grey and mottled, and he was moving with an awkward gait. His eyes seemed vacant as he glanced at Bastion.

'Take these two to the cells in the eastern tower,' said Bastion.

Renko nodded slowly, then bent down and lifted both Leksandr and Felice, who hung limp in his arms. He turned, and left the chamber, a soldier outside closing the door behind him.

'Renko?' said Belinda.

'Indeed,' said Edmond. 'Another who has paid for his transgressions against me. I sentenced him to death upon his return from this world; he had failed me in every conceivable way. However, I then changed my mind, but Lord Bastion had already carried out the sentence. I revived him, but, as you have just witnessed, I was too late.' He glanced at Bastion. 'How long was he dead for?'

'About ten minutes, my lord.'

'And now he is a mindless drone,' said Edmond. 'I expect I'll burn him to ashes once I tire of his presence, but for now he serves as an example that I must not be too hasty in my judgements. It was he who told me that you still lived, and for that I should be grateful to him.'

He turned to the Sextant and walked towards it. 'And now, we have this. A real Sextant; the last in existence. Leksandr told me that you had worked out what was wrong with it. Something is missing, is that correct?'

'I don't know; it was a mere guess on my part.'

He smiled. 'You used to know.'

'I used to know many things.'

'Yes.' He gazed into her eyes. 'There were arguments that passed between us that I wish I could forget; cruel words said by us both that you are better off not being able to recall.'

'Bastion told me the rudiments of our quarrel.'

'Good. He also re-familiarised you with the vow you made me. Of course, there is now the question of whether or not someone can be held to a vow about which they have no recollection. Bastion is of the opinion that you do not have to honour it, whereas I disagree. Isn't that right, Bastion?'

'That remains my opinion, my lord.'

'Yes. Bastion thinks that I should forget the vow and have you executed for treason.' He smiled. 'You are a traitor, after all, and that applies to you both before and after your memory loss. Bastion thinks I am being unnecessarily lenient on you; what do you think?'

Belinda's eyes went from Bastion, who was frowning at her, to Edmond. 'I don't know enough about you to say either way.'

'A good answer,' Edmond said. 'It holds out the implicit promise that you want to get to know me better, thereby delaying any future punishment for your crimes. It doesn't have to be that way. I may be a fool, but I am willing to take you back based upon your word alone. Since I cannot read your mind, your word will have to do. Why did you revive the Holdfast boy?'

'Because I care about him.'

Edmond's eyes clouded over with rage, and Belinda almost flinched. 'As a brother,' she added.

Edmond relaxed. 'Oh. A brother. I see. Well then, that seems a rather trivial offence, hardly one that warrants a restrainer mask. Leksandr also alleges that you deliberately withheld information regarding the location of the salve world. He said that you knew about a certain demigod who had used a Quadrant to travel there, and you didn't let Leksandr or Arete know this.'

'I didn't realise the implications,' said Belinda. 'I thought that a physical Quadrant was required. I didn't know that a person who had used one would do. You must remember that I am having to relearn everything, including matters that may seem obvious to you.'

Edmond glanced at Bastion. 'Do you see? This new Belinda is a lost innocent, blissfully unaware of the consequences of her actions.'

'Or, she's a liar, my lord.'

'Hmm. If anyone else called her that, I would kill them.'

'Yes, my lord.'

'Leave us.'

Bastion bowed. 'Yes, my lord.'

Edmond waited until the Ancient had left the chamber, then he gestured to a long couch. 'Let's sit.'

They walked over and took their places at either end of the couch.

'I want to talk, just the two of us,' he said.

'What about?'

'Us. We were lovers once. We made vows to each other, and then you betrayed me by running away with Nathaniel. It wasn't the cause of the wars, though many believe it was, but it certainly didn't help the situation. You don't remember any of this, of course, but I recall every detail. I can remember the scent of your perfume on the last night we spent together; it haunted my dreams for many years. I also remember the rage I felt whenever I imagined you in Nathaniel's arms. I have a temper at times.'

'Why did I run away with him?'

Edmond stared at her for a long moment, his eyes fixed on hers. 'That, Belinda, is the question I have been asking myself for thousands of years. If I had understood that, then perhaps my pain would have been less. One moment we were together, pledging ourselves to each other, and the next, you had gone. I was in denial at first, imagining that you had been abducted against your will, or that it was all just a silly misunderstanding, but no – you were with him; you married Nathaniel. It broke me into a thousand pieces, and I don't think I've ever managed to put them all back together again.'

'I'm sorry.'

He glanced away, and she thought he was angry, but then he wiped the tears from his eyes. 'I have waited so long to hear you say those words,' he said, trying to keep himself from sobbing. 'You have no idea how much they mean to me, my dear Belinda.' He stood. 'Please excuse me.'

She watched as he hurried from the room. She frowned, wondering if he had left so that he could cry without her witnessing. What did it all mean? Had she betrayed him; had she been in the wrong? She tried to imagine what it had been like to be his lover. He was easily the most beautiful man she had ever seen; he was perfectly proportioned, and his face was truly that of a god. And yet, there was something not right about him. His cruelty towards Leksandr and Felice, despite what they had done to her, was beyond anything she could have conceived. And the way his face had changed when she had said that she cared about

Corthie. He was jealous and spiteful, the opposite of how he appeared on the outside.

Lord Bastion entered the room. He glanced at her.

'Third Ascendant,' he said as he approached. 'The Second Ascendant needs a few moments alone. He has given me permission to ask you a few more questions.'

'Alright.'

Bastion sat. 'How many Holdfasts are on Lostwell?'

'Three.'

He nodded. 'Corthie, the battle-vision warrior?'

'Yes.'

'Kelsey, who can block powers?'

She nodded.

'Then the last one would be Sable, is that correct?'

'It is.'

'Does Sable have powers?'

'Vision powers, yes; from battle to inner.'

'Thank you,' he said. 'We intend to kill them all; how does that make you feel?'

'Angry.'

He raised an eyebrow. 'We also intend to destroy their home world. Mortals with those kinds of powers are a direct threat to our rule. Does that make you angry too?'

'Yes.'

'I see. My final question – will you accede to the Second Ascendant's request to get married? Will you become his bride?'

'I don't know.'

'Why not?'

'I've only just met him.'

He smiled.

'Did you really advise Edmond that I should be executed?'

'Yes,' he said. 'It's nothing personal, but I perceive you to be a potentially bad influence upon the Second Ascendant, and a threat to the stability of Implacatus. On a personal level, I quite like you – you make a refreshing change from the snivelling and grovelling gods that I usually have to deal with.'

'You don't think I could be a loyal and dutiful queen?'

He stood. 'I'm hungry; let's get some lunch.'

She followed him out of the study, and they went to the large dining room on the same floor. Inside, Edmond was sitting at the head of the table, drinking red wine from a large glass. His eyes lit up as he watched Belinda enter.

'That dress,' he said; 'quite spectacular.'

'Thank you,' she said, sitting opposite Bastion.

'I've notified the courtiers, my lord,' said the Ancient; 'lunch should be coming in a few moments.'

Bastion linked eyes with the Second Ascendant, and Belinda sensed the vision conversation going on between them.

Edmond nodded. 'Angry? That's a pity.' He turned to Belinda. 'You see, my dear, I have a plan...'

The sound of a commotion came through the door to the stairwell landing.

'Where's Leksandr?' cried a voice. 'What's going on?'

Edmond chuckled. 'It seems that the blessed Seventh Ascendant has returned. Bastion, would you fetch her, please?'

Bastion stood, bowed, then walked to the door.

'Arete has been off hunting dragons,' said Edmond.

Bastion came back into the dining room, hauling Arete by the arm, her face a picture of raw terror. He pushed her down into the seat along from Belinda, then retook his own place at the table.

'Arete,' said Edmond.

The Seventh Ascendant trembled. 'I should be kneeling; I'm sorry, your Grace.'

Edmond waved a hand. 'Relax.' He looked into her eyes, then shook his head. 'Defeated by two Holdfasts? It seems at times that everything we have tried to do here on Lostwell has been thwarted by that family.'

'But, your Grace,' said Arete; 'I destroyed the Catacombs, killing two dozen dragons as punishment for the escape at the pits.'

'Yes, but then you fled. You were supposed to return with the escaped dragon, were you not?'

She said nothing, her eyes wide.

'Sable Holdfast was in your head, manipulating you; I can see the effects of her powers lingering in your mind. She persuaded you to abandon your mission and return here, and you fell for it like a child. That is the only reason you will be unpunished for your failure – you were up against a stronger opponent. I also see that you had no part in the masking of the Third Ascendant, though I sense that you wish you had been able to participate?'

'Belinda is a traitor, your Grace. Along with the Holdfasts, who are her friends, she has been responsible for our failures here.'

Edmond nodded. 'Lord Bastion has explained to the Third Ascendant that we intend to destroy the Holdfasts on Lostwell, and then, in time, we shall destroy the others on their home world.'

Arete glanced at Belinda. 'Whose side are you on?'

'My own, for the moment,' Belinda said. 'I am weighing up an offer.'

'What offer?'

'None of your business, Arete.'

Edmond smiled. 'Well said, Belinda.'

'Your Grace,' said Arete; 'may I ask what has happened to the Sixth Ascendant?'

'Leksandr is resting in the dungeons,' said Edmond, 'along with Lady Felice. I gave them to Lord Bastion for a few hours, and they will need some time to recover.'

Arete shuddered.

'It's a pity,' said Edmond, 'as it has been a long time indeed since four Ascendants were in the same room together. I have a little announcement, and I suppose three Ascendants will have to do. I have assessed the situation here in Lostwell, and have come to a decision. This world is in its death throes, and I see no reason to prolong its agony; therefore, I have decided to speed up the process. I intend to destroy this world, utterly, starting today.'

The table sat in silence, then Arete let out a low laugh.

'Why not?' she said. 'Most of it's ruined already. I concur, your Grace.'

'Quite right,' said Edmond. 'And, as an added bonus, the destruction of Lostwell will eliminate the three Holdfasts who oppose us.'

Belinda swallowed, unable to take in what the Second Ascendant was saying. Was it even possible to destroy a world? She thought of Dun Khatar. She was the Queen of Khatanax, and the Queen of Lostwell and, despite the catastrophes that had overtaken the world, millions of people still lived there, the majority of them in Alea Tanton. They were her people, whether they knew it or not.

'My lord,' said Bastion; 'what about the salve world? Is still hasn't been located.'

'We have the Sextant, Bastion; therefore we have all we need. We shall take it with us when we return to Serene, and there hand it over to the lore-masters. They have mountains of books; surely one will contain the information we need to activate the device.'

'All the same, my lord,' said Bastion, 'do I have permission to intensify the search for the demigod Naxor? He has within his mind instructions on how to get to the salve world, and was last known to be on a ship heading to Cape Armour. I can have every vision god and demigod in Old Alea looking for him.'

'Granted,' said Edmond.

'How long will the destruction of Lostwell take?' said Belinda, keeping her tone level despite the turmoil in her mind.

'A day or so,' said Edmond.

Bastion got to his feet. 'Then, your Grace, I shall get to work.' He bowed, and crossed the chamber. As he was leaving, a small group of terrified-looking servants were ushered in, their eyes cast downwards. They were pushing trolleys, which they wheeled over to the table.

'Excellent,' said Edmond, rubbing his hands together. 'My first meal in Lostwell.'

One hour after noon, the three Ascendants and Lord Bastion used a Quadrant to travel to the walls that surrounded the high plateau of Old Alea. Three hundred Banner soldiers had been sent on ahead, and were waiting for them, formed in thick ranks to protect the most sacred Second Ascendant. Edmond walked along the north-facing section of walls, stopping when he came to a collapsed turret, where the bare rock of the cliff was visible. He turned to the ocean, and waited for the others to join him. Bastion stood by his right, Belinda his left, and Arete was to the right of Bastion.

Edmond gazed at where the ocean met the vast city of Alea Tanton. Smoke was rising from a few locations, evidence of the continuing dragon-related disturbances.

'I think this might be the ugliest city I've ever seen,' he said. 'A disgusting midden. It seems that mortals can't help but ruin everything they're given. Ungrateful wretches.'

Belinda turned to him. 'Please don't destroy them. I know they fight among themselves, but most of them are poor, and there was a great earthquake a few days ago, and many are destitute and starving.'

'Then I shall be putting them out of their misery,' he said. He looked into her eyes. 'Will you try to oppose me?'

'Would you kill me if I did?'

'Oh, I'd probably devise something worse than death. However, Belinda, I have taken to heart your words on how you are ignorant of many things. Young gods have a tendency to feel pity for the plight of the mortals, and that is because they have not yet gained the perspective of a life that spans centuries, millennia. You remind me of them, and if your memories only go back a few years, then your attitude does not surprise me; indeed, I find it rather endearing. You care; you still care.'

'And you don't?'

'About mortals? No. But I do care, deeply, about many things; and you are among those. Therefore, I have these words for you – if you oppose me, or try to hinder me, then I will be forced to put you back into the mask. I do not wish to do so, but I will have no alternative. Is that clear?'

She said nothing, her heart almost stopping from fright.

'Good,' he said. He turned to the ocean and stretched out his arms, his eyes wide open. His skin shone in the noon light, and he looked like a vision, his robes flowing like liquid silver. He then crouched, placed a hand onto the bare rock of the promontory, and closed his eyes.

Belinda did nothing as she watched him. She was a coward. The powers he was unleashing would bring life on Lostwell to an end, and she was doing nothing to stop him, her fear of the mask paralysing her. Corthie would be ashamed; Silva would be ashamed; she had failed.

Edmond rose to his feet and wiped the dirt of Lostwell from his hand. 'It is done. By sunset tomorrow, Lostwell will be nothing but a memory.'

Belinda fell to her knees, and wept.

CHAPTER 22
HOMEWARD

S outhern Kinell – 3rd Kolinch 5252

'Please,' said Aila; 'just try it.'

Frostback glanced away.

'It's not solely about our comfort,' Aila went on; 'your front limbs would be free if we went on your shoulders. You nearly crushed Kelsey's ribs again yesterday when you carried us; we're fragile.'

'You're not,' said Frostback. 'You have self-healing.'

'Alright, I can recover from getting squashed in your grasp, but Kelsey can't. How can she protect us from the Ascendants if you grip her too tightly?'

Frostback extended her wings. 'I've had enough of listening to your complaints. I am going to scout the vicinity to ensure there are no soldiers still following us.'

She ascended into the sky, then banked to the north and flew away, leaving Aila and Kelsey alone on the high ridge. Below them, the plains of Southern Kinell stretched, a treeless, flat landscape of farms and grasslands.

'Something tells me that didn't work,' said Kelsey, her arms hugging her bruised ribcage.

Aila shrugged. 'She didn't actually refuse.'

'Aye, but you picked the wrong day for this argument. She might have done it if she'd thought no other dragon would see, but we should be reaching the Catacombs today, and I think the embarrassment would kill her.'

A low rumble vibrated through the mountainside.

'Damn earthquakes,' muttered Aila.

Kelsey pointed south. 'Not this time.'

Aila turned to glance in the direction Kelsey was pointing. Twin funnels of smoke were rising above the horizon, sending vast pillars of ash and rock into the sky.

Aila groaned. 'Volcanoes?'

'Looks like it. Didn't Frostback say that lava flowed right past the Catacombs? I wonder if that's normal.'

'Normal? Nothing about Lostwell is normal. Are there volcanoes on your world?'

'Just the one that I'm aware of, but I've never seen it. My father's folk used to believe that an old volcano was a god – Pyre.'

Aila smiled. 'Yeah?'

'Don't mock. Those were simpler times.'

'What about earthquakes? Do you get many of them?'

'Nah. I've never felt one of those.'

'That settles it; I'm going to your world. It would be nice to walk over ground that doesn't shake and rumble all the time.'

Kelsey nodded.

'What about you?' Aila said. 'Are you homesick?'

'Not really. This trip has opened my eyes to the possibilities. There are other worlds out there to explore. I even fancy taking a look at your city-world, now that it's safe from the greenhides. I wasn't that upset when Amalia was threatening to take us there.'

'Wouldn't your mother be sad if you didn't go back?'

Kelsey shrugged. 'As I mentioned before, I'm the most expendable of her children. I've never really fitted in. She'd be disappointed, and then she'd probably forget.'

'I don't believe that.'

'You don't know her.'

'No, but I already know that she won't like me. Karalyn made that quite clear.'

'Part of her will be secretly pleased and flattered that a demigod is joining the family, though she'd never admit that out loud. "Yes, this is my new daughter-in-law. She's immortal, in case you didn't know." She'll love it.'

Aila laughed. 'Daughter-in-law? Malik's ass, that sounds strange.'

'Try "Aila Holdfast" for size. Once the family's sucked you in, there will be no escape.'

Aila fell silent. 'I hope Corthie's alright. If something's happened to him, I don't know how I'd go on.'

'Don't say that; he'll be fine. He's probably getting drunk somewhere.'

'He'd better not be. He's supposed to be looking for us.'

A shadow swooped over them and Frostback landed on the ridge.

'Any soldiers?' said Kelsey.

'I didn't look. I came back when I saw the volcanoes erupt.'

'Aye, we noticed that. Is that not normal?'

'No,' said the silver dragon. 'I've seen them give off smoke and ash before, but never like that. We have to go; the Catacombs may be under threat.'

The dragon reached out with her forelimbs to seize the two women, then paused.

'If the Catacombs are in danger,' she said, 'then I might need to keep my limbs free. I have an idea; climb up onto my back, and I'll carry you that way.'

Aila opened her mouth, but kept quiet at a glance from Kelsey.

'That's a good idea,' said the Holdfast woman.

'Yes, thank you, Frostback,' said Aila.

'So, how do we, uh... climb on?'

The dragon shifted position, and presented a limb for them to scramble up. Kelsey went first, and clambered up until she was perched on the dragon's shoulders, then Aila did the same. It was better than being clutched in a forelimb, but she felt vulnerable atop Frostback with little to hold onto and nowhere to put her feet.

'Blackrose had a harness,' she said, 'and now I can see why.'

Frostback glared at her, then beat her wings and rose into the sky.

'Woah,' said Aila. 'Don't turn too quickly or we'll fall off.'

'It'll be fine,' said Kelsey, her eyes lit with excitement. 'This is great.'

Frostback circled a few times as they ascended, and Aila could see the volcanoes more clearly. Vast rivers of lava were surging across the broken mountainside, and the sky to the south-west was filling with ash and smoke. Even at that distance, she could make out the burning rocks that were raining down on the cliffs by the side of the valley. The dragon moved off, heading south, following the edge of the mountains. The grasslands faded and died the further they went, and the valley floor transformed into a barren wasteland of basalt and deep, ragged ravines. Pools of lava were glowing, and sending clouds of vapours and steam into the valley, filling it like mist. Frostback flew higher, getting above the vapours, and Aila stared at the approaching volcanoes.

'How can anything live here?' she said.

'It's how my father likes it,' said Frostback. 'No humans can approach, which makes it safe.'

'It doesn't look very safe.'

'Something's wrong,' the dragon said. 'The volcanoes have never erupted like this.'

She picked up her speed, and Aila gripped onto the folds on her shoulders, her knuckles white as the wind rushed through her hair. Her eyes were streaming, and she kept them half-closed as the miles unfolded beneath them. The noise from the volcanoes increased, and a few red hot boulders crashed down onto the valley on either side of them.

Frostback let out a cry, and banked, almost sending Aila and Kelsey hurtling off her shoulders. She straightened in time, then circled.

'It's gone,' she gasped.

'What's gone?' said Aila.

'My home; the Catacombs.'

Aila and Kelsey both gazed at the cliffs below them. Lava was flooding down from open fissures in the mountainside, and the slopes were covered in molten rock. Kelsey pointed. At the bottom of the valley was the charred and smoking body of a large dragon, half-covered in debris. A dozen yards from the body, what could have been a dragon wing was poking up from the rocks, burning.

'Amalia's breath,' whispered Aila.

'I lingered too long in the forest,' said Frostback, her voice strained. 'My home... my family...'

Another dragon swooped down from above. It had a dark green body, with blue streaking its wings. Frostback saw it, and the two dragons circled each other.

'Frostback!' cried the green dragon. 'You have returned.'

'Halfclaw,' said the silver dragon; 'what happened?'

'Blackrose and Sable provoked the Ascendants, and they destroyed the Catacombs. Many dragons died. Deathfang and Ashfall survived, though. Come, I will show you.'

The green dragon raced off to the east, and Frostback followed.

'The Ascendants?' whispered Aila. 'Do you think...?'

'Arete?' said Kelsey.

'She might have come here after she lost our trail.'

They crossed the broken valley and came to the slopes on the opposite side. A dozen dragons were in the sky, circling or hovering, while others were gathered in clusters on the barren hillsides.

'I see Blackrose,' said Aila. 'What's she doing?'

'It looks like my father has challenged her to a fight,' said Frostback. 'We must hurry.'

She broke away from Halfclaw and soared down at high speed as Aila and Kelsey clung on. Below them, the large form of Blackrose was facing a huge grey dragon, while others were arranged around them in a wide circle. Blackrose had her claws extended, and flames were dancing over the jaws of both dragons. Frostback surged down, landing a few yards from them.

'Stop!' she cried.

The grey dragon turned to her, his eyes glowing. 'Frostback?'

'Fath... I mean, Deathfang.'

The three dragons stared at each other.

'I am very happy to see you alive,' said Blackrose. 'We thought you fell at Yoneath.'

'I was badly injured, but I survived. Shame has kept me from returning until now. Why are you fighting?'

Deathfang glanced from Frostback to Blackrose. 'Have you seen the Catacombs?'

'Yes,' said Frostback.

'That was Blackrose's doing. She brought the Ascendants down upon us, her and her witch.'

'That is not true,' said Blackrose. 'My only crime was to escape the pits of Alea Tanton.'

'You were in the pits?' cried Aila.

Deathfang and Blackrose glanced up at the two women on Frostback's shoulders, as if noticing them for the first time.

'I was. How did you come to be here, Aila? I thought Amalia had you held prisoner.'

'We escaped too,' said Kelsey.

'And who is this?' said Blackrose. 'Wait. I saw you in Fordamere briefly. Kelsey Holdfast, is that right?'

'Aye, that's me.'

Deathfang emitted a low groan. 'Frostback, why are you carrying a Holdfast witch on your shoulders? The sight saddens me. Has she ensnared you with her powers?'

'Kelsey saved my life,' said Frostback. 'She can block the death powers of Ascendants. We were also attacked, by an Ascendant called Arete.'

'That is the same one who destroyed the Catacombs,' said Blackrose.

'Is my aunt here?' said Kelsey.

'She is,' said Blackrose. 'She is resting at the moment, exhausted after driving the Ascendant away.'

'Let me down,' said Kelsey. 'I have to see her.'

'Of course,' said Frostback. She angled her forelimb awkwardly, and Aila and Kelsey slid down to the barren ground.

The two women hurried through the cluster of dragons. Maddie and a young man were sitting by a shallow cave where Sable was lying. Maddie stood as she saw them approach.

'Aila! Over here.' She ran forward and threw her arms around the demigod. 'You're safe; you're alive! I thought old Amalia was going to kill you or something. Hey, did you know that Corthie's not dead?'

'I certainly hope he's not dead.'

'That's right; you don't know that he was killed. You were snatched before that happened.'

Aila pushed Maddie back. 'What? He was killed?'

'Eh, yeah. By two Ascendants, then Belinda brought him back from the dead. I didn't see it either, but Belinda told Blackrose all about it. Corthie fought the two Ascendants and lost.'

Aila felt tears flow from her eyes. 'Where is he?'

'Sorry; I don't know.'

'He was in Kin Dai,' said a voice.

Aila looked down and saw Sable sitting up. Although Aila had never met the Holdfast woman, she had seen her in vision form, and remembered what she looked like.

'Hello, auntie,' said Kelsey.

Sable grinned and struggled to her feet. 'Hello, niece. What a place to meet.'

Sable embraced her. Kelsey stood stiffly for a moment, then returned the embrace as the others watched.

'Two Holdfast witches together,' said a dark red dragon who was close by.

'This is Sanguino,' said Sable. 'I'm his rider.'

'What?' cried Kelsey. 'How did you get a damn dragon? That's not fair.'

'I saw you ride in on Frostback's shoulders,' said Sanguino. 'Are you her rider?'

Kelsey looked sheepish. 'No, well, no, but I'm, eh, trying. I want to be. How did you do it, Sable?'

'Sable and I have a deep bond,' said the dark red dragon. 'She helped me fly again after I was blinded in one eye.'

Sable swayed a little, and sat back down. 'I'm still tired,' she said, as Aila, Kelsey and Maddie also sat.

'What did you do?' said Aila. 'Blackrose said you drove the Ascendant off. How?'

'I went into her mind and "persuaded" her to go back to Alea Tanton.' She met Aila's eyes. 'I'm sorry about before, you know, when I manipulated your feelings. I shouldn't have done it.'

'It's alright,' said Aila.

Sable turned to Kelsey. 'It's good to see you again, niece, but I have to tell you something.'

'Aye?' said Kelsey.

'I won't be going back with the rest of you to the Star Continent.'

'Oh?'

Sable glanced down. 'I've decided to go to Dragon Eyre with Blackrose, Sanguino and Maddie.'

'And me,' said the young man sitting next to them.

'Yes, and you, Millen. And three other dragons as well. We have our own little army.'

'Wow,' said Kelsey. 'I don't know what to say.'

'Makes a change,' said Sable. 'You might be the only Holdfast who'll care, though. I can't imagine Daphne will lose any sleep over it.'

'What about Corthie?' said Aila. 'Did you say you met him?'

'No, I've yet to lay eyes on my nephew. I saw him via vision, though; like I said, in Kin Dai. He was with Naxor and a couple of Banner officers.'

'Van?' said Kelsey.

'Yes; you know him?'

Kelsey's face flushed.

'How was Corthie?' said Aila. 'Maddie told me he was killed and brought back by Belinda.'

Sable shrugged. 'That's what she told Blackrose. He wasn't in great shape, to be honest. I can't get into his head, but he seemed to be in very low spirits.'

Aila nodded, feeling her heart break a little for him.

'You still don't like Belinda, then?' said Kelsey.

Sable lifted her shirt and showed them a scar across her torso. 'The last time we met, she did this to me.'

'To be fair, though,' said Maddie, 'you did attack her.'

'She's working for the Ascendants.'

'We don't know that for sure,' said Maddie. 'She tried to warn us about the Catacombs.'

'Back to Van for a moment,' Sable said, glancing at her niece. 'Do you have something going on with him?'

Kelsey tried to smile, but it came out strange. 'Not yet.'

'I see.'

'What's that supposed to mean?' said Maddie.

'Holdfast business,' said Sable; 'not Maddie business.'

'Do you have a Quadrant?' said Aila.

'Yes,' said Sable. 'Well, Maddie has it. I'm not allowed to touch it any more. I've been bad.'

'Does anyone know where Corthie is now? Could someone take me to him?'

'Sorry,' said Maddie; 'we don't know where he is.'

'He's not in Kin Dai,' said Sable; 'I checked.'

'Damn it,' muttered Aila.

'Blackrose probably wouldn't allow it anyway,' said Sable. 'After everything she's been through, she's understandably a little reluctant to part with the Quadrant again.'

'Then how am I going to find him?'

'How soon are you leaving Lostwell?' said Kelsey.

'We were meant to be going tomorrow at dawn,' said Sable, 'but with what's happened to the Catacombs, I'm not sure any more. Twenty-five dragons were killed in the attack; it was awful.'

Kelsey blinked. 'Twenty-five? Pyre's arse. And it was Arete? She nearly killed us in the forests of Kinell.'

Sanguino lowered his head into their midst. 'The other dragons have called a meeting to discuss what to do now. You should come along, all of you.'

Millen helped Sable up, and they walked next to Sanguino down the slope to where the dragons had assembled. On one side stood Deathfang, flanked by over a dozen dragons, while Blackrose stood opposite him, with three dragons arrayed behind her. Sanguino joined the smaller group, and the humans stayed close to him. Aila looked for Frostback, and saw her standing alone, separate from both groups. She nudged Kelsey, and the two women walked over to stand next to the silver dragon.

'Is everyone here?' said Blackrose.

'No,' said Deathfang. 'Three dragons are off hunting for food for the little ones, but we cannot delay any longer. We must consider our next move.'

'You know my next move, Deathfang,' said Blackrose. 'I intend to leave for Dragon Eyre, just as we planned.'

'For shame, Blackrose,' said a small yellow dragon standing next to Deathfang.

'That's Burntskull,' whispered Frostback to Kelsey and Aila.

'You would abandon us in our time of need?' the yellow dragon went on.

'I'm not abandoning you,' said Blackrose. 'With us gone, you will have five fewer mouths to feed.'

'And where are we supposed to live?' said Burntskull. 'The caves at this end of the valley are stinking holes.'

'Never mind that for now,' said Deathfang; 'all I can think about is revenge. We should fly to the great city by the sea and burn it to the ground.'

'That would be madness,' said Blackrose. 'The city is well protected, with anti-dragon ballistae, as well as two Ascendants with death powers. If you attack Alea Tanton, you will die.'

'Possibly three Ascendants,' said Sable; 'if Belinda is on their side.'

Deathfang glared at her. 'Silence, insect. You have meddled enough.'

Sable closed her mouth and raised her palms.

'There is another choice,' said Blackrose. 'Perhaps you could consider bringing everyone to Dragon Eyre?'

'Never,' said Deathfang. 'This is where we part, Blackrose, forever. Take your followers and go.'

A sleek grey dragon stepped out from behind Blackrose. 'Father, let us not part this way.'

'You have made your choice, Ashfall. My two elder daughters are dead to me.'

Frostback let out a mournful sound and lowered her head.

Ashfall turned to her. 'You are still my little sister. Are you coming with us, Frostback?'

Frostback said nothing for a moment as everyone turned to her. 'Blackrose is my protector,' she said quietly. 'I will do as she orders.'

'Then I order you to do as you wish,' said the black dragon. 'I will not drag you to Dragon Eyre against your will. Deathfang, I can see that you still love her. Would you take her back if I relinquished my authority over her?'

'I don't know,' he said, keeping his gaze averted from Frostback. 'She disobeyed a direct command.'

'She is young,' said Blackrose; 'she made a mistake.'

'Does no one want me?' said Frostback. 'Blackrose, are you casting me aside because I failed you at Yoneath? I wish I had died that day.'

Kelsey put her hand against the silver dragon's scales. 'I want you.'

'You see?' said Frostback. 'Even an insect values me more than my father or my protector.' She looked down at Kelsey. 'I am sorry; I shouldn't have called you an insect. You saved my life. Thank you.'

'It's alright,' said Kelsey.

'You misunderstand,' said Blackrose. 'I would gladly take you to Dragon Eyre, Frostback, and I know your sister would also be very pleased if you came along. It's just that I sensed a reluctance on your part, and wanted to offer you the chance to go your own way. What do you want, Frostback?'

'I don't know any more.' She raised her head. 'That's not true; I do know, but I am ashamed to say it.'

'Tell us,' said Ashfall.

The silver dragon looked at Deathfang. 'I want my father back.'

'Do you mean that?' said Deathfang, his eyes burning.

'Wait,' said a dark blue dragon standing next to him; 'don't I have a say?'

Deathfang glanced at her. 'But, Darksky…'

'You promised me,' she said; 'you promised that you would never reconcile with Frostback. She caused you nothing but pain and trouble; you said so yourself on many occasions. And now you're thinking of taking her back?'

'With all due respect,' said Burntskull, 'perhaps this should be a private conversation, not one aired before everyone.'

'I agree,' said Deathfang. 'Darksky, Frostback, we shall continue this later. Blackrose, if that is all you have to say, then this meeting is over. I intend to take vengeance upon the gods who destroyed our homes, while you flee to another world.'

Blackrose tilted her head. 'So be it.' She glanced at her followers. 'Say your farewells; we shall leave shortly.'

The dragons dispersed. Ashfall, Sable and Maddie walked over to where Frostback stood.

'All the best, sister,' said Ashfall. 'I hope father takes you back.'

The silver dragon said nothing.

'So this is it?' said Kelsey to Sable. 'We meet, and you're leaving already?'

'Looks like it,' said Sable.

'This is going to annoy Corthie. Could you not spare some time to at least see him?'

'If I knew where he was, maybe, but he could be anywhere. You'll have to just pass on my regards to him.'

'Your regards?' Kelsey sighed. 'Pyre's arse. Will you ever go home?'

'My home is wherever I want it to be. I'm not wanted or needed on the Star Continent, and the Empress might try to enforce her execution order. What would I go back for?'

'How about me?'

'Are you going back?'

'I suppose so.'

'I thought that you and Frostback… well, you said you wanted to be her rider.'

Ashfall laughed. 'My sister with a rider? That's something I'd have to see to believe.'

Frostback glared at her with defiance in her eyes. 'I might take Kelsey as my rider. She has served me well.'

'I think it would be good for you, sister.'

'Why? Are you taking a rider?'

'Me? Not a chance.'

'What about poor old Millen?' said Maddie.

'Deepblue wants him.'

'She does?'

'Yes. She volunteered to take him right before the Ascendant took over her mind. However, I suspect that she is too shy to ask him outright, in case he says no.'

'Can I tell him that?'

'I think that would be a good idea, Maddie; otherwise neither will ask the other.'

Maddie glanced at Aila. 'So long. I know we weren't always the best of friends, but I always liked you the most out of everyone that came from the City. So, and I'm warning you, you're about to get a hug.'

She reached forward and embraced Aila. Maddie frowned mid-hug and glanced down at Aila's midriff.

'Either you've put on weight, or there's something going on that no one's told me about.'

'Aila is going to be a mother,' said Frostback.

Maddie stared, her mouth falling open. 'Is… is… is it Corthie's?'

Aila frowned. 'Yes.'

'Another grandchild for Daphne,' said Sable. 'Congratulations.'

'And,' said Kesley, 'Amalia reckoned she could sense that the baby might be immortal; a demigod.'

'What?' cried Maddie. 'You're joking, yeah?'

Aila shrugged. 'That's what Amalia said. I can't tell yet. And I don't know what it would mean; what would Corthie think?'

'Are you going to tell him?' said Maddie.

'Of course, if I ever actually see him again. It's driving me crazy not knowing where he is, and to think that he died in Fordamere... I'm glad I didn't have to witness that. I owe Belinda the biggest thank you ever.'

Sable raised an eyebrow. 'Be wary of her; at best her loyalties are confused, at worst, she's a traitor.'

'We don't know that,' said Maddie; 'you just don't like her.'

'That's fair,' said Sable. 'I might be wrong about her.'

Blackrose approached. 'Frostback,' she said; 'I sincerely hope that you get what you desire. And, for the record, you did not fail me in Yoneath; you were brave and honourable, and I couldn't have asked for more.'

Kelsey blinked, then started coughing. Aila patted her on the back. 'Are you alright?'

The young Holdfast woman raised her head, her eyes wide. 'Uh... aye, I'm fine.' She turned to Blackrose. 'You're not going straight to Dragon Eyre, are you?'

'No. We have one final errand to run first, though Sable has not yet told us the location.'

'For good reason,' said Sable. She glanced at Kelsey for a moment, her eyes narrow. 'Anything you want to say to me before we go, niece?'

Kelsey leaned over and whispered something in Sable's ear.

The older Holdfast nodded. 'Alright; I get it.' She looked at Blackrose. 'Are we ready to go?'

'We are,' said the black dragon, her head tilted as she glanced at the two Holdfasts. 'I won't pretend to know what that was about. Maddie, climb up. I will also carry Millen, as the third harness he made was destroyed in the Catacombs, along with our supplies.'

'I have an idea about that, Blackrose,' said Sable. She turned, and winked at Aila. 'See you later.'

The dragons and humans who were leaving gathered on the hillside. Deathfang had turned his back to them, and the other Catacombs dragons were watching from a distance. Sable climbed up onto Sanguino, and Maddie and Millen did the same with Blackrose. The large black dragon took to the skies, followed by Sanguino, Ashfall, and two other dragons, the smaller of which Aila assumed was Deepblue. They circled, then Sanguino took the lead, and they set off on a course towards the south-west.

Aila and Kelsey watched as they stood by Frostback.

'What was all the whispering about?' said Aila.

Kelsey glanced at her. 'I might have had another vision.'

'What about?'

'Let's just say that this wasn't the last time we'll bump into Sable on Lostwell.'

CHAPTER 23

DEEP WATER

O ff Alea Tanton, Tordue, Western Khatanax – 3rd Kolinch 5252
'Do you see the coastline on the horizon?' said Van.
Corthie nodded. 'Aye.'

'Follow it from left to right until you reach the square-looking bump sticking up into the sky. It doesn't look like much from here, but that's Old Alea. It's surrounded by high cliffs, and ringed with a wall, and measures six miles by four miles.'

'That's a lot of space for a handful of gods.'

'Yes, but there are thousands of mortals up there too – servants, guards, porters and a whole range of craft-workers: smiths, carpenters, you name it. Right now, there will also be a garrison of Banner soldiers; a few thousand or so.'

'What about the smoke to the left of Old Alea? Where's that coming from?'

Van shrugged. 'Not sure. Probably a riot; there are many of those. The entire city stretches for nearly thirty miles from end-to-end. Most of it consists of slums and shanty settlements, based around three centres, one for each of the three peoples who live there. Each third has, at its heart, their team's fighting pits and arenas. We'll have to get from the port at Old Tanton, and cross twenty miles of those slums to reach Old Alea. We'll take a wagon.'

'And then?'

'And then we'll reach the city fortress at the base of Old Alea, where the road snakes up the cliffside. If we get past that, we'll come to the gatehouse in the walls of Old Alea itself. It was built to withstand a long siege, and we're going to have problems breaking through.'

Corthie leaned on the ship railing. 'We have no chance, do we?'

'Naxor would have been handy.'

'I know.'

'I guess it depends on Belinda,' Van said, after a while. 'If she's prepared to help us, then anything's possible. Presuming she hasn't been arrested or killed, of course. We won't be able to wait; we'll have to act immediately. Every sailor on board this ship has seen you, and word will spread from the moment we arrive.'

'We'll have to be careful when we dock,' said Corthie. 'They may try to keep us on board while someone summons the local militia.'

'We'll charge right past them if we have to.' He gazed down at the water. 'This is insanity. The entire Banner of the Golden Fist couldn't achieve what we're about to attempt.'

Corthie glanced at him. 'You'll make it out alive.'

'Yeah? Ha. I admire your optimism.'

'Kelsey saw you in a vision that hasn't happened yet.'

'Oh, that? Well, it's something to cling onto, I suppose. Either that, or a couple of uncanny coincidences a few years ago persuaded you all that she could tell the future.'

'You still doubt it?'

'Of course I do. I may be many things, but gullible is not one of them. I need to see evidence of these sorts of claims before I'll believe them.'

'Fair enough. I believe it, because I've seen it work. Not from Kelsey, but from Karalyn. Every single vision she had came true, and after a while you just accept it. If I hadn't seen it, I'd probably be like you.'

'Sable can't do it, can she?'

'I don't think so, but I know hardly anything about her, other than what Kelsey and Belinda have told me. One has a tendency to exaggerate, while the other loathes Sable. You know more about her than I do.'

'The only times I saw her was when she was pretending to be a servant. She made excellent coffee, and you always felt at ease in her company. It was only later I realised that she had been playing my mind like a fiddle.'

They stood and watched as the coast drew ever closer. They were behind schedule; the captain's original estimation had placed their arrival at dawn that day, and already the sun was beginning to lower in the western sky.

'What are you going to do if we win?' said Corthie.

'I still need to find your sister.'

'And then?'

'No idea. I can't go back to Implacatus; I'd be executed for treason. I don't want to stay on Lostwell either; the whole place gives off a feeling of unease. It's not as bad as Dragon Eyre, but nowhere's as bad as Dragon Eyre. Lostwell feels more like it's sick, dying from a terminal illness. What about you?'

'I'm going home as soon as I find Aila. Whatever else happens in Old Alea, I'll need to get a Quadrant.'

'And then learn how to use it.'

Corthie smiled. 'Aye. How difficult can it be? Maddie used one without much training.'

Silva appeared on deck beside them, her eyes reflecting a mixture of relief and fear.

'Good afternoon,' said Van. 'Did you have a late lunch?'

'I haven't eaten,' she said. 'Her Majesty has been in contact.'

'Aye?' said Corthie. 'Thank Pyre for that. Is she alright? What happened to her?'

'She wouldn't say; it was a brief message, and the content was dire.'

The two men glanced at each other.

Silva lowered her voice. 'The Second Ascendant is here.'

Van staggered, his eyes wide. 'No.'

'Yes. And, he has Lord Bastion with him. They came to see what the delay was with the Sextant, but, more importantly, they came to see her Majesty. They want to know if she is truly loyal to them. She is in grave danger, but all of us are; every person on Lostwell is doomed.'

Corthie frowned. 'How can that be? Every person?'

'The Second Ascendant has done something. Her Majesty said he placed his hand onto the bedrock of Old Alea, and then announced that all life on Lostwell will end by sunset tomorrow.'

Van closed his eyes and swayed, as if something had struck him.

'I don't understand,' said Corthie; 'how could life end? What can he do?'

'It has already been done, Corthie. I could sense the powers being used, not long before her Majesty contacted me. A vast sweep of flow and stone powers, reaching deep under the oceans into the rock that underpins the continents of this world.' She glanced at the horizon. 'There is every chance that this ship will never dock at Old Tanton.'

Corthie followed her gaze but could see nothing different. The sea looked calm, and there was no sign that world might be ending. He turned back to Van, whose eyes were still closed.

'Hey, wake up. What are we going to do?'

Van gave a grim laugh as he opened his eyes. 'Nothing. There is nothing we can do. It's over. By this time tomorrow...'

'Is there a chance you're both slightly over-egging this?' said Corthie. 'Everything looks the same.'

'Lord Edmond's powers go beyond anything you could imagine,' said Silva. 'Things still look normal, for the moment, but a chain reaction has been put in place, one which is irreversible. Khatanax will be consumed.'

'But all life will die? I can't believe that.'

'Fine, Corthie; not all life will die by sunset tomorrow. There will no doubt be a few species of fish, insect or bird that may survive for a little longer, but the surface of Lostwell is about to be scoured clean.'

Van glanced towards the horizon, where the coastline of Alea

Tanton was becoming clearer. 'We're not going to make it to shore, are we?'

Silva gave a sad smile. 'That would seem unlikely, Van. At least her Majesty is alive. She will be saved, as the Second Ascendant will take her back to Implacatus before the end.'

'Then forget revenge; forget our plan,' said Corthie. 'We need a Quadrant, and there are Quadrants in Old Alea.'

Van pointed. 'Look at the beach. It's supposed to be high tide, but the water's been pulled back.'

Corthie squinted into the horizon. A long, wide stretch of debris-strewn sand was visible right along the coast where the ocean met the city.

'What's going to happen?' he said. 'Should we warn the sailors? Where's Sohul?' He glanced at Van, but the former mercenary was still staring at the coast. 'Van, snap out of it. Forget about tomorrow - how do we survive the next hour?'

A scream came from the rear of the ship, and they all turned. Corthie's mouth dried up as he gazed at the view to the west. A wall of water was approaching, the roar from it slowly building. It stretched for mile after mile, and was sweeping towards the coast, a hundred feet high, towering over the top of the ship's twin masts. It was moving at speed, far faster than the ship was sailing, and the gap between them was diminishing with every second that passed.

'There's no time,' Silva said. She dropped to her knees and clasped her hands together as if praying.

Van's hands went to his waist. 'Unbuckle your belts,' he said, 'then strap yourselves to the railing. Quickly.'

Corthie stared at him as the roar increased. It began to drown out the cries of the panicking sailors until it was the only noise he could hear. Van looped his belt round the wooden beam of the ship's side railing and wound it round his arm. Corthie undid his own belt, his fingers fumbling with the buckle as he tried to ignore the wall of water. The keel of the boat began to judder, then it lifted, the stern high, the bow low, and sailors began falling and skidding down the deck. Corthie strapped his left arm to the railing and hugged the wooden beam, his feet slipping as the gradient of the deck steepened. The hull was still rising, as if an invisible hand was pushing it up. Corthie reached out to grab Silva, but she tumbled away from him, falling towards the bow, along with sailors, crates, and anything that hadn't been secured to the deck. The masts buckled under the pressure, and then they snapped in two, the rigging and sails twisting and tangling over the deck.

Then the wall of water hit them with a deafening crash, and they were engulfed. Corthie clung onto the wooden beam with all his strength, his eyes closed tight as the ocean swallowed them up. Something heavy struck his back, and his legs were lifted off the deck. He held his breath, his head tucked down by the railing, his arms in agony from gripping the beam. Water surrounded him, cold and dark, then the hull of the ship burst through the top of the wave, and he felt the wind on his face as the water drained away from the deck.

He opened his eyes. The deck had been wiped clean of sailors, and the two masts were reduced to stumps. The entire forward deck had been swept away, and the ship was still angled with the stern high. The keel groaned and twisted beneath them, and sections were tearing off as the water battered them. Corthie stared. The ship was riding the wave, and was hurtling towards the coast.

Next to him, Van was sprawled across the planks of the deck, his left arm still strapped to the railing. Blood was coming from a cut across his left cheek, and his eyes were closed. Of Silva, there was no sign.

Corthie turned back to the city of Alea Tanton. The speed of the wave was so great that they had covered most of the distance, and Corthie could look down upon the fields of Tordue that lay beyond the slums. He had survived the initial impact, but that was the easy part, he realised. Once the wave hit the coast, the ship would be flung forwards, and would land somewhere amid the crowded streets. He released his left arm from its grip round the beam, and pulled Van's unconscious body towards him. There was nothing else he could do; nothing but cling on and hope.

The wave struck Alea Tanton with the force of a hundred earthquakes, overwhelming the first mile of densely packed city without pause. The ship's keel levelled as the water level sank, then the bow lifted. Another mile passed, and the ship was pushed down among the debris and bodies that were churning the water. Corthie closed his eyes again as the deck was submerged. The keel struck something, and turned, twisting and grinding off the rooftops of high tenements. It snagged, and the force of the water ripped the hull in two, the bow continuing down into the maelstrom, while the stern came to a juddering halt on the long roof of a housing block.

Corthie opened his eyes again, his breath coming in ragged gasps. He was still strapped to the railing, and had remained with the stern of the ship on the rooftop. Around him, the water level was falling, but still reached the upper windows of the block's highest floor. He tried to stand, but his legs collapsed under him, and he fell back to the deck. His left arm was gripping onto Van, and he released the buckles on the belts that had saved their lives. His right arm fell limp to his side, the muscles cramped and aching. His entire body was in pain, and for a moment, all he wanted to do was lie down and sleep. He stared up at the blue sky. The view looked peaceful, apart from the flocks of squawking gulls that were circling overhead. They would survive the coming catastrophes, he thought, and for some reason, the thought made him want to laugh.

Time passed, though how much was impossible for Corthie to say as he lay on the deck. Sounds came and went – the roar of the water, the screams, the tumble of collapsing buildings, the groaning from the beams of what was left of the ship. The hot sun dried Corthie's face, and he could taste salt on his lips.

'Hey,' said a slow, tired voice; 'are you alive?'

Corthie glanced over. A sailor, his clothes hanging in ragged strips, was leaning over him and Van.

'I think so,' said Corthie.

'What about your friend?'

Corthie pushed himself up into a sitting position. Van was lying on the deck next to him, his chest rising and falling.

'Aye,' said Corthie; 'he's alive.'

'That makes three of us,' said the sailor, his eyes bloodshot. 'Three. The captain's gone, and the officers. It's a miracle any of us are alive. The gods were with us.'

'Aye; I'm sure they were,' Corthie muttered.

He stood, using the railing to support his weight. The water level had fallen further, and now reached halfway up the tenement block. All around, the tops of buildings were poking out of the water like little islands, while between them, green-skinned bodies and floating debris were bobbing in the currents. To their left rose a complex of high, stone buildings, with one shaped into a circle.

'What's that?' he said, pointing.

'The Northern Pits,' said the sailor. 'We landed between that and the walls of Old Tanton, smack into the middle of Fordian territory, or, what's left of it.' He crouched by the railing, his head bent forward in exhaustion. 'I should have died. I'm alive because I disobeyed orders. The captain told us to draw in the sails, and I ran away and hid in a storage locker under the deck.' He shuddered. 'It was like a being in a coffin.'

'What about below deck?' said Corthie. 'Could anyone be alive down there?'

'There is no below deck,' said the sailor. 'It was ripped off when we hit the first buildings.'

Corthie closed his eyes. 'I had a friend down there.'

'*You* had a friend? I had sixteen crewmates.'

Van spluttered, his chest heaving as water surged from his mouth. Corthie helped him sit, leaning his back against the railing.

'Sohul...' he gasped, as he opened his eyes. 'Corthie?'

'You saved me, Van,' Corthie said, 'your advice saved us both, but Sohul was down in his cabin, and Silva was swept away.'

Van's face crumpled, and he started to weep.

'He's in shock,' said the sailor.

'I think we're all in shock,' said Corthie. 'Thousands have just died.'

'Half the city's inundated. It might be more than thousands. I should never have left Cape Armour; I should never have taken this voyage.'

'Cape Armour will be gone too,' said Van, a hollow look on his face as his tears ceased. 'The entire west coast of Khatanax took the brunt of that wave, and more will come. Lostwell is finished.'

The sailor stared at him.

'Edmond did this,' Van went on; 'the accursed Second Ascendant. Bastard.'

Corthie noticed that a small group of Fordian civilians had joined them on the roof, a handful of drenched and bleeding survivors from the housing block where they had landed. Others were on the roofs of the neighbouring buildings, wailing and lamenting as they stared at the flooded city. Corthie climbed down from the ruined deck and stood on the flat roof. He walked to the edge and looked down.

'The water level is falling fast,' he said. 'Van, we need to go.'

Van staggered over to join him.

'Look,' said Corthie. 'Just a few minutes ago, the water was halfway up the side of the building; now it's only a few feet above the ground.'

Van frowned. 'Another wave is coming.'

'What?'

'The ocean is being sucked back, ready to batter the coast again.'

'Then we need to get out of here; head east, away from the coast. How long have we got?'

Van shrugged.

'We can't give up yet,' said Corthie; 'we're alive.'

'Sohul's not.'

'I know; I'm sorry. He was a good man. And Silva too; she...'

'Immortals can't drown,' muttered Van. 'Silva will be fine, for now. She'll float up onto the shore someplace or another, but even she won't be able survive what's coming next.'

'Then we get to Old Alea. If the Ascendants are there, it ought to be the safest place in the city. The wave wasn't high enough to reach up there. If we can...'

'You don't understand, Corthie.'

'Then humour me. You might be right; we might all die today, or tomorrow, but I'm not giving up. Come on, let's get moving.'

Van shook his head.

'Are you just going to stay here?' cried Corthie. 'Are you going to meekly await your death? Have you forgotten your promise to my sister?'

Van glanced away.

'Fine,' said Corthie. 'I'm going. Good luck.'

He turned, and began to hurry towards the stairwell that led into the housing block.

'Wait,' said Van. 'I'll come, even though it's pointless.'

Corthie waited for him to catch up, then they walked to the stairs, passing the ragged band of survivors, who stared at them. Corthie led the way, and they ran down the stairs. Water was cascading from the upper floors, and they were drenched again as they descended into the darkness of the stairwell. Van staggered and slipped a few times, and Corthie took his arm. The water level was only up to their shins when they reached ground level, and was still falling. Corthie checked the position of the sun to the west, and turned in the opposite direction. No one living was out on the street, but it was almost blocked in places by drifting bodies, and mountains of piled-up debris.

'Can you run?' said Corthie.

'No chance,' said Van; 'I can barely walk.'

'Climb onto my back.'

'What?'

'Do as I say. You saved me on the ship, and now I'm going to save you.'

Corthie crouched down, and Van swore a few times, then clambered onto his back. Corthie straightened his legs, pulling on his battle-vision to steady himself. He glanced up the street, and began to run, his boots splashing through the dank, cold and filthy water. It got easier with every step, as the water continued to drain away, and after a few hundred yards, he was running over a paved surface that was quickly drying out in the harsh sunlight. They passed another boat – a small fishing vessel – that appeared almost intact as it sat upon a hill made of debris. The street began to fill with the living, as civilians roamed, looking for survivors, or mourning their losses. A rumble vibrated behind them, and Corthie turned to glance towards the west.

Another wave was coming, its high ridge glistening in the sunlight. If anything, it was even taller than the first wave, and the civilians started to scream and run. Corthie joined them, Van upon his back, as they jostled and stampeded eastward. The screams and the roar of the wave overtook his senses. Civilians fell to the ground and were abandoned where they lay, while others were crushed in the press.

The ground rumbled beneath them, and tiles began to rain down from the buildings on either side of the street, striking the civilians trying to run from the approaching second wave. A rift opened up in the surface of the road, then widened, and people tumbled in, screaming. The front of a building collapsed, sliding down and disappearing into the rift, leaving dozens of rooms open to the air. Corthie came to a halt, unable to move in any direction.

'We need to get higher,' Van shouted, 'and then take cover.'

Corthie nodded, and shoved through the crowds, heading towards a tall stone tower that sat twenty yards away. The rift had split the mass of civilians in two, and those on the side closest to the approaching wave were screaming in fright as the wall of water got nearer while, on the safer side, the crowd was starting to thin as people bolted in the opposite direction.

Corthie kicked down the door and entered the tower. The interior was wet, and debris was strewn across the floor. He ran to the stairs, Van clinging to his back, and powered up the steps, his legs moving as quickly as he was able. Round and round they went, climbing higher with every moment. The tower shook as the wave hit it, and water began pouring in through every window, and great torrents landed on Corthie from above. He closed his eyes and kept going, step after step. The water level rose until they were submerged, and still Corthie kept on, his limbs exhausted as he struggled through the cold darkness, his breath held. They reached a level with an air pocket, and Van's head broke through the water, then Corthie pulled himself up, filling his aching lungs with air. The sound was tremendous, and his ears rang. A body bumped up against them in the semi-darkness, the floating corpse of a boy, his face contorted with panic and pain. Corthie glanced away. Van was shivering above him, his teeth chattering in the intense cold.

'We're going to make it,' said Corthie. 'Don't give up.'

The water level started to rise again, and Corthie took a deep breath and headed back to the stairs. Every stride took all of his strength as he climbed the steps one after the other, and his lungs felt like they were burning. Their heads broke through the surface of the water again, and Corthie realised that it was receding as quickly as it had risen. He collapsed onto the steps, and Van slipped down off his back. They lay there for a while, panting in the dark stairwell as the water reached their knees, then their feet.

'There will be more waves coming,' gasped Van, 'and more earthquakes.'

'We managed to get half a mile in between the first two,' said Corthie. 'We have to keep going.'

'You're insane,' said Van. 'By the end of today, there will be no city left.'

'Old Alea will still be there,' Corthie said. 'I bet the gods and the Ascendants are watching from the battlements, laughing at the mortals as they drown. We might die here, but we'll take down at least one of them first.' He stood, and glanced down the stairs. 'Come on; we'll follow the water as it recedes, and then run again.'

Van looked at him in disbelief. 'You can still run after that?'

'My battle-vision will last the day, and by tomorrow, it probably won't matter.'

They staggered back down the steps, watching as the water drained away before them. They emerged back out onto the devastated street. Huge quantities of water were falling into the giant rift that split the road in two. Another rumble disturbed the ground, sending more fragments of timber, tiles and masonry down into the street, where they joined the piles of bodies and debris in the ankle-deep water. Van climbed back onto Corthie's shoulder, and they set off, Corthie's boots splashing as he ran. The ground started to climb slightly, and the surface dried out again. Corthie turned a corner, and ran into a horse that was galloping wildly towards them, riderless. Van went flying from his shoulders as Corthie stumbled. The horse reared in front of him, and Corthie grabbed the dangling reins. He laughed, his nerves stretched and taut. A horse. Of all the things he could have wished for.

With one hand gripping the reins, he put a foot in the stirrups and swung himself up into the saddle. The horse reared again, and Corthie tugged on the reins, bringing the brown gelding under control.

'You're safe now,' Corthie whispered, as he stroked the side of the gelding's head; 'you're safe. Van! Get up here.'

Van groaned from the ground, and pulled himself to his feet. He stared at the horse as Corthie reached down with a hand. Van took it, and Corthie pulled him up onto the saddle behind him.

'Sorry about the weight,' Corthie said to the gelding. 'It won't be for long.'

He jabbed the horse's flanks with his heels, and the gelding took off, cantering along the street. Corthie guided it between the piles of debris, away from the coast. They reached a wide, level road, and Corthie urged the gelding into putting on some speed. It burst away, racing over the cracked and sodden paving slabs. Ahead, a crowd of survivors was gathering, and Corthie veered away from them, taking the gelding down a succession of side streets. Some were blocked with fallen buildings, but they had gone more than a mile before he heard the rumble from the next wave begin.

'One more effort,' Corthie whispered to the gelding; 'you can do it.'

The gelding was tiring, but it must have sensed the approaching wave, because it managed to pick up its speed again, it hooves clattering off the surface of the road. It settled into a gallop, tearing along the length of a street as the roar grew to a crescendo behind them. They reached a thick line of debris blocking their way, and the gelding slowed as Corthie looked for a way through.

'That line,' said Van; 'that's as far as the last wave got.'

They dismounted, and picked their way through the mountain of debris, Corthie leading the gelding by the reins. On the far side was an old earthen embankment that had supported a carriageway, and they climbed it. A quarter of a mile to the east was the edge of the city, and beyond stretched the fields of Tordue. They gazed in that direction for a moment, then turned. From their vantage point, they saw the third wave strike. It was lower than the first two had been, and by the time it got close to where they stood, the water barely reached its previous furthest point. A small crowd gathered on the embankment next to them, and everyone watched in silence as the wave rolled up to them, then receded again.

'Thank you,' said Van. 'I thought we were finished back there.'

'We're far from finished,' said Corthie, stroking the gelding's flank.

Van glanced at the beast. 'Kelsey told me that your people were horse-lovers.'

'It's been a while,' said Corthie, 'but you never forget.'

'What now?'

Corthie turned to him. 'Now, we go to Old Alea. It's time to make those bastards pay.'

CHAPTER 24

PIG IRON

Falls of Iron, Western Khatanax – 3rd Kolinch 5252

The sun was low in the western sky when Sable told Sanguino to begin his descent. It had taken far longer to fly from the Catacombs to the Falls of Iron than she had expected, and she imagined that Blackrose would have a few words to say about that. Sanguino circled over the ruined town, its buildings flattened by the Ascendants almost four months previously. Remnants of the castle still clung to the cliffside, and Sable told Sanguino to land by the forecourt, which was mostly clear of debris. The dark red dragon brought his wings in and extended his limbs as he landed.

'There's plentiful water by the river,' said Sable, as she climbed down to the ground. 'It's very close, so you should be able to fly there on your own.'

'Then I shall drink, my rider,' he said, and took off again.

The other dragons were beginning their descents, and Blackrose was the next to land.

'You told me that the journey would take three hours,' she said to Sable, her eyes burning. 'That felt more like six.'

'Yes. Sorry about that. I might have misjudged the distance. Anyway, we're here now. Sanguino's gone to get some water from the river.'

'I shall do the same.'

Maddie and Millen clambered down the leather straps from the harness and landed next to Sable, then Blackrose ascended back into the sky. Rather than land in the forecourt, the other three dragons followed her to where the waterfalls cascaded down the steep cliff.

'Six hours on that damn harness,' said Maddie, as she walked with a limp. 'My bum is killing me.'

'That wasn't the fault of the harness,' said Millen.

'I'm not blaming you; I'm blaming Sable.' She glanced around. 'The Falls of Iron? I didn't think I'd be seeing this place again.'

'It's a dump,' said Millen.

'It used to quite beautiful,' said Maddie; 'all these cute little white houses. It's a shame what happened to it. Can you believe the Ascendants destroyed an entire town?'

'They poisoned the farmland too,' said Sable. 'Nothing will grow here for centuries. It'll be swallowed up by the Shinstran Desert in a while.'

'So, this is where the ton of gold has been stashed, eh? Why the Falls of Iron? Were you ever here?'

'This is the first place that Karalyn, Belinda and I travelled to after leaving Gadena's camp. I was only here for a month or so, long enough to see Belinda set off to the salve world, and then Karalyn sent me to Alea Tanton to find a Quadrant. What I remembered most about it were all the caverns burrowed deep into the cliffside. Even back then I thought they'd make a good hiding place.'

Ashfall swooped down and hovered over them. 'Humans,' she said, 'Broadwing has told us that he thinks something is wrong on the coast, so I am going to investigate.'

'What could be wrong with the coast?' said Millen.

'He doesn't know, but says he could feel vibrations coming through the air from that direction. I will be back soon.'

She beat her wings and surged off to the west.

'That was weird,' said Maddie.

They all squinted into the direction of the setting sun, but the shore was too far away to be able to see anything. A large number of birds were in the air, but no people could be seen anywhere across the barren lands surrounding the town.

The other dragons returned from drinking at the river, and they all landed onto the castle forecourt. Sable walked over to Sanguino, and linked her mind to his, filling him with encouragement for having made the short flight successfully on his own.

'I have such bad memories of this place,' said Blackrose, 'for it was here that the witch Karalyn stole the Quadrant that brought us from Pella. And yet, here we are again.' She glanced at Sable. 'I hope we are not staying for too long.'

'That depends,' said Sable.

'On what?'

'On how much mass can be transported by a single Quadrant.'

'It should be able to handle a pile of gold without any difficulty, as well as five dragons and three humans.'

'Yes,' she said, 'but there are other useful things here that we could take to Dragon Eyre. You told us that your world was lacking in metals; well, guess what? This castle is sitting on a massive amount of iron, much of it neatly, and conveniently, stacked into ingots within the caverns. In some ways, it would be a lot more valuable to us than the gold. We could trade it, or turn it into weapons; whatever we fancy. Also, there are piles of supplies in the deeper caverns, including enough grain to last us weeks. This place was stocked for a long siege. Some of it's been looted, but much remains.'

'Iron?' said Blackrose.

'Yes, as much as we can carry.'

'I don't know how much that could be, as I have never seen a Quadrant tested in that manner. For large shipments of materials, a portal was always set up, requiring two Quadrants.'

'What happens,' said Maddie, 'if we try to take more than the Quadrant can cope with?'

'I would be speculating if I tried to answer that,' said Blackrose.

'You might arrive without a tail.'

'Or without a rider.'

'Hmm. Maybe we should test it first; or perhaps we could go in relays? I mean, there's nothing to stop us ferrying stuff back and forward. We could take the gold, and then come back for the iron, or something along those lines.'

'I like your thinking, Maddie,' said Sable. 'That would seem to be the safest course.'

'Here's what we'll do,' said Blackrose. 'Broadwing will patrol the vicinity to the east, Ashfall to the west, while Sanguino and I protect the castle area. Deepblue will accompany the three humans into the caverns as far as she is able, to assist with the extraction of the gold, iron and other supplies, which will be piled up in the forecourt. While that is being done, I can consider the plan of how we take it all to Dragon Eyre. As you know, I hate delay, but after having waited so long already,' her gaze lingered on Sable for a moment, 'a few more hours will make no difference. Let's set our new departure time for dawn tomorrow. Are we agreed?'

'My Queen,' said Broadwing; 'Ashfall is returning.'

They turned, and saw a tiny black speck in the western sky. The sun was on the horizon, and Sable lifted a hand to shield her eyes from its glare.

'She's fast,' said Maddie.

'She is the fastest among us,' said Blackrose, 'but we all have our talents.'

'I noticed a great store of leather in one of the caverns,' said Sable, nudging Millen. 'You might be able to stitch together another harness without all of that horrible tanning business.'

'It's not much use to me if I don't have a dragon.'

Ask Deepblue. She's too shy to approach you, and you'll combine well together; you want to ask her; be brave.

Millen blinked, then glanced at the small blue dragon, who was watching Ashfall approach.

'Maybe I should ask Deepblue,' he whispered.

'That's a great idea,' said Sable. 'You can do it when we enter the caverns.'

Ashfall circled once overhead, then alighted onto the castle forecourt.

'The coast has been inundated,' she said. 'The small harbour town has been swept away, and the ocean has encroached several miles of farmland.'

'How strange,' said Blackrose. 'Perhaps there was an earthquake at sea; they can sometimes trigger large waves. Maybe that's what Broadwing sensed.'

'The damage stretches north and south as far as I could see. I could have gone to look, but I wanted to come back with the news first.'

'I have assigned you to patrol our western flank while we remove the supplies from the caverns. It would be wise to take a closer look; please do so.'

Ashfall tilted her head. 'I shall.'

Sable gestured to Maddie. 'We'll be on our way if that's everything agreed.'

'Report back to me within the hour,' said Blackrose, 'so I can judge the extent of materials to be transported.'

'No problem, boss.'

'Do not refer to me as "boss," Sable. "Your Majesty" or "my Queen," those titles I find acceptable, but not boss.'

Sable smiled, then nodded to Maddie and Millen. 'This way. Deepblue, you can follow us in. The caverns on this level are all big enough for you.'

She led the way towards the ruined castle gates, Millen and Maddie by her side, and Deepblue a few paces behind. Huge fragments of masonry were littering the courtyard beyond the shattered gates, and of the keep, only a single high wall was still standing, the rest having been reduced to a great pile of rubble at its base. Sable turned left, and walked towards the cliffside, where there were several openings in the rockface.

She paused by the entrance to the closest cave and crouched down. 'Someone's been here.'

'Who?' said Maddie.

Sable gave her a look. 'I cannot tell that by a single footprint.'

Millen hovered his foot over the mark on the ground. 'It's about the same size as my boot.'

'So, it's probably a man, then,' said Maddie. 'A looter? You told us that some supplies have been looted. Malik's ass, I hope they haven't plundered the gold.'

'I'd expect a lot more footsteps if that were the case,' said Sable. 'I don't see any going out. Let's be wary in here; we might not be alone.'

'But he might attack us,' said Maddie.

Sable rolled her eyes. 'We have a dragon with us, remember?'

'Shall I burn any who approach?' said Deepblue.

'Not unless they're hostile. It might just be some poor refugee from the town, taking shelter in here; but be ready, just in case.'

They entered the first cavern. It had a ceiling so high that any single one of the dragons could have fitted inside. On the opposite wall were several other openings, but Sable walked over to a pile of refuse to the left. She leaned over, pulled away a tattered cloth and picked up a lamp that she had placed there months before. She lit it, angled the shutters to point ahead, then strode to the second tunnel from the left.

'Follow me,' she said.

The tunnel was just large enough to take Deepblue, though she had to stoop low to fit. They emerged into another cavern, and Sable lit a couple of wall lamps.

'This is where we leave you, Deepblue. Millen, you stay here as well. Maddie and I will descend into the depths together.'

'Why do I have to go?' said Maddie. 'Isn't Millen going to be carrying anything?'

'He'll be needed, all right, but first I want to bring up some samples to show Blackrose, and take a count of how much is down there.' She glanced at Deepblue. 'We won't be long. Twenty minutes at the most.'

The dragon nodded, then Sable led Maddie down a flight of stairs burrowed through the rock. The lantern lit their way, and they descended into the heart of the cliffside, passing side chambers and junctions.

'Am I supposed to remember the way?' said Maddie. 'I'm already lost.'

'We'll mark the floor on our return journey,' said Sable. 'Right, here's our first stop.'

She turned into a landing and they entered a wide but low-ceilinged chamber that stretched back into the distance. Sitting on the ground were row upon row of large bins, each filled to the top with grey ingots.

'There you have it,' she said; 'several thousand tons of pig iron. Each bin would probably take us a day to move up to the forecourt, unless, of course, you want to use the Quadrant to do it. Think of your poor arms and legs, and how tired you'll be after each trip.'

'Knowing my luck,' said Maddie, 'I'd end up appearing in the middle of the cliff.'

Sable put her hand out.

Maddie frowned. 'Blackrose would not approve.'

'I'll show you how to do it; that's all.'

Maddie withdrew the Quadrant from her shoulder bag, then hesitated. 'By the sacred breath of Amalia, if you vanish when I give you this...'

Sable laughed, and took it from her hand. 'Alright,' she said; 'are you watching?' She hovered a finger over the copper-coloured surface. 'You're not travelling far, so you just need to indicate direction, and then distance; like this.' She moved her finger. 'That will take you into the cavern where Deepblue and Millen are. And you know how to get back here, yes? Just indicate that you wish to return to your previous location and you'll turn up down here again. Got it?'

'How do I take a bin of iron with me?'

'Just grab onto it with your free hand; I haven't the time to explain the complexities of transporting other objects to you.'

Maddie nodded, and Sable gave her the Quadrant back. 'Thanks. Eh, please don't tell Blackrose what just happened.'

Sable looked shocked, and placed a hand to her mouth. 'You're asking *me* to keep a secret about the Quadrant from Blackrose? What a disgraceful suggestion; are you trying to get me into trouble?'

'Shut up,' Maddie muttered.

She walked to the nearest bin of ingots and placed her left hand on it, then her thumb moved over the surface of the Quadrant and she vanished, along with the bin.

Sable sat on the steps and lit a cigarette.

'You can come out now,' she said; 'I know you've been following us.'

Naxor emerged from the shadows of the stairs above her. 'Hello.'

Sable patted the space on the step next to her. 'Cigarette?'

'Yes, please.' He trotted down the stairs to join her. 'I ran out a couple of days ago.'

She shook her head at him. 'There is literally tons of tobacco sitting in one of the lower caverns; what have you been doing with your time here?'

'Hiding,' he said, taking a cigarette.

She lit it for him. 'It goes without saying, of course.'

'Yes, yes, I get it. If I try to take Maddie's Quadrant, you'll do something awful to me. How long have you known I was in here?'

She shrugged. 'A few minutes. I sensed your battle-vision. At first I thought someone might attack us, but then I realised it was only you.'

'I needed it to see in the dark.'

'So, you're in hiding? Did my nephew finally threaten to kill you?'

'Might I say how kind it is of you to refrain from dragging this information out of my head? You weren't quite as accommodating the last time we met.'

'How did Belinda react when she found out that you'd propositioned me?'

He shrugged. 'I'm still alive.'

'That was very forgiving of her.'

'It was a close run thing. So, what are five dragons and three humans doing in the Falls of Iron? Apart from stealing iron from my dead cousin, of course. Actually, it could be my iron. If I remember correctly, when I obtained the Falls of Iron for Count Irno, I'm sure I added a clause to the contract that stated that the county would revert to me in the event of his untimely death.'

'I'll fight you for it.'

'Is that how things are done where you're from? You disregard laws and contracts, and take what you want by force? I don't begrudge you a bit of iron, but I would like to know what you intend to do with it.'

'We're taking it to Dragon Eyre.'

'How odd.'

'Not if you consider that Dragon Eyre has a shortage of metals. That iron would be worth an awful lot there.'

He smiled. 'I knew you would have an ulterior motive.'

'I don't – I was perfectly honest with Blackrose. Let's go back to my earlier question; did you and Corthie have a falling out?'

'Corthie and I have had many disagreements during the time we have known each other, but he is not the reason I am in hiding. You see, my dear, I have discovered that the Ascendants are after me.'

'What do they want with you?'

He tapped the side of his head with a finger. 'They want what's in here. I have used a Quadrant to travel to the City, I mean the salve world, many times, and apparently my brain remembers the finger movements necessary.'

'And that's all they need?'

'Precisely. They still haven't managed to get the Sextant to work, so I guess I'm the next best thing.'

'And where is my nephew?'

'He'll probably be in Alea Tanton by now, I'd think.'

'What's he going there for?'

'To do Corthie-type things; fighting and so on. Dying once wasn't enough for him.'

'Did he send you away?'

'No, I fled. Not my proudest moment, but self-preservation has always been a talent of mine, and a priority.'

She darted into his head as he smoked the cigarette.

'How much do you want for the salve?' she said.

'How do you know... wait, that's a stupid question. You couldn't resist, could you?'

'At least I'm offering you a price for it; I could have just knocked you out and taken it. Is it the same jug you had when you healed me in Old Alea?'

'It is, yes. Nine-tenths of it remain.'

'How much would be a fair price? I have plenty of gold, as you've probably seen.'

'That gold is yours? I might have known. Where did you get it?'

'Lots of places. That Quadrant I took from Felice proved to be very lucrative.'

'Then why did you hand it over to Maddie?'

'It was the price of going to Dragon Eyre.'

He laughed. 'And why, in Malik's name, would you want to go there? It's infested with lizards, gods and Banner soldiers.'

'It sounds like fun.'

'Suit yourself. You can have what's left of the jug for five hundred gold sovereigns, standard Implacatus weights, of course; and a favour.'

'What favour?'

'Get me out of here.'

'Where do you want to go?'

'Home, ideally; back to the City with my tail between my legs, where I shall offer my services to the new king and queen.' He sighed. 'How my hopes have fallen, that I would view such a fate favourably.'

'It'll be up to Blackrose,' she said. 'I can ask her, or you can ask her yourself.'

He shook his head. 'I already know what she'll say.' He eyed her. 'Maybe, when Maddie gets back, we could...'

'Haven't you tried this approach before? And anyway, I'm on my last warning with the big black dragon. One more transgression and she'll roast me.'

The air by the stairs shimmered, and Maddie appeared.

'Hi,' said Naxor.

Maddie clutched the Quadrant to her chest and stepped back. 'What's he doing here?'

'Hiding from the Ascendants,' said Sable. 'I've warned him about the Quadrant, but stand away from him, just in case.'

Maddie narrowed her eyes at the demigod. 'The last time I saw you, you tried to steal the God-Queen's Quadrant, in the cavern at Fordamere.'

Naxor spread his palms out. 'I was trying to stop her leaving.'

'Yeah, right.'

'How did it go upstairs?' said Sable.

'Fine. Blackrose sniffed the pig iron for a minute and pronounced it satisfactory. She wants to look at some gold next.'

Sable stood. 'Then let us give her Majesty what she desires.'

'What about him?'

'I'm sure he can tag along. I'll stay between him and the Quadrant.'

She picked up the lantern and led them down one more flight of stairs, and then into a long, cold passageway. They came to a door, and Sable pushed it open, then shone the lantern inside. Maddie gasped. The chamber was filled with gold. Most of it consisted of coins, piled up in bags and chests, but there was a heap of ingots in the centre of the floor.

'You stole all this?' said Maddie.

Sable smiled. 'Yes.'

'You are quite the entrepreneur,' said Naxor. 'Some of that bullion appears to have come from bank vaults in Kin Dai.'

'That's right.'

'You broke into a bank?'

'I had a Quadrant; what else was I supposed to do with it?' She gestured to Maddie. 'Pick up an ingot, and we'll walk back up to the iron bins. I could show you how to get out of here using the Quadrant, but I don't want to place temptation in Naxor's way.'

Maddie lifted one of the gold ingots. 'It's heavy.'

'Give it here,' said Sable.

She passed it over, and the three of them returned to the cavern filled with pig iron. Maddie took out the Quadrant, and Sable took hold of her arm, while Naxor placed his hand on Sable's shoulder. Maddie swept her fingers over the surface of the device, and they appeared in the chamber next to Deepblue and Millen.

'Who's that?' said Millen.

'This is Naxor,' said Sable. 'Don't trust him.'

'Should I burn him?' said Deepblue.

'Not yet. Let's see what Blackrose has to say first.'

They all walked out of the caverns and emerged into the dim light of evening. They crossed the courtyard and went through the broken gates to where the other dragons had gathered. Ashfall was talking to Black-rose, but stopped as the others approached.

'Things may be worse than we'd feared,' said the black dragon. 'Ash-fall has patrolled up and down the coast. It is in ruins. Enormous waves have battered the entire shoreline. Cape Armour is no more; the entire settlement is under water, and it is the same to the north.'

'How far to the north?' said Naxor.

Blackrose paused, staring down at the demigod. 'Naxor? What a surprise. I haven't seen you since your foolish behaviour at Fordamere.' She glanced at Maddie.

'We know; he's not to get close to the Quadrant.'

'He is already too close to it, in my opinion. Step a few yards to the right, Naxor, just to ease my nerves a little.' She watched as Naxor did so. 'Now, what was your question?'

'The waves you mentioned; did they reach Alea Tanton?'

'I didn't go that far,' said Ashfall.

'Should I check?' said Sable. 'Naxor doesn't have the range to reach.'

'If you must,' said Blackrose, 'though the fate of that city does not particularly interest me.'

'Yes, but Naxor said that Corthie is on a ship, headed in that direction.'

'I see.'

Sable glanced around, then went and crouched by Sanguino's crossed forelimbs. She leaned against him, and sent her vision out from her body. It sped west to the coast, then turned north-west, cutting out the bulk of the mountains in the way. She passed high cliffs, and things seemed normal. She started to relax. Corthie would be fine; she was worrying over nothing. She rounded the coastline and turned to the north-east, where the cliffs receded, and had her first glimpse of the destruction that had been wrought upon Tordue. Mile after mile of coastline lay flooded and under water, and every building along the shore, to a depth of three miles, was in ruins. It was growing darker, but the moon was out, and the flooded fields were reflecting its light.

She reached the city, and slowed. The coastal strip had been devastated, and over half of Alea Tanton was under the rolling waves of the ocean. On the eastern side, the destruction almost reached the inland edge of the city, and crowds of survivors were clustered on the drier land. Despite the water, fires were raging in some districts, and many buildings had collapsed. Along the shore, the wrecks of dozens of ships were lying twisted and broken. Across the whole city, only one area was untouched by the calamity – Old Alea. Sable's sadness grew. All those lives, snuffed out, thousands, maybe hundreds of thousands, dead; and where was Corthie?

She pulled her vision back and slowly got to her feet.

'Naxor, tell me again; why was Corthie going to Alea Tanton?'

'Belinda had pleaded for his help,' said the demigod. 'He was reluctant at first, but decided to go along with it. He intends to fight the Ascendants again.'

'And Belinda? Whose side is she on?'

'I don't know. I suspect she might have been trying to trap Corthie, but he wouldn't listen to me.'

'And the giant waves? Could the Ascendants have done that? Were they trying to kill my nephew?'

'What do you mean? How was Alea Tanton? I assume you saw it.'

Sable glanced around at everyone. 'Alea Tanton has been destroyed. The entire city is in ruins, except for Old Alea; that's fine, but the rest? It's gone.'

The others stayed quiet for a moment.

'The whole city?' said Millen.

'That's what I said; it's... gone. The waves...' Sable took a breath, feeling a weight of confused emotions battering her.

'The Ascendants could have done it,' said Naxor.

'But why?' said Blackrose. 'It is unfortunate, but might this not have been a natural disaster?'

'Either way,' said Sable, 'my nephew's in the middle of it.'

'He should have arrived this morning,' said Naxor; 'well, according to the shipping timetable in Cape Armour. If his ship docked on time, he would have been there when the wave struck.'

'I know he is your nephew, Sable,' said Blackrose, 'but he has been in danger before.'

'Are you implying that I don't care?' said Sable, her temper rising. 'When he appealed for help in Yoneath, who urged you to go to his assistance? Me. I even went myself. I was going to help him, but I had to save Maddie, and then I was injured.' She put a hand to her face. 'And Aila's pregnant; I feel sick.' She remembered what Kelsey had whispered to her, took a deep breath, then turned back to Blackrose. 'I have to go; I have to see for myself if he's dead, and help him if he's not.'

'No,' said Blackrose.

The forecourt fell into a chill silence.

Sable turned to Sanguino. 'My dragon, will you take me to Alea Tanton?'

'I forbid it,' said Blackrose.

'You are my mother,' said the dark red dragon, 'but my love and loyalty belong to my rider before they belong to you. Yes, Sable, I will take you.'

Blackrose bared her teeth, and the claws on her forelimbs shone. 'No. This will not happen again. If you leave this company, then I swear to you that I shall take the rest of us to Dragon Eyre without you; do you understand?'

'But...' said Ashfall.

'Silence!' She glared at Sanguino, who stood his ground. 'Do you understand?'

'I do,' he said.

Sable climbed up the harness onto the shoulders of Sanguino and secured the strap round her waist.

'I'm sorry, everybody,' she said. 'I can't abandon Corthie. Good luck.'

'Wait,' cried Maddie, but it was too late. Sanguino extended his wings and bore Sable up into the sky. The moon was in the east, and they soared away. Sable glanced down at the four dragons. Among them, the three humans were staring up at them. She wiped a tear from her eye.

'Take me to Alea Tanton, Sanguino.'

'For you, my rider, anything.'

CHAPTER 25

THE MISSING PIECE

Alea Tanton, Tordue, Western Khatanax – 3rd Kolinch 5252

Belinda's vision roamed the devastated city. The scenes of destruction and death were filling her with despair, but she couldn't look away. Aside from a thin strip on the eastern side of Alea Tanton, the rest of the city was in ruins; flooded, collapsed, burning. The waves had ceased in the afternoon, but the earthquakes and tremors had continued beyond sunset, and were getting stronger with every hour that passed.

Old Alea had remained like a rock amid a storm, solid and secure, with only a few vibrations shaking the crystal chandeliers in the Governor's residence. Edmond had sent Belinda to her quarters when they had returned from the battlements; he was embarrassed by her tears, and had told her that they made her face look unattractive. He had also set a vague departure time, announcing that they would leave for Implacatus in the morning as, by that time, Old Alea itself would become unstable. He hadn't asked her if she wanted to leave with him, and she hadn't refused to go, her spirit defeated. Lostwell had been Nathaniel's creation, and Edmond was taking a certain pleasure from destroying the work of his rival's hands.

She watched as another earthquake opened up a crack in the

ground by the Central Pits. The stone buildings had been packed with refugees following the giant waves, but the collapse of the main arena had killed many and had driven the others away, sending them eastward to spill out into the countryside beyond the city limits, where thousands of other survivors had clustered. A solitary greenhide had lived through the destruction of the Blue Thumbs training facility, and was stalking the broken neighbourhoods, cutting down any Torduan it could find, and pausing to eat the flesh of those who had fallen.

The crack in the ground widened, and an entire row of tenements plunged into the hole as the ground beneath them buckled and rose. There were no screams, for the street had already been emptied of anyone still alive and, apart from her, there was no one there to witness its destruction.

She had searched for the ship that had been carrying Corthie and Silva, but there were dozens of such vessels littering the submerged coastline; broken hulls and snapped masts lay strewn by the new edge of the ocean, the wind fluttering the ripped canvas of the sails that sat half-buried in mud. The waves had borne thousands of bodies out to sea, and were in the process of pushing them all back inland again; they bobbed along with the tons of flotsam and debris clogging the wide bay.

She stilled, trying to listen for any signs of powers being used, but her skills at detecting other gods or mages were crude and unpractised. She could sense if a god in the same room as her was using vision, but over an area as large as that of Alea Tanton, any such signal was lost in the background noise of destruction. Silva could be alive, she knew; her self-healing powers should have ensured her survival if the ship had been hit by one of the waves, but she could be anywhere. The currents could have thrown her miles out to sea, or she might be one of the bodies bobbing in the bay, still too weak to swim to shore. Belinda moved away from the coast, and looked down on the fields and roads that lay to the east of the city. Every farmhouse had collapsed in the succession of earthquakes, but it was still the safest place to be, and exhausted, ragged groups of civilians had gathered there in their thousands. Granaries and barns had been plundered in the survivors' search for food, and several farmers and their families had been murdered by desperate and hungry bands of looters. As well as the brutality, many small acts of generosity and kindness had been on display – people sharing what food and drink they had with strangers, and cases where men and women had run back into collapsing buildings to rescue those who had been trapped.

Finally, after searching for hours, she found Corthie. He was on foot, leading a horse southwards along the farm tracks to the east of the city. A man was with him, the same man who had persuaded her to revive Corthie in the cavern of Fordamere. He was limping and looked exhausted, but Corthie was urging him onwards, his will undimmed, and Belinda's heart filled with love and pity at the sight. She wished she could enter his mind, to tell him to keep going, to tell him not to give up, but that wouldn't have been fair. Like everyone else on Khatanax, Corthie was doomed.

She sensed a knock on her door, then realised it had been going on for some time. Her vision snapped back to her head and she sat dazed for a moment, the image of Corthie leading the horse imprinted into her mind.

'Your Majesty?' said a voice from through the door.

She stood. Her chambers were in darkness, as she had been using her powers throughout the evening and had not bothered to light any lamps. She walked through the shadows to the front door of her quarters and opened it.

Two men in Banner uniforms were standing outside. By their feet were two crates – one long and narrow, the other tall and wide.

'Good evening, your Majesty,' said one as they both bowed their heads.

'Have you been knocking long? I'm sorry; I was... distracted.'

One of them glanced at her face, and she realised that her cheeks were wet from tears. She wiped them and tried to smile, but the muscles around her mouth wouldn't respond.

'We have a delivery for you, your Majesty,' said the soldier. 'The chief artificer sent us up here to make sure you received the goods in person.'

'A delivery?'

He gestured to the two crates. 'Should we bring them inside for you, your Majesty?'

She narrowed her eyes for a moment, then nodded, and the two men lifted the crates and carried them into her living room. They set them down on the rug by a low table, and bowed again.

'Have you been given any orders to evacuate?' she said.

The two soldiers glanced at each other.

'No, your Majesty,' said one.

She nodded. 'Thank you for bringing me... whatever it is you've brought me.'

The soldiers bowed again, then left her quarters. She closed the door behind them and lit a wall lamp. The small flame grew, its light flickering around the grand chamber. She sat on a couch and looked at the crates. She leaned over and lifted the lid off the long, narrow one first. Inside, nestled upon a bed of straw, was the rebuilt Clawhammer. Its new handle glowed in the lamplight, the etchings and engravings standing out. Leather had been wrapped round one end as a grip, while at the other end, a new metal headpiece had been attached. It had been formed into the shape of a skull, and two of the three greenhide talons were protruding from the eye sockets, while the third was jutting out from the jaws. At the rear of the skull was a short, curved steel spike. She lifted it from the crate. In many ways, it was a different weapon from the one that Corthie had wielded in the City of Pella and the Falls of Iron, but the greenhide claws were the same as those he had taken on his first day beyond the Great Walls. She wept as she held it; the work had been in vain.

She set it back down, wiped her face and removed the lid from the taller crate. She pulled out the loose straw and frowned down at the contents. The artificer had made her a new set of armour, and the pieces were stacked inside. She withdrew a shining steel breastplate, and held it up to her chest. It was edged in burnished bronze, and looked like it would fit her perfectly. Why would the chief artificer send her such a gift? Was he trying to curry favour with an Ascendant? Perhaps he had seen or heard about the state of her old leather armour, with the hole through the cuirass that Sable's sword had made outside Yoneath. That old armour had served her well for years, but had given her the appearance of a common soldier rather than the Third Ascendant. The steel armour would change that, if she ever decided to wear it. She doubted she would – what need would she have for armour once she had been enslaved as Edmond's wife?

She shuddered at the thought, then her mind went back to Corthie and the horse. A new determination began to arise in her. What if she could get her hands on a Quadrant? She would only need a second to grab one, and then she could be gone. She could rescue Corthie and they could flee the destruction of Lostwell together; perhaps hide in the City of Pella, anywhere, as long as Edmond wasn't there. She realised how much she hated the Second Ascendant. The devastation of Alea Tanton had so consumed her thoughts that she had almost overlooked his role in it. He had murdered a million mortals, and had set in motion a process that would kill everyone else.

She replaced the lids on the two crates and stood. Edmond had a Quadrant, and so did Lord Bastion. Arete also had one, while Leksandr's would be located somewhere in the residence. Four Quadrants; surely she was capable of stealing one of them. She walked to the door of her quarters and went out onto the landing. Two guards were at their posts, while a small cluster of her servants were standing by the stairs, having been banished from her rooms when she had arrived back from the sea wall. They bowed to her, but she ignored them and ascended the steps to the top floor of the tower.

Two soldiers were standing outside the door to Leksandr's old rooms, where Edmond and Bastion had taken up residence.

'Is the blessed Second Ascendant in?' she asked the soldiers.

They bowed.

'His divine Grace has gone up onto the roof, your Majesty, along with Lord Bastion and the Seventh Ascendant,' said one.

'I think I shall join them. How do I get onto the roof?'

One of the soldiers walked to a small side door and opened it, revealing a set of stairs going upwards.

'Thank you,' said Belinda.

She went through the doorway and climbed the narrow stairs. At the top, she emerged onto a wide, flat roof with a low wall ringing the perimeter. Chairs had been carried up, and Edmond was sitting with his feet up on a stool, drinking red wine as he gazed down over Alea Tanton. Bastion was standing by his shoulder, his hands clasped behind his back, while Arete was sitting next to Edmond, a glass also in her hand. She was laughing, then stopped as she noticed Belinda.

'Ah, there you are,' said Edmond. 'I didn't think we'd see you again this evening. How are you feeling? Are you still upset? Would you like some wine? Bastion, pour her a glass.'

Belinda sat on an empty seat across from Edmond, and took the glass of wine that Bastion had prepared for her.

'Thank you,' she said.

'We've been amusing ourselves by watching all the fun,' said Edmond. 'Mortals are so predictable; shrieking and wailing, and running around like frightened sheep.' He paused, waiting for a reaction from her, but she kept her features impassive. 'Many are probably praying to me,' he went on; 'can you imagine? I was thinking of saving one or two of them; maybe a couple of the green-skinned variety, to take back to Serene as specimens for the lore masters to dissect. What are they called again; those green people?'

'Fordians, my lord,' said Bastion.

'Yes, that's right; another of Nathaniel's clever inventions. He was so inventive. Imagine coming up with salve, not to mention another world populated by mortals with powers. So very, very inventive.' He glanced down at the city and frowned. 'Those fires in the Shinstran district appear to be going out; we can't have that.' He raised a hand, and the flames around the Southern Pits grew in size, spreading from rooftop to rooftop in a roaring inferno. 'There, that will keep them going for a while. Not that it matters; by this time tomorrow, there will be nothing left to burn. Isn't that right, Bastion?'

'Yes, my lord.'

'I still haven't decided what to do about our two prisoners,' Edmond went on. 'What do you advise, Belinda?'

'Which prisoners? The cells under the residence are full.'

'Our immortal prisoners – Leksandr, and the other one.'

'Felice, my lord,' said Bastion.

'That's right. Felice. My instinct is to save the Ascendant and let the other one perish in the destruction of Lostwell, as a little reminder to the loyal inhabitants of Serene that even gods can die if they cross me.'

'I agree, your Grace,' said Arete.

'Do you?' said Edmond. 'I can sense from your thoughts that you secretly harbour a desire for Leksandr's death, as this would mean one fewer Ascendant to compete with for my favour. Such thoughts are unbecoming, my dear Arete.'

Arete's cheeks flushed and she lowered her gaze. 'Apologies, your Grace.'

'You can't help your feelings, I suppose. There, I have decided. Bastion, ensure Leksandr is brought to our chambers in the morning in time for our departure.'

'Yes, my lord.'

Edmond's eyes narrowed, and he stood.

'Is something wrong, my lord?' said Bastion.

'No, not wrong. I have just sensed someone using battle-vision down in the city. An extremely virulent strain. There are no self-healing powers associated with this use of power, therefore I must assume that it is Corthie Holdfast I am detecting. Bastion, can you also sense it?'

The Ancient turned his gaze to the city. 'Yes, my lord. Faint, but definitely battle-vision. He's using it to stay alert, not to fight.'

'Indeed. Send a full regiment of Banner soldiers after him. Tell them that the soldier who brings me his head shall receive a reward of five thousand gold sovereigns.'

Bastion bowed his head. 'At once, my lord.'

Edmond smiled as Lord Bastion descended the stairs. 'I shall mount it upon the wall of my bedchamber at home,' he said, 'where you, my dear Belinda, will be able to gaze at it every day, at least until it rots away.'

Arete narrowed her eyes.

'I can sense what you're thinking,' said Edmond, 'so it is time to let you in on our secret. Belinda and I will be marrying upon our return to Serene.'

Arete's mouth fell open.

Edmond laughed. 'You seem surprised, but this wedding has been a long time coming. We shall invite every Ancient to celebrate with us, in order to share our joy, and then we shall rule as husband and wife; the Second and Third Ascendants.'

'But...' said Arete.

'What's the matter?' said Edmond. 'Are you jealous? Do you wish you were becoming my bride, Arete?' He laughed again. 'Don't look so terrified; I'm only teasing you.'

Belinda glanced at him. 'I hadn't given you my decision.'

'I know, but is there really anything to decide? Choose now. It's either marriage or the mask, so choose wisely.'

'You will put me back in the mask if I say no?'

'That's right; that's what happens to people who break their vows to me.'

'Then I will marry you, Edmond.'

He sighed. 'Excellent. Now, I've been thinking about the Sextant. I must say, your idea was a very clever one; I have inspected every inch of the device, and I also believe that a part is missing. I am going to ask you to think very deeply for me, my dear. I know that you can remember nothing prior to the Holdfasts wiping your mind, but I wish you to consider everything that has occurred since. It would make sense that the missing part would be something that could be easily found, therefore I believe that you would have hidden it in plain sight. Has anyone given you anything since you arrived in Khatanax? An heirloom of some kind, or a trinket? It could be anything, but I suspect it would be made of metal. Does any of that seem familiar?'

'No,' she said.

'That answer was too quick. Either you didn't think it through, or you already know what the missing part is, and you're keeping it from me. Which is it?'

'Neither, Edmond. I had already considered this, and I can't think of anything that fits the description.'

He stared into her eyes. 'I wonder what secrets are in there. Not being able to read your thoughts makes you all the more enticing to me, and you enflame my desires like no other woman ever has. I would lie with you this night but, alas, I must stay here to supervise the annihilation of Lostwell. Tomorrow night, my dear, when we are safely back in Serene, I will show you how much I love you, and you will love me in return.'

Belinda said nothing, as fear gripped her heart.

'You'll make a lovely couple,' said Arete.

'Indeed, we shall.'

Belinda got to her feet. 'I think I will retire for the night.'

'That's a good idea,' said Edmond. 'Get some rest.'

She turned and walked to the stairs, amazed at her ability to hide her true feelings. She had wanted to scream when Edmond was telling her his plans for the following night, and yet she had kept her face steady throughout. He must realise that she was unwilling, she thought; he had to, didn't he? Or was he delusional, believing that she was as besotted with him as he was with her? Her thoughts turned to escape as she descended the steps. Running away would mean her death in the ruins of Lostwell, but death sounded a better prospect than either the mask or getting married to Edmond. She reached the landing and went down the main stairwell to her own quarters, ignoring the cluster of servants standing outside. She went in, lit a few lamps, and sat on a couch, her head in her hands. It would be simpler to end her own life, but she didn't know how. The Clawhammer was lying in its crate, but she doubted she would be able to use it to kill herself. What else did she have?

A sword, she thought; she had a sword.

She frowned. The Weathervane. A chill ran down her back, then she sprang up and ran to her bed chamber. She threw open the doors of the wardrobe, and pushed past her old, battered leathers to find the sword in its sheath at the back. She grabbed it, and drew it from the scabbard. Its dark metal blade glimmered in the lamplight.

She stared at it. The Sextant's missing part; it had to be, and it had been sitting in her wardrobe the entire time. Did Edmond already know, or had he been trying to trick her into revealing it? If so, then he was probably watching her at that moment, and she had just given him the information he needed. She sheathed the sword and hurried back into the living room, half-expecting the front door to crash open.

If she was right, then what would Edmond do next? He wouldn't come downstairs himself; he would send a lackey. He would send Bastion. She knelt by the tall crate and opened it, gathering up the loose straw and throwing it to the side. She laid out the pieces of armour on the rug, then began to strap them on over her clothes. She had no mail or padding, but the pieces fit her well, and weren't too uncomfortable. She attached the Weathervane to her belt, then stood and looked at her reflection. The armoured woman in the mirror frowned back at her, her eyes seared with a ferocious determination.

She would not be marrying Edmond, and she would not be abandoning Lostwell without a fight. It was her realm, and she was its Queen. If the land died, then so would she, fighting in its defence.

Her front door opened.

'Third Ascendant,' said Bastion; 'come with me.'

'No.'

He smiled. 'Found your courage at last, have you? I wondered when you'd break. The Second Ascendant is blinded by his love for you, but I can see the fear and hatred in your eyes whenever you look at him. How long have you known that the sword was the piece required for the Sextant to function?'

Belinda said nothing, her eyes still on her reflection.

'Third Ascendant, I order you to hand over the sword.'

She turned to face him. 'Come and take it.'

Bastion moved to the side, and a tall warrior in armour walked in, a studded club gripped in both hands.

'Renko,' said Bastion; 'take the sword from her.'

The dead Ancient lifted his empty eyes towards Belinda, then charged at her. He swung the club at her head, and she leapt backwards, her battle-vision flowing. He swung again, and the club glanced off the armour on her right shoulder, missing her head by an inch. She drew the Weathervane, and caught a glimpse of Bastion's eyes narrowing as he watched. Renko swung again, his longer reach keeping her back. She ducked under a fourth swing, then darted forward, gripping the Weathervane in both hands as she powered it through the air. It connected with the steel collar protecting Renko's neck and sliced right through and carried on, severing his head. The corpse fell to its knees, then toppled over onto the floor, the head rolling to a stop by Bastion's feet.

Bastion glanced down at it. 'The Second Ascendant is watching,' he said. 'I hoped that you would betray yourself by your actions, and you have proved me right. By attempting to keep the sword from us, you are deliberately disobeying a direct command of the Second Ascendant, and I'm sure you appreciate that there will be consequences.'

'Shut up, Bastion,' said Belinda. 'Admit that you're scared to fight me. If you come any closer, I will kill you, and you know it. You are nothing without your death powers, nothing but Edmond's slave.'

'We'll see if a month in the mask changes your attitude,' he said. 'If it doesn't, then perhaps a year would suffice? A century? A millennium? We have time; we can wait. Imagine, Belinda, what that length of time in the mask would do to you. I have seen proud gods on their knees begging for death to release them; you will be no different.'

Rage burned through Belinda, and she lunged forward, the dark blade swinging, but Bastion was fast, as fast as she was, and he calmly moved aside, a smile on his lips.

'You are doomed,' he said, 'and the last thing you will see before the mask is fitted onto your face, is me laughing.'

She raised her hand without knowing what she was doing, as anger flooded her. She reached within herself, pointed at Bastion, and willed him to die. A surge of raw power burst from her, a power she had never sensed or used before, and Bastion's body flew back from the impact. He collided with the wall in the hallway outside her rooms, his skin melting from his body like wax. Belinda went after him as he struggled to his feet, blood dripping from every part of him.

She raised her hand again. 'Die.'

Blood showered the hallway as Bastion's body was slammed backwards. He tottered on the edge of the lift shaft, the remnants of his skin hanging from him in ragged strips, then fell. Belinda rushed to the edge and looked down. His body was lying crumpled on the lift platform two floors below, a mangled mess of blood, bone and naked tissue. A soldier cried out in horror and leaned over the body. A bloody hand, stripped of its skin, reached out and grabbed hold of the soldier's arm. The soldier screamed in agony, and seemed to crumple before Belinda's eyes, while the body of Bastion began to regenerate. The soldier's cries ceased, and his dried-up, withered body fell onto the lift platform. Bastion reached out again, plucked a vial of salve from the soldier's tunic and drank it all. He stood, his skin re-forming, and glanced up.

Belinda froze, then ran for the stairs, leaping up them two at a time. She reached the landing by Leksandr's old rooms and cut down the two soldiers standing guard by the entrance, the Weathervane's keen edge ending their lives in seconds. She burst through into the study, and locked the door behind her. She shoved the couch over to block the entrance, then piled up everything she could find, her heart racing in panic. She upended a table, and rammed it between the couch and the door handle, then stood back, panting.

They would be coming; she didn't have long.

She turned to face the Sextant. The room was in semi-darkness, the only light coming from an open window, and she walked through the shadows towards the huge device, the Weathervane in her right hand.

She had the key to make it work, but she had no idea where it was supposed to go. She crouched by the Sextant, scanning its surface, looking for anywhere the dark blade of the sword would fit. It was impossible. The device was too big; there were too many places the sword could go, and she didn't have time to try even a small fraction of them.

Sounds echoed from outside the room, and from the stairwell came the thud of boots on the stone steps.

They were coming for her, and for the sword.

She stood, and turned to face the door she had blocked. She had battle-vision, and fire powers, and now she also had death powers.

She readied herself. Let them come.

CHAPTER 26

LORD OF THE CATACOMBS

Torduan Mountains, Khatanax – 3rd Kolinch 5252

Aila awoke in pitch darkness to the sound of grinding rock. The ground was shaking under her body, and she felt stones land on her from above.

'Everyone out of the caves!' shouted a loud dragon voice over the thundering rumble.

Aila scrambled upright, lost in the darkness. 'Kelsey! Where are you?'

'I'm right here,' said a voice next to her, and a hand grabbed hold of hers.

'Out, out!' called Frostback. 'The caves are collapsing.'

Aila was thrown back to the ground as the earth shuddered, and the noise sounded like the entire mountainside was uprooting itself. A large, clawed forelimb grasped her waist and she was lifted into the dust-choked air. She was shaken about in Frostback's grip, and then they were outside again, and she could see the moon and stars shining down from above. Frostback flew for a hundred yards, then set Kelsey and Aila down onto a narrow stone ledge near the bottom of the valley.

'Remain here,' the silver dragon said, 'I must return to help the others.'

She beat her wings and flew off, heading back towards the caves where they had been resting.

'Are you alright?' said Aila.

'I think so,' said the young Holdfast woman, shaking the dust from her hair. 'You?'

'Is Arete back? Has she come to finish the job?'

'I can't sense any powers being used, so hopefully not.'

They sat down on the cold ledge and stared in the direction of the cliffside. It was hard to see anything in the moonlight, but Aila could make out the silhouettes of several dragons flying above the ridge, and others swooping down, or ascending into the sky. She shivered in the cold night air, wishing she had a blanket or warmer clothes.

'Did you get any sleep?' she said.

'None,' said Kelsey. 'I was lying awake thinking about Sable and Corthie, and everything that's happened to us. And then the ground moved and a chunk of the cave's roof fell on me; a small chunk, luckily. How about you?'

'I think I'd just managed to drift off.'

'Pyre's arse, what a mess. I hope everyone's alright.'

The ground rumbled again, and the ledge where they were sitting juddered for a moment.

'I hate this place,' said Aila, clinging onto the rock as it settled. 'All of it; Lostwell, Khatanax, this hideous valley. Damn it; where's Corthie?'

'He's in Alea Tanton.'

Aila stared at her. 'What?'

'Do you remember I told you that I'd had a vision? I'm not going to say anything else about it, but I can tell you that he's alive and in Alea Tanton. He was in the vision, briefly.'

'And when were you going to tell me this?'

'I wasn't sure if I should. I mean, now you're all agitated. Knowing doesn't help.'

'No, Kelsey; it does help. Alea Tanton? Why would he go there? Does he think we're there?'

'I can't answer any of those questions.'

'Do you think we could ask Frostback to take us?'

'Let's wait and see what the dragons decide to do next. We still don't know what's going on over at the caves.'

'Was he hurt? In your vision, was he hurt?'

Kelsey sighed. 'I knew I shouldn't have told you. Look, Sable sees him; that's all I can say. It was through her eyes that I had the vision, and that's why I told her about it. Corthie didn't seem hurt, but it was only a flash.'

'Sable's in Alea Tanton as well? Good. That makes me feel a little better.'

'I still can't believe that Sable has her own dragon. She must have used her mind powers to trick him.'

Aila raised an eyebrow. 'Don't change the subject.'

'I was hoping you wouldn't notice.'

Frostback soared towards them and landed a few yards away, down the slope from where the two women were sitting, so that her head was level with them.

'Grim news, humans. The earthquake claimed the lives of another nine dragons. The entire network of caverns has collapsed. Some of the others are digging, looking for more survivors; it will be some time before they are finished.'

'Is your father alright? And Darksky and the children?' said Kelsey.

'They were sleeping close to the entrance of a cave; they got out uninjured.'

'Thank Pyre for that. I can't sense any gods close by; I think the earthquake might have been natural, or maybe it was caused by the eruption of the volcanoes by the Catacombs.'

'That was one of the questions I came to ask you. The others are worried that an Ascendant has returned, and I told them that you had the power to sense them.'

'No; I think we're in the clear. If I sense any powers being used, I'll shout out and let you know.'

'Thank you.'

Aila glanced up at the moon. 'Is it midnight yet?'

355

'Not yet,' said Frostback. 'It will be here in another hour or so.'

Aila nodded. 'How long would it take to fly to Alea Tanton?'

Frostback tilted her head. 'Why would you ask that?'

'I was just wondering.'

'I don't know for certain; maybe five or six hours?'

'We'll let you go back to the others,' said Kelsey; 'I'm sure you're busy.'

'I am. I will pass on your message that you can sense no gods, and will return when I can.'

Frostback extended her wings and ascended into the dark night sky, her shadow blotting out the stars as she flew.

'Could you not have waited?' said Kelsey. 'Nine dragons have just died, and all you care about is going to Alea Tanton?'

Aila said nothing. It was unfortunate that the dragons were dead, but Corthie was alive; and that was all that mattered to her.

Kelsey and Aila spent an hour sitting on the ledge in the cold, as the dragons continued their efforts to search for survivors inside the collapsed caverns. When they had finished, Frostback returned to the ledge, and picked them up in her forelimbs. She carried them a few miles to the south, where the other dragons had assembled on a low hilltop close to the wide empty expanses of the Fordian Wastes. The moon was shining down upon them, and Frostback's silver scales were radiant in the light. She landed, and the two women scrambled free.

Deathfang had positioned himself on the summit of the barren hill, and the other dragons gathered round in a semi-circle.

'This has been a calamitous day for us,' he said, his voice reaching the ears of every dragon; 'the worst day we have seen in a century. Some of you came with me when we escaped from the pits of that accursed city on the shore of the ocean, while others were already living in the Catacombs when we arrived. Still others were born in the Catacombs but, regardless of our origins, we are one kin; one family. As your lord, I have failed you.'

Many of the dragons looked surprised, and Burntskull seemed almost offended by the suggestion.

'It was I,' Deathfang went on, 'who allowed Blackrose to stay in the Catacombs, and so set in motion the events that have destroyed us. I nearly came to blows with the black dragon earlier today, but she had a point – she escaped from the pits, and it was not her fault that the Ascendants decided to retaliate. Nevertheless, had I not allowed her to remain in the Catacombs, we would still be there, living in peace. I take full responsibility, and will step down as leader. To make it easier for my replacement, I will fly into exile, alone.'

There was an outcry. Several dragons tried to speak at the same time, most of them objecting loudly to Deathfang's words. The huge grey dragon said nothing from where he sat on the hill's summit, his eyes looking over the small crowd.

'May I speak?' cried Burntskull above the noise. 'I have been Death-fang's closest advisor for decades; I have a right to speak.'

The shouts died away, and the yellow dragon stepped forward, his eyes on Deathfang.

'You are our lord, until we say different. You cannot relinquish your authority.'

'I can, and I have.'

Burntskull's eyes widened. 'But, my lord, please. No one here can replace you.'

'I'm sure you'll find someone.'

Burntskull turned to the other dragons. 'Do any here wish to claim the lordship? Is there one among you who thinks they could do a better job than Deathfang?'

No one uttered a word.

'You see, my lord?' said Burntskull. 'You are our leader. We beg you to reconsider.'

'You beg me?'

'We do; please stay.'

'If I did,' said Deathfang, 'would you all swear to follow my every command?'

'We shall,' said Burntskull. 'Does anyone object?'

Again, no one spoke.

'In that case,' said Deathfang, 'I reluctantly accede to your wishes.'

The dragons breathed out in collective relief. Aila shook her head, quite sure that the argument had reached the conclusion that Deathfang had intended from the beginning.

Burntskull bowed his head. 'Command us, my lord.'

'Our home has been destroyed,' Deathfang said, 'and that requires two responses. The first is that we must find somewhere new to live. The valley here has hidden us well for a long time, but there are other places in Khatanax where a colony of dragons could thrive and yet remain safe at the same time. One or two here among us remember the old days, before Dun Khatar was destroyed. South of that ruined city are forested mountains...'

'I've been there,' said Kelsey.

The dragons turned to look at her.

'Sorry,' she said; 'carry on.'

Deathfang's eyes narrowed for a moment, then he turned back to the other dragons.

'It will be a long and hard journey,' he went on, 'especially for the little ones, across wastes and deserts with no water, but we cannot remain here.'

The ground rumbled as he spoke, then the hill shuddered, sending half of the dragons into the air in fright, while Aila and Kelsey fell over. Behind them to the north, a fissure had opened in the side of a mountain, and lava was seeping from it. The ground vibrated again, and then a huge roar echoed across the hills as the side of the mountain exploded, blowing thousands of tons of rock into the sky. Lava poured out like a river bursting its banks, and spewed down the slopes towards where the dragons had gathered, lighting up the night sky.

Deathfang looked at the broken mountain in disgust. 'This land is dying. Follow me.'

He took off, and the other dragons followed. Frostback gathered up Aila and Kelsey in her forelimbs, and joined the others in the sky. Deathfang turned to the west, and they crossed back over the valley to the south of the Catacombs. The volcanoes there were still active, and their intensity had increased. Ash filled the air, and Deathfang was forced to turn away. He led them further south until they came out of the dense ash cloud, and followed the mountain chain until they reached a peaceful ridge a few miles from the edge of Tordue. Deathfang circled, then landed, and the others joined him.

'I can still feel the tremors through my boots,' said Kelsey, as she and Aila walked to where the dragons were arranging themselves into a ring. The younger dragons looked worn out, and so too were those who had been carrying the infants. Darksky remained to the rear of the circle, her three infants sleeping under her wing. She had said nothing during Deathfang's resignation speech, and Aila had seen her cast several angry glances at Frostback.

Aila sat on the ground. The air was chill, and she longed for a warm bed. She glanced up. She had become used to the stars above Lostwell, but missed the purple skies of the City at night.

The dragons talked about Dun Khatar for a while. As Deathfang had said, he and a few of the other oldest dragons remembered the city from their youth, before the gods of Implacatus had destroyed it. From the way they spoke, it seemed that they had been on friendly terms with the old rulers of Khatanax before the invasion.

'There might be problem with Dun Khatar,' said Burntskull, who was one of those who had been to the city as a young dragon.

'Yes?' said Deathfang.

'To the south of the city are mountains, just as you said, my lord. But some of those mountains are volcanoes. If volcanic activity is increasing in Khatanax, then perhaps it might be too dangerous there.'

'Then where do you propose?'

'I don't know, my lord; I have no alternative suggestions.'

The arguments continued, with various dragons offering their opinions regarding Dun Khatar or other sites where they could potentially settle on the continent of Khatanax.

Kelsey glanced up at Frostback. 'Why are you not getting involved in the discussion?'

'There are two reasons. Firstly, there is nowhere in Khatanax where I think we can settle; and secondly, there is only one thing I want to talk about, and my father has so far avoided it.'

'Oh. Is this about you and him?'

'Yes. He still hasn't answered my plea.'

'Maybe you should speak to Darksky first,' said Aila. 'If you can win her over, then things might go easier for you and your father.'

'I cannot; she hates me. I have had a troubled relationship with Darksky. Some of it was my fault; I have behaved badly toward her, but she made it very difficult.'

'Aila's right,' said Kelsey. 'We could come with you if you want?'

Frostback lowered her head for a moment. 'Very well, but you must stay back and say nothing. Darksky dislikes all humans.'

The silver dragon edged round the outside of the crowd until she reached Darksky, with Aila and Kelsey keeping up behind her. The dark blue dragon eyed Frostback as she approached.

'What do you want?' she said.

Frostback tilted her head. 'To make my peace with you, Darksky.'

The dark blue dragon took a step forwards, to shield her children from Frostback. 'I'm sure you do, now that you want something from Deathfang. You disrespected me daily in the Catacombs, and disobeyed your former father's commands; but now that your unwise choices have rendered you alone and without a protector, you want to come crawling back? You should have thought of that before you went off with Blackrose.'

The silver dragon's claws gouged tracks into the ground, but she bowed her head. 'I apologise for all of the times I failed to show you the respect you were due.'

'Fine words, Frostback, but that's all they are – words.'

'I promise that I will never disrespect you again.'

'Of course you do, now that you're desperate.' She glanced at Aila and Kelsey. 'I see you've brought your pet insects along; Blackrose has infected you with feelings for those vile creatures. You should get rid of them. My children are hungry; give me the insects so that my children may eat.'

Frostback's red eyes burned. 'No.'

'So, you disrespect me again? You would take food from my children's mouths?'

'I do not own the humans, so they are not mine to give; but, if you try to hurt them, Darksky, then I will protect them.'

Flames lapped round Darksky's jaws, and she tensed.

'What's happening here?' said Burntskull, barging between the two dragons. 'Darksky?'

'Frostback is behaving in her usual manner – disrespectful and threatening.'

'That's not true,' said Frostback; 'I came here to make peace and apologise. Darksky wants to feed the humans to her children.'

'One of the insects is a witch,' said Burntskull; 'she can sense the approach of the gods. We cannot kill her; she is useful to us.'

'What about the other one?' said Darksky.

Frostback growled. 'I will not allow it.'

'Would that not be a fair compromise?' said Burntskull. 'You'll get to keep one of your insects.'

'No,' said Frostback. 'Aila is going to be a mother, and I am her protector. I will defend her; I swear it.'

From behind Frostback's half-raised forelimb, Aila could see that every dragon was watching.

'Did you notice,' said Darksky, 'how she uses the insect's name? She has fallen in love with these creatures. The insects are the reason we had to hide in the Catacombs; they infest the land and build ballistae to kill us, and yet Frostback thinks they are worth more than the lives of my children.'

'You twist everything,' cried Frostback. 'I will go hunting, and bring back food for your children, but I will not let you kill the humans.'

'Yes, leave,' said Darksky. 'Take your insects and go, but don't bother coming back.'

Frostback glanced around at the watching dragons. 'If no one wants me here, then I'll go.'

Aila searched for Deathfang among the silent dragons, but couldn't see him anywhere.

'I want you to stay,' said the young green dragon with blue wings. 'I missed you when you were gone.'

'Thank you, Halfclaw,' said Frostback. She looked in vain for her father, then lowered her head.

'I lost my mother in the Catacombs, and have no other family left,' Halfclaw went on. 'If you're really leaving, then I'll come with you.'

Halfclaw strode through the dragons towards Frostback and stood by her side.

'Let's consider this carefully,' said Burntskull.

'What is there to consider?' said Frostback. 'If everyone except for Halfclaw thinks as little of me as Darksky does, then I would be better off leaving.'

'No one's leaving!' thundered Deathfang, as he shoved his way through the crowd from where he had been skulking.

'There you are, my lord,' said Burntskull, moving out of the way as Deathfang came to a halt next to Darksky.

'I was staying back,' the huge grey dragon said, 'hoping that Darksky and Frostback would be able to settle their differences peacefully, but I was mistaken.' He stared at Frostback and Halfclaw. 'No one is leaving. Look around; see how few of us remain. We cannot afford to lose two healthy young dragons approaching their prime. This is how the insects beat us; they divide us and we turn on each other. If we are to survive, we must stay together.'

'I will stay,' said Frostback, 'if you call me daughter.'

Deathfang's gaze remained on the silver dragon, but he said nothing.

'We discussed this earlier in the caves, Deathfang,' said Darksky, 'and I believe I made my feelings on this known to you.'

'You did, my love, but my heart is torn.'

'What about the compromise?' said Burntskull. 'Perhaps if Frostback was to give up one of her pet insects in order to feed the three infants, then everyone could be happy.'

'But I offered to go hunting for her,' said Frostback. 'I will not surrender Aila to be ripped to shreds before my eyes. She is carrying a child...'

'An insect child,' said Darksky; 'a child that will grow into yet another enemy we will have to face.'

'Not all humans are evil; I learned this in the forests of Kinell. Kelsey used her powers to protect me from the Ascendant, and Aila used her cunning to provide me with good advice. They are my friends.'

Some of the gathered dragons gasped in horror at her words.

'Your "friends?"' said Darksky.

Frostback held her head high. 'Yes. One of them, I may choose to be my rider.'

'She condemns herself with her own words,' said Darksky. 'Those of us who escaped from the fighting pits of Alea Tanton, do you recall the way the insects jeered and mocked us in the arena? How they spat on us and laughed when we were injured?'

'Some humans are evil,' said Frostback; 'that I will not deny. But if we are civilised beings, then we must be able to discriminate between the good and the wicked. Kelsey and Aila are not wicked.'

Darksky turned to face the others. 'Hear me. I am prepared to accept the compromise offered by Burntskull. If Frostback surrenders one of her insects to me, then I will not object to her presence among us.'

Deathfang's eyes beseeched Frostback. 'Well? What do you say?'

Frostback turned from his gaze. 'No.'

Burntskull turned to Halfclaw. 'Speak up. Do you think this is right? Will you leave with Frostback, knowing that her heart has been corrupted by her friendship with these creatures?'

'That is up to her,' said Halfclaw. 'I loathe the insects, but I respect Frostback's decision. Without a protector here, I will be at the mercy of any older dragon who wishes to throw their weight around.'

'Do not listen to him,' said Darksky; 'he is clearly besotted with Frostback; he has always chased after her. He is looking for a mate, and is not thinking clearly.'

Halfclaw looked aggrieved at her words, but didn't deny them.

'If that is all there is to say,' said Frostback, 'we shall go.'

She turned, ensuring that Kelsey and Aila remained shielded behind her forelimbs, then nodded to Halfclaw. The other dragons backed off, clearing a space for them. Halfclaw extended his long blue wings, their surface gleaming in the moonlight.

'Wait,' cried Deathfang. 'Wait, my daughter.'

Frostback froze, then slowly turned her head. 'I will not give up either of my humans.'

'I know that, but yet I claim you as my own. Do not leave us. You broke my heart once before, when I had to send you into exile, and now Ashfall has also left me. Do not break my heart again.'

Darksky gave him a look of contempt, while a few of the other dragons muttered.

Deathfang turned on them, his eyes full of rage. 'A short time ago, you all pledged your loyalty to me as your chief and lord. Are your promises worth so little, that you would oppose me at the first hurdle? If you want me as your leader, then you have to accept my commands; that is the bargain we struck.' He raised a giant forelimb, the claws extended. 'Does anyone intend to break their vows to me?'

No one spoke.

'Then, my word has the force of law. Frostback, you are my daughter once more, without conditions. You can keep your pet insects and, as my daughter, what is yours now comes under my protection. Halfclaw, I also pledge to protect you; the loss of your mother in the Catacombs was a bitter blow, but you shall not come to harm because of it.' He turned to Darksky. 'My love, I know that this is painful for you to accept. Frostback has not given you the respect you deserve. That will change, I assure you.'

Darksky refused to meet his eyes, and turned her head away. Death-fang gazed at her, then nodded.

'Father,' said Frostback, 'thank you. I will stay.'

Halfclaw pulled his wings back in. 'I also thank you, my lord.'

'It's settled,' cried Burntskull. 'The Lord of the Catacombs has spoken.'

Darksky strode away, leading her children with her, and the dragons began to disperse.

'Remain here,' said Deathfang, 'for I have not finished.' He waited until everyone was watching him again. 'Earlier, I spoke of two responses to the destruction of our home, and we have only discussed one of these. I now wish to turn to the other.' He paused, making sure he had everyone's attention. Darksky glanced over, her irritation evident. 'It carries risk,' he went on, 'but must be done. The god who ruined our home is currently luxuriating in comfort within the palaces of Alea Tanton. In order to restore our honour and our pride, I shall lead a pack of our strongest and fastest, and we shall deliver vengeance unto our enemies. The high promontory known as Old Alea shall be our target. We shall strike, and burn their palaces to the ground.'

'But, my lord,' said Burntskull, 'won't those same gods use their death powers upon us?'

Deathfang turned to Frostback. 'Your insect; you said that she can block these powers?'

The silver dragon nudged Kelsey forward. 'Tell them.'

Kelsey stood amid the massive dragons, her eyes wide.

'Hello,' she said. The dragons stared back at her. 'Thanks for not eating me or Aila. I know that we humans must seem a little ridiculous to you at times, but...'

'Get on with it,' boomed Deathfang.

'Of course. Right. It's true; I can block the powers of the gods. Not all powers; I can't prevent them using earthquakes or fireballs, but death powers – those I can stop. And, I can shield any dragon that stays within a hundred yards of me; if we stick close together, then no death powers will affect you. That's the key – a hundred yards. Within that circle, no gods will be able to harm us.'

Deathfang stared at her. 'You will accompany us.'

Kelsey gulped.

'We are taking an enormous risk,' said Burntskull. 'Can we trust what the insect says?'

'I am a witch, like Sable,' said Kelsey. 'I am a Holdfast.'

'And I am a living witness that she speaks the truth,' said Frostback. 'Were it not for Kelsey, the Ascendant would have killed me in the forests of Kinell. I will carry Kelsey upon my back during the attack.'

'Then you agree with my plan, my daughter?' said Deathfang.

'I will follow your lead, father.'

Aila stepped forward, her eyes darting from dragon to dragon. 'I also want to come.'

'Why?' said Burntskull. 'What use will you be?'

'None, but the father of my child is in Alea Tanton. His name is Corthie Holdfast, Kelsey's brother, and he is the greatest mortal warrior alive. He is fighting the Ascendants, as you intend to do. We could join forces with him.'

Deathfang pondered for a moment. 'Will you carry her also, my daughter?'

'I will, father.'

'Then, it is agreed. The children will remain here in this valley, along with those assigned to protect them, and I will lead the attack, with Frostback by my right shoulder, and every other dragon capable of making the journey. Darksky, I appoint you to lead those who remain.'

Darksky tilted her head. 'I shall do as you command, my lord.'

'And I?' said Burntskull. 'Perhaps I should remain too, in order to help with the children.'

Deathfang laughed. 'No, my old friend. You shall be on my left when we descend to Old Alea, to deliver flame and death to our enemies.' He scanned the crowd. 'Dragons, my beloved kin, prepare yourselves, for we will leave shortly. It shall be a red dawn, a bloody dawn of screams and terror; one that shall never be forgotten.'

CHAPTER 27

THE BROKEN CITY

Alea Tanton, Tordue, Western Khatanax – 4th Kolinch 5252

Corthie and Van stole down the farm track, passing a burning barn on their left, the flames rising up into the night sky. The gelding was frightened of the flames, but Corthie urged him on with soft words and a firm hand on the reins. They were on foot again, after having ridden the gelding on and off for most of the journey south. The remains of the city of Alea Tanton were on their right, a mile or two away over the fields, which were crowded with the survivors of the waves and earthquakes. Beyond, huge flames were coming from an area of the city that Van had told him was the Shinstran district, and many injured civilians were lying out in the open, screaming and wailing from burns they had received in the inferno.

Van stumbled, and Corthie shot out his free hand to grab him before he could fall.

'Do you need to go back on the horse again?' he said.

'No, I'm fine,' said Van; 'just keep going.'

Corthie frowned at the former mercenary. He looked far from fine. They had travelled over twenty miles since the last wave had struck the city, and Corthie had kept up a fast pace, hurrying towards the high promontory of Old Alea. He could see it clearly in the distance, the light sandstone cliffs reflecting the glow from the fires raging through the slums at its base.

He squinted. 'Are there faces carved into the side of Old Alea?'

Van blinked, exhaustion etched into his features, along with the dried blood from the cut across his cheek.

'Yes,' he said, 'the faces of the gods who ruled Alea Tanton. I think a few of them might be dead.'

'They carved their own faces into the rock?'

'You may not have realised this,' said Van, 'but some of the gods have a high opinion of themselves.'

Corthie gave a wry smile.

'Can we stop for a moment?' Van said. 'Just long enough for me to have a cigarette? It might be my last.'

They came to a halt once they had cleared the barn. Corthie looped the horse's reins round a gate post as Van sat on the ground and lit a cigarette.

'I can't believe you handed over a gold sovereign to buy those things.'

Van shrugged. 'The world is ending; what else am I going to spend my money on?'

The ground shook, and the horse whinnied in fear.

'It's alright,' said Corthie, stroking its flank as the tremors settled.

'But it's not, though, is it?' said Van. 'The earthquakes are coming every few minutes. We passed the location of the Southern Pits a little while ago. You used to be able to see them from here, they were so tall, but they've gone, completely gone. Who knows what will be left by dawn?'

'Old Alea will be left,' said Corthie.

'And how are we going to get in? I reckon that, by now, thousands of refugees will have tried to escape to the heights of Old Alea, but none of them will have made it through the gates. I've seen them; they're as well protected as the fortifications in the Falls of Iron.'

'We'll think of something.'

Van nodded, but his eyes were disconsolate.

Four men emerged from the shadows of the burning barn, each armed with homemade weapons.

'Your horse,' cried one, brandishing a long, curved knife; 'hand it over.'

Corthie eyed them. 'Or what?'

'We need that beast,' the man shouted; 'our families are starving.'

'You'll have to look elsewhere for food, lads,' said Corthie. 'The horse is mine.'

'I don't want to have to kill you; just give us the horse.'

'He can't be reasoned with,' snapped another, wielding a blacksmith's hammer; 'he's made his decision. Get him!'

Corthie decided not to wait. He clenched his fists and charged into them, his battle-vision singing. A single punch flattened the man with the hammer, then he dodged a jab from an improvised spear. He grabbed two men by the hair and cracked their skulls together, felling them both. The last man backed off, holding out a butcher's knife in front of him, then turned and fled.

Corthie leaned over and picked up the spear. It had been fashioned by strapping a knife blade to the end of a broom handle. He frowned and tossed it away.

'I don't think they even noticed I was here,' said Van.

Corthie picked up the blacksmith's hammer and tucked the handle into his belt, as Van stubbed out his cigarette and struggled to his feet.

'We need to find you some salve or something,' said Corthie, watching as Van held his back and winced.

'I would have slapped you if you'd suggested that a few days ago,' said Van. 'The thought of getting addicted to salve again chills my blood. But now? If we're all going to die, then I might as well have some.'

They walked on for another hour, as they inched their way towards the foot of Old Alea. They were forced into a detour that took them round a series of fields where two rival gangs were battling each other in the glow of the fires.

'Torduans against Shinstrans,' muttered Van as they watched from a distance. 'Even now, they hate each other.'

They turned, and skirted the far end of the field, leaving the warring factions to their rear. Ahead, the sound of the regular thump of boots could be heard approaching along the farm track.

Van halted. 'Wait.' He inclined his head to listen. 'That sounds like soldiers.'

Corthie glanced over his shoulder. Behind them, the battling gangs were only twenty yards away, while irrigation trenches lined the banks of the track, their deep water reflecting the moonlight.

'Dammit,' muttered Van, 'there's nowhere to run.'

'It'll be fine,' said Corthie. 'What are the chances the soldiers are after us? They'll be going to the fields to break up the fight.'

They moved to the side of the track as the thud of boots grew louder, then Corthie noticed steel armour glinting in the moonlight. The lead ranks of the Banner soldiers slowed as they saw Corthie and Van.

'It's him!' one of the officers shouted. 'Right where the blessed Second Ascendant told us he would be. Remember, lads, it's five thousand gold sovereigns for the one who brings me his head!'

Van glanced at Corthie. 'You were saying?'

Corthie leaped up onto the saddle of the horse, then pulled Van up after him. Taking the reins in both hands, he turned the gelding and urged it into a gallop. The horse responded, its steel-clad hooves clattering off the stones of the track as the soldiers began to chase them. Van clung on to Corthie's waist, his fingers gripping his belt as the gelding sped along the track. Corthie guided the horse into the field where the two gangs were fighting, and people dived out of their way.

Corthie brought the horse to a halt, and glanced around at the angry faces of the gang members.

'The Banner is coming!' he yelled, pointing towards the track. 'They're coming to kill us all!'

The first soldiers burst into the field, and several began loosing their crossbows in the direction of Corthie. A Shinstran was hit, the bolt ripping across his face, and a young Torduan standing by the horse took a bolt in his guts.

'Fight!' cried Corthie from the horse. 'Defend yourselves!'

Many members of the two gangs were staring in shock as more soldiers entered the field, but a few clutched their weapons and rallied. Bolts were being loosed into the crowd, and more fell amid screams, panic, and a rising tide of anger.

Corthie raised his arm. 'Follow me!'

He charged at the soldiers, and the mob roared, and followed him. A dozen more were hit by bolts as they crossed the distance, and then the gangs were in amongst the Banner soldiers, and all semblance of order and control was lost. Corthie leaned over in the saddle and smashed the hammer into the face of a soldier, but then the gelding was struck by a bolt and stumbled, sending Corthie and Van flying to the ground. Corthie rolled and picked up a shield from a soldier lying with a pickaxe lodged in his back, then sheltered behind it as more crossbow bolts were aimed at him. All around him was blood and chaos, as the gangs tore the soldiers to pieces. The Banner troopers, outnumbered ten to one, tried to withdraw, but the narrow track became a crowded bottleneck, and any who had entered the field were cut down in the carnage. Corthie drove forward, using the shield to batter any soldier who stood in his way. The blood-soaked hammer slipped from his hand, and he picked up a sword. Battle-vision flooded his senses, and he cut his way into the heart of the Banner regiment, memories of the Falls of Iron and Fordamere shining in his mind. Behind him, the gangs cheered him on, and rushed to follow, and like savage beasts they ripped through the soldiers, until the survivors broke and fled, throwing away their shields and running down the track to safety.

Corthie raised his sword, and the mob roared in victory, their old rivalries temporarily forgotten.

'We beat the Banner!' yelled a man covered from head to foot in blood.

Strangers slapped Corthie's back, while the bodies of the dead soldiers were looted, their weapons and armour stripped from them.

Corthie blinked as his battle-vision receded. Van. He turned, his eyes scanning the ground, then he hurried back the way he had come. He saw the gelding first. It was lying on its side, blood seeping from several bolt wounds, its lifeless eyes open. Van was propped up next to it, leaning against the dead horse's flank. Corthie crouched down by them.

'Are you alright?'

Van coughed up some blood, then hugged his ribs. 'It might be time for some of that salve you were talking about.'

'But how will I get any out here?'

'The Banner soldiers,' gasped Van; 'they might be carrying some. Check their pockets for a small vial.'

Corthie rushed back across the field of dead. He searched through the pockets of the first few soldiers he came to, but found no salve on them. He noticed a soldier with officer insignia on his helmet, and ran over to the body. A Shinstran civilian was pulling the boots from the officer's feet as he approached, and the man nodded to Corthie as he started to look through his pockets.

His fingers found a glass vial, and he took it out and held it up to the moon. Inside, a silvery liquid was swirling. Corthie ran back to Van and handed him the vial.

'None of the troopers had any,' Corthie said, 'only the officers.'

'They must be running low up on Old Alea,' Van said. He removed the stopper, lifted the vial to his lips and drank.

Corthie watched as Van's body writhed for a moment, his face contorted. Colour returned to his cheeks, and he groaned.

'That was amazing,' he gasped. 'I feel like I could take on the Ascendants on my own.'

'Give me the rest of it,' said Corthie; 'you know, to keep temptation out of your reach.'

Van glanced at the half-full vial, and hesitated for a moment before handing it over. Corthie tucked it into a pocket.

'I already want more,' Van said. 'Nothing feels as good, nothing.'

Corthie frowned at the mercenary, wondering if he had done the right thing.

'Hey, you,' cried a voice; 'the big guy.'

Corthie turned to see a group approaching him. Half were wearing assorted pieces of looted Banner armour, and all had swords.

'Aye?' he said.

'We saw you lead the attack on the soldiers,' the man said. 'Are you a demigod?'

'I'm a man, like you.'

'I'm handy in a fight, but I'm nothing like you. You moved like you had battle-vision.'

Corthie noticed that the group around him was growing. 'What do you want from me?'

The man gestured back towards the flames of the ruined city. 'The waves,' he said, 'the fires, the earthquakes... Some of us here think that the gods have done something to destroy Alea Tanton. I thought maybe you were a demigod; I thought maybe that you'd know.'

Corthie stood. 'I am mortal, but I know what's happening.' He waited as the crowd listened. 'Up in Old Alea, the Second Ascendant is watching over his handiwork. He has decided to destroy all of Lostwell. The devastation you witnessed here today is going on all over Khatanax, and it will get worse.'

'Why?' the man cried.

'None of your lives mean anything to the gods,' said Corthie. 'They don't care about you; they're up there drinking and laughing while they watch millions die. I'm going to do something about that. I'm going to walk up to Old Alea, and show the gods that not all mortals are yet beaten. If any of you want to, you can follow me.'

The crowd around him stood in silence, as if stunned that anyone would suggest opposing the gods. Van got to his feet next to him, and they began walking towards the track, the crowd parting before them. Van stopped, and pointed at the body of a tall Banner soldier.

'That breastplate might fit you, Corthie,' he said.

Van crouched down and started unstrapping the armour from the body as the crowd grew and grew.

'Who are you?' shouted a young man.

Corthie glanced up. 'My name is Corthie Holdfast.'

'You're not a Shinstran, or a Torduan, and you certainly ain't a damn Fordian.'

'I am not from Khatanax, and Alea Tanton is not my city, but I will fight the gods who did this. I fought Banner forces at the Falls of Iron and in Yoneath, and I have killed three gods. This night, I hope to kill more.'

Van stood, the breastplate in his hands, and strapped it over Corthie's chest, as the masses of gang members and civilians stared at him.

'There you go,' said Van, stepping back. 'Shield, sword and breastplate. You could almost pass for Banner. All you need is a helmet.'

'Then I'd better do without one. The last thing I want is anyone to mistake me for Banner.'

'The soldiers are only doing their jobs, Corthie.'

'I know. I've no doubts that they have good men and women in their ranks, but tonight, they're the only ones standing between us and Old Alea. Tonight, they are the enemy.'

He began walking along the track, and again the crowd parted to let him pass. He crossed the threshold where the last bodies lay, and carried on. Next to him strode Van, his demeanour completely altered by the dose of salve. He seemed alert and strong, and his eyes were wide.

Behind them, Corthie became aware that at least some of the crowd was following. Hushed whispering reached his ears, along with the clank of ill-fitting armour.

'What will the Banner soldiers do next?' said Corthie.

'Their orders seemed clear enough,' said Van. 'They were after you, and I heard the sum of five thousand gold sovereigns mentioned. That would be enough for any soldier to retire on. My guess is that they'll retreat for half a mile or so and then re-group. They'll sneak scouts along either side of this track, who will run back and report our position as soon as they've seen us, and then they'll probably set up ambushes. That's what I'd do.'

Corthie picked up his pace. 'Then we run, and deny them the time they need to organise.'

He broke into a sprint, his shield covering his left side, and his head down. He powered his battle-vision to a higher intensity, and wondered if salve would help prolong it, or even heighten it. He could take it whenever he began to tire, or if he got injured; whichever happened first.

He charged along the track, his senses picking up the sound of Van running a few paces behind him, and a large body of soldiers ahead. In front of him, the track opened out onto a wide farmyard, where the Banner had paused in their flight from the mob. Soldiers were standing in groups, catching their breath in the light of the moon and the flames. Many had their backs to the track, while officers tried to re-organise their ranks. A few shouted warnings as Corthie raced into the yard, and for a moment panic gripped them as they assumed that the mob had closed with them. Corthie charged into them, his shield battering soldiers from his path, but the soldiers closed ranks, their discipline holding them together.

Corthie abandoned himself to his battle-vision, his limbs moving automatically, but he wasn't fighting greenhides in the wastes beyond the Great Wall, and within moments, the professional soldiers were flanking round his sides to surround him, their shields raised. He glanced back at the track, but Van was nowhere to be seen, and then he had to concentrate on nothing more than staying alive as the ring around him began to close in.

He had made a mistake. If he had been wearing his old set of steel armour, and had been wielding the Clawhammer, then it would have been different, but his back and his limbs were unprotected against the swords of the Banner soldiers.

'Cut him down,' cried an officer, 'and every man here will receive his share of the reward!'

A loud roar rose up from the yard. At first, Corthie thought it had come from the soldiers around him, but then he noticed many of them glancing back towards the track in alarm. It was the mob. Hundreds of armed civilians were flooding the yard, pushing the Banner soldiers back, and the lines of soldiers bent, buckled, then broke under the pressure. They tried to retreat from the yard, but many were cut down as they fled, the mob's momentum unstoppable.

'You idiot,' cried Van, as he reached Corthie's side. 'Were you trying to get yourself killed?'

Corthie lowered his sword, panting. 'It seemed like a good idea at the time.' He pointed at the fleeing soldiers as they scattered back towards Old Alea. 'And look, it worked.'

'Only because I ran back and told the civilians to move their asses.'

'You did that? Thanks.'

The yard was packed with armed civilians, and they cleared a space around Corthie and Van.

'You asked them to follow you,' said Van. 'Now you'll have to lead them.'

Corthie turned to gaze up at the high cliffs of Old Alea. 'What's next?'

'The garrison had a fort at the base of the promontory, but it was next to the ocean, and most of it will be under water. The start of the ramp that leads up the slope emerges from the gates of the fortress, and this whole side of the cliffs has a low wall at the bottom to stop anyone getting to the ramp any other way.'

'Can we climb this wall?'

'Yes. It has no parapet, but once we're past it, we'll be in range of the ballistae up on the walls at the top of the cliff. If you lead the civilians that way, it will be a massacre.'

'Take us there,' said Corthie; 'I want to see for myself.'

An hour later, Corthie, Van, and several hundred civilians reached an area where the ground had been cleared. The slums of the Shinstran district came to an abrupt halt twenty yards from the low wall that Van had mentioned. To their right, the high battlements of the garrison fortress towered above the roofs of the slum dwellings, and the line of the ramp was visible as it snaked up the side of the cliff towards Old Alea. Corthie told the gang leaders to wait in the shadows of the slums, and he and Van ran to the low wall, and climbed up to take a look. Beyond, a large garden had been laid out next to the steep cliffside, but it looked as though it had been neglected for years, and was overgrown and withered.

'Every inch of land here,' said Van, 'can be seen by the soldiers up on the battlements, and the walls on this side of Old Alea have dozens of ballistae, designed to repel any uprising by the locals.' He pointed up, and Corthie squinted into the darkness. At the top of the ramp was a huge gatehouse, its strong gates firmly closed.

'What about the other sides?' he said. 'Are they unprotected?'

'Yes, but for the simple reason that it's impossible to climb up any of them.'

'It can't be impossible.'

'You and I might be able to scale the cliffs, but then we'd reach the wall at the top, and there's no way through that.'

'Then we'll have to charge the gatehouse.'

'It would be a slaughter, Corthie. The civilians wouldn't get halfway up the ramp.'

They jumped off the wall, landing back onto the side of the Shin-stran district.

'We have no choice,' said Corthie. 'We can't just sit here and wait to die.'

Van nodded, his eyes dark, then his body shook and he fell to one knee.

'Van!' cried Corthie.

The mercenary glanced up, his eyes glazed over. 'Hello, nephew.'

Corthie stumbled back a step, his eyes wide.

'I only have a minute, so listen carefully.'

'Sable? What the... How...?'

'How do you think, nephew? I'm in his mind; a place I've visited several times. I'm on my way, but it'll be another hour or so before I reach Alea Tanton; I'm just having a quick break, and thought I'd try to find you. Forget your stupid plan; all it will do is get you and Van killed, and dear old Aila would be most upset, not to mention Kelsey.'

'You've seen them? They're alive?'

'Alive and well, nephew. Now, listen to me. There is another way up onto the promontory, one that I spotted months ago when I was living there. I know it works, because I sent Millen that way when he needed to escape from Old Alea.'

'Millen?'

'Never mind. I've imprinted the route into Van's brain, so that when he awakes, he'll know which way to go. I'll meet you up there, and then we'll get you a Quadrant.'

'The Ascendants are destroying Lostwell, Sable; all of it. The Second Ascendant...'

'I already know this, Corthie; I'm in Van's mind. I may have been wrong about Belinda. Get up there, and break into Old Alea, and together we'll wreak some havoc. Got it?'

'Eh, aye, alright.'

'Bye.'

Van slumped forward and groaned. 'Sable...' he muttered; 'again.'

Corthie crouched by him. 'Did you hear what she said?'

'Of course I heard; her voice sounded like a bell ringing through my mind.'

'Do you know the way?'

He nodded. 'It's been stamped into my head like a boot in the face.'

They hurried back to the shelter of the ruined slums that edged the Shinstran district. Waiting for them was the leadership of the mob, made up of gang bosses from the Blue Thumbs and Bloodflies supporters, their enmities forgotten in the chaos and violence of the previous day and night.

Corthie stood before them. 'Wait here,' he said. 'Van and I will open the gates from the inside. When that happens, bring everyone up to Old Alea. Of all the places in the city, it will be the last to be destroyed.'

'How will you break in?' said a grizzled old Bloodflies supporter in stolen armour.

'We have been shown the way. Rest, gather weapons, and collect the strongest force you can. Then, go over the wall and up the ramp, once you see the gates open.'

'Is this really the end of Tordue?' said a Blue Thumb.

Corthie gazed at their expectant faces. 'It is the end of Lostwell.'

It was three miles from the edge of the Shinstran district to the place at the base of the cliffs that Sable had imprinted into Van's head, on the southern flank of Old Alea. In the darkness, Corthie could see no way up the steep cliffs, but Van led him to a shallow cave, where a path ascended the slope. Above them stretched a high aqueduct that brought fresh water all the way from the Torduan Mountains to the residences of the gods.

'The entrance is up there,' said Van, pointing, 'where the aqueduct crosses the walls. This path must have been built so that workers could repair the waterway.'

They sat for a moment, resting, and Van lit a cigarette.

Corthie took the salve from his pocket. 'Should we have some?'

Van eyed the vial, his desire for its contents written into his features. At length, he shook his head.

'Save it for when we need it.'

Corthie nodded. 'My battle-vision should last a little bit longer, but after that, I'm going to need to sleep for a month.'

'If we don't stop the gods, we'll be sleeping for a lot longer than that.' He frowned. 'How is Sable getting here?'

'I don't know. On foot? She said she was a couple of hours away. She knows where Aila and Kelsey are, so our priority is getting a Quadrant.'

'And what about all of the civilians?'

Corthie lowered his gaze. 'Pyre knows how many have already died.

I don't know, Van. If we can't stop the gods from destroying Lostwell, I don't know how we can save them.'

Van stubbed out his cigarette. 'When I first heard about this operation, I gambled everything on getting a place on it. I borrowed money from Sohul, and used up every favour that was owed to me. I even bribed a doctor to forge a note saying that I was in good health. I thought we were going to be in and out, a quick operation that would help pay off some of my debts.' He shook his head. 'No one on Implacatus will care about the destruction of Lostwell. The Banners will mourn their losses, but none of the gods will raise an eyebrow at the annihilation of an entire world.'

Corthie got to his feet and glanced at the steep path that snaked up the side of the cliff face.

'It's our job to stop that happening,' he said. 'Come on; let's pay the gods of Old Alea a visit they'll never forget.'

CHAPTER 28

THE GATES OF OLD ALEA

South of Alea Tanton, Tordue, Western Khatanax – 4th Kolinch 5252

Sanguino glanced down at Sable. 'Did you find your nephew?'

'Yes,' she said, rubbing her temples, 'and just in time; they were about to charge up the ramp of Old Alea to their deaths.'

'Then we did the right thing.'

Sable looked up at the dark red dragon. 'I'm so sorry about what happened, Sanguino. You chose me over Blackrose, and I know how much that decision has cost you.'

'Do you think they have already left Lostwell?'

'I don't know; maybe? It will take them time to transfer all of the iron and gold up to the forecourt, but after that there will be nothing to delay them.'

Sanguino lowered his head. 'I don't regret it. I wanted to go to Dragon Eyre, but I'd rather be with you.'

Sable stood and stretched her arms. Looking north from the foothills of the Torduan Mountains, she could see a dull red glow on the horizon. Alea Tanton was burning.

'Are you ready for the final stretch?'

'Yes,' said Sanguino.

'We'll follow the line of the aqueduct that crosses the plain. Keep low, in case any god is watching.'

'And then?'

'Then, we go to war.'

The ground rumbled under them, and a series of rockslides cascaded down the high slopes to their rear. They had flown over freshly-made ravines that were pulsing out lava into the heart of the mountain range, and had witnessed high, barren peaks collapse as the ground had writhed in torment. Sable hadn't understood it at the time, but after reading Van's thoughts, she had realised what was happening.

'When the sun comes up,' she said, 'it will herald Lostwell's final day.'

'What do you mean?' said Sanguino.

'The Ascendants have destroyed this world; I read it from Van's mind. By tomorrow night, there will be nothing left. By leaving Blackrose, I may have killed us both.'

The dragon said nothing.

'I have made many mistakes, Sanguino.'

'You didn't know, my rider. It's not your fault.'

She tried to smile. 'Yes, but even if I had known, I would still have left the Falls of Iron. My sister's son needs our help.'

'Then let us find him.'

She turned from the red glow on the horizon and climbed up onto the harness, buckling the strap round her waist. Sanguino extended his great wings and rose into the night sky. He circled once, then surged to the north. He angled to the left and descended a little, soaring above a tall stone aqueduct that crossed the plain. Sections of it had collapsed, and fresh mountain water was pouring from the broken stonework. The miles rushed below them as Sanguino flew at his top speed, and Sable had to narrow her streaming eyes to see anything amid the wind that struck her face. She pushed her vision out, relying upon it rather than her physical sight, and scanned the tormented and broken countryside ahead of them. She found a battery of anti-dragon defences, but it had been abandoned, and the nearby barracks block was on fire, its roof collapsed. Slaves were roaming the fields, after having freed themselves in the chaos. They were trailing south and south-east away from the city that had kept them in chains for so long. To them, the waves and earthquakes had been a blessing, an act of god that had set them free. Corpses also littered the fields – those of slave masters and guards, cut down by their former chattel. Farms had been gutted, and every large barn was in flames, or had fallen to the ground in a heap of debris.

'For years,' said Sanguino, 'I have wished to see Tordue suffer, but now that it has happened, I feel nothing but pity in my heart. I looked down, and glimpsed the hope and joy upon the face of a slave child, a child who will be dead before the sun sets tomorrow. The Ascendants must have known the pain their actions would bring, and yet they did it anyway.'

The city appeared in the distance, marked by the high cliffs of Old Alea. The promontory looked at peace, while flames were rising from the slums at its feet. Sable pushed her vision round the flanks of the cliffs, and saw the ramp. On the battlements above the gates, hundreds of soldiers stood ready next to their large ballistae, each pointing down at the approaches to Old Alea, while at the bottom of the slope, over a thousand armed civilians had gathered behind the shadows of a low wall, the place where Sable had seen Corthie and Van. An earthquake rumbled through the city as she watched, and more buildings crashed to the ground. The tremors were so violent that they reached the cliffs of Old Alea, and with a crack that split the sky, the face of one of the carved gods detached itself from the rockface and tumbled down. It struck the gardens below, exploding into a thousand fragments of sandstone amid a cloud of dust that spiralled up into the night sky.

Sable guided Sanguino along the route of the aqueduct, keeping low, and she turned her attention to the narrow path that snaked up to where the stone water-bearing channel cut through the wall at the top of the cliffs. Close to the summit were two men.

'I see them,' said Sanguino. 'I assume the taller of the two is your nephew?'

'Yes,' said Sable, 'and the other is Van, a former mercenary, whose loyalties now lie with all those opposed to the Ascendants. We shall draw attention away from their position, and cause some trouble elsewhere in Old Alea. The more soldiers we can pull away from the gatehouse and the Governor's residence the better.' She used her vision to look over the huge mansions dotting the high plateau. 'Lady Felice's old palace; that will do.'

She drew her vision in as the promontory rushed towards them. Sanguino banked to the left, following the line of cliffs away from the aqueduct, then soared up and over the walls. Soldiers were patrolling the streets, ensuring the large civilian population remained in their homes, and the dark red dragon was spotted within seconds.

Sanguino surged over the narrow terraced houses and wide, open estates until they reached the sprawling palace where Felice had her home.

'Burn it, my love,' said Sable; 'burn it to the ground.'

'With pleasure, my rider.'

Sanguino soared across the meadows and parkland of the estate, then opened his jaws. Sparks flew, followed by a great burst of dark flames, red, tinged with blue, and the central wing of the mansion exploded as it was enveloped in fire. Soldiers screamed as they fled the inferno, and Sanguino hovered for a moment, moving his head in a shallow arc as the flames spewed out of his jaws. A tall tower ignited, its stones glowing red, then it toppled into the western wing of the palace, driving through the tiled roof into the interior below with a crash that rang through Sable's ears.

A few crossbow bolts whistled by them, and Sanguino lowered his gaze to the soldiers in the gardens beneath them. He opened his jaws again, consuming a dozen in a flash of orange flame.

'That should do it,' said Sable; 'we have their attention. Ascend out of range.'

Sanguino beat his great wings and soared upwards, and Sable glanced down at the promontory. Soldiers were rushing towards the location of Felice's mansion, along with companies of fire fighters and their water wagons.

'Alright, back to the aqueduct.'

Sanguino banked and headed to where they had last seen the two men. A large, walled reservoir stood close to where the aqueduct pierced the walls, and Sanguino alighted onto the roof of a low building next to it. Sable unbuckled the waist strap and dropped down to the roof.

'Fly straight up; I'll contact you once I've spoken to Corthie.'

Sanguino tilted his head, then soared back up into the sky. Sable watched him for a few seconds, then climbed down from the roof, and hurried to the side of the reservoir. She followed the stone channel that fed it, turned a corner, and ran into Corthie and Van.

They stared at each other.

Sable put a hand on her hip. 'So, I've finally found you at last, nephew? Better late than never, I suppose.'

Corthie grinned, then wrapped his wide arms around her and squeezed. 'Auntie.'

Sable pushed him away with a laugh then glanced at Van. 'I hope you've been looking after my sister's boy, and not leading him astray.'

'Not at all, Sable,' said Van. 'From what I've heard, it seems that you're the bad influence.'

Sable squinted at him. 'Have you been smoking keenweed? Have you got any?'

'No.'

'Are you sure? You look... unusually alert.'

'I've had a dose of salve.'

'Ah. I see. Well, I'm glad you've taken something; we have a lot of work to do.'

'How did you get here?' said Corthie.

'Never mind that for now. I'm guessing our priority is to obtain a Quadrant, so we can escape from Lostwell?'

'Aye; that, and to take down as many gods and Ascendants as possible. And, we need to help Belinda.'

'If she wants to be helped.'

'I've heard from lots of people that you two hate each other, but Belinda is like a sister to me.'

'It pains me to hear that, nephew.'

'I guessed it might. My plan was to attack the gatehouse from the rear, and open the gates. There are hundreds of armed Blueflies and... whatever the others are called.'

'Bloodflies and Blue Thumbs,' said Van.

'Aye, them. There are hundreds waiting at the base of the ramp. If we can open the gates, they'll flood into Old Alea, and we might have a chance of getting inside the Governor's residence. That's where Belinda is, and the gods' Quadrants will be there too.'

'And the Sextant,' said Sable. 'If we can take that with us, we can stop the Ascendants finding our world. I like your plan, Corthie; I'm sure your mother would be very proud of you.'

'Come on,' said Van, shaking his head. 'How are three of us going to storm the gates? Even from the inside, they'll be heavily defended.'

'Sable has battle-vision,' said Corthie.

'Even so. We haven't a chance. Maybe we should just try to sneak into the residence. Sable and I both know the layout well.'

'You're right,' said Sable, 'except for one thing – there are four of us, not three.'

Corthie frowned. 'Do you mean Belinda?'

'No, not Belinda.'

Sanguino, descend to me. Land by the banks of the reservoir.

'Who else is here?' said Van. 'Have you brought another all-powerful Holdfast?'

'Not quite. He'll be with us in a moment.'

The two men glanced at each other, then their eyes widened in alarm as a huge shadow appeared overhead. Sanguino landed a few yards away, tucked his wings in, then extended his neck towards them.

'You called, my rider?'

Corthie staggered back. 'You have a dragon?'

'I'm his rider; I don't "have" him, or, at least, we have each other. His name is... Sanguino. What do you think of our odds now, Van?'

'I would say,' mumbled the mercenary, as he stared up at the dragon, 'that they have improved considerably, ma'am.'

She laughed. 'Don't call me "ma'am." Well, not unless you want to. We'll follow Corthie's plan. Sanguino and I will deal with the gatehouse, while you two make your way to the Governor's residence. Don't try to get in until the gates of Old Alea are open, and then we'll join you. We'll stay outside, causing a commotion, and you get a Quadrant, and Belinda too, I suppose; but please, I implore you, be wary of her. Once we're all out, Sanguino can hit the western tower of the residence, where the Sextant will be, and destroy it, if we can't take it with us.'

'That all sounds fine,' said Corthie, 'except for one point. Blackrose tried to burn the Sextant in Fordamere, and it was completely undamaged. I don't think it can be destroyed.'

'Damn it,' Sable muttered. 'Alright, that part of the plan we may have to improvise. If I need to talk to you, I'll land and speak to Van.'

'Can't you talk to us from the air?'

'No. I need my powers to fly.' She turned towards the harness. 'Good luck, boys. See you at the residence.'

Sanguino ascended back into the night sky.

'Keep to the walls by the south side,' she said. 'There are fewer soldiers guarding that stretch.'

'I shall, my rider. Why did you tell your nephew that *you* needed powers to fly? The opposite is true; I need you.'

'What is it with dragons and their obsession with lies?' she said. 'What I said was technically true; if it weren't for my powers, then I wouldn't be able to fly on your back, so I wasn't actually lying.'

'You were defending me; you didn't want them to pity or mock me.'

'My truth is open to interpretation.'

'Your entire relationship with the truth troubles me at times.'

'Just concentrate on the job at hand. If we survive, we'll have plenty of time to philosophise about the nature of truth.'

Sanguino banked to the left, following the wall as it turned north. The battlements over-looking the ramp were packed with soldiers. Most were gazing down at the city, but several caught sight of the approaching dragon. Some were trying to reposition their ballistae to meet the new threat, but the machines seemed to be fixed to aim down towards the ramp.

'They are at our mercy,' said Sable; 'show them none.'

'Yes, my rider.'

Sanguino unleashed a long burst of flames as they soared over the line of battlements. Soldiers fell screaming, engulfed in the river of fire as it consumed the walkway atop the walls. The large gatehouse was halfway along the stretch of battlements. It had a roof platform filled with ballistae, and Sanguino rose up and delivered another volley of fire, incinerating everything. He hovered for a moment, turning his attention to the courtyard directly behind the gates. Some soldiers were fleeing, but others were trying to organise a response, and several crossbow bolts were loosed at the dragon. Sanguino opened his jaws, filling the courtyard with flames.

'Now the gates,' said Sable; 'bring them down.'

Sable felt the heat around her rise as the dragon descended into the burning courtyard. He turned his head towards the thick, iron-framed gates, and blasted fire at them. They ignited, the wood blistering and splitting, the iron beams glowing red hot. Sanguino enveloped them in fire, and the gates buckled under the force of the flames, then exploded outwards, sending fiery fragments spinning into the night sky.

A crossbow bolt struck Sanguino's right flank, and he grunted, then turned. Banner soldiers were gathering to his rear, forming into lines, and he swooped down at them, using his claws to sweep through their ranks, ripping the soldiers to shreds. He sent out another burst of fire, consuming a squat barracks block. The windows blew out, and the roof collapsed in the inferno. Sanguino rose up again, and Sable glanced down. Beneath them, nothing was moving, and charred and smoking bodies filled the yard.

Sable guided Sanguino back up to the walls, and he soared over the remaining stretch of battlements until the last ballistae had been reduced to burning ruins. At the base of the ramp, hundreds of civilians were staring up at the walls, watching the destruction of the defences.

With a roar, they surged forwards, breaking into the gardens and spilling up the slope towards the ramp. More were emerging from the shadows of the ruined streets, armed with farm tools and stolen Banner weapons, and the hundreds turned into thousands, a vast mob of vengeful humanity.

Sanguino turned away from the battlements. Companies of soldiers were rushing through the streets of Old Alea from the direction of the Governor's residence, and more ballistae were being prepared from the backs of several wagons.

'Quickly, Badblood,' Sable said; 'get them before they can loose at us.'

Sanguino beat his wings and surged through the air, crossing the narrow terraced streets of Old Alea where the mortals lived. He sent a long stream of flames down the centre of the road, engulfing the wagons and the ballistae operators, and sending the companies of soldiers scattering for cover. The dark red dragon banked as he approached the edge of the huge structure of the Governor's residence.

Sable glanced at the building, her gaze lingering on the western tower where she had killed Maisk. A solitary figure was standing on the roof of the tower, his skin seeming to give off its own light, as if a star had descended from the skies.

'The Second Ascendant,' she gasped. 'Turn; get us away from the residence.'

'Is this not our chance to kill him, my rider?'

'His death powers will kill you first. I'm immune, but you're not.'

Sanguino banked again, and the figure on the roof raised his hand. The dragon let out a cry of agony, and Sable could feel his pain through her connection to him. She urged him on, and he soared away, nearing the estate of Felice, where the mansion was still burning. He began to descend, his strength failing, and they tumbled towards the ground. Sable clung on as he crashed into the gardens of the estate, his limbs buckling under his weight and ploughing furrows across the grass as he skidded to a halt, unconscious.

Sable released the waist belt and slipped to the ground, her legs shaking. She drew her sword and scanned the gardens. A few people were staring across the parkland at them from the vicinity of the burning mansion, but no soldiers were approaching. She placed her left hand onto Sanguino's side, and felt the beat of his heart; it was weak, but persisting. She circled the dragon looking for threats, knowing that soldiers would be diverting to their location. A powerful feeling struck her temples and was rebuffed, and she realised that the Second Ascendant was trying to access her mind. Having failed, he would likely guess her identity as a Holdfast, and send everything he had against her and the dragon.

She leaned against the still form of Sanguino to catch her breath, then heard the sound of boots in the distance. Glancing up, she saw ranks of soldiers entering the gardens from the direction of the residence. They took a few moments to form up into a thick line, creating a deep shieldwall, then began their advance.

Sable drew on her remaining battle-vision. If she was going to die, then she would do so defending her dragon. With some surprise, she realised that she loved Sanguino more than she loved any human. He understood her, and yet accepted her the way she was; he hadn't tried to change her, and treated her as his equal. She glanced at the crossbows that bristled from the front of the approaching shieldwall.

'Come on, you bastards!' she cried.

She cursed her luck, and cursed the words that Kelsey had whispered to her in the valley close to the Catacombs. She had met her nephew, as Kelsey had foreseen, and with the prophecy fulfilled, there was nothing to prevent her death.

'Sorry, Badblood,' she whispered. 'You should be on Dragon Eyre with the others. What have I done?'

The ranks of soldiers had crossed the first stretch of grass, and were approaching the range where they would be able to cut her down with their crossbows. Another rumble of noise grew nearer, and she turned, expecting to see yet more soldiers close in on her position.

She was wrong; it was the mob from the city. Hundreds of armed civilians, many with blue sashes or red armbands, were entering the gardens through a different gate. They raced across the parkland, among the neat lines of trees, and slammed into the side of the Banner formation. The outnumbered soldiers kept their lines intact, but were pushed back, their shieldwall contracting under the strain as the mob swarmed round them.

A few of the mob peeled off from the others and reached where she stood next to the fallen dragon.

'We saw you go down,' said one with a blue sash over his shoulder. 'Is your dragon alive?'

'He is,' she said, watching as the Banner forces retreated back across the gardens, their numbers lessening as they attempted to withdraw.

'We shall protect him,' said the man; 'and you. You broke down the gates.'

'You'll protect him? You swear it?'

'We swear it, miss.'

Another civilian, with a red band round his arm looked closer at the dragon. 'It's Sanguino!'

The other rebels gasped.

'You can't trust the Blue Thumbs to protect him, miss,' cried the Shinstran. 'They wanted to kill him in the arena.'

'We did,' said the Torduan, 'but that seems a long time ago now.'

Two men pushed their way through the crowd.

'Are you both alright?' said Corthie, his eyes wide.

Next to him, Van was staring at the fallen dragon.

'I'm fine, nephew,' she said, 'but Sanguino...'

Corthie rushed forwards, his hand fumbling in a pocket. He took out a small vial, and opened the dragon's jaws with his free hand, his heels digging into the ground as he strained. He emptied the contents of the vial onto Sanguino's tongue and stood back.

The dragon shook, causing the crowd to edge away a few feet, then he opened his eyes. He glanced around at the crowd, then his gaze settled on Sable.

'You're safe,' she said. 'Corthie used his salve on you.'

The Shinstrans in the crowd cheered, while a few Torduans looked nervous.

'Thank you, Corthie,' said the dragon. He turned to Sable. 'We should fly, my rider. My heart aches for vengeance against that damned Ascendant.'

'No,' she said. 'If you go up again, he will strike you down again, and that was the last of the salve.'

'None of us can get close to the Governor's residence, miss,' said a Torduan. 'Anyone who tries has their skin melted off.'

Sable glanced at Corthie. 'You're like me, aren't you? Immune.'

He nodded.

'Van,' she said, 'stay here with Sanguino; protect each other. Corthie and I will go to the residence.'

'But, my rider,' said the dragon; 'I fear for you.'

'This is the only chance we've got. On foot, Corthie and I might be able to break into the residence. The death powers of the Ascendants cannot harm us.'

'No,' said Van, 'but a crossbow bolt through the throat would.'

'Then do your job,' she said. 'The job of everyone here is to keep the soldiers busy.' She glanced around the crowd. 'Do you hear me? Keep the soldiers' attention over here. Loot, burn and destroy the mansions of the gods, but leave the homes of the mortals untouched. Corthie and I will do what needs to be done. Are you with me, nephew?'

'I'll be right by your side.'

She smiled, then glanced back at the crowd. 'If we're successful, we'll bring Quadrants back with us, and everyone left alive will be saved.'

'But where will we go?' said a Shinstran. 'Corthie told us that Lost-well is being destroyed.'

'I don't know yet,' said Sable; 'one thing at a time.'

She walked over to Sanguino and placed her palm against the dark red scales. 'Wait here for me, my beloved. You will draw the soldiers to you. Van and the other humans will fight by your side today.'

'Please, my rider, be careful.'

She kissed the side of his head. 'I will.'

'Folk of Alea Tanton,' cried Corthie; 'the dawn that approaches will be the last that Lostwell sees. This night, let Torduans, Shinstrans and Fordians fight as one, alongside the red dragon. If we survive this, you can quarrel again tomorrow; but for now, your unity is all that will save you.'

Van stuck out his hand. 'Good luck, Corthie.'

He shook it, then he and Sable raced away, running towards the gates leading to the residence, the thick crowds parting to let them through.

'What's the plan?' said Corthie, as they entered the streets outside Felice's estate.

'Kill everything in our path until we have a Quadrant in our hands.'

'Do you know how to use one?'

'Come on, Corthie; this is Auntie Sable you're talking to. Of course I know how to use a Quadrant.'

They turned a corner and saw the huge residence ahead of them. They ducked into the shadows along the side of the street and slowed their pace.

'This is it,' he said. 'Are you ready?'

'The world is ending,' she said, 'and millions are dead; I'm ready for anything.'

CHAPTER 29

THE KEY

Alea Tanton, Tordue, Western Khatanax – 4th Kolinch 5252

Belinda paused behind the smoking ruins of the barricade by the door, allowing her powers time to heal the wounds inflicted by the three crossbow bolts. Hundreds had been loosed at her in a barrage that had lasted minutes, but her new armour had deflected most. Beyond the barricade, the bodies of the soldiers were piled so deep that they were blocking the landing leading to the stairwell. The attack had been brought to a halt, but her escape route was sealed off.

She didn't care. She would go down with Lostwell, and her only hope was to prevent the Second Ascendant from being able to take her or the Sextant back with him when he returned to Implacatus.

The massed soldiers with their bows had been the second wave that had attempted to breach Leksandr's old study that night. The first had been a team of demigods, each equipped with battle-vision and death powers, and she had cut them down and thrown their bodies from the window, the Weathervane singing in her hands as she had wielded it.

She glanced outside, searching in vain for signs of the coming dawn, then sat down next to the Sextant, the Weathervane across her knees. She paused for a moment, then turned back to the window. Lady

Felice's estate was ablaze, and more flames were coming from the vicinity of the gatehouse that guarded the approach to Old Alea.

She stood to get a better look. As she did so, the air shimmered behind her. Without hesitating, she rolled to the floor, as Arete lunged forward with a sword, a Quadrant clutched in her left hand. Belinda sprang back to her feet, the Weathervane held out.

'Leksandr got me that way,' she said. 'Did you think I wouldn't have learned?'

Arete said nothing, her eyes tight.

'Are you going to flee, now that your little plan has failed?' Belinda said. 'Are you going to run back to Edmond?'

'Bastion was right; you've gone completely insane. What are you trying to accomplish? You cannot hope to win.'

'All I need to do is stop you from winning.'

Arete laughed. 'You fool. Did you know that, even now, the blessed Second Ascendant thinks you can be saved? He doesn't realise that it's much too late for that.'

'You should be careful what you say; he's probably in your head right now, Arete, watching you fail to kill me.'

'Oh, I'm sure he is. At least he'll see the extent of your treachery. You've already killed four demigods this night, not to mention putting Renko out of his misery.'

'They were sent here to arrest me, to place me in chains, or put me back in the mask.'

'Lord Edmond wishes to offer you a deal.'

'He does? Then why did you strike as soon as you arrived? Did he expect you to fail?'

'Perhaps he did. If you leave this chamber voluntarily, he promises that you can walk free from the residence. Despite his feelings, the Sextant is worth more to him than you. What do you say to that, Belinda? I think it's the best offer you're going to get tonight.'

'Do you believe his promises, Arete?'

Arete smirked. 'What I believe is immaterial.'

395

'If you give me the Quadrant, I'll let you live. Do you believe me?'

Arete's eyes wavered for a moment, and Belinda struck. She surged forward, swinging the dark blade in both hands. Arete raised her sword, but the Weathervane sliced through the steel blade as if it wasn't there. Arete's fingers brushed over the surface of the Quadrant just as the Weathervane connected with her neck. Her body vanished from the room, but her head remained. It fell to the floor and rolled onto the rug.

Belinda looked away, then bent down and picked it up by the hair, then hurled it through the open window. She wiped the blade on the rug, smearing it in blood.

She had just slain an Ascendant, one of the most powerful and ancient beings in existence, but she didn't feel any different. Arete's death hadn't given her any joy or satisfaction, nor had it repelled her. Her only regret was that she had been a fraction of a second too slow. Any quicker, and she would have obtained a Quadrant, and now it was back in Edmond's possession, along with the headless body of the Seventh Ascendant.

She sat down, her back to the Sextant. No sound was coming from beyond the half-burnt and smouldering barricade, and she wondered who would be coming next to try to defeat her. Bastion, perhaps? She could scarcely believe that Edmond would put himself at risk; he would prefer to send minion after minion, but what would happen when he tired of that? He had the power to destroy the entire western tower, crushing her under a thousand tons of rubble. She glanced at the Sextant. During a lull between the first and second waves of attackers, she had spent some time probing the device with the sword, looking for places where it could snugly fit. She had found a couple, but the device had remained inactive. Was it supposed to spring into life if she found the right spot? Some of the parts inside the device seemed to be made of the same dark metal as the sword, and she presumed that they were significant in some obscure way. She peered closely at the interior, her mind trying to make sense of the jumble of cogs and pipes. It looked fragile, but she had seen what it had gone through in Fordamere. If

Edmond did decide to collapse the tower, the Sextant would probably be the only thing that would survive.

The chandelier above her tinkled as another earthquake rumbled through Alea Tanton. She longed to send her vision out to investigate, but if Bastion arrived with a sword and a Quadrant while she was gazing out onto the city, her resistance would be brought to a swift end.

She remembered the flames rising from the gatehouse in the walls; what did they signify? Were the mortals rising up against their overlords and assaulting Old Alea? She hoped so. If they were all doomed to die, then it was better that they met their ends with defiance in their hearts rather than despair. Her people were being exterminated, like vermin, so that Edmond could wash his hands of Lostwell; her Lostwell. Nathaniel may have made it, but she was its Queen.

A long, slow hour passed. The tower was in silence, though she could hear sounds coming from the streets of Old Alea. Fighting was going on, and she guessed she had been correct about there being an uprising, but she had remained in the seat, her eyes continually scanning the room, her right hand gripping the hilt of the Weathervane.

Where was Edmond? The last place she had seen him was up on the roof of the tower, but she doubted that he would still be there. Perhaps he was dealing with the uprising, knowing that Belinda was contained within Leksandr's old rooms. Maybe the death of Arete had scared him, and he had already abandoned Lostwell to its fate. No, he wouldn't have left without the Sextant, for it was his only route to securing the supply of salve. She suppressed her frustrations; she needed to stay alert, ready.

She heard a soft sound come from beyond the barricade. She got to her feet and raised her left hand, preparing her powers. A figure peered over the smoking couch blocking the entrance.

'Corthie?' she cried.

Belinda ran forward as the figure clambered into the room. She threw her arms around him, tears coming to her eyes.

'Belinda,' he said, 'are you alright?'

'You're alive,' she said, stepping back to look up at his face. 'When Edmond sent the Banner out against you, I thought...'

'You thought what?' said another voice.

Belinda turned, and her eyes narrowed. 'What are you doing here?'

'What do you think?' said Sable. 'We're trying to get off this world before you crazed Ascendants destroy it. Do you have a Quadrant?'

'No.'

'What have you been doing in here?' said Corthie. 'The stairwell is full of bodies.'

Sable strode past them and stood before the Sextant. 'She's been defending this... thing.'

'Yes. If I can stop Edmond taking it, I will. I've been here for hours. They've sent soldiers and demigods against me. Even Arete.'

Sable turned. 'You fought Arete?'

'I killed her.'

Corthie's eyes widened. 'You killed an Ascendant on your own?'

'I am an Ascendant, Corthie; the Third. You should know that I have death powers now.'

'They won't work on us,' said Sable.

'And why would you think I'd want to use them on you?'

'You tried to kill me the last time we met.'

Belinda's temper bubbled to the surface. 'You attacked me, Sable. You didn't give me a chance to explain what I was doing; you lunged at me with your sword. And didn't you have a Quadrant? What happened to it?'

'I gave it to Blackrose.'

'Is Blackrose coming?' said Corthie.

'No. She, and the rest of them, will be in Dragon Eyre by now. Only I was stupid enough to come here.'

'What's happening outside?' said Belinda.

'Sable broke open the gates,' said Corthie, 'and the Banner soldiers are fighting thousands of civilians who came up the ramp. The residence seems deserted; we hardly met any resistance on the way here, apart from a squad at the entrance. If we can get a Quadrant, we can come back here and take the Sextant with us. We'll need to pick up Van and Sanguino first, then Aila and Kelsey, and anyone else we can find; and then we can go home.'

Belinda felt her chest constrict. 'I am home, Corthie. Lostwell is my home.'

'Yeah?' said Sable. 'Well, your home is in the process of tearing itself to pieces. Do you want to live or not?'

'I want to get the Sextant working.'

'What's wrong with it?' said Corthie.

Belinda raised the Weathervane. 'It needs this. This is the missing piece, the key. Only, I don't know where it's supposed to fit.'

'Is that the sword that Silva gave you?'

'Yes, though she had no idea of its true significance. All she knew was that I had told her to keep it safe.'

Corthie walked up to the Sextant. 'This brings back some bad memories,' he said. He glanced at Belinda. 'You saved me, back in Fordamere. Thank you. The two Ascendants... they...'

'I know, Corthie,' she said. 'I watched it happen.'

'They were too good for me.'

'You tried to fight two at the same time.'

Sable crouched by the huge device. 'If we can get this beast working, can we use it as a Quadrant?'

'Yes.'

'Then stop talking and get that sword over here. I can see several places where a blade would fit.'

'That's the problem,' said Belinda, as she walked over. 'I've tried many locations.'

'Corthie,' said Sable; 'watch the stairs.'

'Actually,' said Belinda; 'Corthie, go down one flight of stairs and into my rooms. Look for a long crate on the floor. There's something inside for you. A gift.'

Corthie frowned. 'Use your vision first; see if anyone's there.'

Both women turned to the doorway.

'It's clear,' said Sable.

'Yes,' said Belinda, 'but be quick. I don't know where Edmond is.'

Corthie clambered over the barricade and slipped from the room.

Sable and Belinda gazed at the Sextant.

'Are all your powers back?' said Sable.

'I'm missing flow and stone.'

Sable half-smiled. 'You've got all of the important ones, then. Are you really thinking of sacrificing yourself for this stupid world?'

'Aren't you doing the same thing? I thought you would have taken the chance to leave with Blackrose? Wasn't that your plan? Why did you come back?'

'For Corthie.'

'You're doing the same as me. We're risking everything to try to save what we love. For me, it's Lostwell; for you, your nephew.'

'We're not the same, Belinda. And Lostwell's doomed; Corthie isn't. I intend to live through this, and find somewhere for me and Sanguino to settle. I wanted it to be Dragon Eyre, but right now, anywhere would do, even the damn Holdings. I don't like you, Belinda, but Corthie loves you. Don't throw your life away for a world that cannot be saved.'

'My realm.'

'In a matter of hours, your realm will consist of nothing but dust and corpses. If you could only...'

Sable's voice tailed away as another strong rumble shook the tower. Dust floated down from the ceiling, and a painting fell from the wall, clattering over the polished floorboards. The chamber settled for a moment, and the two women glanced at each other, then the ceiling collapsed at the same time as the floor gave way. The walls tumbled in and the tower fell. Belinda lunged forwards as rubble bombarded them and covered Sable with her body, pushing her next to the Sextant as everything in the chamber plunged downwards. Darkness enveloped them amid the thunderous roar of collapsing masonry. The impact with the ground drove the breath from Belinda's lungs, then a stone block struck her back and head, and she lost consciousness.

———

She awoke in the ruins of the tower. Light was flickering through the gaps in the rubble, the light of flames. She felt groggy, but her self-healing was thrumming, and her body had repaired itself. The armour had helped, she thought, pushing herself up. Beneath her lay Sable. Belinda placed a hand against the woman's face. She looked uninjured, but Belinda's healing senses could feel the crushed ribs and broken bones. She shot a surge of healing into Sable's body, then pushed up again, using her battle-vision to move the heavy blocks and shove them to the side. She climbed up from the wreckage and saw a figure glowing ahead of her.

'Like a god, you arise from the ashes,' said Edmond, standing a dozen yards away at the edge of the mountain of rubble. 'I should have guessed that toppling the tower wouldn't kill you.'

'Do you want to kill me?'

'I didn't, but then I saw what you did to the Seventh Ascendant. You butchered one of the most ancient beings alive, someone who has survived countless wars; someone who was there with us at the beginning. If only you could remember. You've changed, Belinda. The old you would never have slaughtered one of your own kind.'

'I am the Queen of Lostwell.'

Edmond laughed. 'What?'

'I am the Queen of Lostwell, the world you decided to destroy. Fight me.'

'Don't be ridiculous, Belinda. I will not stoop to fighting you. You will step aside and allow me to take possession of the Sextant, and then you will accompany me to Implacatus, where you will become my bride. That is your future; it is inescapable. You will also be punished for what you did to the Seventh Ascendant; that is also inescapable.'

'You will not take the Sextant, and you will not take me.'

'Where is the sword, Belinda?'

'I dropped it when the building fell.' She gestured to the rubble. 'I imagine it's somewhere in there.'

Edmond's eyes glazed over for a second, and a company of Banner soldiers approached. The ruins of the western tower had fallen into the rear yard of the residence, and a stretch of the mansion's main wing had been damaged by collapsing masonry. Belinda glanced around. A hundred soldiers were fanning out behind Edmond, while another company was approaching from the other side of the mansion, with Bastion and a fully-healed Leksandr leading them. Beyond the perimeter wall of the residence, flames were rising from several directions, and the sounds of fighting rang through the air. To the east, a faint light was building, and the moon had set.

'Belinda,' snapped a voice behind her. 'Get over here; I've found Corthie.'

She turned for a moment. Sable was crouching a few yards away in the rubble, her hand clutching something. Belinda edged over, dreading to see what it was. She crouched down next to Sable. It was Corthie. He was breathing but, like Sable, he had suffered several broken bones in the fall of the tower. She shifted a massive stone block that was crushing his legs, and touched his hand, sending a great burst of healing powers into him.

'This is for you,' said Sable, holding out the Weathervane. 'It was buried next to the Sextant.'

Belinda took the sword as Corthie's eyes opened.

'What happened?' he said. 'Everything went dark.'

Belinda smiled. 'Edmond brought the tower down, and hundreds of soldiers are surrounding us.'

'Then why are you smiling?'

'Because you're alive. I thought... well, I tried not to think about you. You are the one constant in my life, Corthie. You were there with me, in the attic, in the beginning. You are my first memory.'

'We should get ready to fight,' said Sable; 'otherwise he'll also be your last.'

Belinda and Sable stood, and then Corthie pulled himself to his feet, his right hand gripping something made of steel. He ripped the Clawhammer from the rubble, and the three of them stood side by side on the summit of the ruined tower. Soldiers had moved into position around the rubble, their shields forming a thick wall. Behind them, Edmond stood.

'Belinda!' he cried. 'Do not make me do this; I beg you. What do you want? Say it, and it shall be yours; only step aside and give me the Sextant. I will even spare the lives of the two Holdfasts by your side. They can come back with us to Implacatus; they can be your mortal servants, honoured and safe; just stand aside. I understand your feelings of confusion. I made a mistake with Lostwell, I can see that now. It was your realm, and I shouldn't have destroyed it. Let me make it up to you. With the Sextant, I can create for you a brand new world, and fill it with whatever makes you happy. Would that be enough for you? Speak, I implore you; say something.'

'Go back to Implacatus, Edmond,' she said; 'without me, and without the Sextant. That is all I want from you.'

'I cannot, my dear, and you know the reason why. Salve. All this death and destruction, that is what it has been for – salve. Thousands of gods depend upon it, Belinda; from the Ascendants and Ancients down to the lowliest demigod; it has returned our youth and vigour, and has given a second life to the rulers of the worlds. To return empty-handed would destabilise the order I have struggled for centuries to restore. You must understand.'

'You are frightened,' she said. 'You fear the gods will rise up against you once the stocks run out.'

Edmond bowed his head. 'You shame me. Even so, my love for you remains undimmed. You were right before, you are a Queen. As my wife, we would rule together, and your kindness would temper my...'

'Cruelty?'

'Yes! The millennia have jaded my sympathies, but you are young again; you would be the greatest Queen in the history of Implacatus.

With that kind of power, you could help me remake our rule, transform it into something better.'

'He wants to marry you?' said Corthie, the Clawhammer gripped in both hands.

'He does,' said Belinda. 'He thinks he loves me.'

Edmond's face contorted with rage. 'You made a vow! You promised that you would be my bride, Belinda, you promised. The things I did for you, the crimes I committed so that you could be with me; if only you could remember, I...'

'Your Grace,' said Bastion; 'perhaps now is not the time for such secrets to be aired.'

Edmond faltered for a moment. 'You are right, Bastion. When the Third Ascendant and I are alone, then I will tell her, then, I will confess.'

'She has made her decision, your Grace,' Bastion said. 'Old Alea is weakening with the coming dawn; it will soon become too unstable to remain here.'

'Yes.' He took a breath. 'I tried; so be it. Destroy the Holdfasts and bring me Belinda.'

Bastion bowed, then gestured to Leksandr. Both men raised their right hands, and Belinda felt their death powers swirl around her and the two Holdfasts.

'They are immune to such things,' snapped Edmond. 'Burn them out.'

Bastion nodded. He turned to the south, where thick flames were rising over the grounds of an old palace. He and Leksandr lifted their hands again, and the fires twisted up from the blaze in two long channels. They intertwined in the skies above the ruined tower, then surged down. Belinda raised her left hand, using her fire powers to deflect the oncoming roar of flames. They hovered over their heads for a moment, just yards away, then Belinda sent them into the main wing of the residence. The flames smashed into the tall building, ripping through the fine tapestries and marble-lined hallways in a crescendo of fire that lit up the night sky.

Bastion's face remained expressionless. He signalled to an officer of the Banner. 'Advance.'

Belinda watched as the soldiers surrounding the mountain of rubble locked their shields together and began to close in. Corthie stood to her left, the rebuilt Clawhammer ready, while Sable was on her right, a Banner-issue sword in her right hand. Belinda could see more reinforcements arriving through the main gates. They looked worn out, their lines ragged, and Belinda realised that their appearance could only mean that the rebels in Old Alea were gaining ground. Bastion saw them, and ordered them into position, bolstering the ranks of those surrounding the tower.

A whistle blew, and the soldiers stopped the advance and readied their crossbows.

Belinda didn't wait for them to loose. She raised her hand again, and sent out a dense wave of death powers into the tight lines, and the soldiers gasped, clawing their throats as she stopped their hearts and lungs from working. A great groaning cry arose as hundreds of soldiers collapsed around them, their crossbows clattering off the paving slabs, and their steel armour grinding together. Silence fell over the courtyard, and Belinda felt a pang of guilt at the deaths of so many by her hand.

Beyond the ring of corpses, only three figures still stood, reflecting the three on top of the heap of rubble – Edmond, Leksandr and Bastion.

Bastion laughed, shattering the silence. He raised his arms, and the bodies of the soldiers began to twitch then, slowly, they got back to their feet, their eyes lifeless and dull.

'Swords,' Bastion cried, and each soldier drew their weapon.

'No flow powers, you said?' muttered Sable. 'You could have blown their heads off with flow powers. Now we're going to have to fight the dead.'

Belinda aimed her death powers at the advancing soldiers, but they had no effect. She switched to fire, and tried to channel the flames down from the burning residence, but Leksandr and Bastion diverted them so that they fell harmlessly to the rear of the courtyard.

'Yes,' she said; 'we'll have to fight.'

'About time,' said Corthie.

'Resist the urge to charge into them,' said Belinda; 'we fight back to back, to the end.'

Corthie hefted the Clawhammer. 'Aye, to the end.'

Sable frowned. 'Whose end, exactly?'

Belinda kept her eyes on the advancing soldiers. 'To the end of the world.'

CHAPTER 30

THE LAST DAWN

A lea Tanton, Tordue, Western Khatanax – 4th Kolinch 5252

Aila and Kesley huddled together on Frostback's shoulders. For hour after hour they had soared through the cold night air, and both women were shivering under their thin clothes. They had crossed the Torduan Mountains and then, with Deathfang leading the raiding party, they had flown over the long miles of the plains of Tordue. The moon had set, and the darkness had been almost complete.

'We are nearly there,' said Frostback, 'I can see the city in the distance.'

Kelsey squinted ahead. 'Can you?'

'Yes. It is burning.'

Behind them, a faint patch of light was growing on the horizon, and the features of Tordue grew visible out of the shadows and gloom. Aila frowned as she peered down. Bands of people were roaming the fields, all heading away from the city, and every farmhouse and barn appeared to have been destroyed. Smoke was rising from some, while others had been flattened as if a giant hand had crushed them.

'More earthquakes,' muttered Kelsey.

'Not just earthquakes,' said Frostback. 'Much of the city appears to be underwater, as if it has slid into the ocean.'

Aila stared ahead. Towering columns of smoke were rising above the horizon, and as the light in the sky behind them grew stronger, she began to pick out the flames tearing through the slums of Alea Tanton. To their left, the high promontory of Old Alea stood clear of the lower districts, but flames were also rising from there.

'Every building has been destroyed,' said Kelsey.

'Not every building,' said Frostback. 'Several within the walls of Old Alea still stand.'

Deathfang banked, and the other dragons joined him in circling over the edge of the ruined city.

'We have arrived,' he cried out, 'but it seems we shall find no vengeance here. The accursed city has already been destroyed. Their anti-dragon defences are in ruins, and the ragged survivors are at our mercy, but what damage could we do that has not already been done?'

'Then, my lord,' said Burntskull, 'should we return to the ridge in the mountains?'

'Wait,' said Frostback; 'Old Alea yet remains. Smoke is rising from its palaces, but they have not been touched by the earthquakes. That is where the gods shall be; that is where we can take our vengeance.'

'You are right, my daughter,' said Deathfang; 'let us scour the cliff tops of Old Alea.'

'Remember the hundred yards, my lord,' said Burntskull. 'We must stay within that distance from Frostback, or else the gods will strike us down.'

'Indeed,' said Deathfang. 'I shall go, with Frostback and Halfclaw; the others shall retreat a few miles and rest.'

'But, my lord...'

'I have spoken, Burntskull; do as I bid.'

The huge grey dragon peeled off, and Frostback and Halfclaw moved into a tight formation behind him.

'Stay close,' said Deathfang, 'and go where I go. I did not win back a daughter only to lose her.'

He surged off towards the promontory, skirting the edge of the Shinstran district. Aila stared at the devastation. As Frostback had said, miles of the city were submerged under the waves, with only the tops of the ruined buildings poking up from the dark water. A long strip of city had remained above sea-level, but every building seemed to be on fire, or had collapsed into rubble. Thousands of refugees were streaming out of the city, heading into the relative safety of the fields, but earthquakes were continuing to rip and buckle the land. A new river of lava had burst through the surface, and was spouting molten rock and ash into the sky a few miles to the north.

'What's happening?' Kelsey whispered, her eyes wide.

'I don't know,' said Aila. 'I thought that the volcanoes and earthquakes were only affecting the valley of the Catacombs. This is... something else, something terrible.'

A thunderous roar ripped through the ground as they approached Old Alea, and the last faces of the gods carved into the rock face collapsed, showering the ramp below with rubble, and killing dozens of civilians who were trying to make their way up onto the plateau. At the top of the ramp, the gates had disappeared, and the gatehouse was in smoking ruins. Deathfang led them up and over the line of walls that surrounded the promontory, passing smouldering heaps of burning ballistae and piles of charred corpses. Beyond, the streets were in chaos. Armed bands of civilians were battling small detachments of Banner soldiers, and bodies lay scattered upon every road. A mile ahead of them, an enormous palace set amid huge gardens was burning, the flames reaching up into the growing light as dawn approached.

Behind them, the sun breached the horizon, sending its rays across the surface of Old Alea, and the extent of the slaughter became clear.

'I can sense powers,' said Kelsey.

'Where?' said Frostback.

'Ahead and to the right, next to that huge building with the tower. Death powers, and fire.'

'Father,' Frostback called; 'Kelsey has located the gods.'

Deathfang slowed a little, careful to remain close to the silver dragon. 'You take the lead from here, my daughter; guide us to them.'

'Yes, father.'

Frostback powered her wings and moved to the front of the formation, Deathfang to her right, Halfclaw to her left. Aila stared at the ground as they approached the building. Was Corthie somewhere down there among the carnage?

'I see Sanguino,' called Halfclaw; 'he is in the gardens of the burning palace.'

'Leave him for now,' said Deathfang; 'we shall check on him once we have dealt with the gods.'

Aila leaned to the left, her fingers gripping the folds on Frostback's shoulders. She caught a brief glimpse of the dark red dragon, surrounded by dozens of humans, who appeared to be fighting Banner soldiers alongside him. A blast of fire rose up from the gardens, incinerating a group of soldiers who had ventured too close to where Sanguino was standing.

'He seems to be holding his own,' said Aila, 'but I can't see Sable.'

'I can see her,' said Kelsey, staring directly ahead.

Aila turned. At the western end of the huge building, a tower had collapsed. Surrounding it was a swarm of soldiers, scrambling up the slopes of rubble to confront three figures upon the summit – Sable, Belinda and Corthie.

'Frostback!' cried Kelsey. 'Sable's down there, in the centre of the rubble, and my brother is with her.'

'Is he the one with the clawed hammer?'

'Aye.'

Deathfang closed in on their right. 'Look at them fight! I am tempted to leave them to it; I have never seen humans fight like that.'

'Help them,' said Aila; 'please.'

'There are three gods down there, too,' said Deathfang.

'Kelsey will block their powers, father,' said Frostback. 'We must act before the soldiers' numbers prevail against Kelsey's kin.'

'And this will work, you can assure me, daughter?'

'It will, father.'

'If you are wrong, we will all die.'

'You must trust me.'

'Very well, daughter; lead on.'

Frostback swooped down, the other two dragons staying close to her flanks. They opened their jaws together, and unleashed a flood of flames onto the soldiers scaling the heap of rubble. They circled the mound once, incinerating the thick ranks of armoured humans, then turned for the gods.

All three raised their arms as the dragons approached. Deathfang flinched, but nothing happened, and the dragons opened their jaws again. Flames exploded over where the gods stood, and they were engulfed in the blast of fire.

'Run, gods, run!' laughed Deathfang. 'Taste my vengeance and burn!'

The flames cleared a little as the three dragons banked together. One of the gods had vanished, and of the two that remained, one was fleeing on foot, his hair and robes alight, while the other was trying to crawl away. Deathfang peeled off to chase the fleeing god.

'No, father,' cried Frostback; 'you must stay close to Kelsey.'

Deathfang pulled short at the last moment, and they watched as the running god ducked into the smoking building. Then they turned to the one who was crawling along the ground. His clothes were hanging in burnt, tattered strips, but his skin was regenerating. The three dragons hovered over him, aimed down, and enveloped the god in flames. The paving slabs cracked and split, and a scream rose up with the intense heat and smoke, but the dragons were relentless, their streams of fire combining into a white hot inferno. At last, Deathfang closed his jaws, and the other two did the same. Not a trace of the god remained amid the glowing slabs.

'Today,' Deathfang said, 'we have slain a god, and sweet vengeance is ours.' He turned to Kelsey. 'You, girl, are a true wonder, and I was wrong about you. Frostback, your rider will always be honoured by me, from this moment forth; I swear it.'

'My rider?' said Frostback. 'Yes. My rider. Kelsey, do you wish it to be so?'

'Of course I do!' cried Kelsey

'Then I accept you as my rider.'

'Let us land,' said Deathfang; 'the other two gods have fled, as cowards are wont to do.'

They circled one more time, then descended into a clear area of the vast yard. Aila slid and clambered down from Frostback's shoulders and ran towards the heap of rubble. The charred and blackened bodies of the soldiers were spread across the remains of the tower, and she struggled up the slope. Corthie saw her, shouldered the Clawhammer and rushed down towards her. He scooped her up in his arms and held her close, the stench of death and ash filling the air around them. She didn't care, her head buried into his chest as he held her tight. He kissed her face and her neck, then pulled back so he could gaze down into her eyes.

'I was supposed to rescue you,' he said; 'and here you are, with three dragons.'

'And Kelsey,' she said; 'your sister's here too.'

'You again?' said Sable, as she reached them.

'When we parted,' said Aila; 'did you know we'd meet here?'

'I knew there was a fair chance. Sanguino's a mile away; I need to go to him.'

Deathfang approached. He turned to Halfclaw. 'Go, and fetch Sanguino. Remember his blindness, take it slowly, and guide him here.'

Halfclaw tilted his head. 'Yes, my lord.' He beat his blue wings and rose into the bright morning sky, then flew to the south.

Belinda walked down the slope and went to gaze at the place where the god had been consumed by flames. Corthie, Aila and Sable joined her.

'Which one was it?' said Corthie.

'Leksandr,' said Belinda. She glanced up at the two dragons. 'You killed an Ascendant.'

'Did we?' said Deathfang. 'The glory of this morning shall never be exceeded! An Ascendant!'

'Don't celebrate just yet,' she said. 'Old Alea is crumbling. Lostwell has only a few hours left to exist.'

'What?' said Aila.

'The Second Ascendant has destroyed Lostwell,' said Corthie. 'Did you see the rest of Alea Tanton?'

'We did, but… Lostwell… I can't believe it. Why?'

'Edmond hated Lostwell,' said Belinda, 'because Nathaniel made it.'

'Has he gone?' said Aila. 'The Second Ascendant? Did he have a Quadrant? When the flames died down, there were only two gods there, not three.'

'Yes,' said Belinda. 'The one who ran away on foot was Bastion. He also has a Quadrant; perhaps he's on his way to collect it now.'

'We need to find him before he does,' said Aila; 'otherwise… otherwise, what happens next?'

'We all die,' said Sable.

Kelsey joined them. 'I have a dragon,' she said, her eyes glowing; 'did you hear? Brother, it's good to see you and everything, but I have a dragon!'

Aila frowned. 'Not for long, it seems. Lostwell is in the process of being obliterated. We have hours to live.'

Kelsey staggered back a step. 'What?'

'We still have the Sextant,' said Sable; 'it's our last chance.'

They returned to the mountain of rubble, and enlisted Frostback to assist with clearing the boulders and broken masonry from around the Sextant. Despite the collapse of the tower, it appeared to be without a single scratch.

'How's it supposed to work?' said Kelsey, as they gathered round it.

'Belinda's sword,' said Sable; 'that's the key. It has to be inserted somewhere into the mechanism, and then, I guess, it activates.'

Kelsey frowned. 'A sword?'

Belinda drew the Weathervane. 'This.'

'There are lots of places where it could fit,' said Kelsey, as she crouched by it.

'I know,' said Belinda. 'We've tried more than a dozen.'

Kelsey extended her hand. 'May I?'

Belinda handed her the weapon hilt-first, and the young Holdfast woman took it.

'Excuse me,' said Sable, glancing up; 'my dragon's here.'

She scrambled back down the slope, passing Frostback, who was watching the Sextant closely, and reached the bottom as Sanguino descended. Halfclaw was only yards from him as he flew, and they landed together.

Sable ran up to the dark red dragon, just as Sanguino opened a fore-limb, releasing Van from his grip. The former mercenary collapsed to his knees, and Sable reached out a hand and helped him up.

'More dragons?' he gasped.

Sable pointed at the heap of rubble. 'There's a young woman up there whom I believe you are looking for.'

Van squinted. 'Kelsey?'

'Yes. And see that silver dragon close by? Whatever else you do, I recommend that you are very polite to her. She and Kelsey have bonded.'

Aila watched from the top of the heap as Van hurried towards them.

Kelsey hefted the Weathervane as she peered into the mechanism. 'What about this side? Have you tried here?'

'No,' said Belinda, 'not yet.'

'Kelsey!' cried Van, as he reached the top of the heap.

She raised a finger. 'One moment, Van; I'm concentrating.'

The former mercenary looked a little disappointed, but said nothing, and they all watched as Kelsey slotted the dark-bladed sword into the side of the Sextant.

'Nope,' she said, trying another place; 'nope, nope, nope.' She tried a fifth position, halfway up the side. She pushed the sword in, and the Sextant began to emit a low hum. She glanced up, and winked at Belinda.

'Everyone, stand back,' said Belinda. She approached the device and stretched out her hand towards it. She slid one finger under the glass panel on the top of the Sextant, and lifted the entire device clear of the ground. She laughed, then placed her palm onto the surface of the device, her eyes closing.

'Is it working?' said Aila.

Belinda nodded, as a tear slid down her cheek. 'I can sense... everything; everywhere. I can see the endless plains of the Holdings, where horses are running over the grass, and I can see the Great Fortress in Plateau City, and the Empress.' The tears came quicker, and Belinda's head fell a little. 'I'm sorry, Bridget, for all the pain I caused you. I can also see the City of Pella,' she went on, 'and all of the empty spaces in the Bulwark. The greenhides bodies have gone, but so have the Scythes. And, I can see other worlds too, many other worlds, including Dragon Eyre.'

'This Sextant made Dragon Eyre?' said Sable, who had returned to the top of the heap.

'Yes, but not by Nathaniel, by another hand, many long millennia ago. I can also see Lostwell. There is no hope for my realm. In the east, the same fate that destroyed Alea Tanton has also happened to Kin Dai, and the forests of Kinell are burning from one end to the other. The Southern Cape, too, has been obliterated by lava flowing down from the mountains behind Dun Khatar. Everywhere I look on Lostwell, there is nothing but death and destruction.'

'Can you get us off this world?' said Corthie. 'I'm sorry that your realm is ending, but can you save us?'

'I can do more than that, Corthie. With the power of the Sextant, I can save the survivors of Alea Tanton; I can see every person up here on the plateau of Old Alea – gang members, Banner soldiers, and the thousands of servants who used to serve the gods.'

'What about Edmond?' said Aila. 'Can you see him?'

'No. He's gone.' Her eyes snapped open. 'I know what I have to do.'

'What?' said Corthie.

'With this device, I can send people, living people, from here to any of the worlds created by this Sextant. There are over forty thousand up here; survivors from the desolation below us. I can save them, and I can save the dragons. I saw a small group of them in the Torduan Mountains, sheltering.'

'They are my kin,' said Deathfang. 'Who are you? How has such power come to you?'

'I am the Third Ascendant and the Queen of Khatanax.'

The huge grey dragon's eyes burned. 'Queen Belinda?'

'Do you remember me?'

'I never saw you, but I used to visit Dun Khatar in my youth, before the gods destroyed it. Are you truly the wise old queen?'

'I am, though I don't think I'm very wise any more.'

The dragon hesitated for a moment, then tilted his head. 'Your Majesty. The light of my youth was filled with happy days, and for many years I have longed to return to that time. Everything went wrong when the gods invaded. We were imprisoned, and made to fight in the pits.'

'And now, before the end of Lostwell, it will be my privilege and honour to save you and your kin.'

'Where will you send them?' said Kelsey.

Belinda thought for a moment. 'A short time ago, I visited Queen Emily and King Daniel in the City of Pella, and they asked me about dragons. They also suffered terrible losses from the greenhides. I shall send the survivors there, both humans and dragons.'

'You're sending them to the City?' said Aila.

Belinda glanced around at the small group. 'Can anyone think of a better place?'

'Wait,' said Kelsey. 'Are you sending Frostback too?'

'I would want my daughter to accompany me to this City,' said Deathfang; 'I do not want to lose her again.'

Kelsey glanced at Frostback, then turned to Corthie. 'Brother?'

He turned to her. 'Are you and this silver dragon close?' he said. 'Like Sable and Sanguino?'

'Aye. She's only just accepted me as her rider. I don't want to be separated from her.'

'Nor I from you,' said Frostback. 'Come with us to this new world, Kelsey.'

'What about me and Sanguino?' said Sable. 'Where should we go? Can you send us to Dragon Eyre?'

Belinda chewed her lip, then placed her hand onto the Sextant and closed her eyes as the others watched in silence. For a few moments, nothing happened, then the air above the residence crackled and spat out sparks of lightning. The immense form of a dragon appeared overhead, and the air stilled.

Blackrose looked down at the mountain of rubble. 'You called me, Belinda, and I am here.'

'Sable and Sanguino want to return with you to Dragon Eyre,' said Belinda. 'Will you take them?'

The black dragon descended, and Maddie jumped down from the harness. Blackrose opened one clawed forelimb, and Naxor stumbled out.

'Were you in Dragon Eyre?' said Corthie.

'For about two hours,' muttered Naxor; 'and, believe me, that was enough.'

'It's beautiful,' cried Maddie; 'you should see it; the oceans, the sunshine, the little islands; it's perfect.' She glanced at Sable. 'But it wasn't the same without you and Sanguino. Blackrose feels really bad about the way you parted...'

'I do not,' said the black dragon. 'I behaved correctly in every respect. I have, however, decided to return Naxor to you; he does not belong on my world.'

'Quite right,' said Naxor, brushing down the front of his clothes.

Blackrose glanced around. 'This city is in ruins.'

'Lostwell is dying,' said Sable.

'What?' said Naxor. 'Hold on, this wasn't part of the deal.'

'Hush, cousin,' said Aila. 'Everything will be fine.'

The black dragon lowered her gaze to Sable. 'Have you accomplished what you set out to accomplish?'

'We have.'

'Are you ready to leave? Truly ready, this time? No more delays?'

'I am.'

'Then, let us depart. Millen, no doubt, will be overjoyed to see you.'
She looked around at the others. 'Our time together on Lostwell is at an
end. Farewell, all of you.'

Sable embraced Corthie and Kelsey.

'Thanks for coming back for me,' said Corthie. 'This is hard for me
to take; I've only just met you, and you're leaving already.'

'Look after Aila,' said Sable, 'and stay out of trouble. I'll see you all
again one day.'

She climbed up onto Sanguino's harness, and the dark red dragon
lifted into the sky. Maddie gave a sad wave to the others, and climbed up
onto Blackrose's back, and she rose up next to Sanguino.

Belinda placed her palm back onto the Sextant, closed her eyes, and
the two dragons and their riders disappeared with a loud crack.

She opened her eyes again. 'It's time to save the others, even Naxor.
Kelsey, are you going to the City with the dragons and the survivors of
Alea Tanton?'

The young Holdfast woman looked from Frostback to Corthie, her
eyes wide.

Van walked up to her. 'If you go,' he said, 'then I will too. There's
nothing for me on Implacatus, except for a hangman's noose.'

She gazed at him, then lowered her eyes and nodded.

'What will I tell mother?' said Corthie.

Kelsey started to cry. 'Tell her I'm happy. And tell her I'm sorry.'

Corthie embraced her. 'I'll miss you.' He turned to Van. 'You'd better
be good to my sister.'

'I will ensure that,' said Frostback. 'I have my eye on you, Van.'

The former mercenary officer tried to smile. 'I only wish Sohul were
here. He would have liked a new adventure.'

'What happened to him?' said Naxor. 'And Silva? I don't see her
anywhere.'

'They didn't make it,' said Van. 'The waves took them.'

'I know it's not much consolation, but you'll have me for company
again. Back to the City, eh? I can hardly believe it.'

Belinda placed her palm onto the flat surface of the Sextant. Overhead, the sky seemed to swirl, and jagged forks of lightning tore through the air over Old Alea, growing in intensity with every second that passed.

'Goodbye, Corthie,' said Kelsey, then she, Van, Naxor and the three remaining dragons vanished in a harsh crackle of noise amid a smell of smoke and iron.

'It's done,' said Belinda, opening her eyes. 'Listen.'

'I can't hear anything,' said Corthie.

'Exactly. I have removed every survivor from the surface of Old Alea and transported them to the fields behind the Great Wall, where the Scythes used to live. Over forty thousand people, and a dozen dragons. I pray that Queen Emily forgives me when she finds out.'

Aila looked around. Only she, Corthie and Belinda remained in the yard. For all she knew, they might be the only people left alive in Tordue.

'What now?' said Corthie.

Belinda frowned. 'In truth,' she said, 'I do not wish to return to the Star Continent. Despite the love I feel for you and Karalyn, I have always felt out of place there.'

'But you can't stay here,' said Aila, as another fierce rumble shook the ground. At the other end of the yard, the eastern tower collapsed in an explosion of rubble and dust.

'Vana was in there a few minutes ago,' said Belinda, 'but before you ask, Aila – yes, she's safe. Your sister is back in the City with the others.'

The air shimmered a few yards away and Edmond appeared, Lord Bastion and four other gods by his side. Every one of them was clad from head to foot in steel armour, and they were wielding long swords.

'Belinda,' Edmond cried; 'did you think you had seen the last of me? And now your dragon friends are gone, and so too is Kelsey Holdfast. Who will save you this time?'

The air shimmered again a few yards to Edmond's left, and two armed ballistae appeared, each crewed by Banner soldiers.

'If the Third Ascendant's hand moves towards the Sextant,' said Edmond; 'bring her down.'

Corthie clutched his Clawhammer, while Aila looked around in vain for a weapon. Belinda was also unarmed, and Corthie pushed them both behind him. Aila's eyes moved from the loaded ballistae to Edmond and his armoured gods. Belinda had no sword, and any attempt to use her death powers would be met with two ballista bolts. Edmond's eyes were shining; he had them trapped, and he knew it.

'Corthie,' said Belinda, her right hand flexing, 'tell Karalyn that I love her, and tell the Empress that I'm sorry.'

'What?' said Corthie. 'No; tell her yourself.'

'This is the end for me, my brother, but not for you and Aila. I've tried my hardest to be the best person I could be, and I know I didn't do a very good job at times. Throughout it all, you stuck by me, and that means more to me than you'll ever know.'

She pushed Aila out of the way and threw herself towards the Sextant, her hand slapping down on it as two ballista bolts sped through the air. The air around Aila shimmered, and the last thing she saw were the bolts piercing Belinda's armour, a spray of blood, and the Ascendant's body crashing to the ground.

Aila screamed, but it was lost in the silence and darkness.

CHAPTER 31

DISLOCATION

C olsbury Castle, Republic of the Holdings – 16th Day, Second Third Autumn 531

Darkness enveloped Corthie and he seemed to be floating. He had just seen Belinda struck down by a pair of yard-long steel ballista bolts, but before he had been able to react, the air around him had shifted. Panic began to grow within him, then the sky appeared above, a lightening sky with seven stars and no moon, and he fell to the ground, landing on a grassy slope by a lake. The impact winded him, and the Clawhammer slipped from his hands.

He lay on the grass, dazed, staring up at the sky. The light was growing above the steep mountains behind him, and the sky was beginning to turn blue. A chill wind rustled through his hair.

'Corthie?'

He lifted his head, still groggy, and saw Aila a few yards from him. She was struggling to her feet on the grassy slope, trying to reach him. He groaned and sat up, rubbing his head.

'That felt...'

'...terrible,' she finished for him; 'like being hit over the head.'

'Belinda,' he said.

'I know.' Aila reached his side and sat down. 'She did it for us. Look.'

She pointed down the hill. Near the bottom, where an unpaved road ran by the shore of the lake, the Sextant was lying on its side.

'It must have rolled down the hill,' she said. 'Where are we?'

'I don't know, but do you see the stars?'

They glanced up. The seven stars were just visible in the darkest part of the sky, above the mountains on the other side of the lake.

'I'm home,' he said.

'Are you sure?'

'Aye, unless there are other worlds with only seven stars.' He shook his head. 'We need to get the Sextant working; we need to rescue Belinda.'

Aila glanced at him.

'We can't leave her.'

'Oh, Corthie; she sacrificed herself to save us. I don't think she had any intention of leaving Lostwell; she made her decision, and maybe we should respect that.'

'I can't,' he said, getting to his feet, and slinging the Clawhammer over his shoulder.

He ran down the hillside, his boots slipping on the dewy grass, until he reached the Sextant. The hilt of the Weathervane was still poking out from the side, and Corthie placed his palm on the upper glass surface, just as Belinda had done.

Nothing happened.

'Damn it,' he muttered; 'work, you stupid thing.'

Aila appeared next to him.

'You try,' he said.

She nodded and pressed her hand against it.

'I'm sorry, Corthie. I don't feel anything.'

He started to cry, softly at first, then great sobs were torn from his chest as the tears spilled down his face. Aila put her arm round his shoulders and held him.

'All the times she's saved me,' he said, 'and I couldn't save her.'

'She saved thousands; let that be her legacy. She also managed to put the Sextant somewhere the Ascendants will never find it. The way she handled the Sextant; she was like a true god, saving as many of her people as she could; putting their lives before hers. She was a hero in the end; the saviour of thousands.'

Corthie tried to digest her words, but the pain was too raw. If only he had been able to say goodbye.

'Can I help you folks?' said a voice.

They glanced over to the path. An old, dark-skinned woman was leading a donkey, which was pulling a cart loaded with bales of hay.

Corthie stared at her. The woman, noticing his tears, reached into a pocket and passed him a handkerchief.

'Thank you,' said Aila. 'Do you know where we are?'

The woman squinted at them. 'I do, but it seems clear that you don't. Where have you come from, then? Who are you?'

'My name is Aila, and this... this is Corthie Holdfast.'

'A Holdfast, eh? Or is he "of Hold Fast," my dear?'

'I'm sorry; I don't understand.'

'I'm the son of Daphne Holdfast,' he said.

'Oh, a proper Holdfast, then. Your sister lives close to here; I often see her when I visit the market in the castle, when she's out with her little ones.'

'A castle?' said Aila. 'Where?'

'That'll be Colsbury Castle, my dear, and it's not far; just round the corner. I'm going that way; shall I take you?'

'Yes, please,' said Aila.

'Right you are, my dear.'

Aila leaned over and pulled the Weathervane from the side of the Sextant and a low hum that Corthie hadn't been aware of fell silent.

'Better safe than sorry,' she said.

They walked with the old woman along the path as the light grew stronger. The sky was mostly clear, but a cold wind was pushing in dark clouds over the lake from the west, and within a few minutes, it had started to rain. Corthie and Aila both paused on the path for a moment, letting the raindrops roll down their faces.

'You two look like you've never seen rain before,' said the old woman.

'It's been about six months,' said Aila.

'Months? What are those, then?'

'She means thirds,' said Corthie.

They turned a corner in the path, and a fresh stretch of the lake opened up before them. Two hundred yards from the turn, a slender bridge extended from the shore, running across the water to an island, which was ringed with a high curtain wall, above which tall towers were rising.

'There it is, my dears; Colsbury Castle. The home of her Highness, Princess Shellakanawara.'

'Shella lives there?' said Corthie.

'You know her?' said Aila.

'She's my mother's friend.' He glanced at the old woman. 'Do you know where my mother is?'

'And how would I know where Holder Fast is, young man? She's the Herald of the Empire; she could be anywhere.'

They walked on, and approached the bridge. A tall woman was waiting for them there, leaning back against a high post at the start of the bridge, a cigarette in her hand.

'Brother,' she said.

The old woman nodded to Karalyn, and kept on walking, while Corthie and Aila halted on the road.

'Sister.'

'You made it back. Where's...'

'Don't start, Karalyn,' he said. 'You have no idea what we've been through.'

'I do, actually; I read it from Aila's mind. Listen, before we argue, let me say this – I'm sorry for what happened; truly, I am. My mind was twisted by grief and rage, and all I wanted to do was come home for my children. The guilt has eaten me up ever since; all I've thought about is abandoning you, but I couldn't leave my children again. That's why I agreed to Kelsey going. She wanted to go, and if Aila's memories are correct, she's happy where she is. She has a dragon. And Sable is also where she belongs. Did she give her Quadrant to Blackrose?'

Aila nodded. 'Yes.'

'Good. That makes up partly for what I did.' She straightened her back. 'Let's go inside, and we can talk about Belinda and the Sextant.'

Karalyn turned and began walking across the stone bridge. Corthie and Aila glanced at each other, then followed.

'Holy crap,' cried Shella, as she walked into the warm chamber; 'you've grown.'

'Hi, Auntie,' said Corthie, getting up from the chair by the fire.

'Sit down,' she said, as she walked to a side table and poured herself a brandy. 'Five and a half years,' she chuckled; 'your mother's going to go mental.' She sat opposite Corthie and Aila and lit a cigarette. 'And you're Aila, eh? I've heard a fair bit about you; none of it good. You officially took the blame for Karalyn not bringing Corthie back, but don't worry; I'm sure you'll win old Daffers round. And, if you don't, all you have to do is wait for her to die. You're immortal, yeah?'

'I am a demigod.'

Shella shrugged. 'Whatever that means.'

The air wavered in the far corner of the chamber, and Karalyn appeared with the Sextant. Aila and Corthie stood.

'The sword,' said Karalyn, holding out her hand.

Shella joined them as they walked over to the huge device. Aila handed the Weathervane to Karalyn, and the Holdfast women crouched and slotted it into place. The device started to hum again, and Karalyn placed her hand on it and closed her eyes.

'What's it supposed to do?' said Shella.

'It can create worlds,' said Aila, 'and transport people between them.'

'Is that how you got back?'

'Aye, said Corthie. 'Belinda...' He stopped, fighting the tears that threatened to re-emerge.

'Belinda saved us,' said Aila. 'She used the Sextant to send us, and it, here.'

'Is she dead?' said Shella.

'We don't know. The last we saw of her, she was hit by two steel ballista bolts.'

Karalyn opened her eyes.

'Well?' said Corthie. 'Can we rescue her?'

Karalyn shook her head. 'Lostwell is no more. I cannot see it or reach it; all that's in its place is a void. Belinda's gone.' She lowered her gaze. 'I'm sorry.'

They stood in silence for a moment, then Corthie sat and put his head in his hands. Aila stood by his shoulder, a hand on the back of his neck.

'I do have some good news,' Karalyn said. 'I can use the Sextant; it responds to me the same way that Quadrants used to. I saw the other worlds it has created, and I saw Kelsey and Sable; one in the City, and the other on Dragon Eyre. They're both in one piece. I can also see the potential this device brings us. We could use it to travel between the worlds, if we wished, or, we could even create a new world. I need time, a lot of time, to study it. Shella, I intend to keep it here.'

'Eh, it seems a bit dangerous.'

Karalyn withdrew the Weathervane. 'It's useless without this. We'll keep them separate unless I'm using it.'

The door to the chamber opened and two young children ran in, a boy and a girl. Karalyn laid the sword down on top of the Sextant and crouched next to them.

'Kyra, Cael; this is Corthie, your uncle.'

The boy frowned at him, while the girl looked shy.

'Hello,' said Corthie. He wiped his eyes, stood, then got down to one knee. 'I've been away, but I'm back now. What have you been doing?'

'Playing in the gardens,' said the boy. 'Do you want to play?'

'Aye,' he said. 'That sounds like fun.'

'Later,' said their mother; 'we're going to visit grandma today, as a surprise.'

The girl's face flushed. 'Will... will Aunty Thorn be there?'

'I expect so, Kyra.'

The faces of both children lit up. Karalyn smiled, but Corthie could see the pain that their response had caused her.

'I'm staying here,' said Shella. 'As much as I'd love to see old Daffer's face when she realises her boy is back, I think I'll leave this one to the Holdfasts.'

Karalyn picked up the Weathervane. 'Stand by me, children,' she said.

'Where are we going?' said Aila.

'The Hold Fast estate,' said Karalyn.

The air wavered round them and they appeared on a wooden porch. It was freshly-painted in white, with chairs and tables laid out under the sloping roof. To one side stretched the flat grasslands of the Holdings, illuminated by the morning sunshine, and Corthie gasped. Home. He stared at the view for a moment, then turned towards the rear of the large mansion. White arches and colonnades were stacked up, and the grand building stretched out before them. Close by were other structures – stables, barns, and down a little slope was a row of cottages for the estate workers.

'You lived here?' said Aila. 'It wouldn't look out of place on Princeps Row in Tara.'

Corthie said nothing, his eyes taking everything in.

'Give me a moment,' said Karalyn. 'Take a seat.'

Aila and Corthie sat down on a couch facing the view of the plains, and a few moments later, a young woman walked out onto the porch.

'You called?' she said. 'Oh, you've brought the twins.'

The young woman crouched down, and the two children ran into her arms.

She laughed. 'Yes, it's lovely to see you too.' She glanced up at Karalyn. 'As much as I adore seeing them, I wish you had called ahead to let me know. It's only been four days since your last visit, and you said you would leave at least ten days before bringing them back here. I...'

'Sorry, Thorn. You're right; I should have let you know, but, well, guess who's back?' She glanced over to the couch.

Thorn turned, and her eyes widened. 'Is that...? Corthie?'

He stood, and her eyes glanced up at his height.

'He's just arrived back,' said Karalyn.

'And Kelsey? Sable?'

Karalyn shook her head. 'They're both fine, but they went their own way.'

Thorn stood, holding a child's hand in each of hers.

'This is Thorn,' said Corthie, 'my sister-in-law.'

'Hello,' said Aila, getting up.

Thorn glanced at Aila for a second, then her eyes went back to Corthie.

'She's a soulwitch,' said Karalyn.

'What's that?' said Aila.

'It means she has the same powers as Amalia,' said Corthie, 'except, of course, she's mortal like the rest of us. It's good to see you, Thorn.'

'And you. You've... grown.'

'Would you mind looking after the twins for a little while?' said Karalyn. 'I want to take him to see mother.'

'Of course. Will you be staying?'

'I might head back to Colsbury later, but Corthie and Aila will be staying; mother will insist.'

'Then there will probably be a party tonight. Keir's here.'

'And how is my brother?' said Corthie.

'Doing well,' said Thorn. 'Celine's been showing him how to run the estate, so that he can take it over one day.'

Karalyn gestured to Corthie and Aila. 'We'll see you soon, Thorn.' She crouched down by the twins. 'Aunty Thorn will look after you this morning; alright?'

Cael smiled, while the little girl had already buried her face in the folds of Thorn's dress.

Karalyn led Aila and Corthie into the mansion through the rear door.

'She was looking after your children,' said Aila, 'while you were... away?'

'Aye,' said Karalyn, her eyes reflecting the pain she felt, 'but what I thought was going to be a few thirds turned out to be four years. Sometimes, I wish I could cut off all contact with her, but the twins love her, and it wouldn't be fair on them. It hasn't been easy, but we're getting there, slowly.'

'The twins are beautiful,' said Corthie.

Karalyn nodded.

'What powers does your mother have?' said Aila, as they walked along the marble floor of the hallway.

'Vision,' said Corthie; 'the whole range.'

'Will she be able to read my thoughts?'

Karalyn eyed her, and they came to a halt in the passageway. 'Good point; we can't be having that.' She looked into Aila's eyes. 'Not any more; I've sealed your mind to her. It'll annoy her, but tough.'

'You sealed my mind?'

'Just to vision mages; it's impossible to seal your mind from me, I'm afraid.'

'You mean that no vision... mage, or god, will be able to see my thoughts again?'

'That's right.'

'Malik's ass, I could have done with that in the City.'

'Try not to curse in front of my mother if you can help it. Are you ready? I've got an idea. We'll walk into her office, but I'll hide you from her. She won't be able to see you until I say so.'

'Is that wise?' said Aila.

Karalyn shrugged, and they approached a set of tall, double doors, which Karalyn pushed open. They walked into a large, high-ceilinged office. The white walls were adorned with a large collection of maps covering almost every part of the Star Continent. At one end of the room, next to a large bay window, was a desk, behind which a woman was sitting, working her way through a large pile of paperwork.

'Good morning, dear,' the woman said, without looking up.

'Good morning, mother. Busy?'

'Rather. I have a meeting with the Empress via vision in five minutes. Urgent, apparently, so you'll have to be quick.' She glanced up, frowning. 'Did you bring the twins?'

'Aye.'

The woman sighed. 'After what we discussed? The more Thorn sees of them, the harder it will be, not just for her, but for you and the children too. It's not fair. You said...'

'I know what I said, mother, but I have a surprise for you.'

The woman lit a cigarette. 'Yes?'

'You might have to prepare a guest room.'

The Holdfast matriarch frowned. 'You've brought a visitor? Have you found yourself a boyfriend at last?'

'No, mother, and I wouldn't hold your breath on that front, if I were you. I know it's been four and a half years since Lennox died but, to me, it's only been a few thirds.' She cleared her thoughts and smiled. 'Anyway, say hello to your son.'

Daphne Holdfast narrowed her eyes for a moment, then stared as Corthie and Aila appeared before her. She screamed and fell off her chair, sending paperwork flying as she landed on the hard floor. Corthie laughed and strode forwards, leaning over to help her up. She stood, staring at him, then her face dissolved in tears and she threw her arms round him, sobbing into his chest.

'Hello, mother,' he said. 'I'm sorry I took so long.'

'Five years!' Daphne cried. 'Let me look at you. You're taller than your father was, and almost as broad-shouldered, and just as handsome.' She glared at Karalyn. 'Are you trying to give me a heart attack?' she sobbed.

'Sorry; I couldn't resist.'

'Well, never mind that now. Sit down, Corthie. Corthie...' She fell into tears again, sat, and wept.

Corthie put a hand on her shoulder. 'Listen, mother. Kelsey has decided not to come back.'

Daphne glanced up at him. 'What?'

'She's safe, and well. She's gone to the City where I lived for a while, with friends. She's a dragon rider.'

'A what-rider?'

'Dragon,' said Karalyn. 'They're like winged gaien, only they can talk.'

'A talking gaien?'

'We can discuss that later,' said Corthie. 'Sable's also not coming back.'

'Is she a dragon-rider too, is she?'

'Aye, she is.'

Daphne sighed. 'Every time someone returns from Lostwell, they leave someone else behind. My little Kelsey.'

Karalyn placed the Weathervane on the desk. Daphne wiped her face and raised an eyebrow.

'Keep a hold of this for me, mother,' said Karalyn. 'It's the key to the Sextant; a huge device that can send people between worlds. Corthie brought it back with him. I have a feeling that you might be able to operate it, so, when we have time, I'll show you, and you'll be able to see Kelsey.'

'And why do I have to keep the sword?'

'The Sextant doesn't work without it, and it's an extremely dangerous device. If you keep it here, I can come and take it whenever I need to, but otherwise it'll remain inactive.'

Daphne nodded. 'Tell me all about it later.' Her eyes flickered towards Aila. 'And you are?'

'This is Aila,' said Corthie.

'I see.' Daphne composed herself and frowned at the demigod. 'This is the woman you stayed for? This is the woman who prevented you from coming home thirds ago?'

'Don't blame her,' said Karalyn; 'it was my fault.'

'I am perfectly capable of assigning blame on my own, thank you very much.' She stood and walked to the front of the desk. She was the same height as Aila, and she stared into her eyes. She frowned.

'I blocked her,' said Karalyn. 'I didn't want you having an unfair advantage over her.'

'I can see that,' said Daphne. 'You did the same with Thorn; you seem determined to undermine me.'

'It seems fair to me,' said Corthie.

'You would think that,' said Daphne. 'Well, what are your intentions? I assume it must be serious. Are you married, or are you planning on getting married?'

'Well...' began Corthie.

'Hush, son; I was asking her.'

'I don't know,' said Aila. 'We talked about marriage once, but things have been a little hectic recently.'

'I can marry you,' said Daphne. 'As Herald of the Empire, I have the authority to do so. That reminds me; I'm supposed to be sending my vision to Plateau City to talk to the Empress. Oh well, she'll have to wait. Family is family. Right, so, Aila; you're a god, I believe?'

'A demigod. My mother was mortal.'

'And how long have you been alive?'

'Almost eight centuries.'

Daphne puffed out her cheeks. 'That's longer than the recorded history of the Holdings. Eight centuries? By the Creator, you're positively ancient. How long can you be expected to live?'

Aila frowned. 'I... I'm not sure, exactly. The oldest gods have been around for over thirty thousand years.'

'And why are you interested in a mortal?'

'I love Corthie.'

'Yes, but you must have been in love before now, surely? Do you have any children? Do you plan on having any? Will you remain young-looking, while we all age around you? What will happen when Corthie grows old; have you thought of that?'

'I've thought of little else,' said Aila. 'Every single person, with the exception of one, has told us that our relationship is a bad idea; that it's doomed from the start. I don't believe that. If I did, I wouldn't be here.'

'Who was the one who thought it was a good idea?'

'My aunt, Yendra. She told me to follow my heart.'

Daphne pulled a face. 'Follow your heart? That doesn't sound very practical. Do you have any powers associated with being immortal?'

'I can heal myself, of course, and I can make people think I look different.'

'Show me.'

'It won't work in front of us,' said Karalyn, 'but it will among normal folk. It's a bit like me making myself invisible; she can persuade others to think she looks like someone else.'

'That could be very useful indeed,' said Daphne. 'Perhaps there is a place for Aila within the Imperial intelligence division. Do you have any experience of subterfuge?'

'A fair bit,' said Aila, 'but I was hoping for some peace and quiet.'

'Are you going to tell her?' said Karalyn.

Aila nodded. 'I'm pregnant.'

Daphne put a hand to her face. 'And I was hoping you were just carrying a little extra around the midriff. Pregnant. Dear me. That settles it; I'll marry you later today, or perhaps tomorrow, once our hangovers have gone. I have a whole crate of whisky that we can open; I think the occasion demands it. I certainly need a drink.'

'There's more,' said Karalyn, 'but I'm not sure if Aila herself knows.'

'What?'

'The baby that is growing within her – I can already sense its self-healing powers.'

'What does that mean?' said Daphne.

'The child will be immortal; a demigod.'

Daphne fell into a chair.

'Are you sure?' said Aila.

'Aye. Positive,' said Karalyn. 'Congratulations, Corthie – you're going to be the father of a god.'

Corthie and Aila sat on the back porch, drinking whisky, the bottle on the wooden flooring next to the couch. In front of them, the endless plains of the Holdings swept away into the distance, and the sun was hanging over the horizon, transforming the western sky into a dozen shades of red and pink.

'Should we go back inside?' said Aila. 'The others will be wondering where we are.'

'Not yet,' said Corthie; 'let me savour the peace for a moment.'

'It's been some day.'

'Aye. This morning we were fighting Ascendants, and now we're here, in Hold Fast. It's been six years since I've been in this house, but nothing seems to have changed. My family... well, you've seen what they're like.'

'They seem nice.'

'They are, most of the time. Even Keir. But...'

'Are you alright?'

'I miss Kelsey,' he said, 'and Sable. And Belinda. It doesn't seem right, us being here after what she did to save us, but no one has asked about her; no one has said anything about her. They all think of her as a traitor; the crazy woman who betrayed the Empress; they don't care what happened to her.' He hung his head, weeping. 'No one cares.'

He felt Aila's hand take his. 'You care, Corthie, and that's all Belinda wanted. She loved you as a brother. What she did, she didn't do for me; she did it for you, so you could go home.'

'It's not fair.'

'I know, Corthie, but life isn't fair. All you can do is try to protect the people you love from everything life throws at you. Your whole life is still ahead of you, and you are surrounded by people who love you. In a few months, we're going to be parents and a whole new chapter of our lives will begin. If you want to honour Belinda, then be the man she wanted you to be; live your life.'

'I thought I would be the one to defeat the Ascendants; I thought I had a grand destiny.'

'You do, only it's here, with me and your family.' She stood. 'Come on; let's go back to the party.'

'You go,' he said. 'I'll just be a minute.'

She nodded, and slipped back into the mansion.

Corthie stared into the west as the sun dipped below the horizon. Aila was right; his future belonged with her and the child that was growing within her. It was a future that Belinda had sacrificed herself to give him, and he couldn't waste it. He tried to think of the hundred things he would soon be doing – finding somewhere for him, Aila and the baby to live, finding work, seeing all of the places on the Star Continent that he had never visited, but it seemed too soon to be dwelling on such matters while his memories were so raw.

He needed time and, thanks to Belinda, he had it.

Corthie raised his glass to the darkening sky. 'To you, Belinda, wherever you are.'

He drained the whisky, got to his feet, and went back inside to join his family.

NOTE ON THE CALENDAR

The Divine Calendar is used on every world ruled by Implacatus (for example, on Lostwell and Dragon Eyre). As all inhabited worlds were created from the same template (and rotate around their sun every 365.25 days), each year is divided into the same seasons and months as that of Implacatus itself.

Each month (or 'inch') is named after one of the Twelve Ascendants (the original Gods of Implacatus). Through long years, the names have drifted some way from their originals, but each month retains its connection to the Ascendant it was named after.

In the Divine Calendar, each year begins on the 1st day of Beldinch.
- Beldinch (January) – after Belinda, the Third Ascendant
- Summinch (February)– after Simon, the Tenth Ascendant
- Arginch (March) – after Arete, the Seventh Ascendant
- Nethinch (April)– after Nathaniel, the Fourth Ascendant
- Duninch (May) – after Edmond, the Second Ascendant
- Tradinch (June)– after Theodora, the First Ascendant
- Abrinch (July) – after Albrada, the Eleventh Ascendant
- Lexinch (August) – after Leksandr, the Sixth Ascendant
- Tuminch (September) – after Tamid, the Eighth Ascendant
- Luddinch (October) – after Lloyd, the Twelfth Ascendant
- Kolinch (November)– after Kolai, the Fifth Ascendant
- Essinch (December) – after Esher, the Ninth Ascendant

AUTHOR'S NOTES

APRIL 2021

Farewell, Lostwell and farewell, Belinda, Queen of Khatanax.

Thank you for reading Gates of Ruin, which completes the second of the three Eternal Siege 'trilogies.' I hope you enjoyed Gates of Ruin. I found the ending to be a particular challenge - trying to stitch the storylines together was tricky - as tricky as drafting the endings of Sacrifice, Renegade Gods and The Prince's Blade.

With the passing of the Lostwell Trilogy, it is time to also say goodbye (for now!) to some of the characters who have been the backbone of the series so far - Corthie, Aila, Maddie and Sable, for instance. They will all be returning later in the overall Magelands Saga. For the City Trilogy (Books 7 - 9), we shall be journeying to the City of Pella, Tara and the Great Wall with Kelsey, forty thousand refugees, and twelve dragons...

RECEIVE A FREE MAGELANDS ETERNAL SIEGE BOOK

Building a relationship with my readers is very important to me.

Join my newsletter for information on new books and deals and you will also receive a Magelands Eternal Siege prequel novella that is currently EXCLUSIVE to my Reader's Group for FREE.

www.ChristopherMitchellBooks.com/join

ABOUT THE AUTHOR

Christopher Mitchell is the author of the Magelands epic fantasy series.

For more information:
www.christophermitchellbooks.com
info@christophermitchellbooks.com

Printed in Great Britain
by Amazon